ADVENTURE TIME™

PIXEL PRINCESSES

PUBLISHED BY KaBOOM!

ROSS RICHIE ~ CEO & Founder

JACK CUMMINS ~ President

MARK SMYLIE ~ Chief Creative Officer

MATT GAGNON ~ Editor-in-Chief

FILIP SABLIK ~ VP of Publishing & Marketing

STEPHEN CHRISTY ~ VP of Development

LANCE KREITER ~ VP of Licensing & Merchandising

PHIL BARBARO ~ VP of Finance

BRYCE CARLSON ~ Managing Editor

MEL CAYLO ~ Marketing Manager

SCOTT NEWMAN ~ Production Design Manager

DAFNA PLEBAN ~ Editor

SHANNON WATTERS ~ Editor

ERIC HARBURN ~ Editor

REBECCA TAYLOR ~ Editor

CHRIS ROSA ~ Assistant Editor

ALEX GALER ~ Assistant Editor

WHITNEY LEOPARD ~ Assistant Editor

JASMINE AMIRI ~ Assistant Editor

MIKE LOPEZ ~ Production Designer

HANNAH NANCE PARTLOW ~ Production Designer

DEVIN FUNCHES ~ E-Commerce & Inventory Coordinator

BRIANNA HART ~ Executive Assistant

AARON FERRARA ~ Operations Assistant

JOSE MÉZA ~ Sales Assistant

ADVENTURE TIME: PIXEL PRINCESSES, November 2013. Published by KaBOOM!, a division of Boom Entertainment, Inc. ADVENTURE TIME, CARTOON NETWORK, the logos, and all related characters and elements are trademarks of and © Cartoon Network. (S13) All rights reserved. KaBOOM!™ and the KaBOOM! logo are trademarks of Boom Entertainment, Inc., registered in various countries and categories. All characters, events, and institutions depicted herein are fictional. Any similarity between any of the names, characters, persons, events, and/or institutions in this publication to actual names, characters, and persons, whether living or dead, events, and/or institutions is unintended and purely coincidental. KaBOOM! does not read or accept unsolicited submissions of ideas, stories, or artwork.

A catalog record of this book is available from OCLC and from the KaBOOM! website, www.kaboom-studios.com, on the Librarians Page.

BOOM! Studios, 5670 Wilshire Boulevard, Suite 450, Los Angeles, CA 90036-5679. Printed in USA. First Printing.
ISBN: 978-1-60886-329-7, eISBN: 978-1-61398-183-2

Created by **PENDLETON WARD**
Written by **DANIELLE CORSETTO**
Illustrated by **ZACK STERLING**
With **TESSA STONE**
COREY LEWIS
CHRYSTIN GARLAND
PAULINA GANUCHEAU

Inks by **STEPHANIE HOCUTT**
and **AUBREY AIESE**
Tones by **AMANDA LAFRENAIS**
Letters by **KEL MᶜDONALD**

"The Mind of Gunter" by **MEREDITH MᶜCLAREN**
Tones by **AMANDA LAFRENAIS**

Cover by **STEPHANIE GONZAGA**

Assistant Editor **WHITNEY LEOPARD**
Editor **SHANNON WATTERS**
Designer **HANNAH NANCE PARTLOW**

With Special Thanks to Marisa Marionakis, Rick Blanco, Curtis Lelash, Laurie Halal-Ono,
Keith Mack, Kelly Crews and the wonderful folks at Cartoon Network.

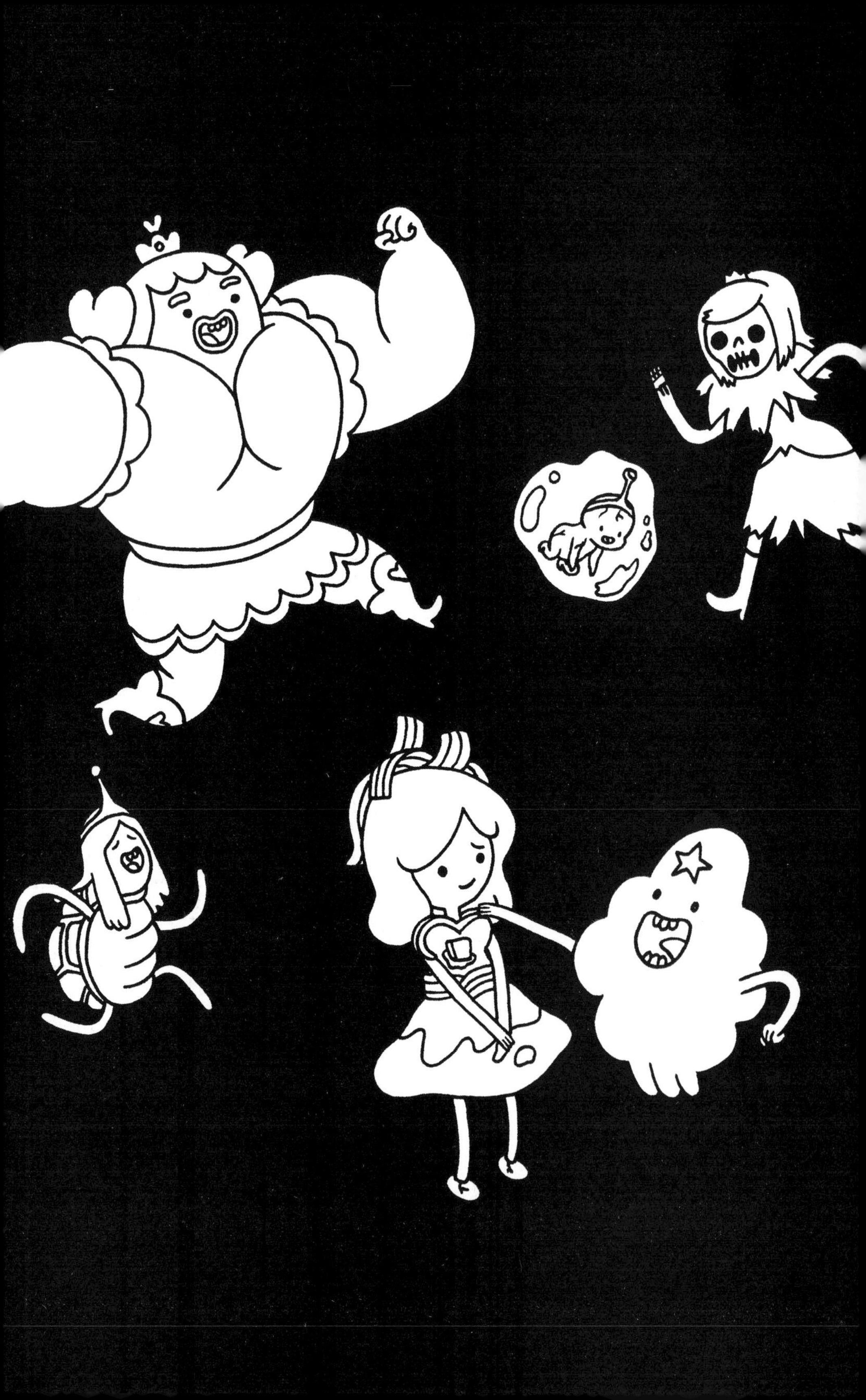

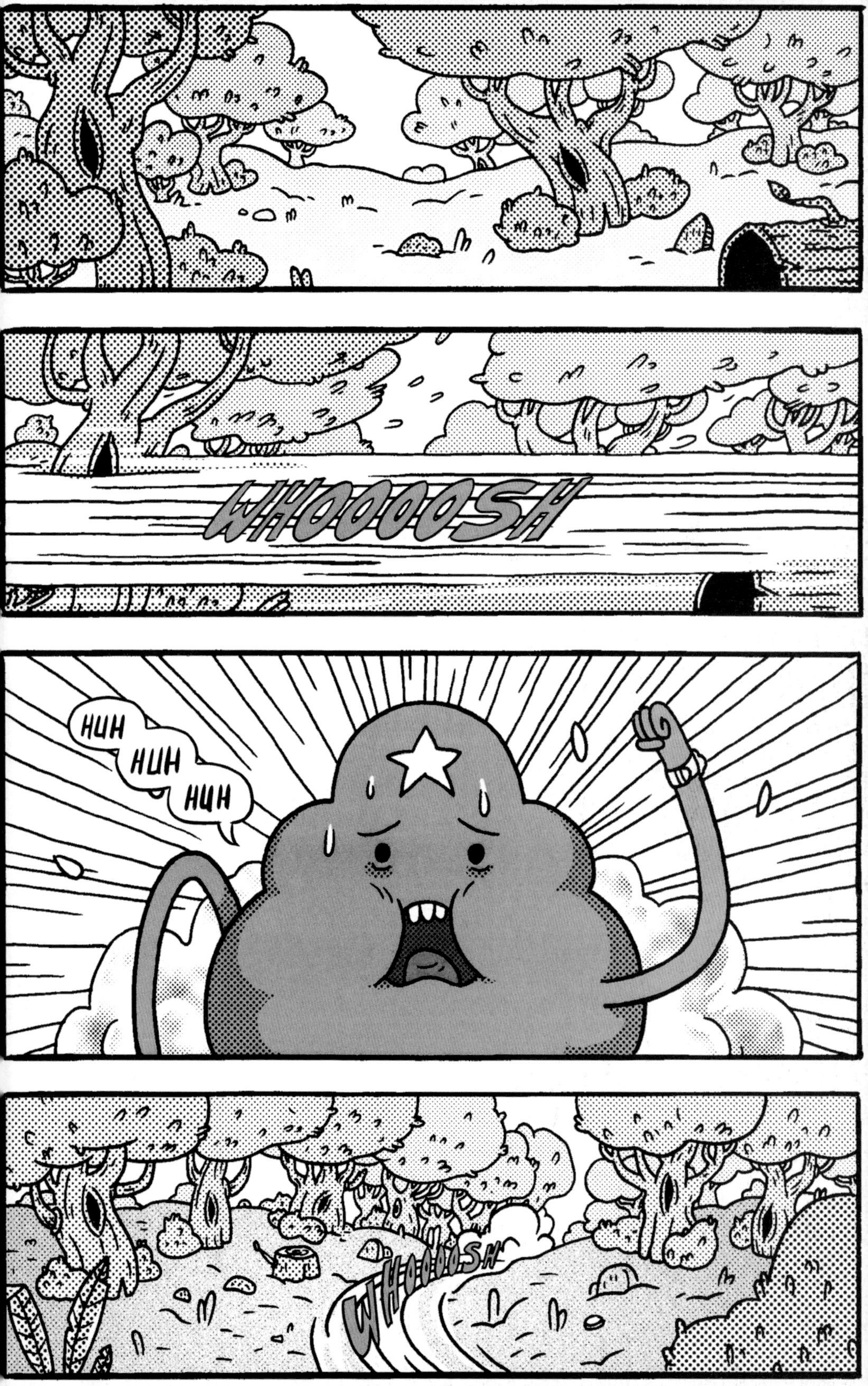
WHOOOOOSH
HUH
HUH
HUH
WHOOOOSH

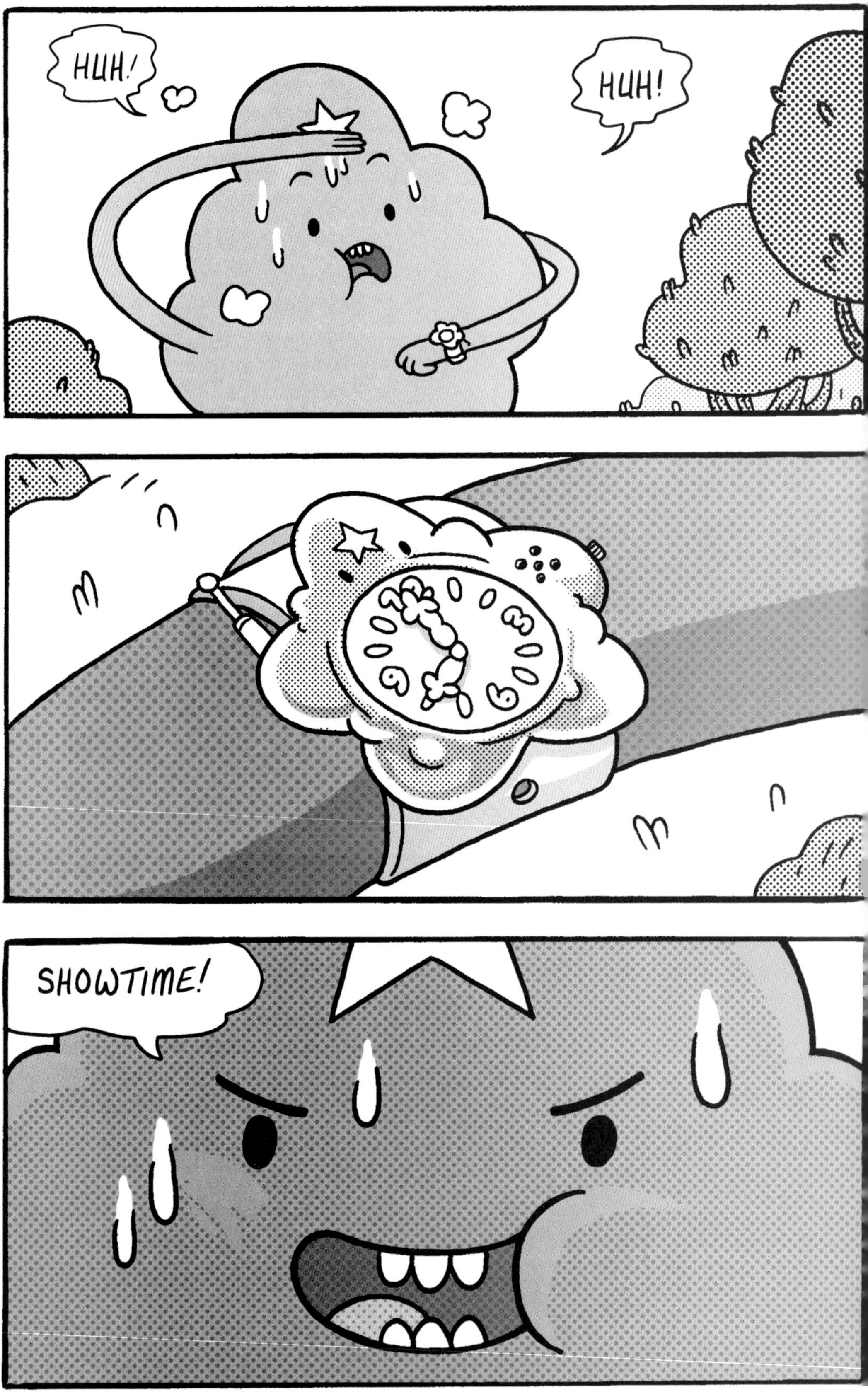
HUH!
HUH!
SHOWTIME!

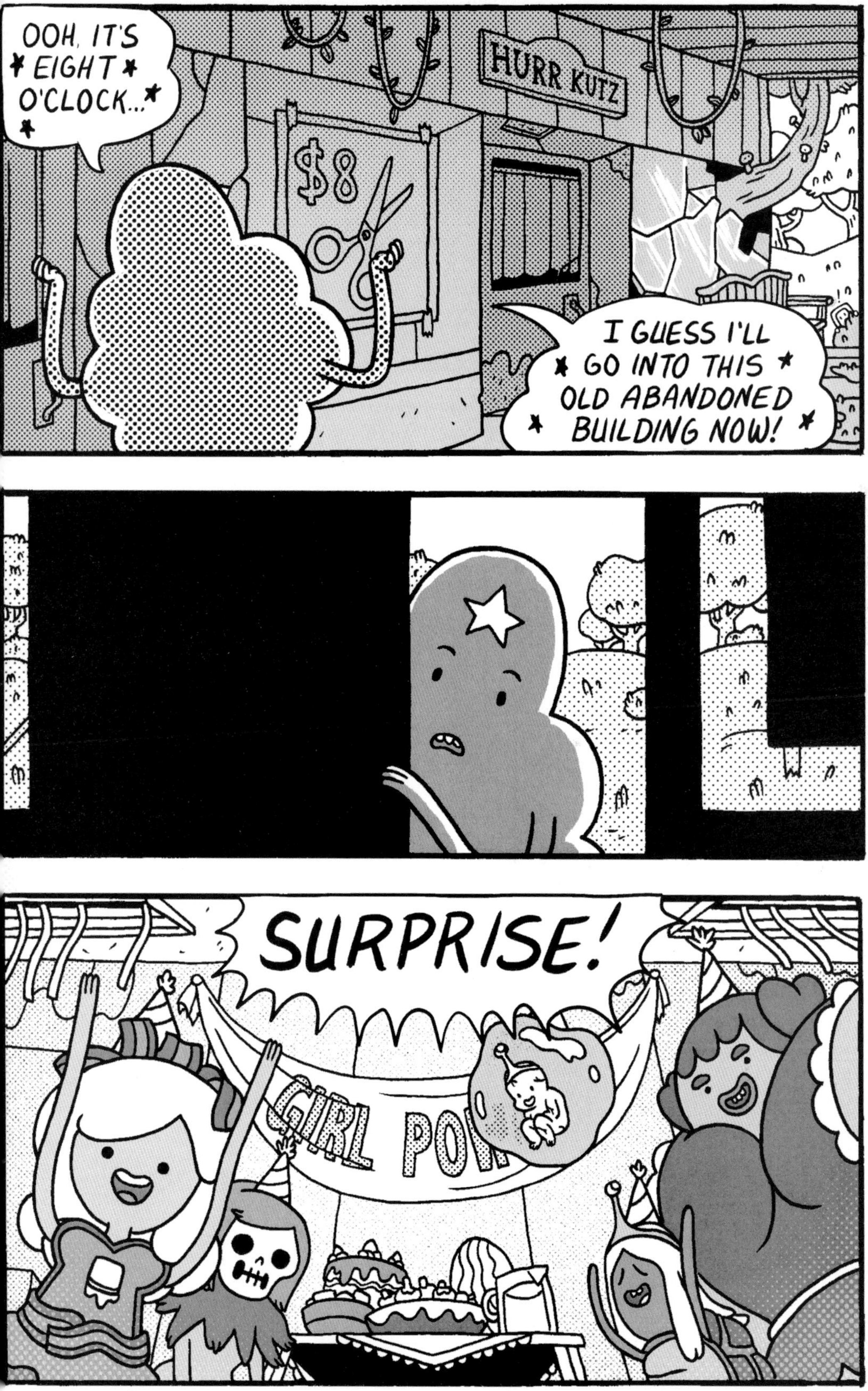
OOH, IT'S EIGHT O'CLOCK...
HURR KUTZ
$8
I GUESS I'LL GO INTO THIS OLD ABANDONED BUILDING NOW!
SURPRISE!
GIRL POW

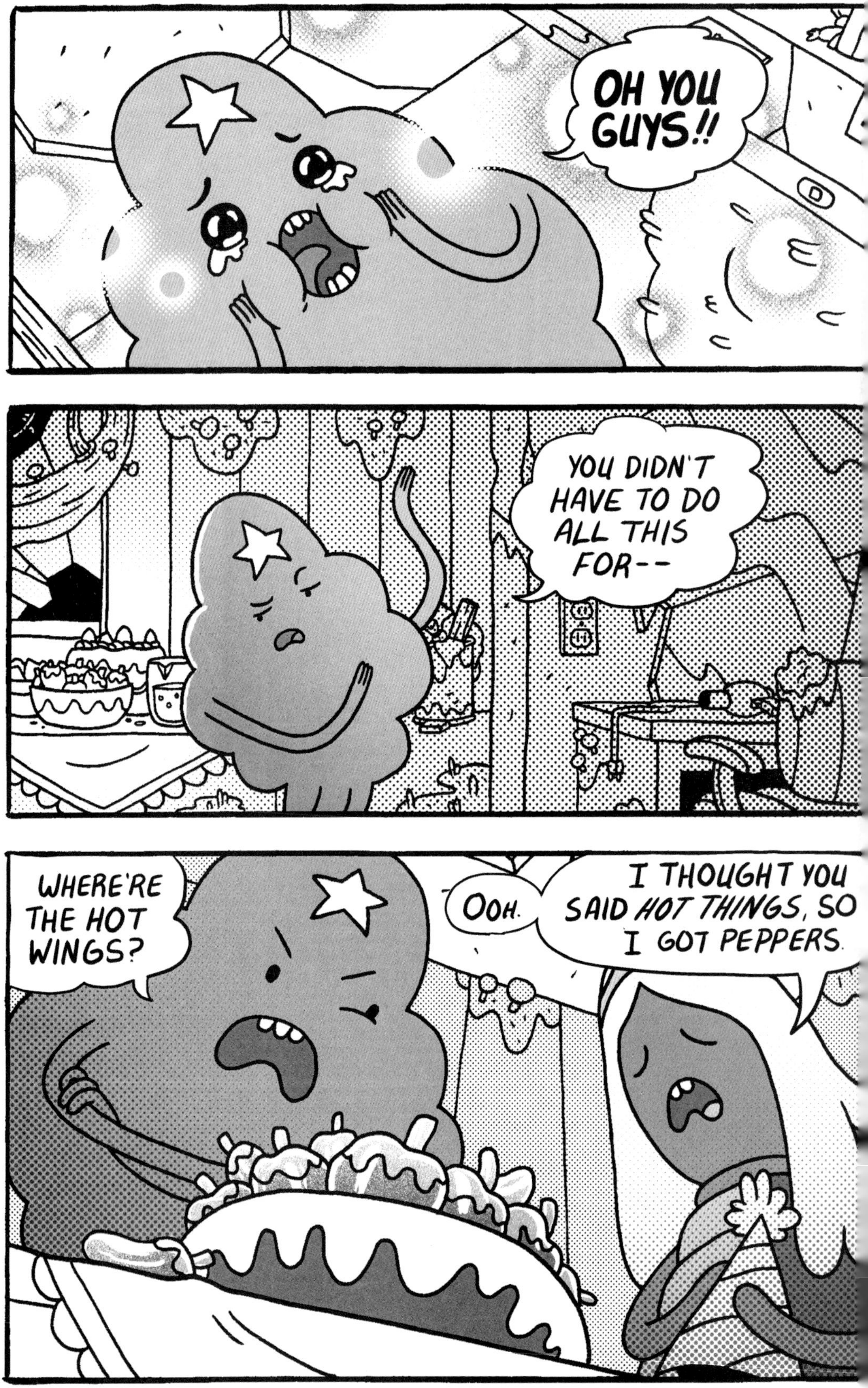
OH YOU GUYS!!
YOU DIDN'T HAVE TO DO ALL THIS FOR--
WHERE'RE THE HOT WINGS?
OOH.
I THOUGHT YOU SAID HOT THINGS, SO I GOT PEPPERS.

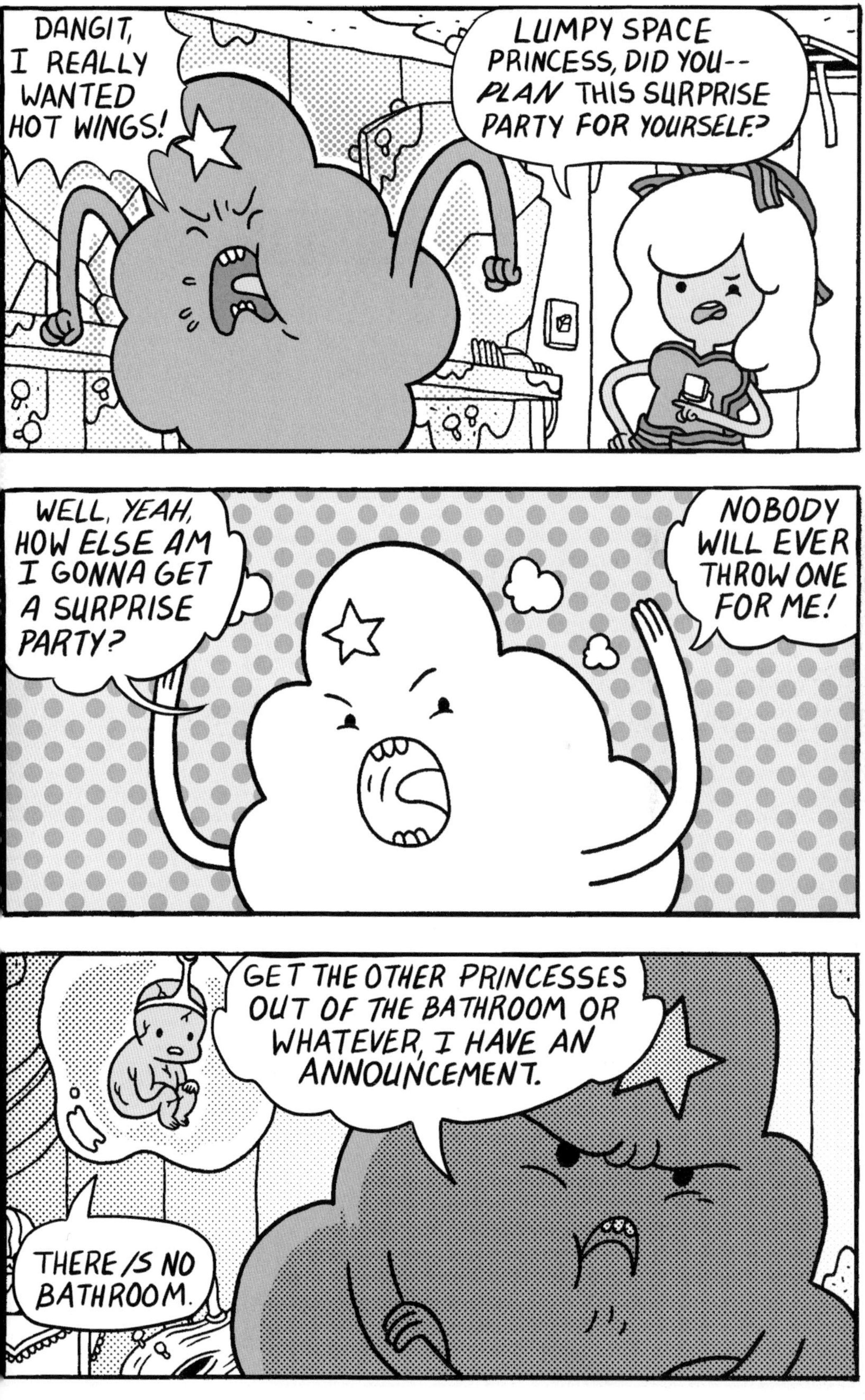
DANGIT, I REALLY WANTED HOT WINGS!
LUMPY SPACE PRINCESS, DID YOU-- PLAN THIS SURPRISE PARTY FOR YOURSELF?
WELL, YEAH, HOW ELSE AM I GONNA GET A SURPRISE PARTY?
NOBODY WILL EVER THROW ONE FOR ME!
GET THE OTHER PRINCESSES OUT OF THE BATHROOM OR WHATEVER, I HAVE AN ANNOUNCEMENT.
THERE IS NO BATHROOM.

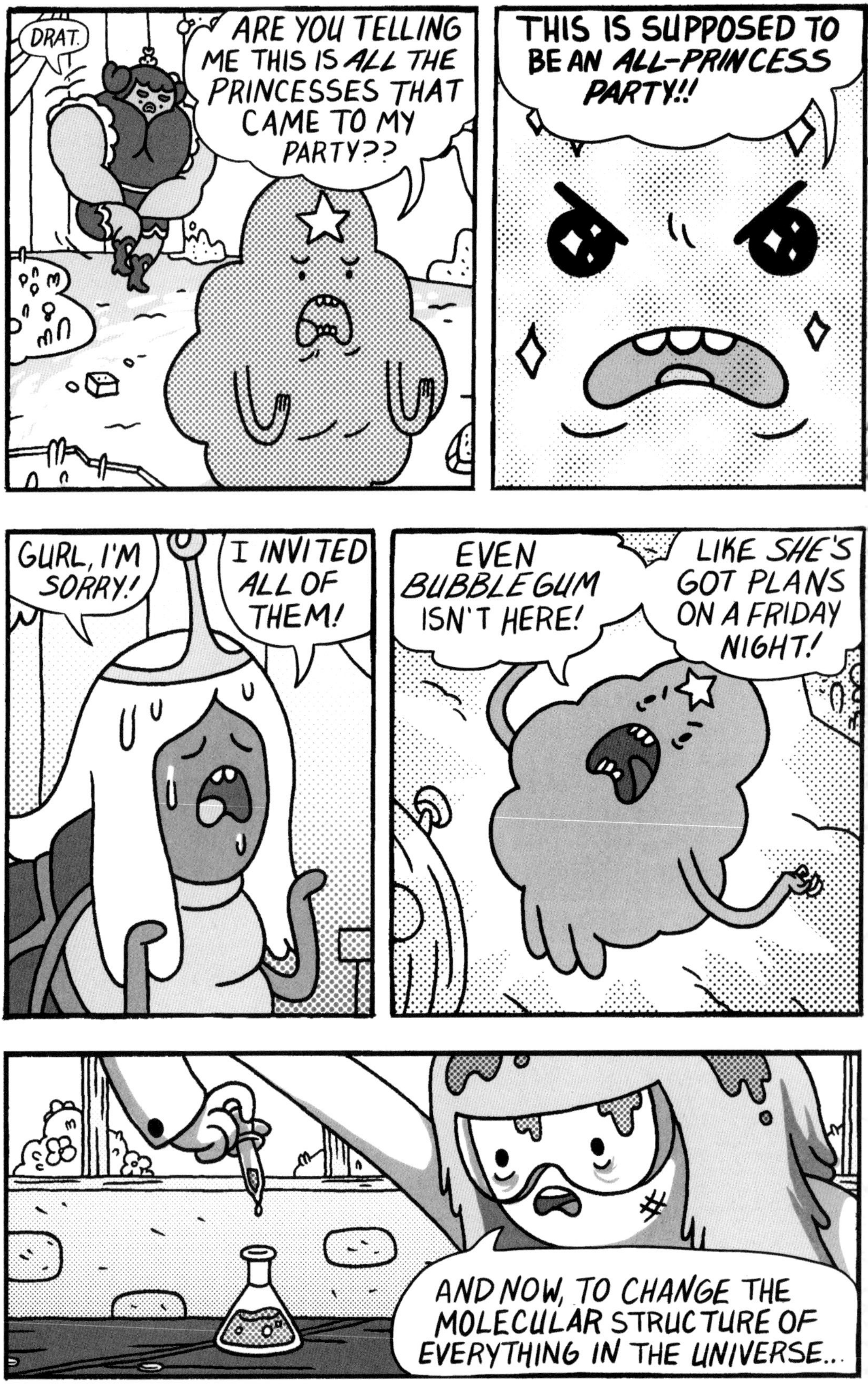
DRAT.
ARE YOU TELLING ME THIS IS ALL THE PRINCESSES THAT CAME TO MY PARTY??
THIS IS SUPPOSED TO BE AN ALL-PRINCESS PARTY!!
GURL, I'M SORRY!
I INVITED ALL OF THEM!
EVEN BUBBLEGUM ISN'T HERE!
LIKE SHE'S GOT PLANS ON A FRIDAY NIGHT!
AND NOW, TO CHANGE THE MOLECULAR STRUCTURE OF EVERYTHING IN THE UNIVERSE...

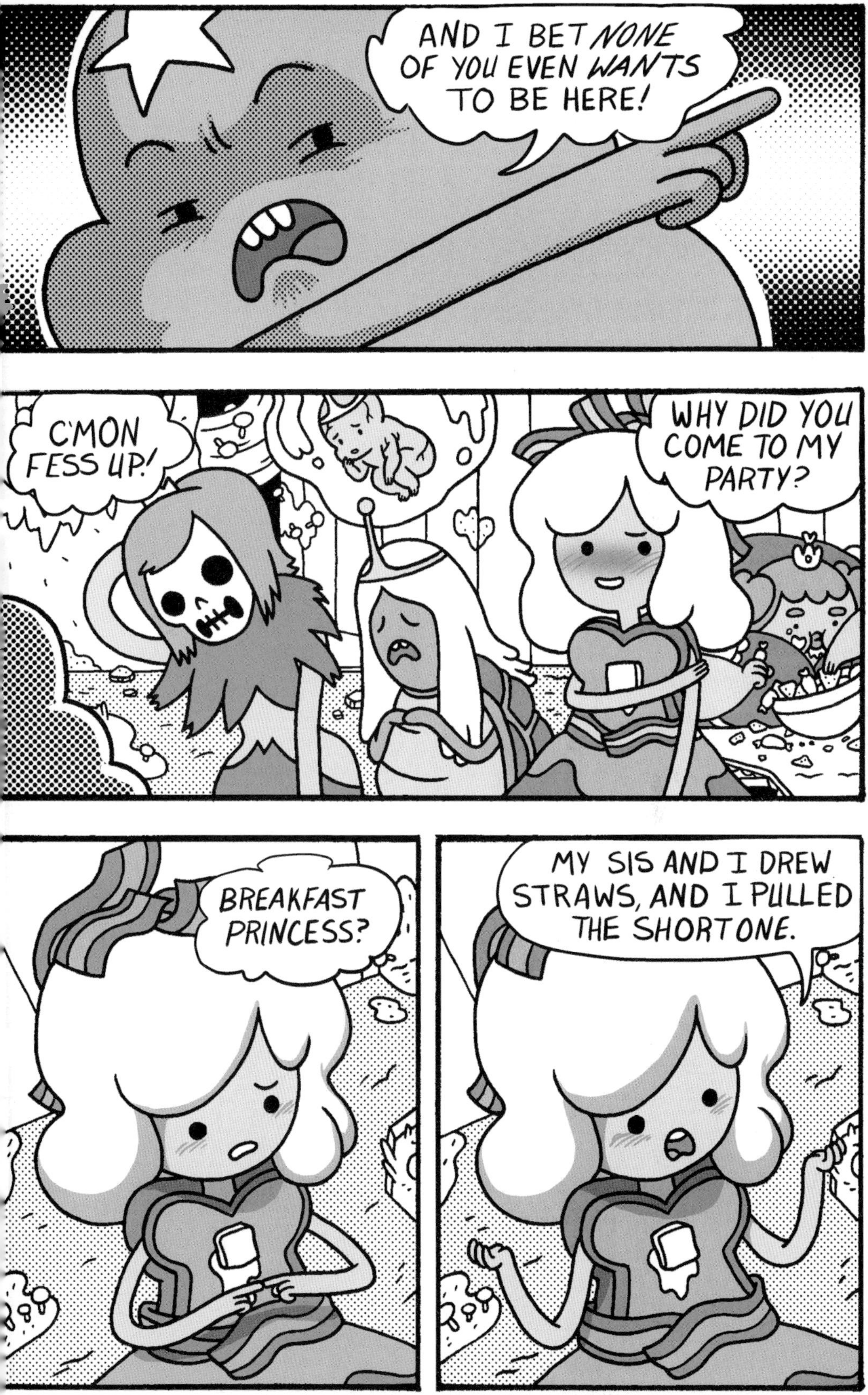
AND I BET NONE OF YOU EVEN WANTS TO BE HERE!
C'MON FESS UP!
WHY DID YOU COME TO MY PARTY?
BREAKFAST PRINCESS?
MY SIS AND I DREW STRAWS, AND I PULLED THE SHORT ONE.

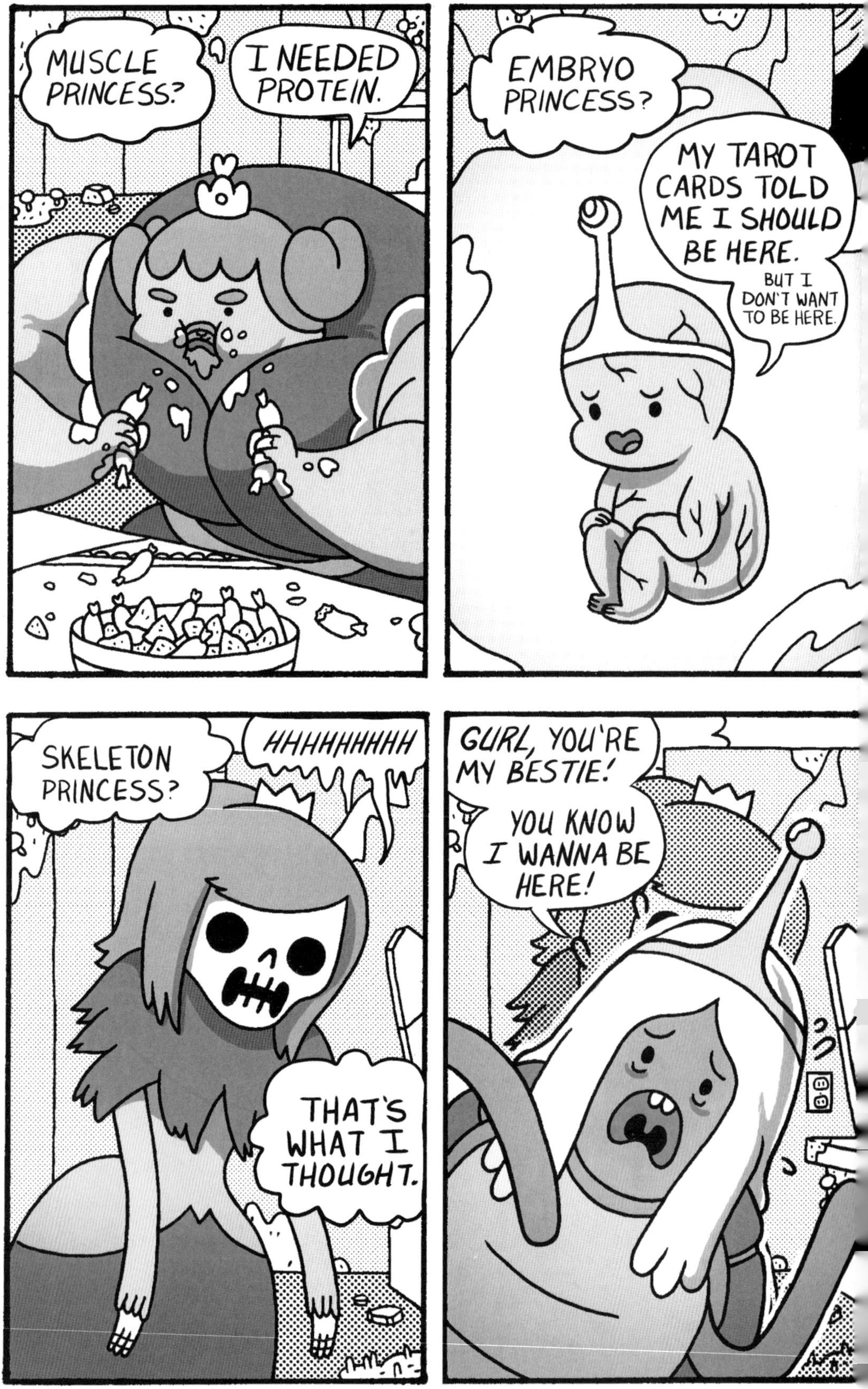
MUSCLE PRINCESS?
I NEEDED PROTEIN.
EMBRYO PRINCESS?
MY TAROT CARDS TOLD ME I SHOULD BE HERE.
BUT I DON'T WANT TO BE HERE.
SKELETON PRINCESS?
HHHHHHHHH
THAT'S WHAT I THOUGHT.
GURL, YOU'RE MY BESTIE!
YOU KNOW I WANNA BE HERE!

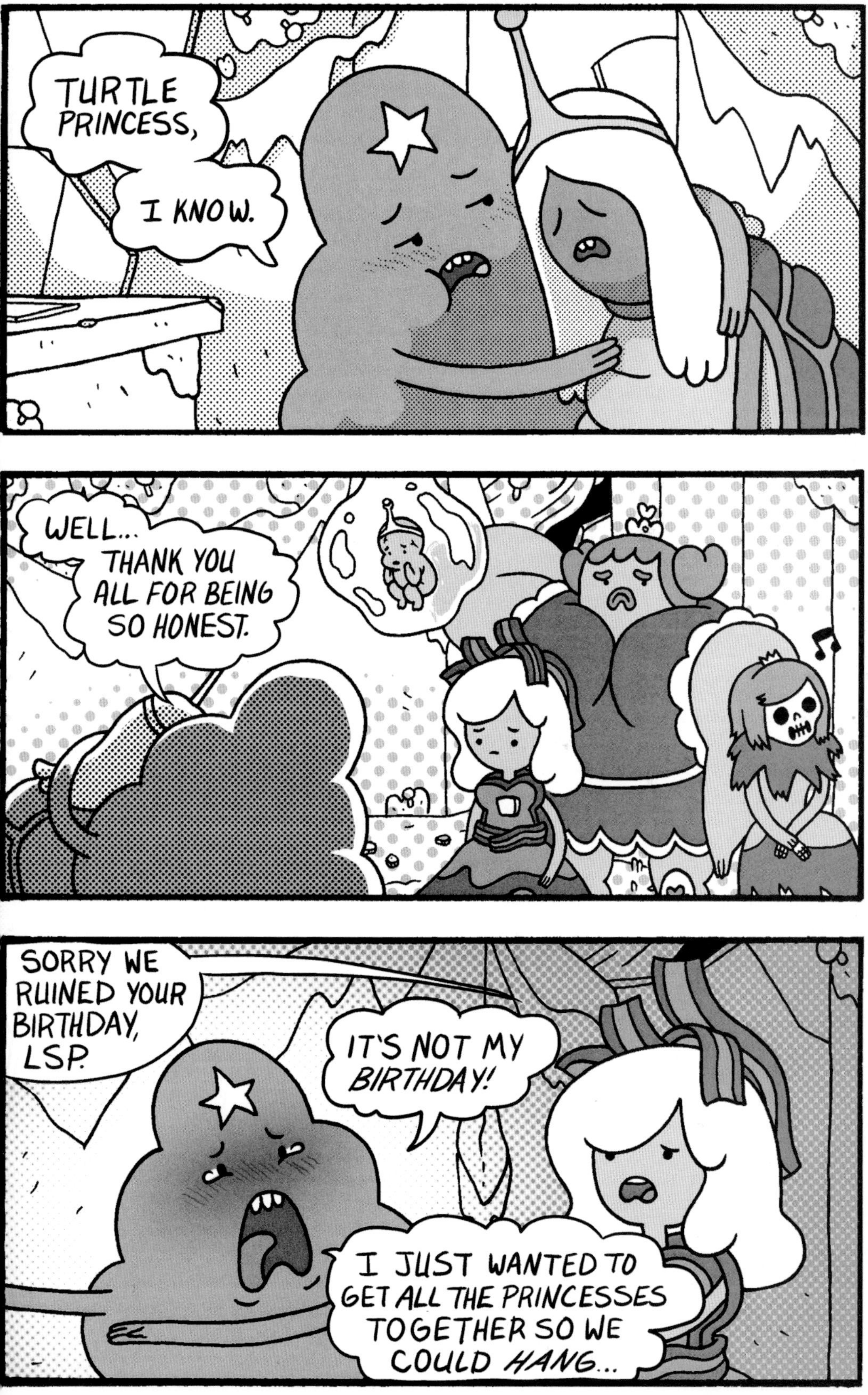

TURTLE PRINCESS,
I KNOW.
WELL...
THANK YOU ALL FOR BEING SO HONEST.
SORRY WE RUINED YOUR BIRTHDAY, LSP.
IT'S NOT MY BIRTHDAY!
I JUST WANTED TO GET ALL THE PRINCESSES TOGETHER SO WE COULD HANG...

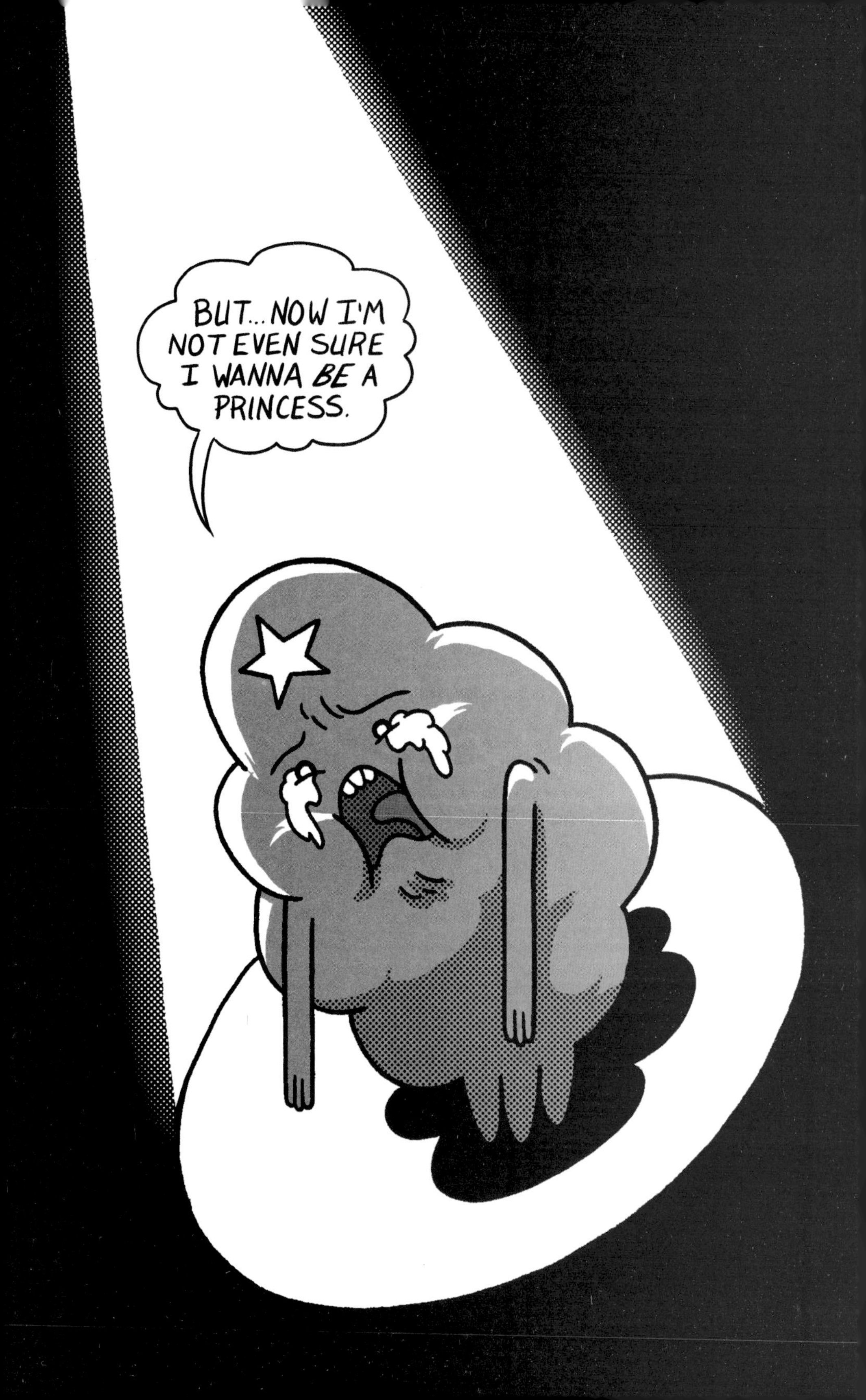
BUT... NOW I'M NOT EVEN SURE I WANNA *BE* A PRINCESS.

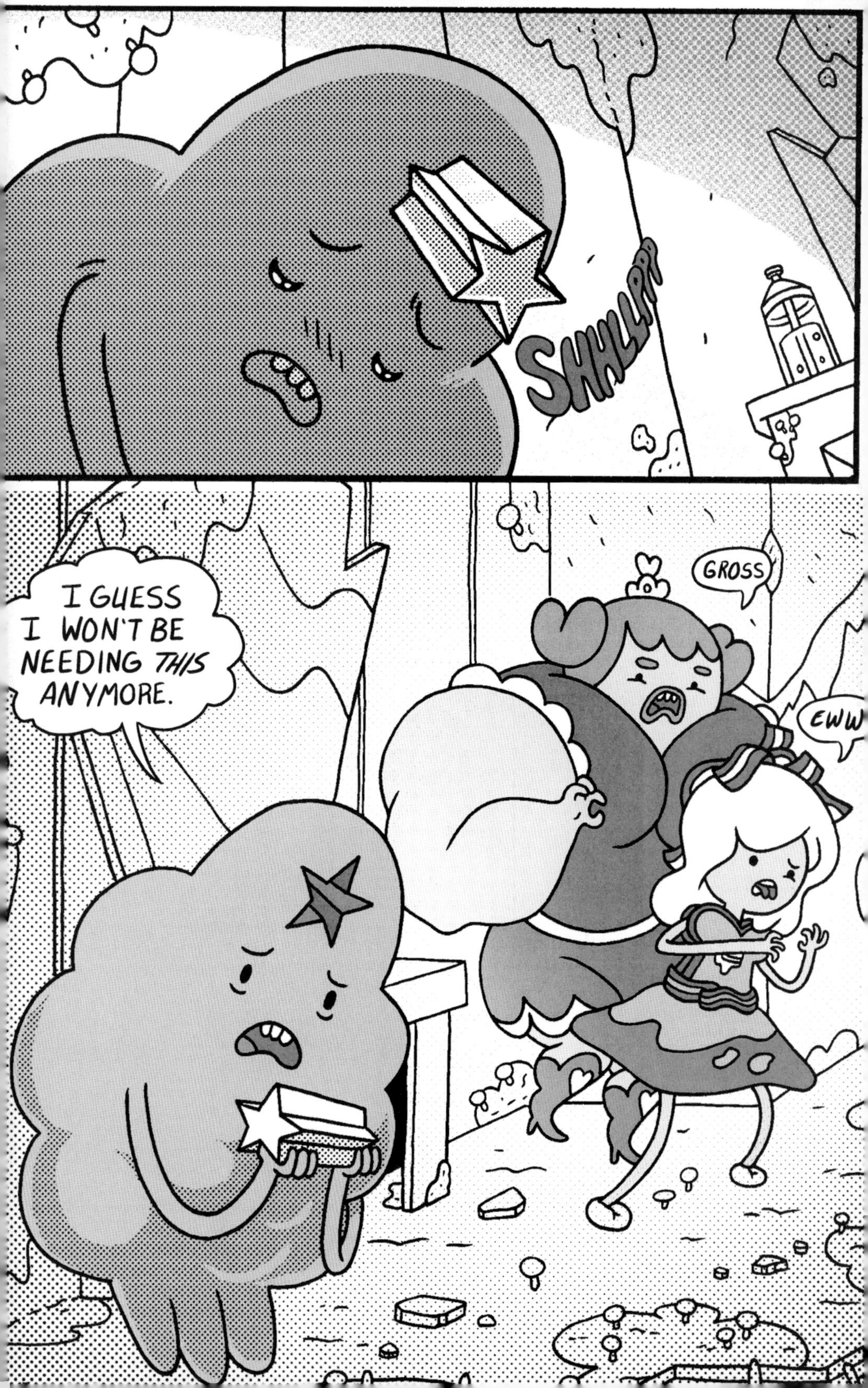
SHHLLPPP
I GUESS I WON'T BE NEEDING THIS ANYMORE.
GROSS
EWW

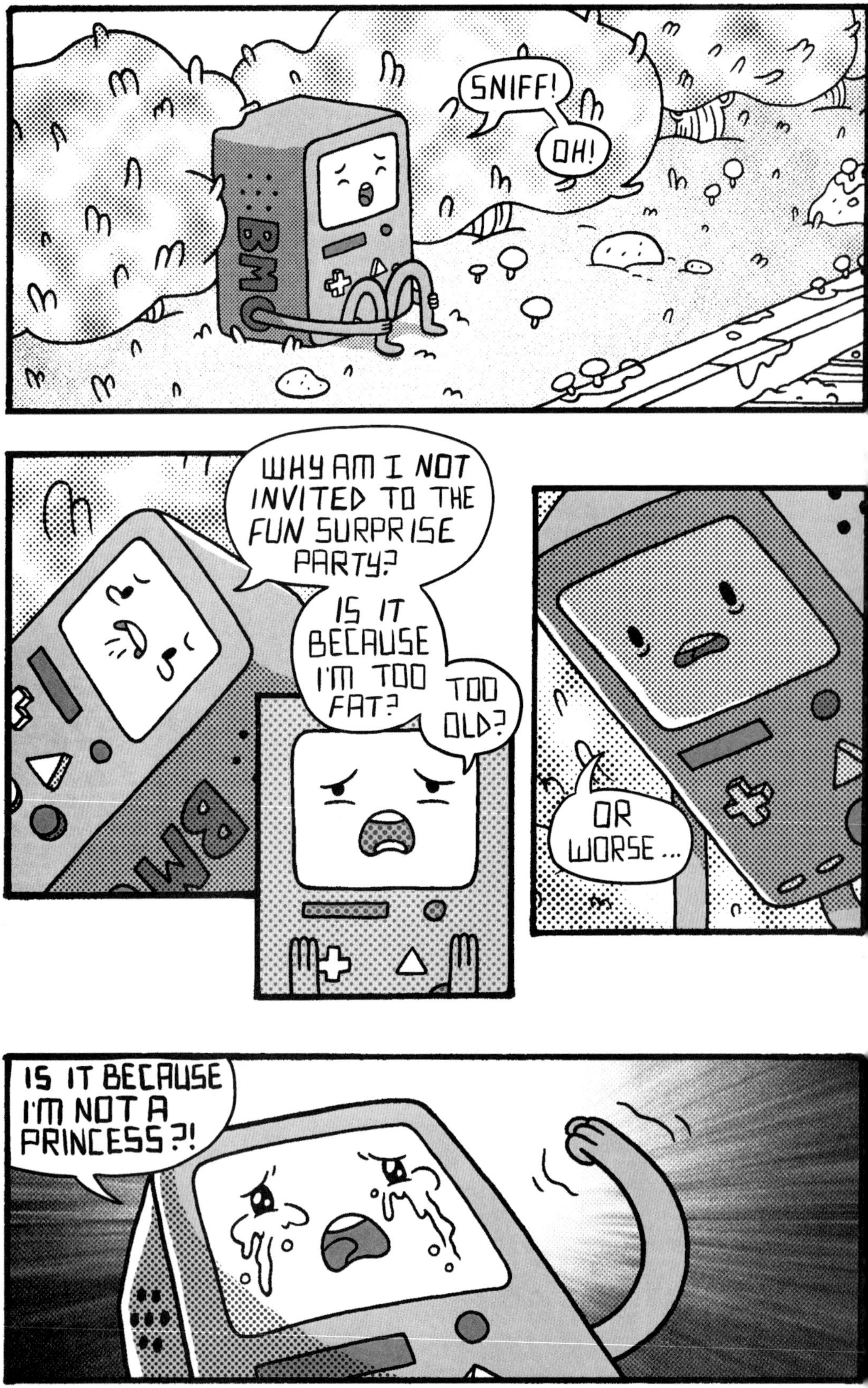
SNIFF!
OH!
WHY AM I NOT INVITED TO THE FUN SURPRISE PARTY?
IS IT BECAUSE I'M TOO FAT?
TOO OLD?
OR WORSE...
IS IT BECAUSE I'M NOT A PRINCESS?!

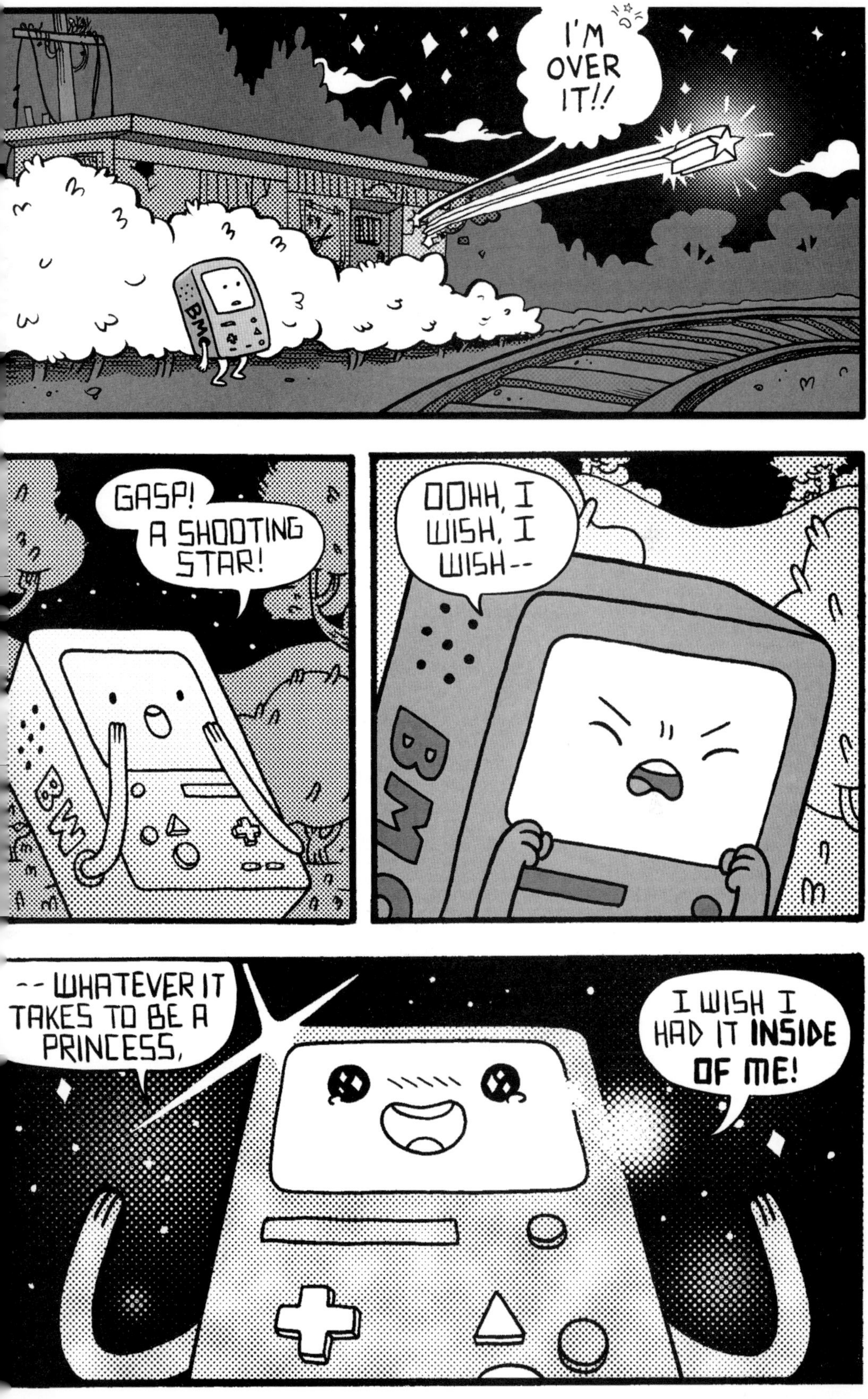
I'M OVER IT!!
GASP! A SHOOTING STAR!
OOHH, I WISH, I WISH--
--WHATEVER IT TAKES TO BE A PRINCESS,
I WISH I HAD IT **INSIDE OF ME!**
BMO

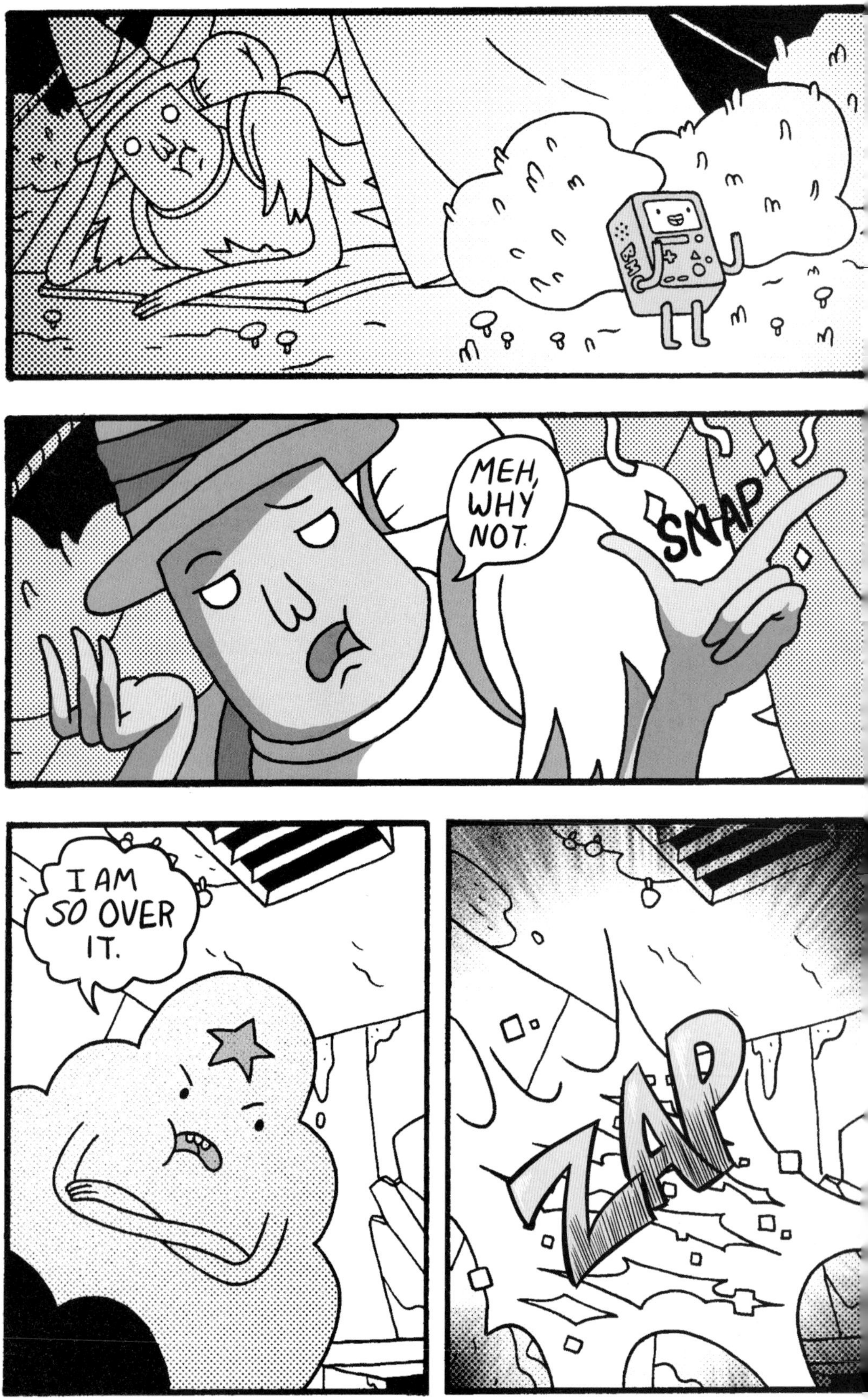
MEH, WHY NOT.
SNAP
I AM SO OVER IT.
ZAP

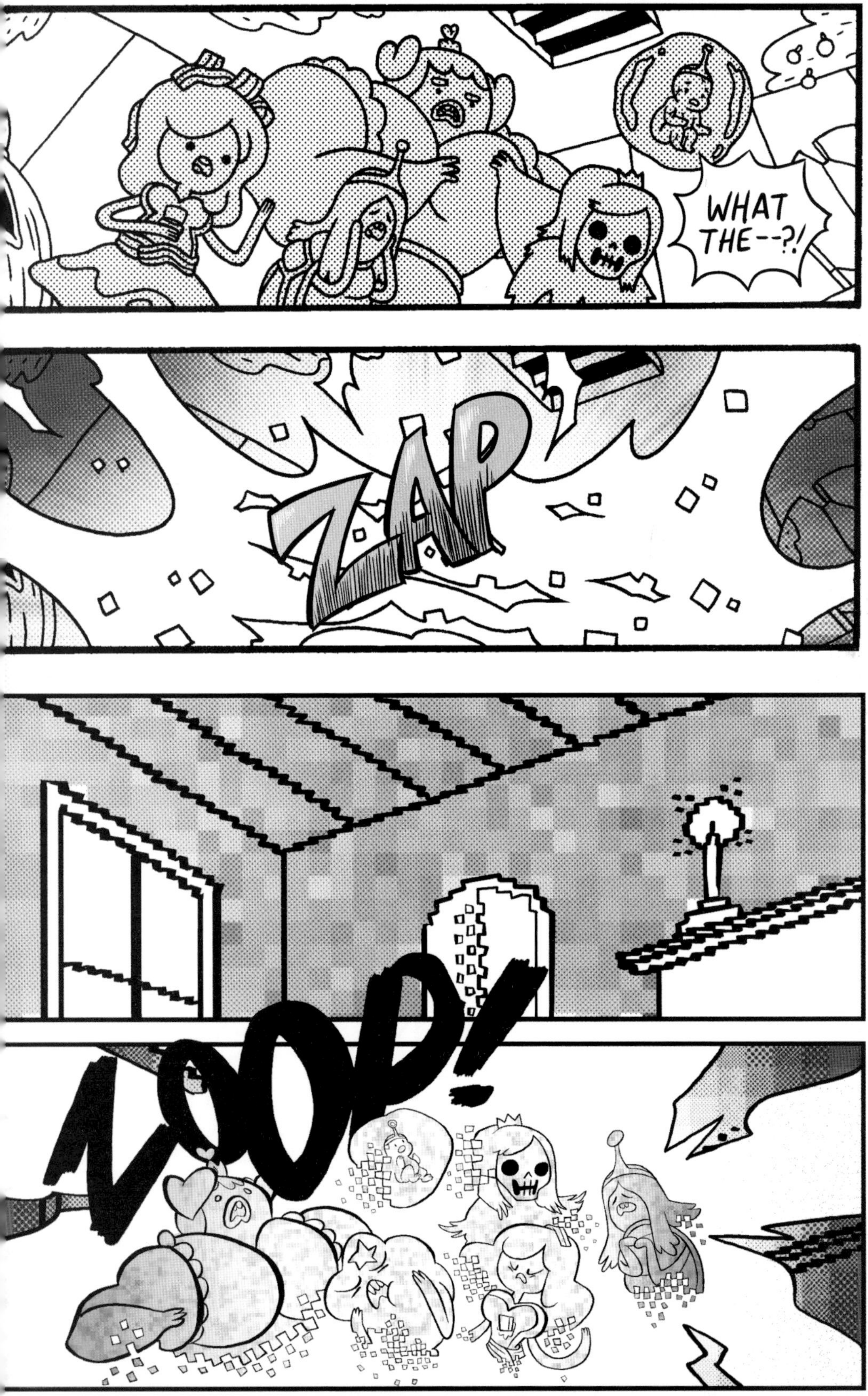
WHAT THE--?!
ZAP
ZOOP!

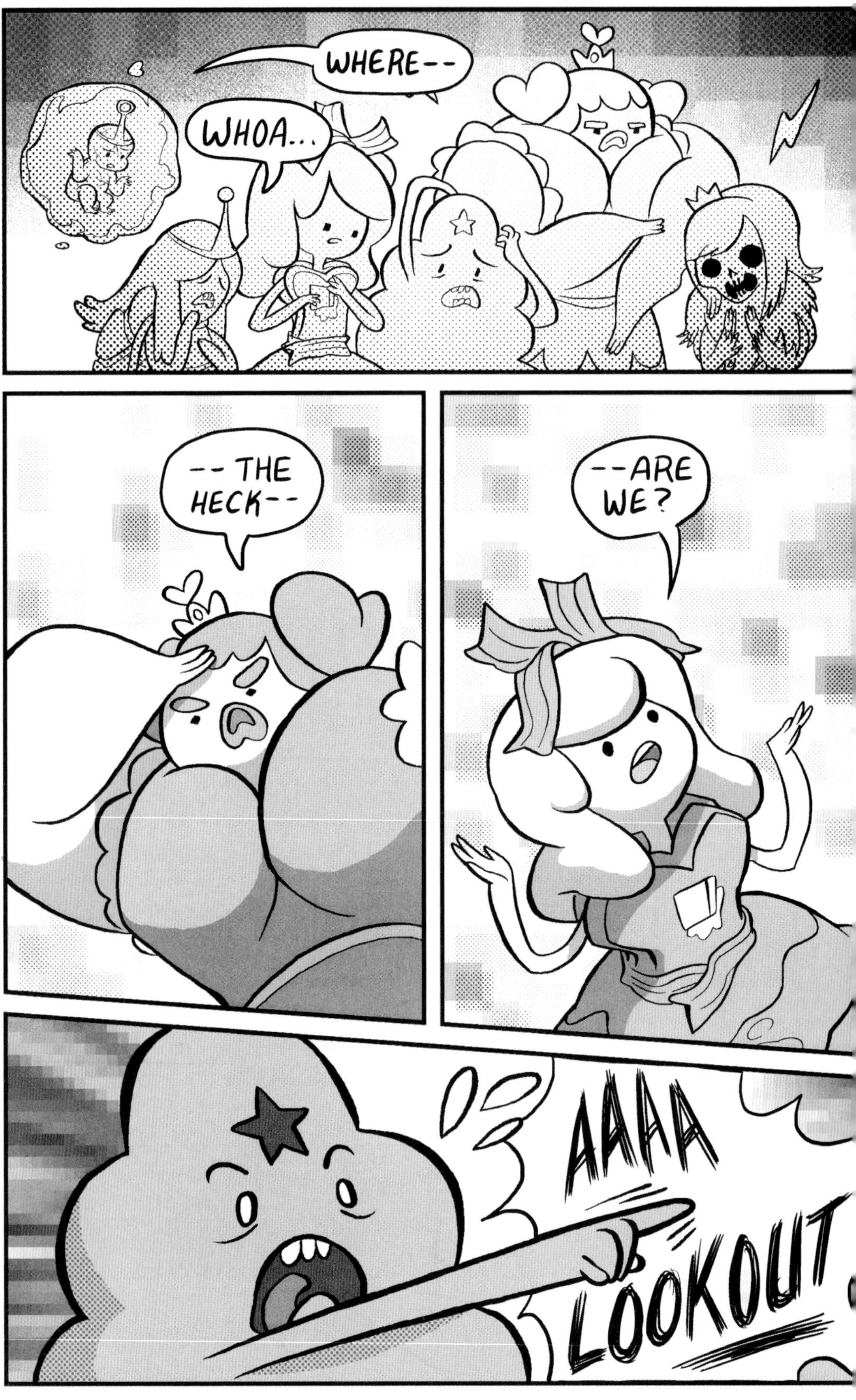
WHERE--
WHOA...
--THE HECK--
--ARE WE?
AAAA
LOOKOUT

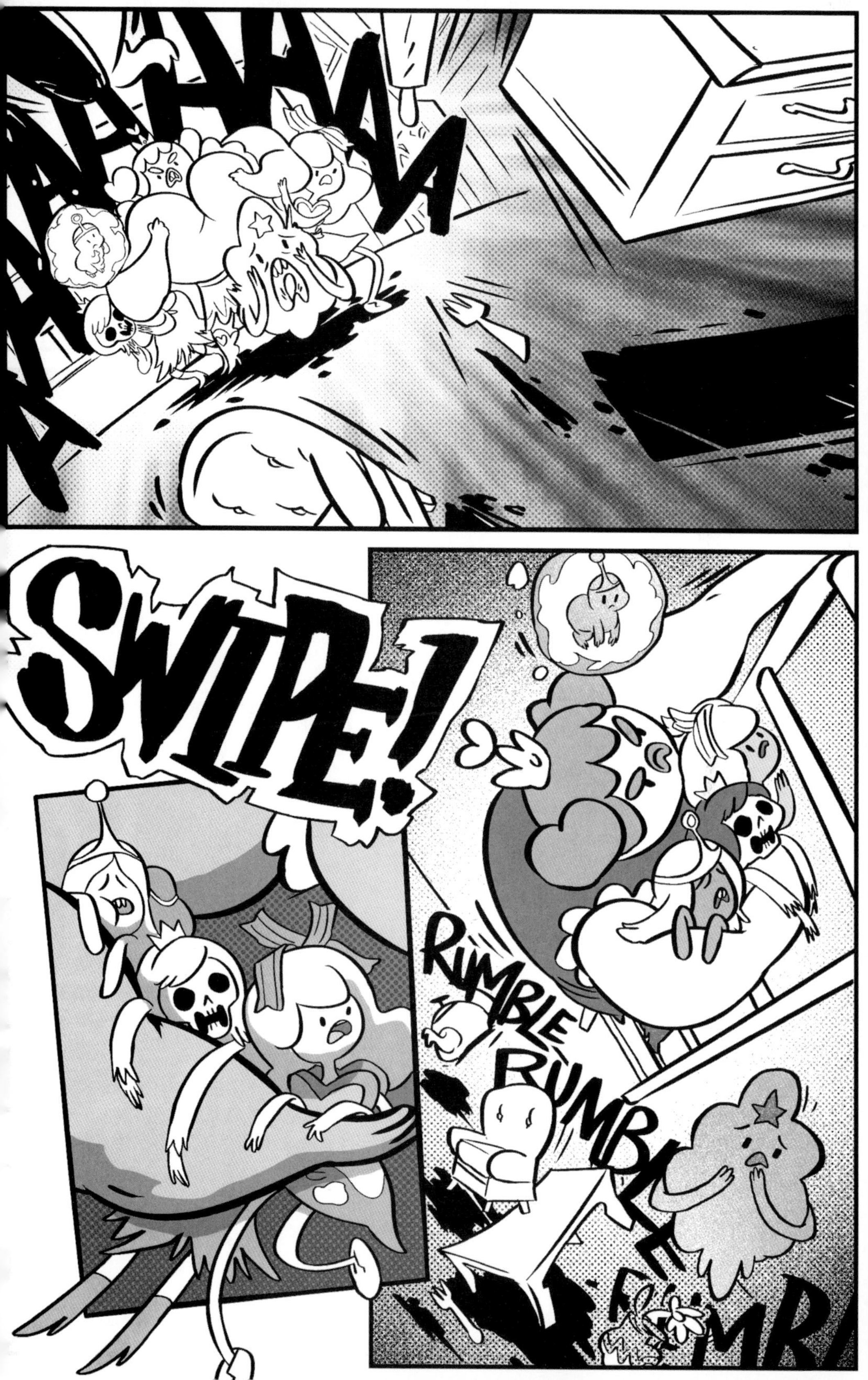
SWIPE!
RUMBLE
RUMBLE

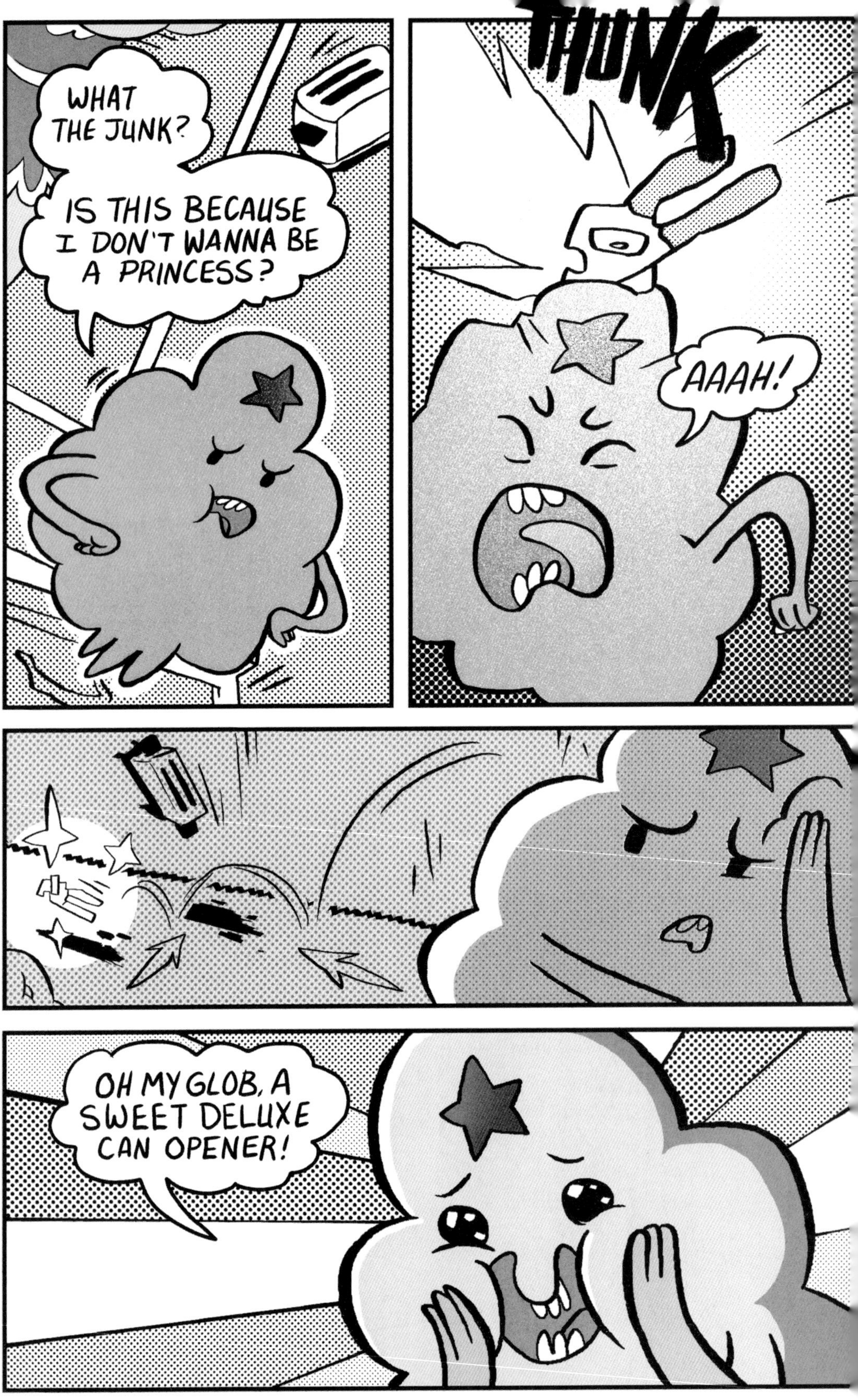
WHAT THE JUNK?
IS THIS BECAUSE I DON'T WANNA BE A PRINCESS?
THUNK
AAAH!
OH MY GLOB, A SWEET DELUXE CAN OPENER!

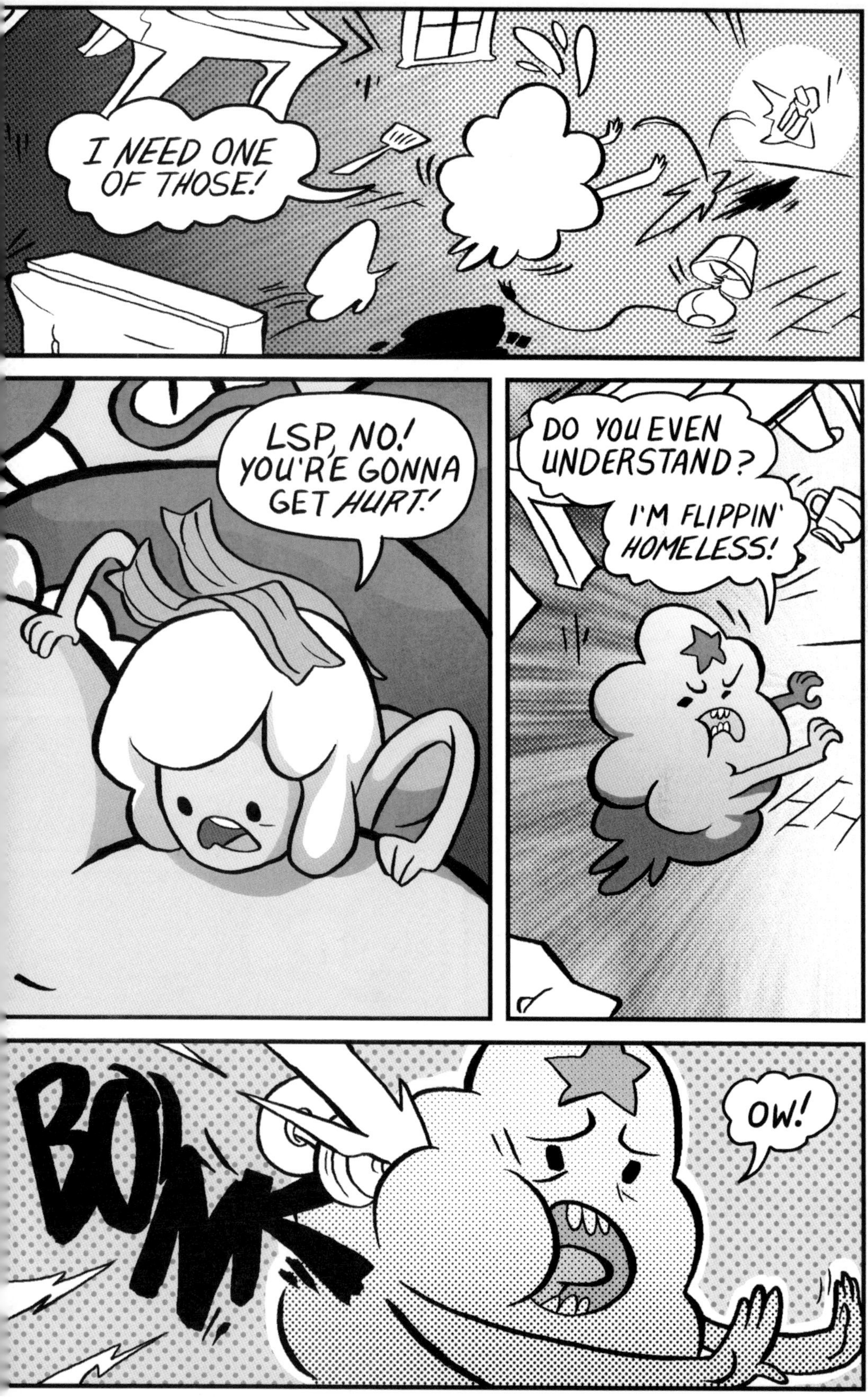
I NEED ONE OF THOSE!
LSP, NO! YOU'RE GONNA GET HURT!
DO YOU EVEN UNDERSTAND?
I'M FLIPPIN' HOMELESS!
BONK
OW!

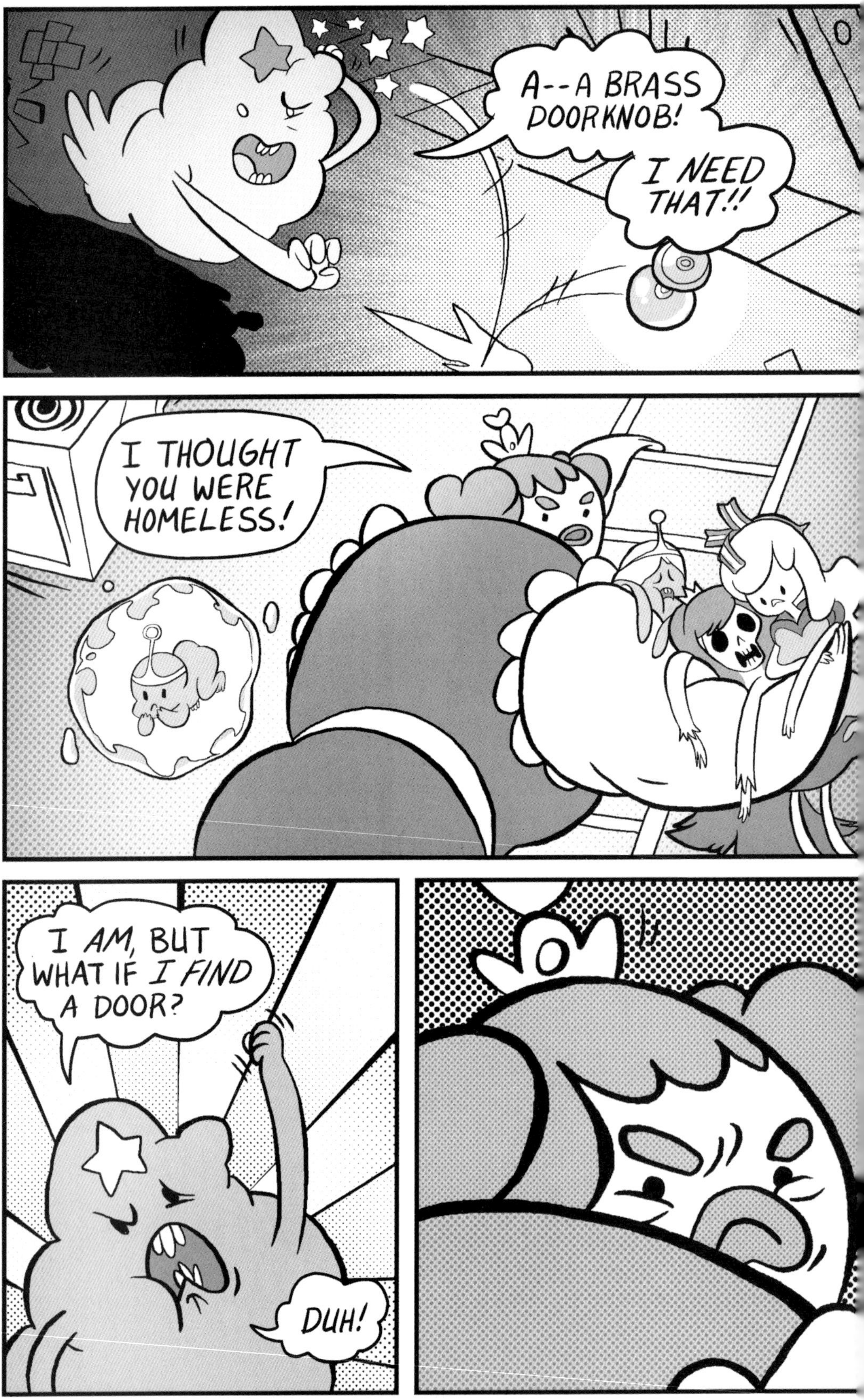
A--A BRASS DOORKNOB!
I NEED THAT!!
I THOUGHT YOU WERE HOMELESS!
I AM, BUT WHAT IF I FIND A DOOR?
DUH!

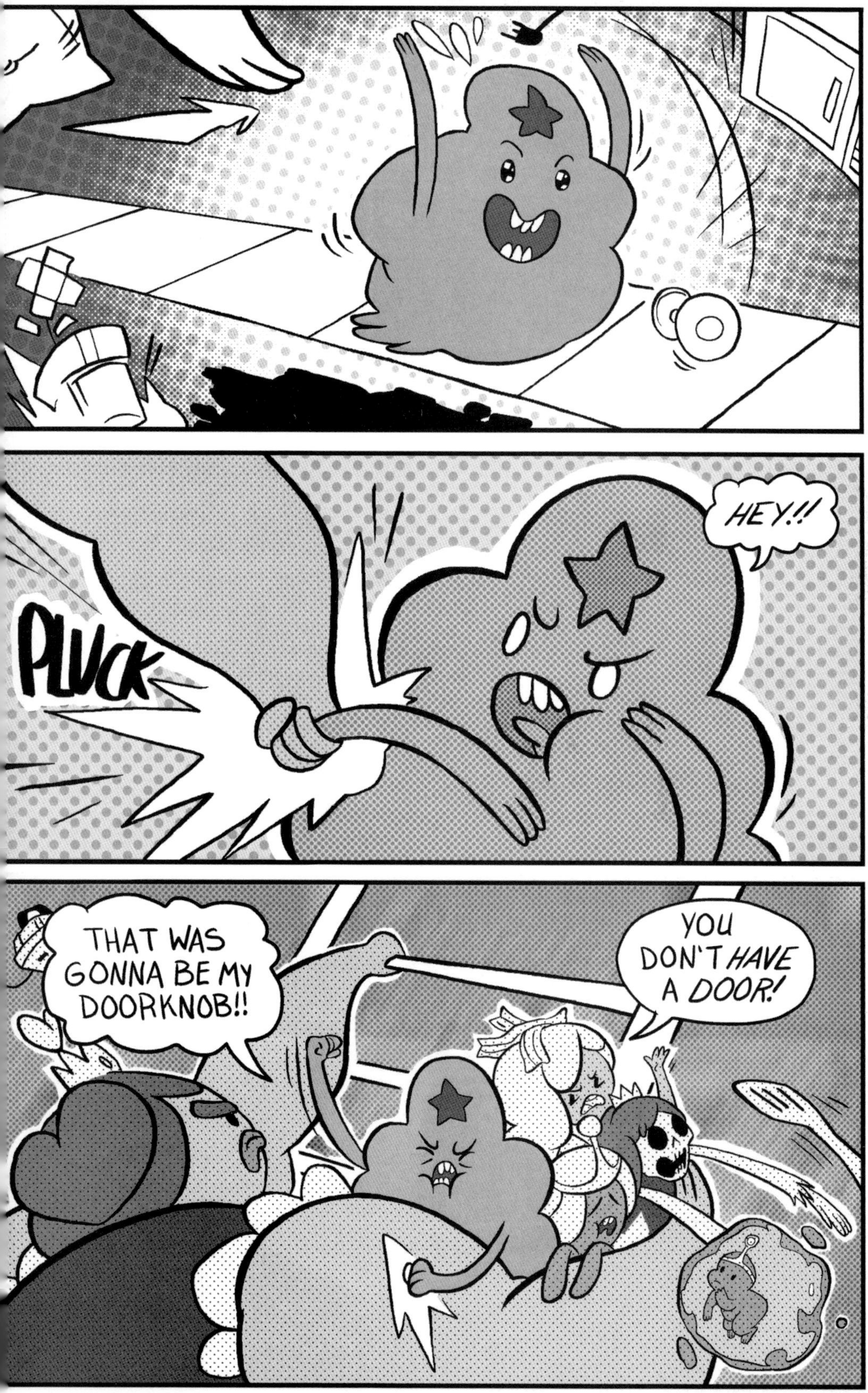
HEY!!
PLUCK
THAT WAS GONNA BE MY DOORKNOB!!
YOU DON'T HAVE A DOOR!

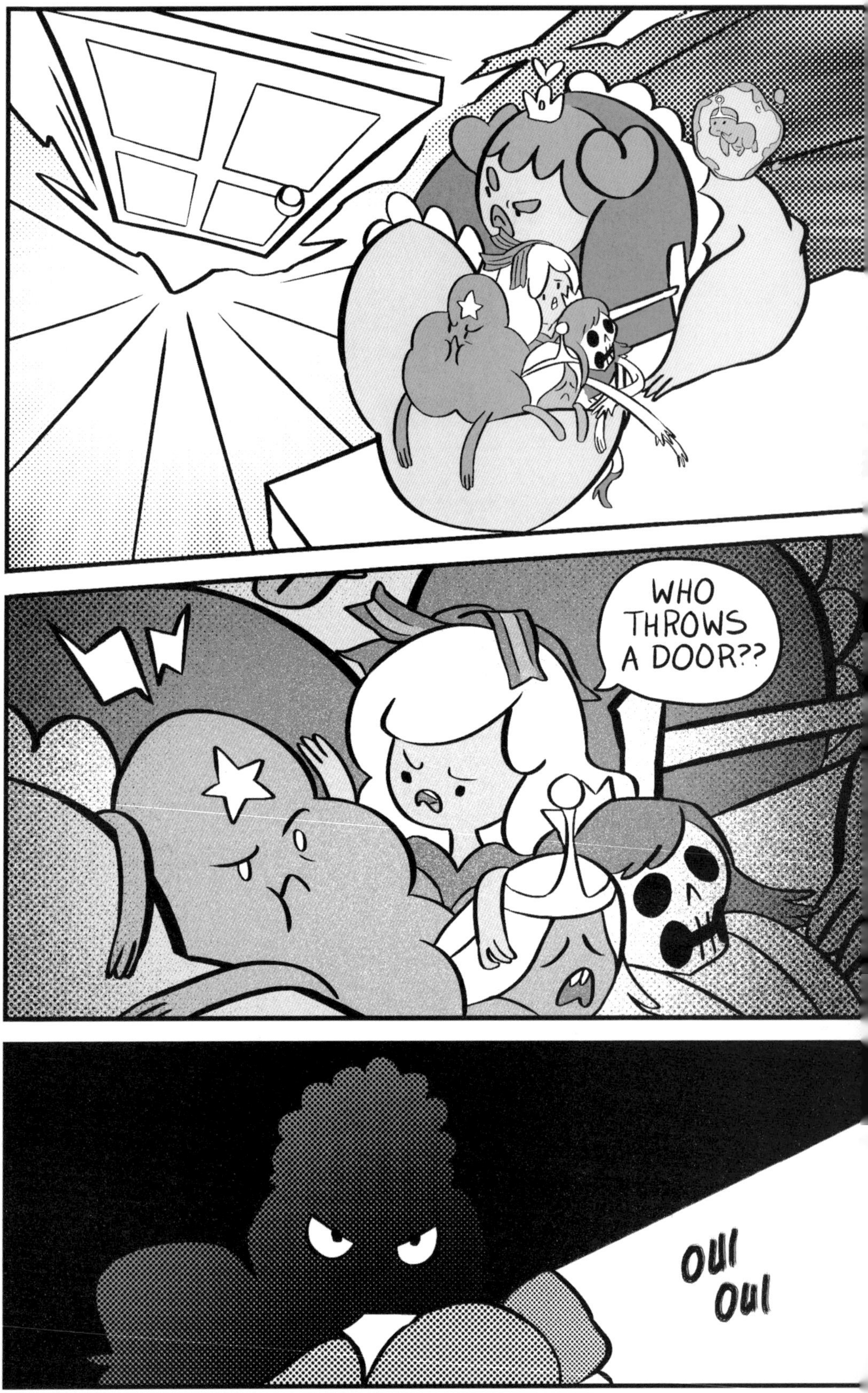
WHO THROWS A DOOR??
OUI OUI

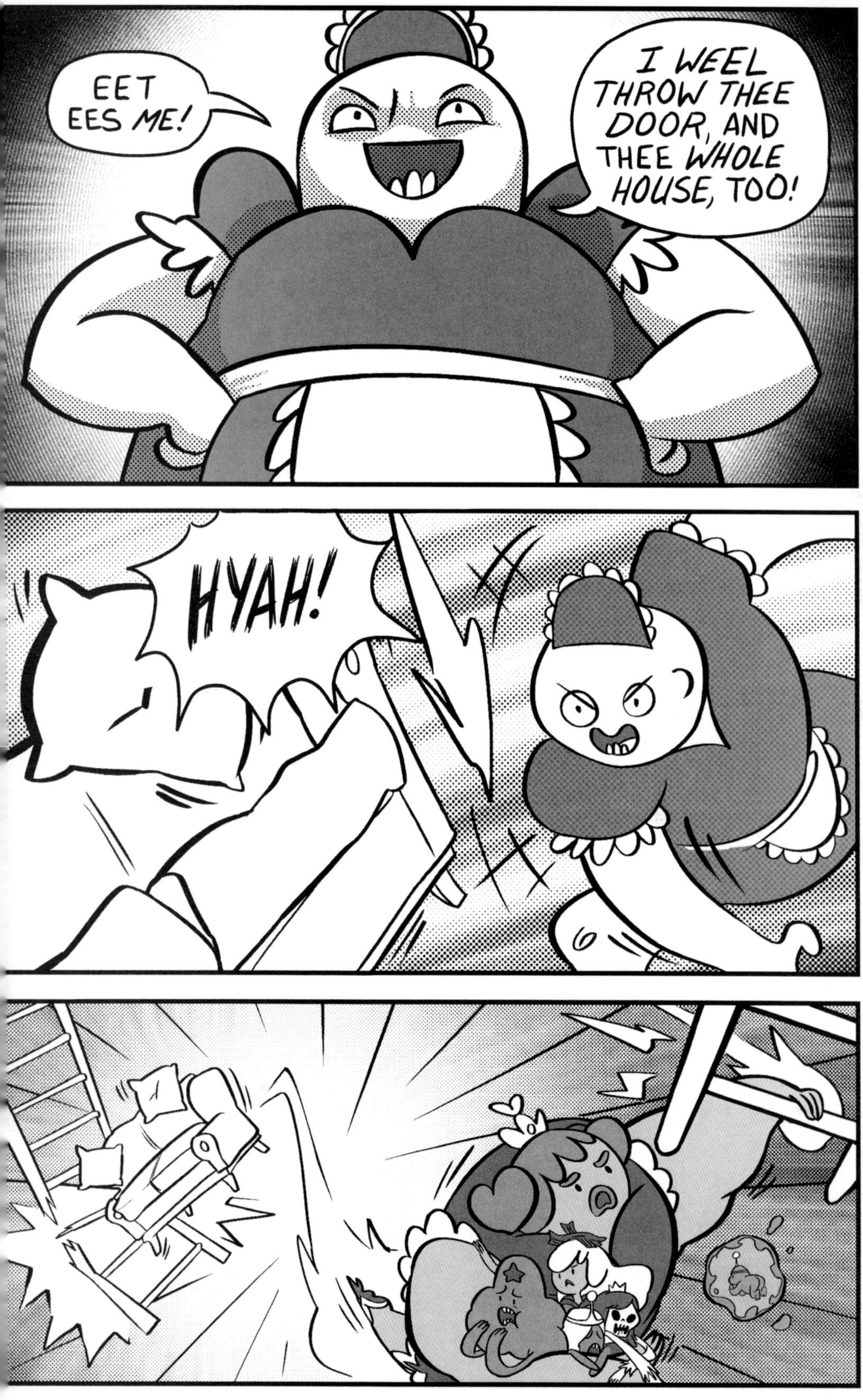
EET EES ME!
I WEEL THROW THEE DOOR, AND THEE WHOLE HOUSE, TOO!
HYAH!

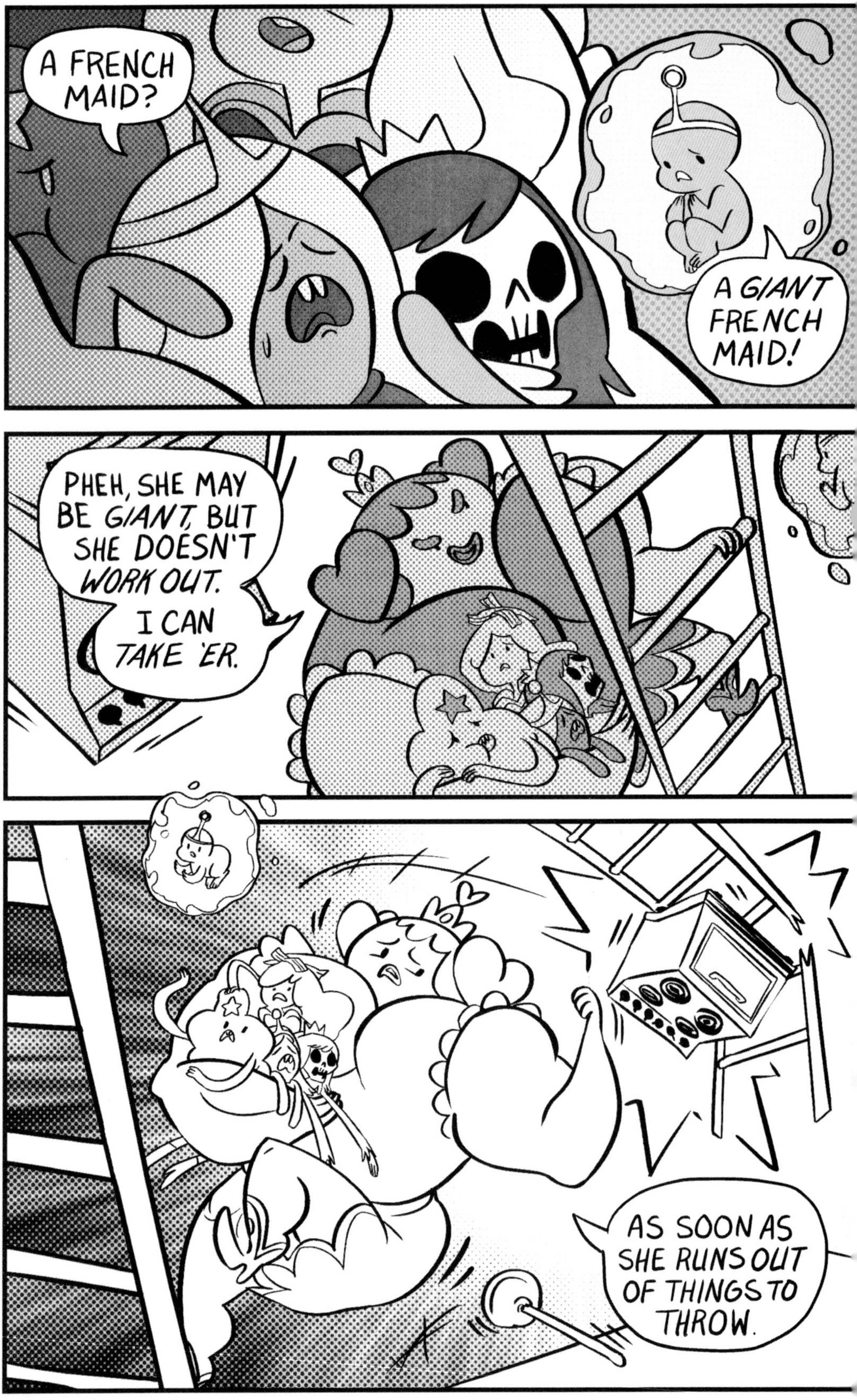
A FRENCH MAID?
A GIANT FRENCH MAID!
PHEH, SHE MAY BE GIANT, BUT SHE DOESN'T WORK OUT.
I CAN TAKE 'ER.
AS SOON AS SHE RUNS OUT OF THINGS TO THROW.

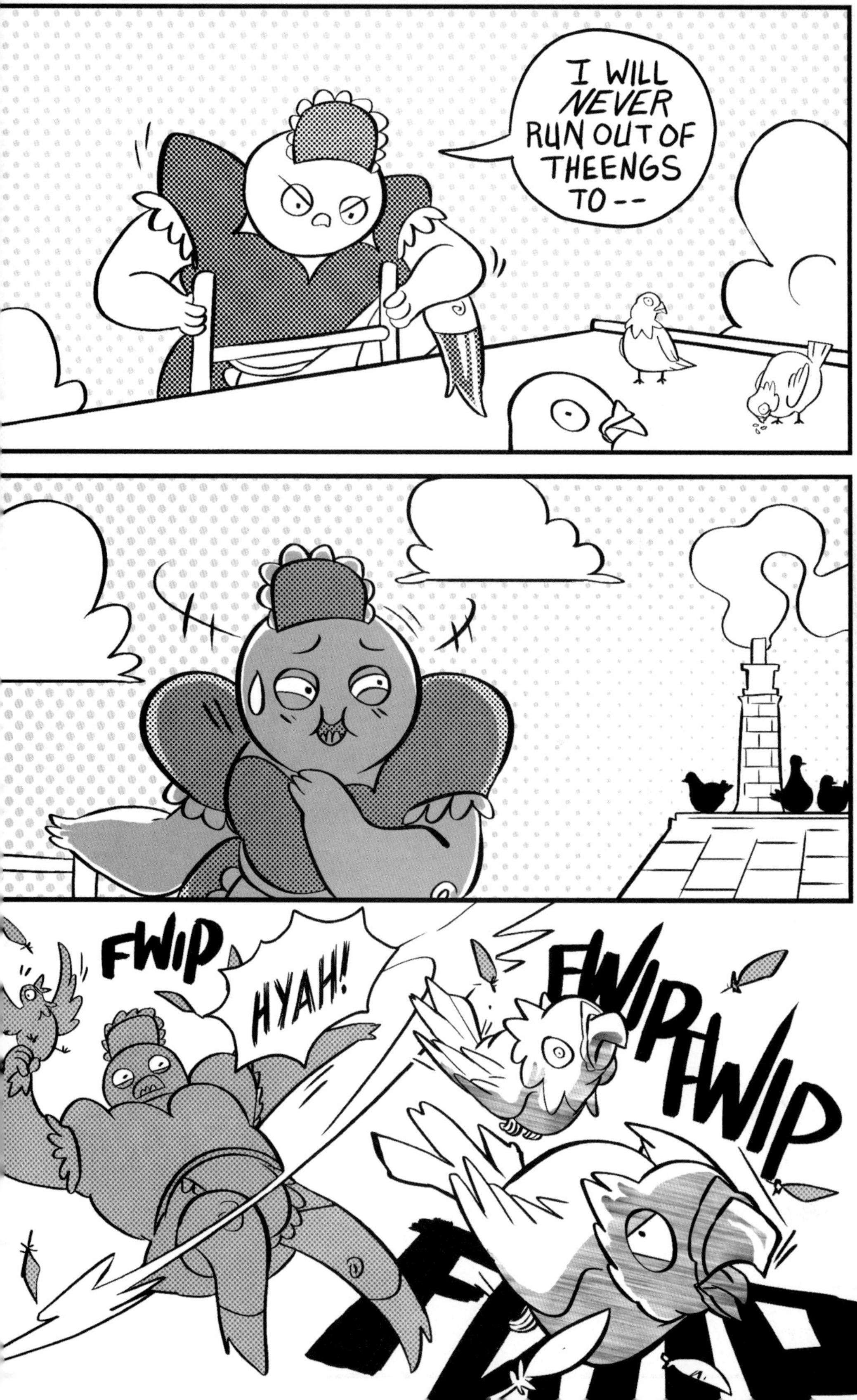
I WILL *NEVER* RUN OUT OF THEENGS TO --
FWIP
HYAH!
FWIP FWIP FWIP

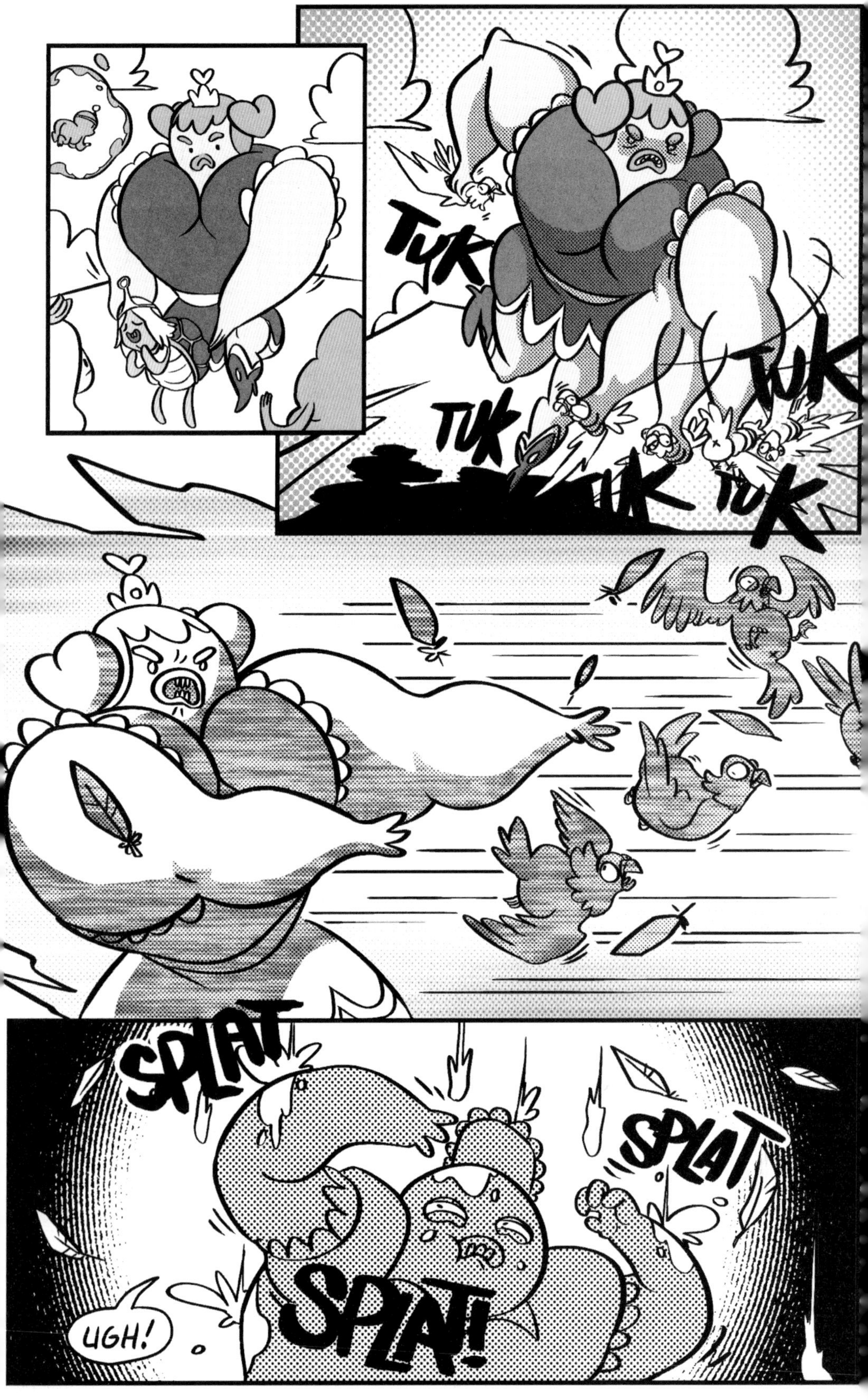
TUK
TUK
TUK
TUK
TUK
SPLAT
SPLAT
SPLAT!
UGH!

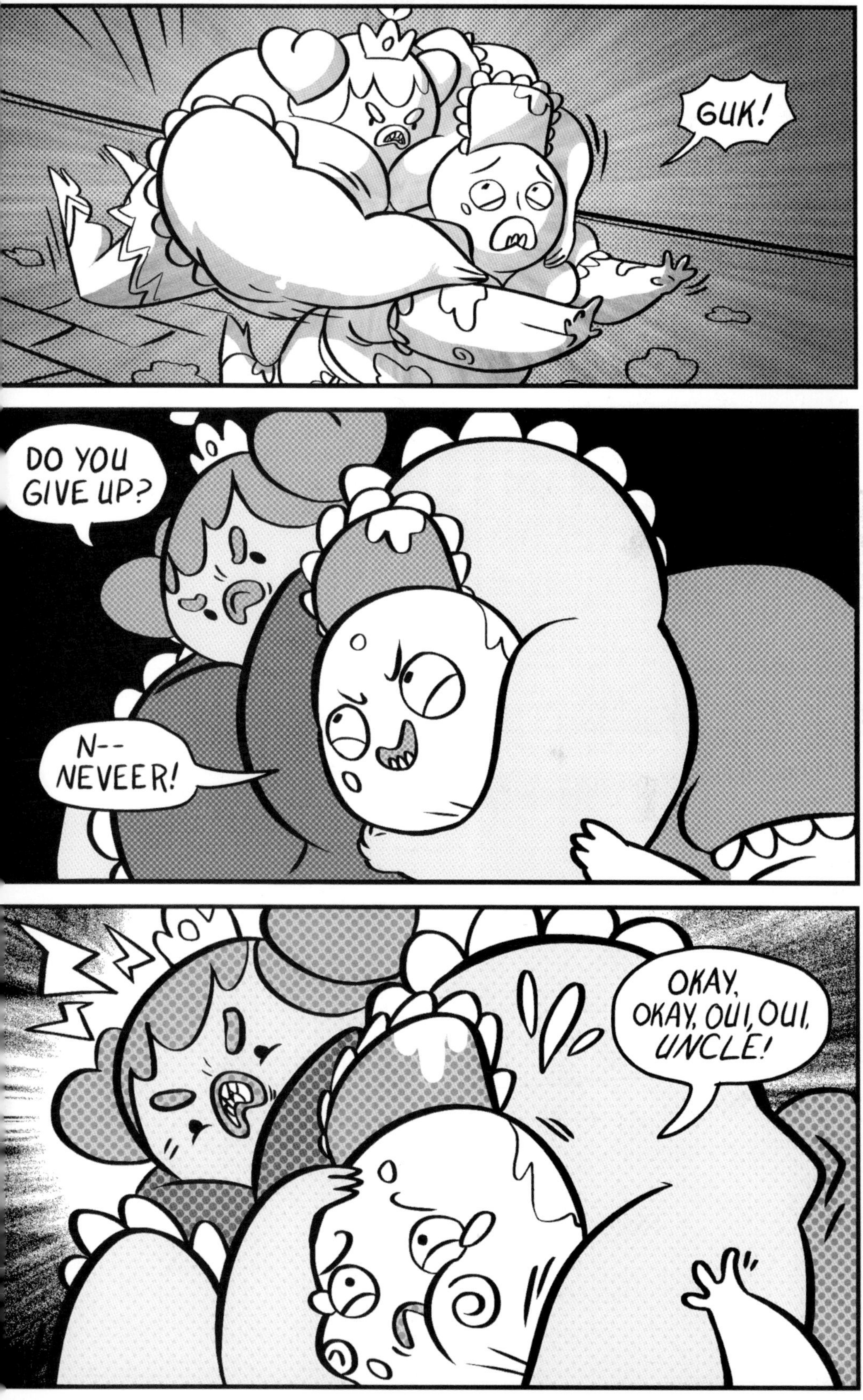
GUK!
DO YOU GIVE UP?
N-- NEVEER!
OKAY, OKAY, OUI, OUI, UNCLE!

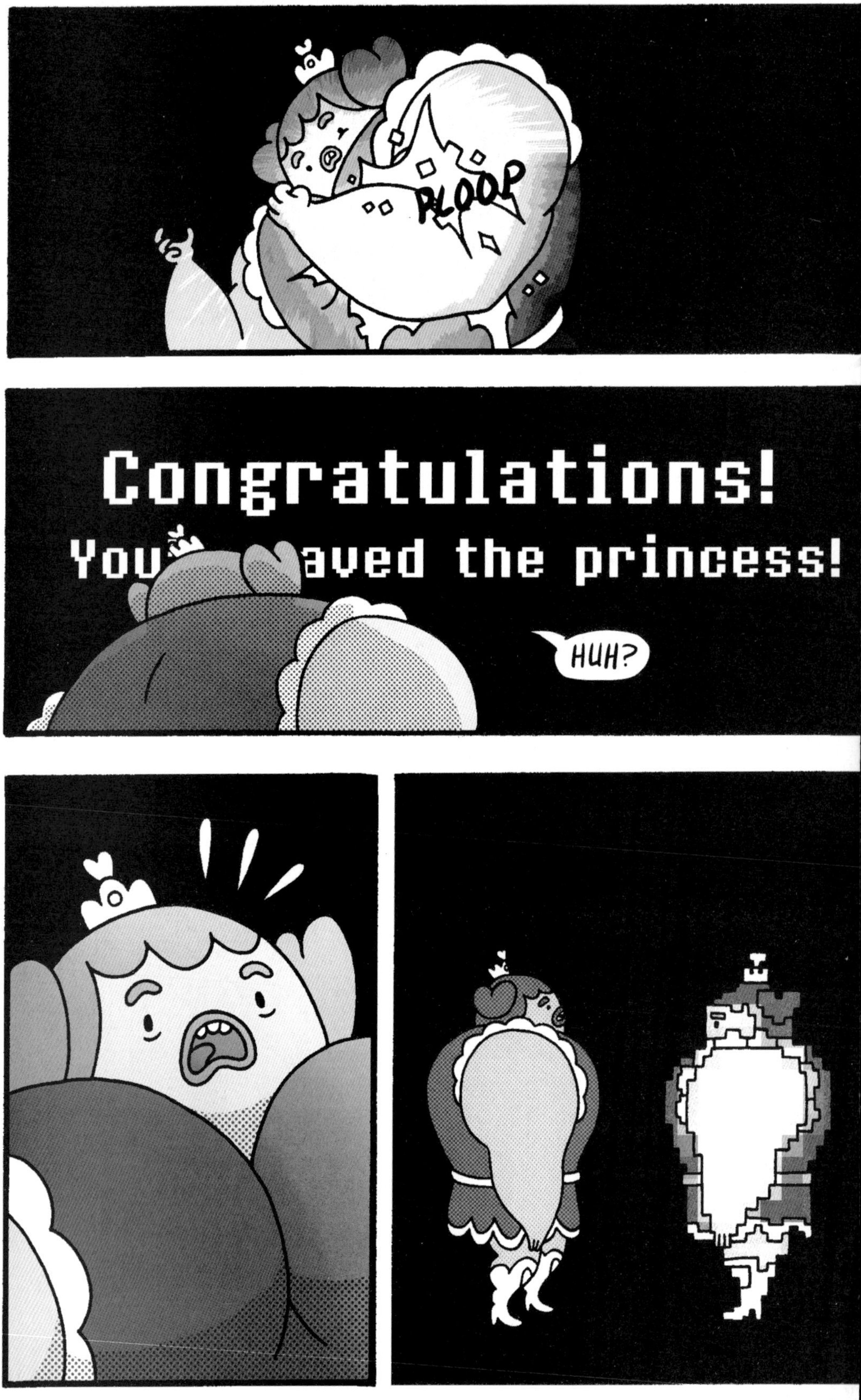
PLOOP
Congratulations!
You saved the princess!
HUH?

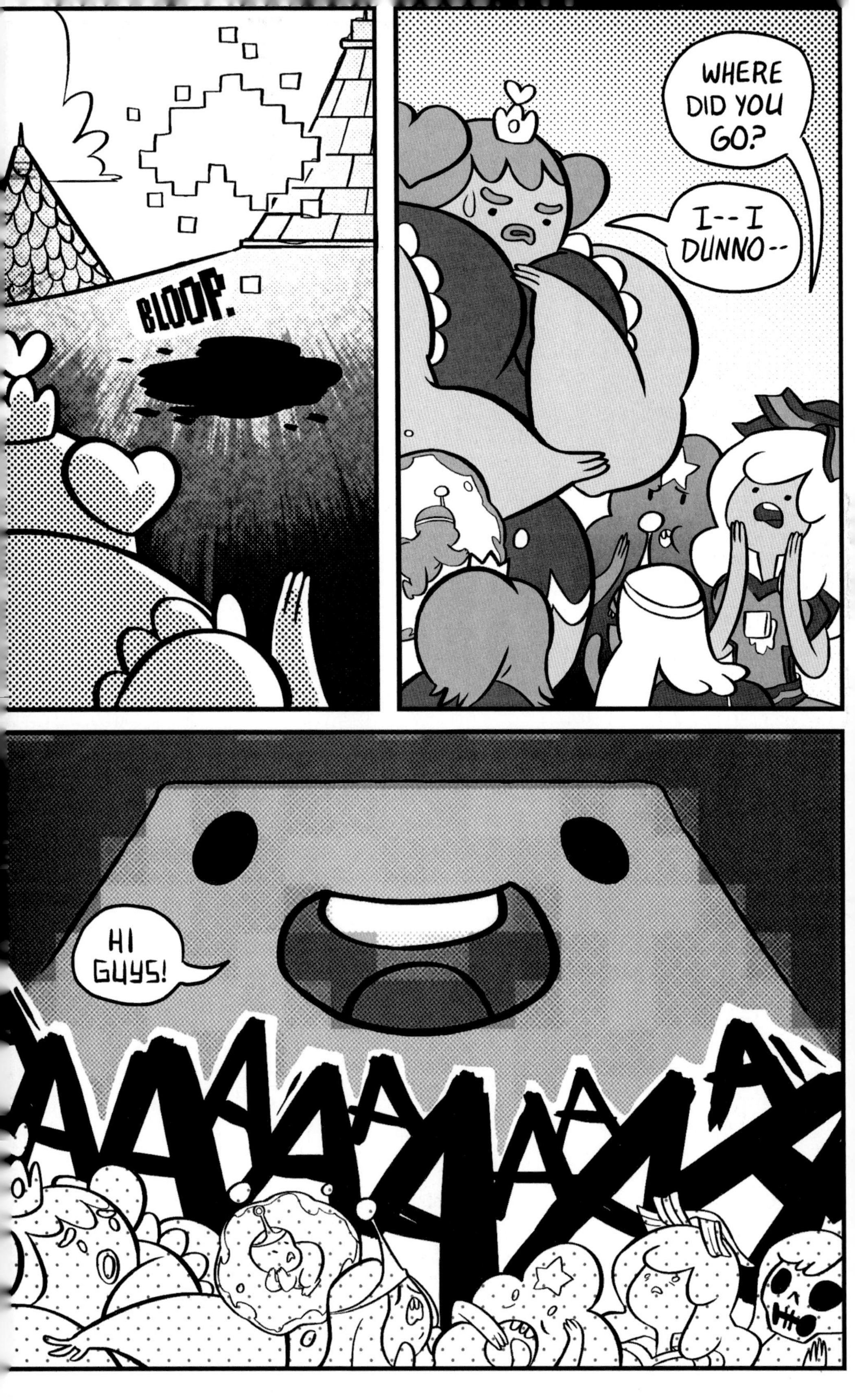
BLOOP.
WHERE DID YOU GO?
I-- I DUNNO--
HI GUYS!
AAAAAAAAAAA

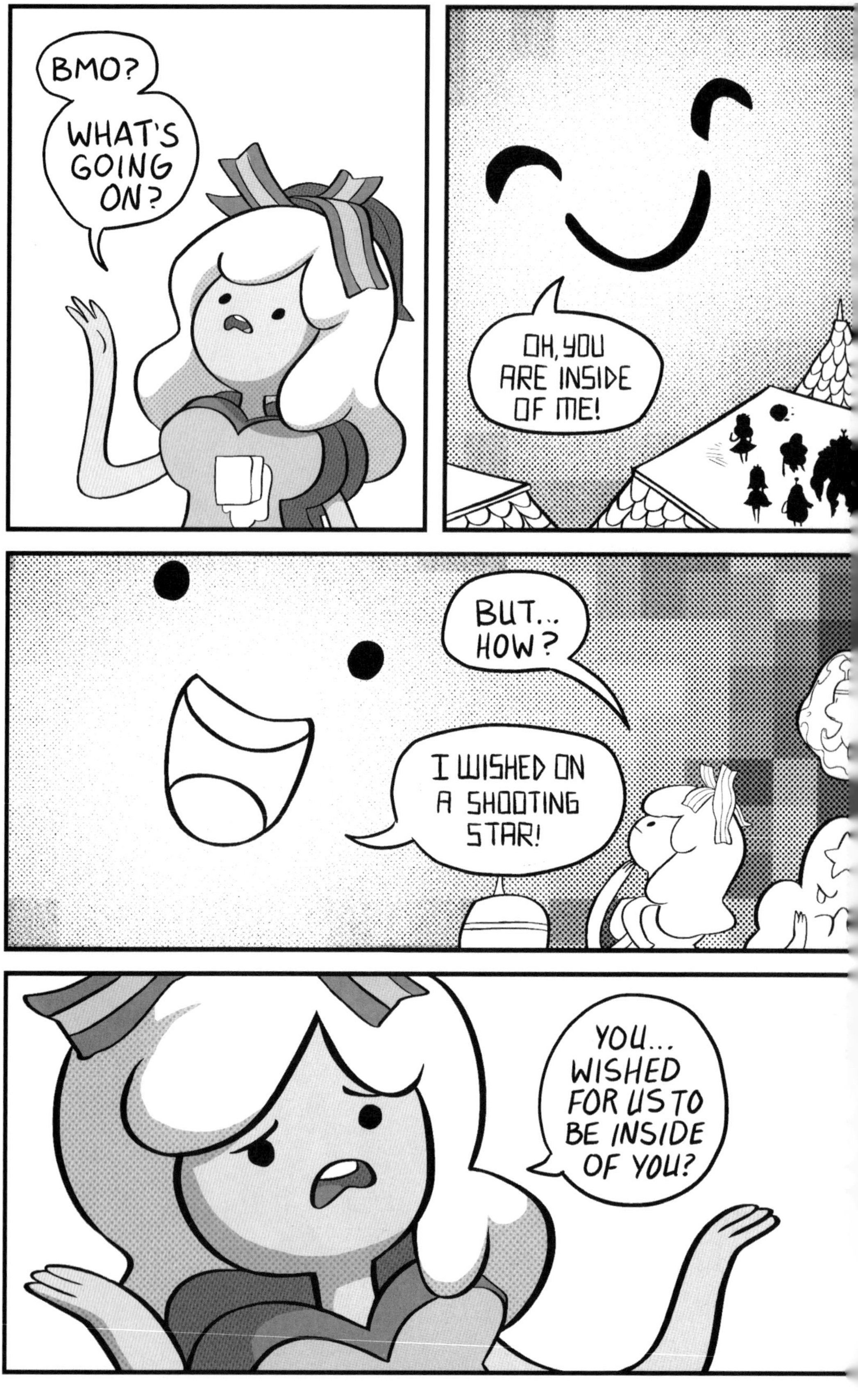
BMO?
WHAT'S GOING ON?
OH, YOU ARE INSIDE OF ME!
BUT... HOW?
I WISHED ON A SHOOTING STAR!
YOU... WISHED FOR US TO BE INSIDE OF YOU?

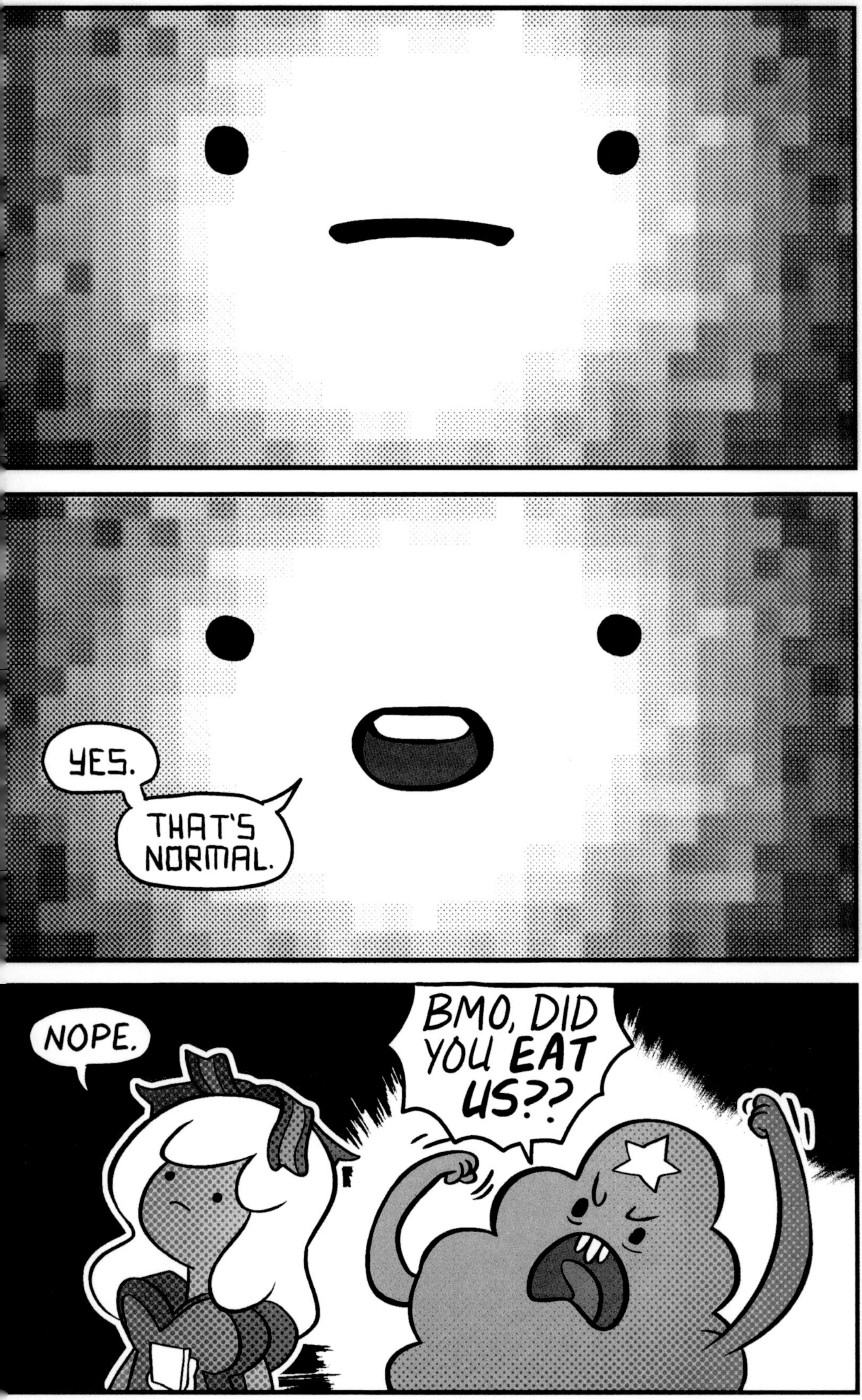
YES.
THAT'S NORMAL.
NOPE.
BMO, DID YOU EAT US??

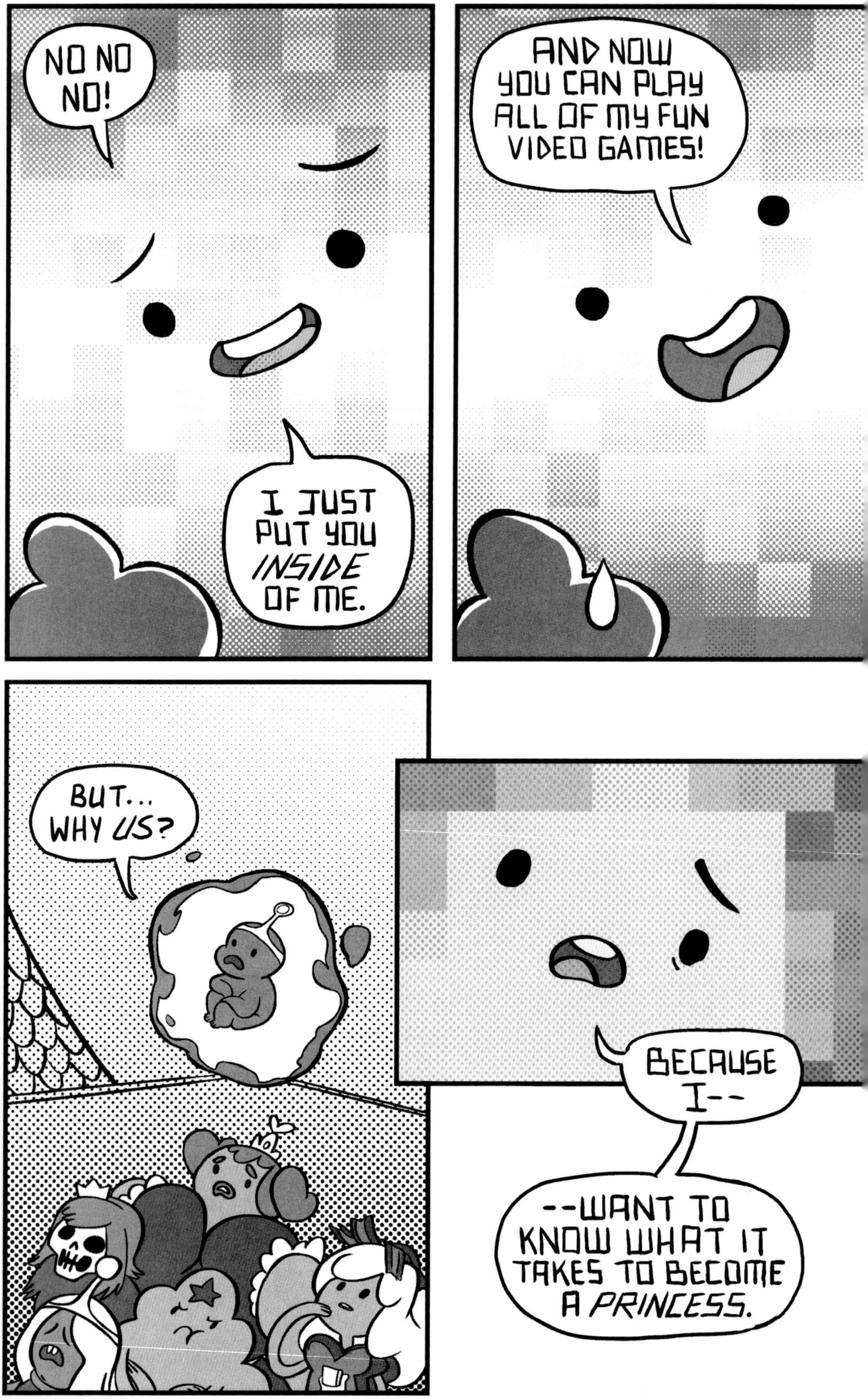
NO NO NO!
I JUST PUT YOU INSIDE OF ME.
AND NOW YOU CAN PLAY ALL OF MY FUN VIDEO GAMES!
BUT... WHY US?
BECAUSE I--
--WANT TO KNOW WHAT IT TAKES TO BECOME A PRINCESS.

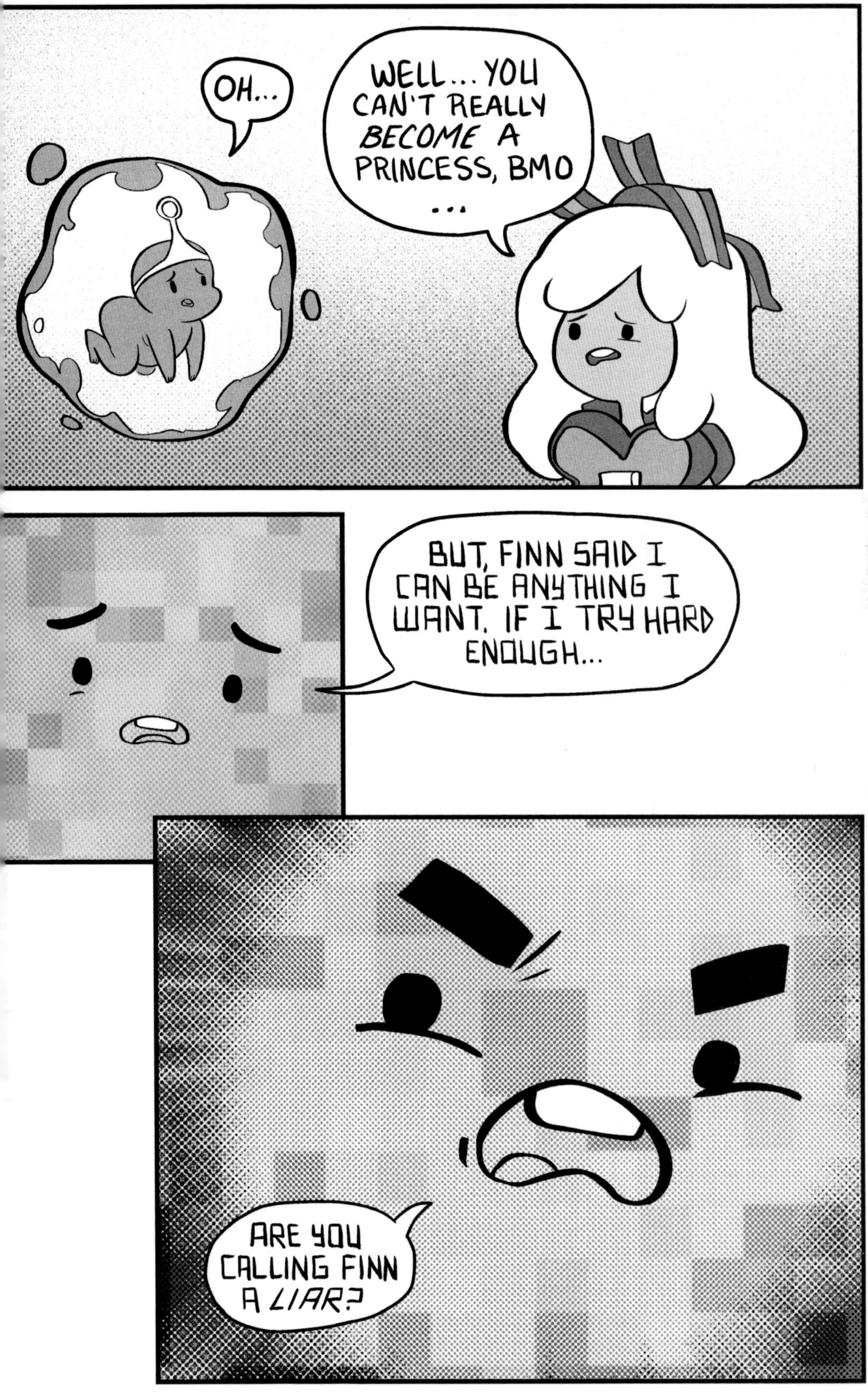
OH...
WELL... YOU CAN'T REALLY *BECOME* A PRINCESS, BMO ...
BUT, FINN SAID I CAN BE ANYTHING I WANT, IF I TRY HARD ENOUGH...
ARE YOU CALLING FINN A *LIAR?*

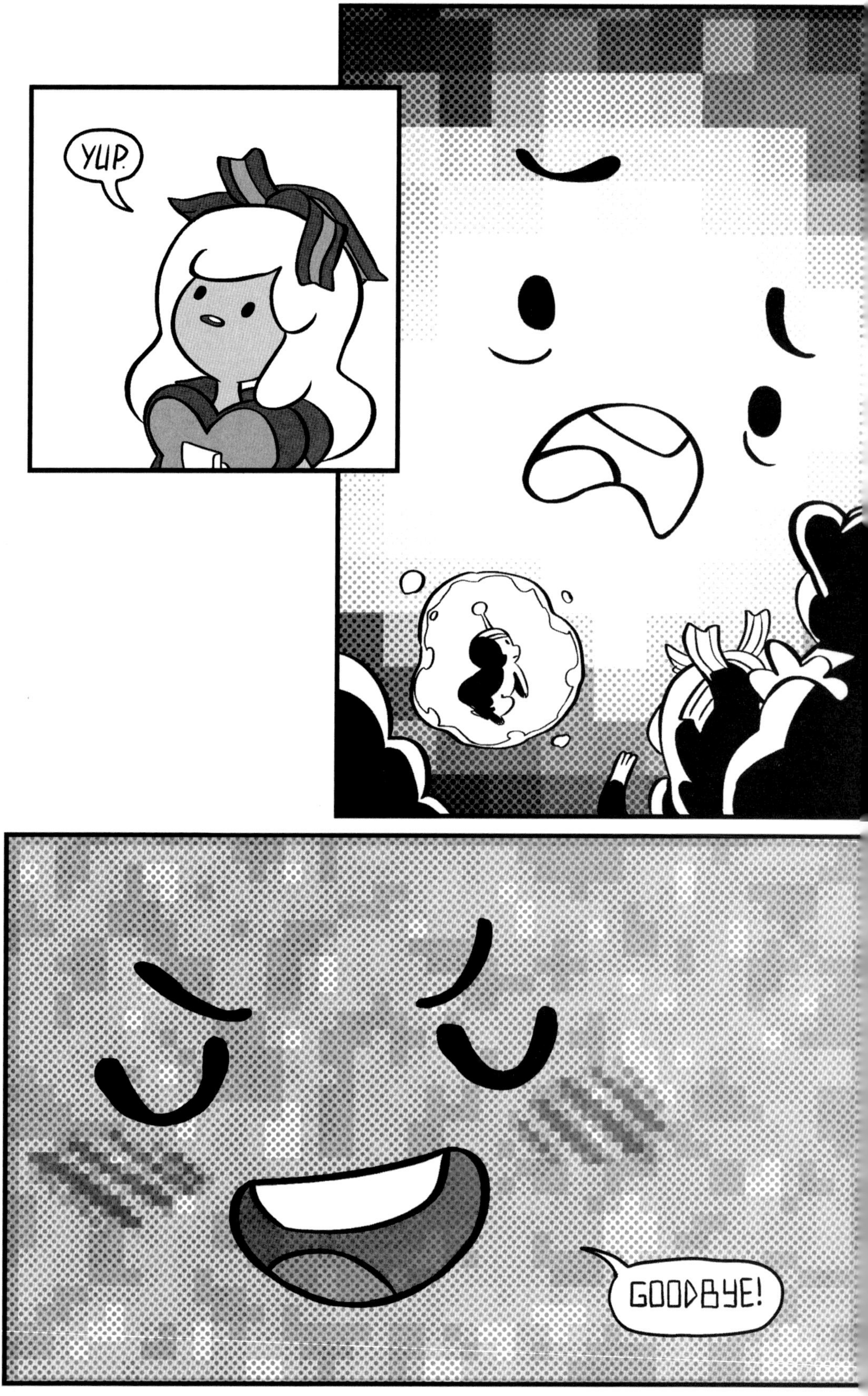
YUP.
GOODBYE!

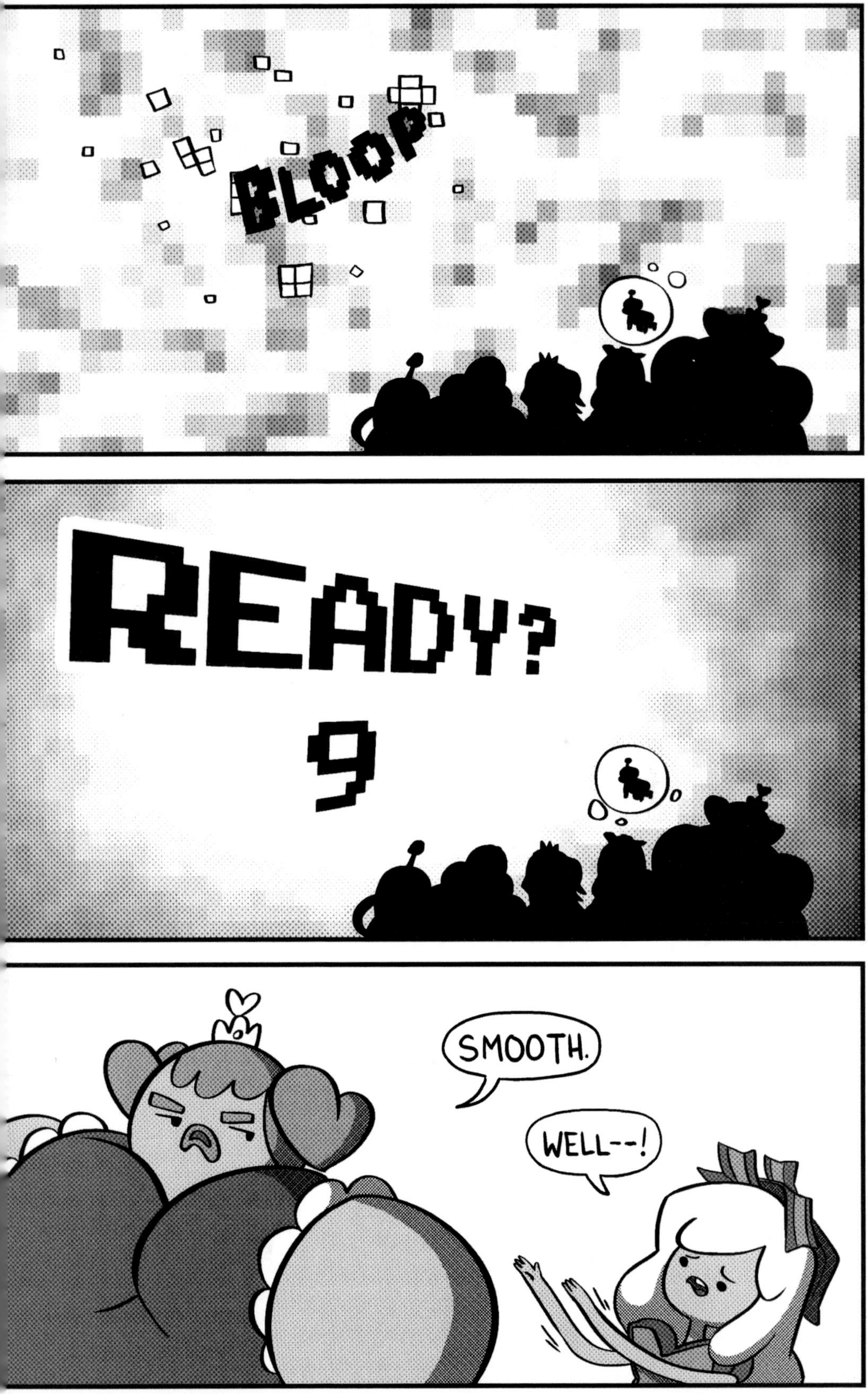
BLOOP
READY?
9
SMOOTH.
WELL--!

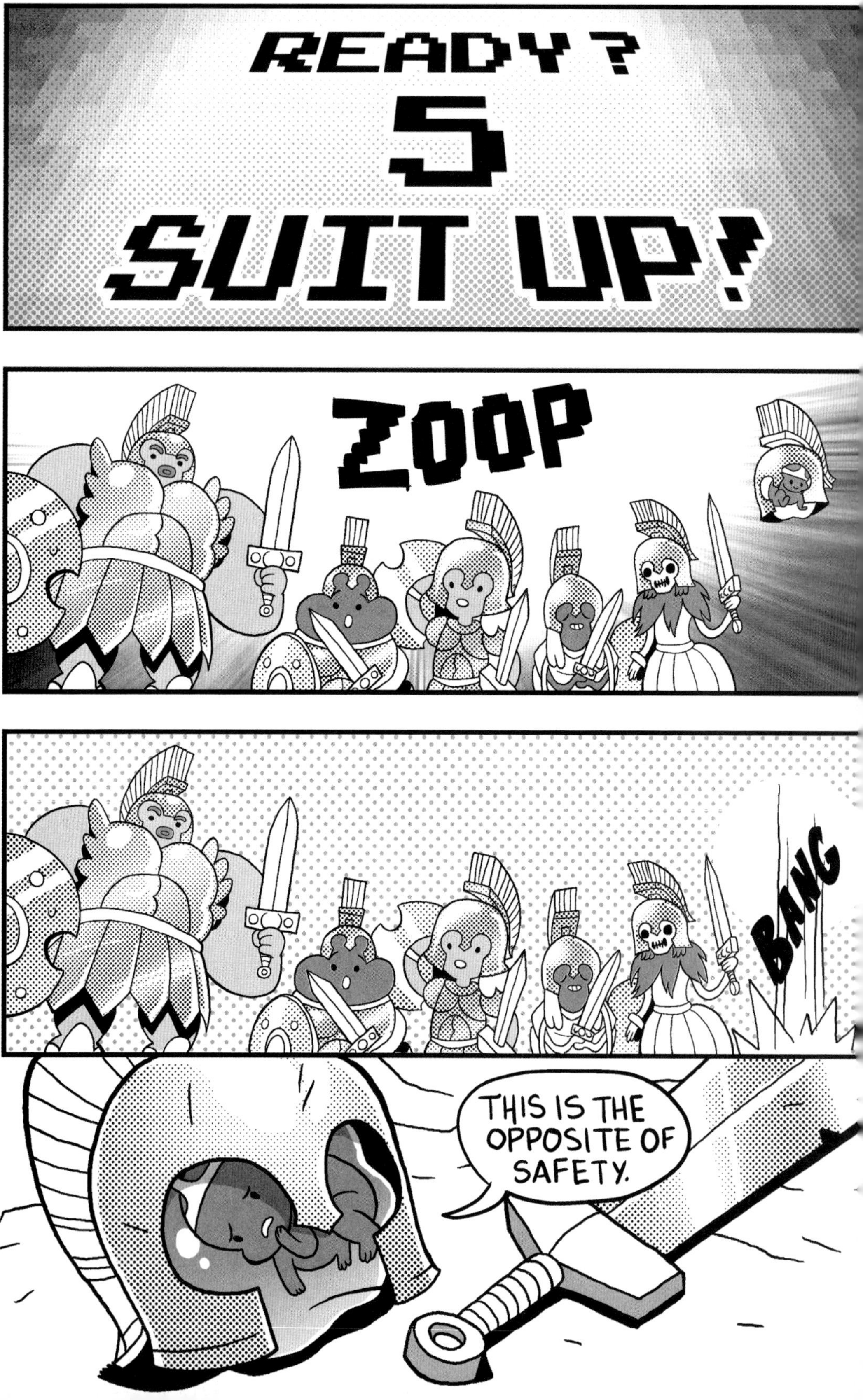
READY?
5
SUIT UP!
ZOOP
BANG
THIS IS THE OPPOSITE OF SAFETY.

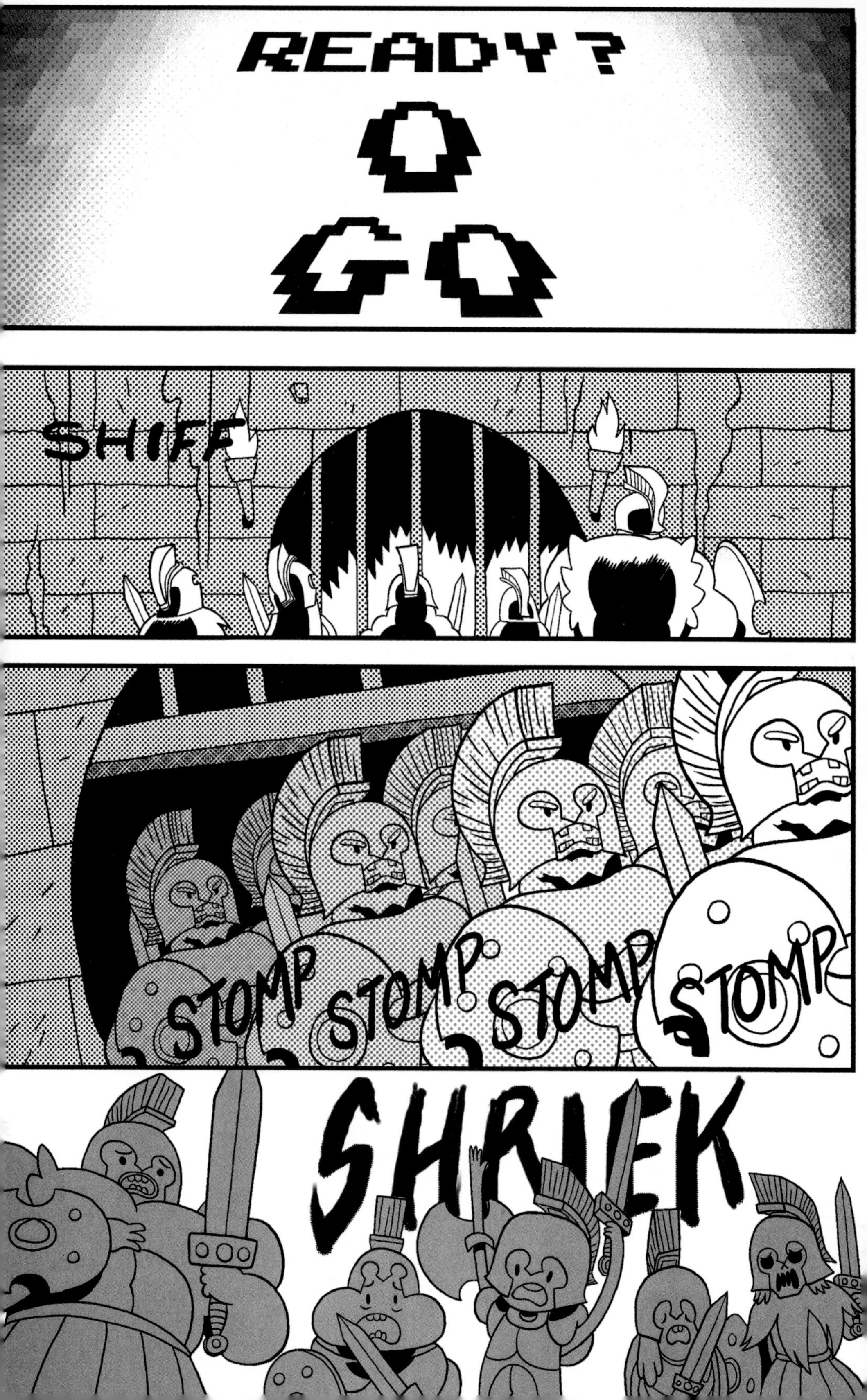
READY ?
GO
SHIFF
STOMP
STOMP
STOMP
STOMP
SHRIEK

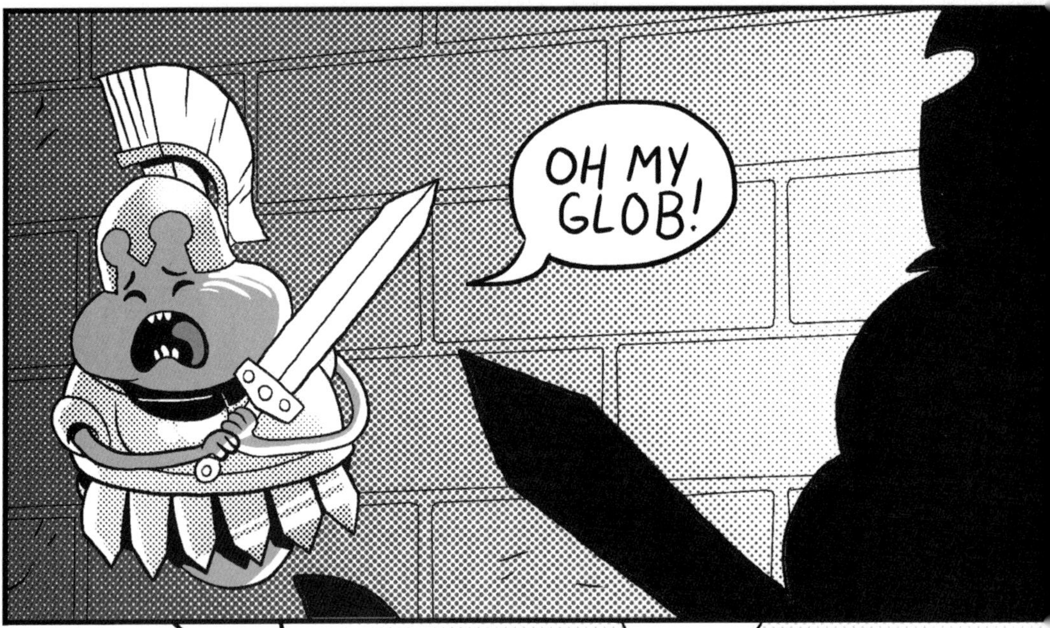
OH MY GLOB!

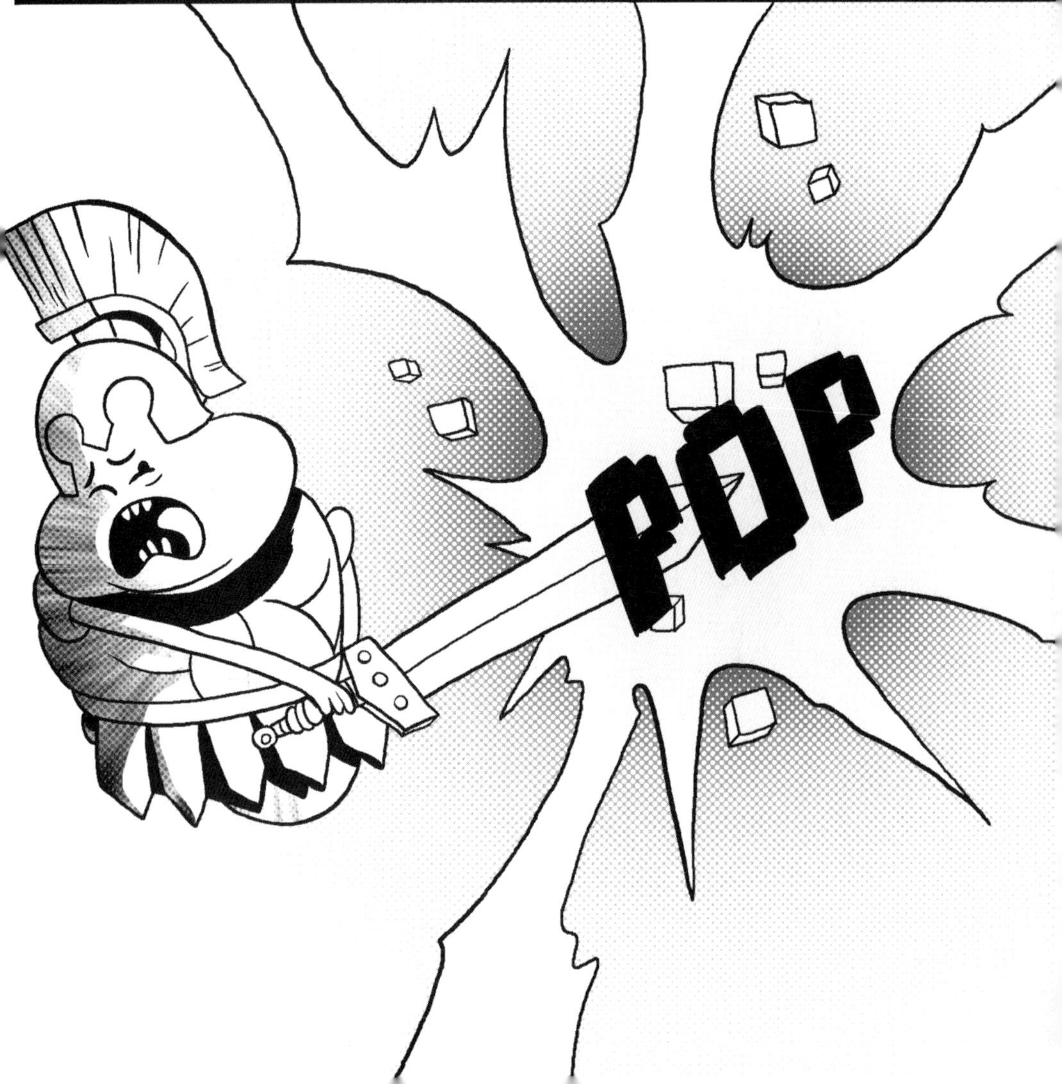
POP

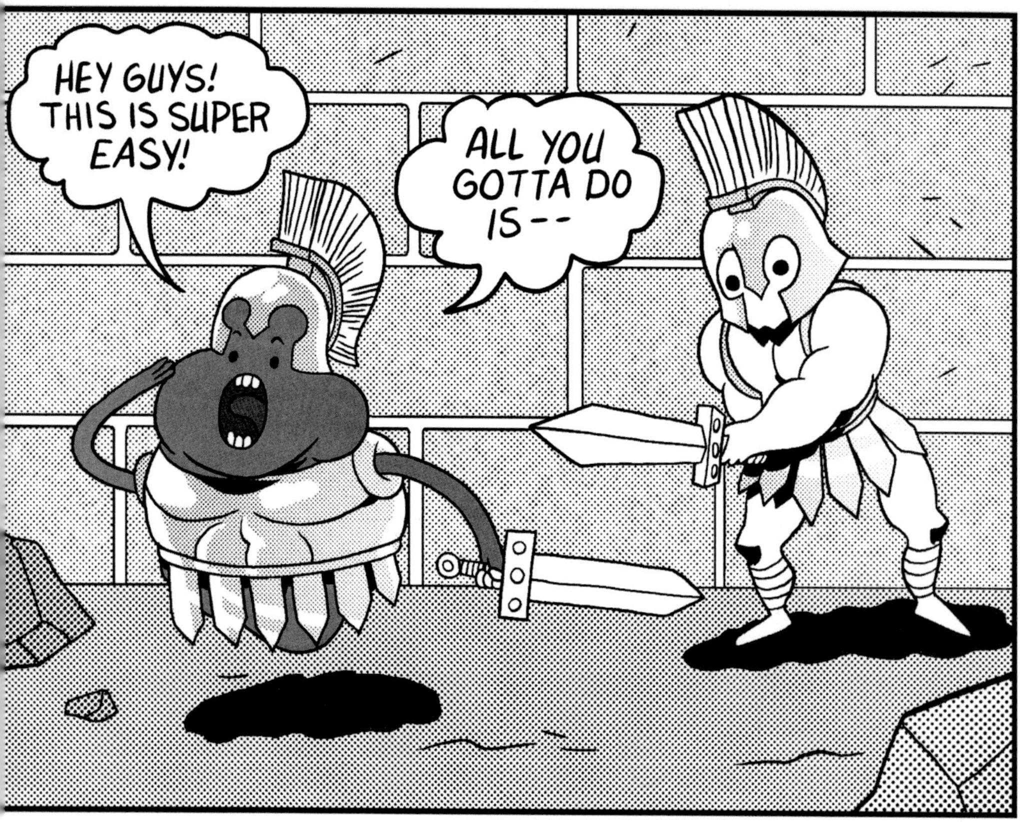
HEY GUYS! THIS IS SUPER EASY!
ALL YOU GOTTA DO IS--

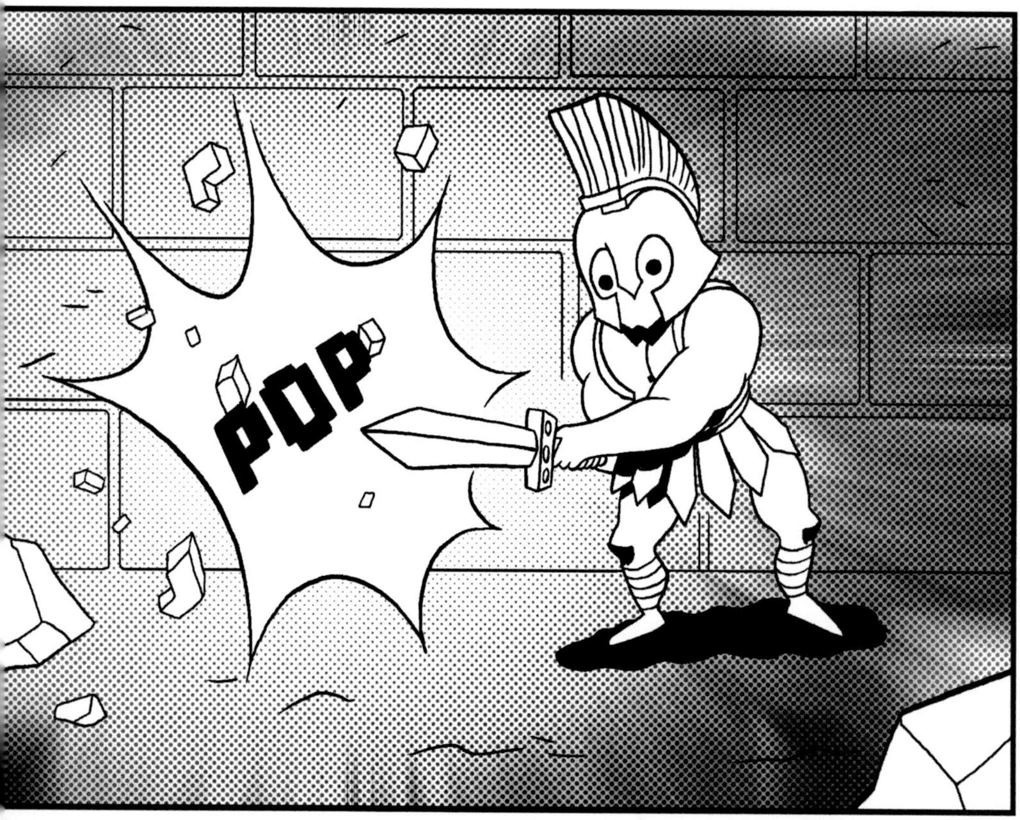
POP

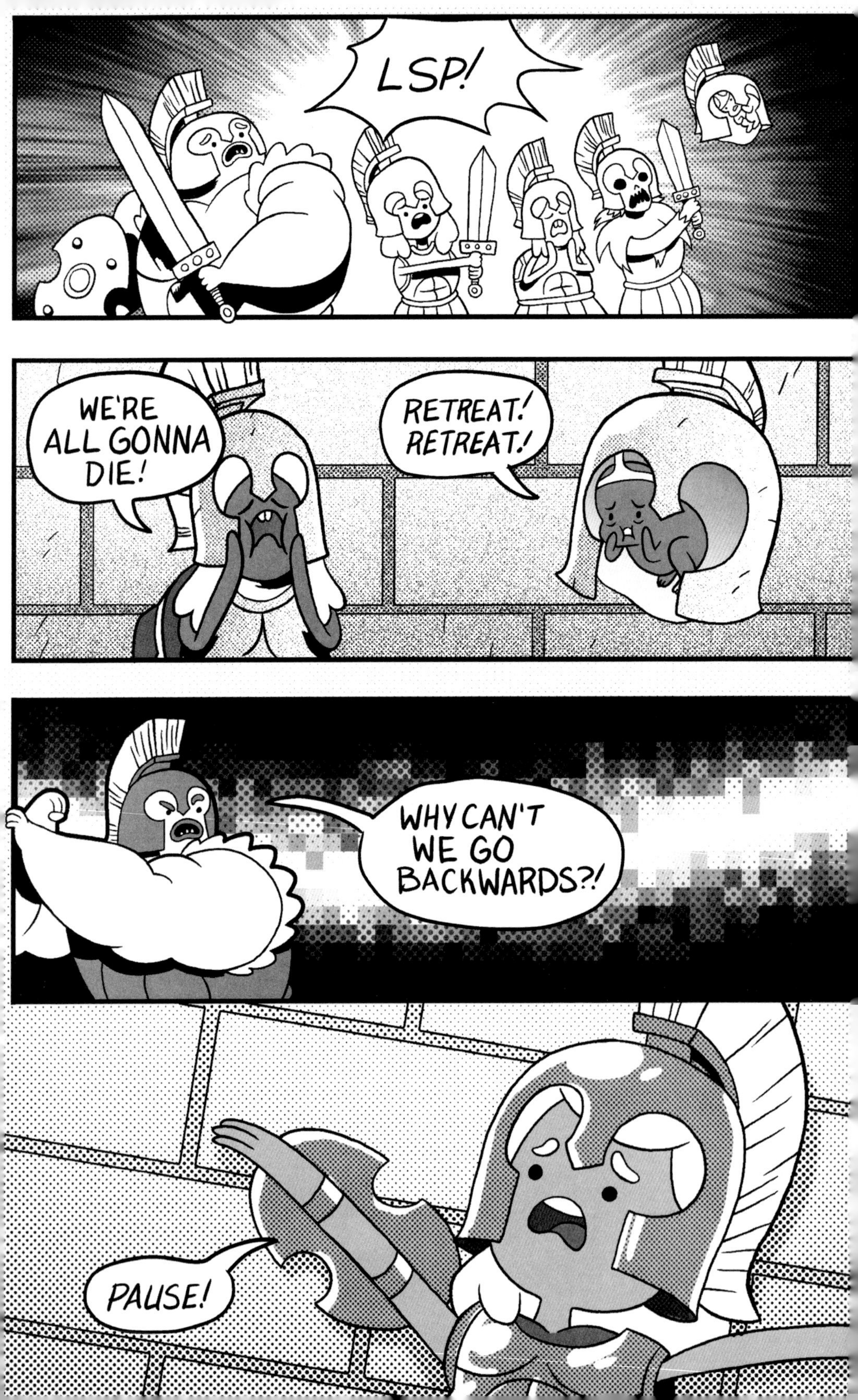
LSP!
WE'RE ALL GONNA DIE!
RETREAT! RETREAT!
WHY CAN'T WE GO BACKWARDS?!
PAUSE!

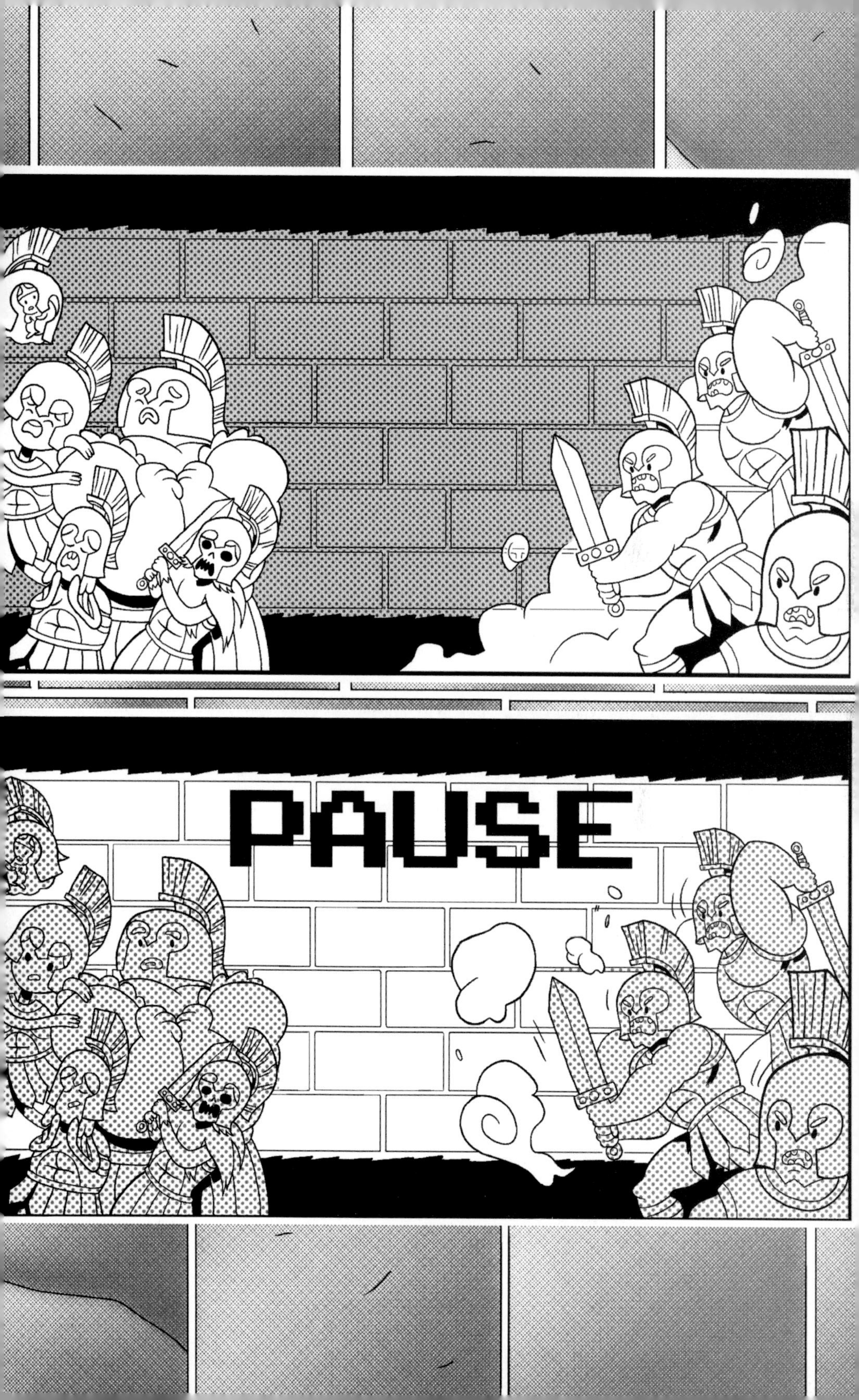
PAUSE

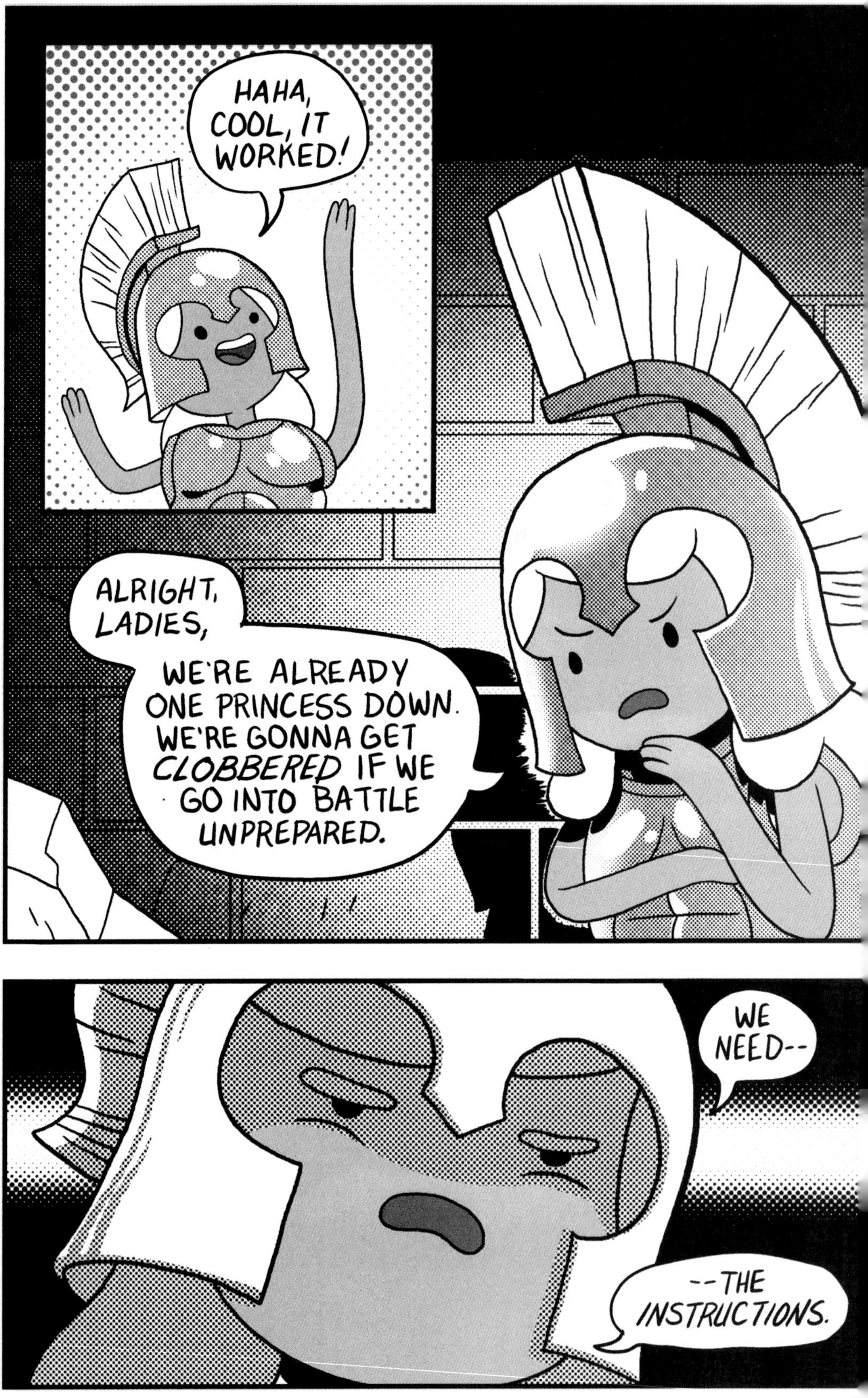
HAHA, COOL, IT WORKED!
ALRIGHT, LADIES,
WE'RE ALREADY ONE PRINCESS DOWN. WE'RE GONNA GET CLOBBERED IF WE GO INTO BATTLE UNPREPARED.
WE NEED--
--THE INSTRUCTIONS.

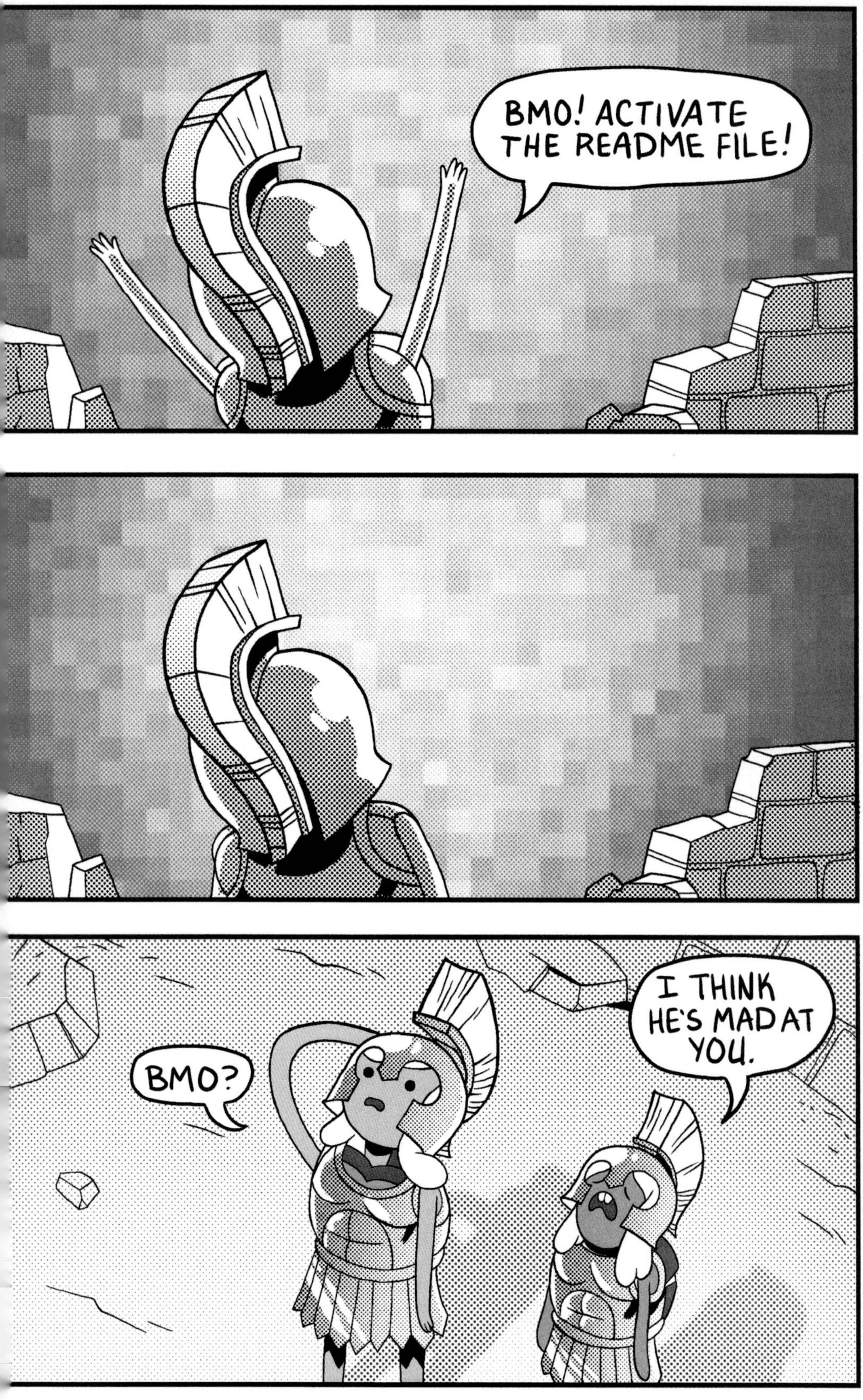
BMO! ACTIVATE THE README FILE!
BMO?
I THINK HE'S MAD AT YOU.

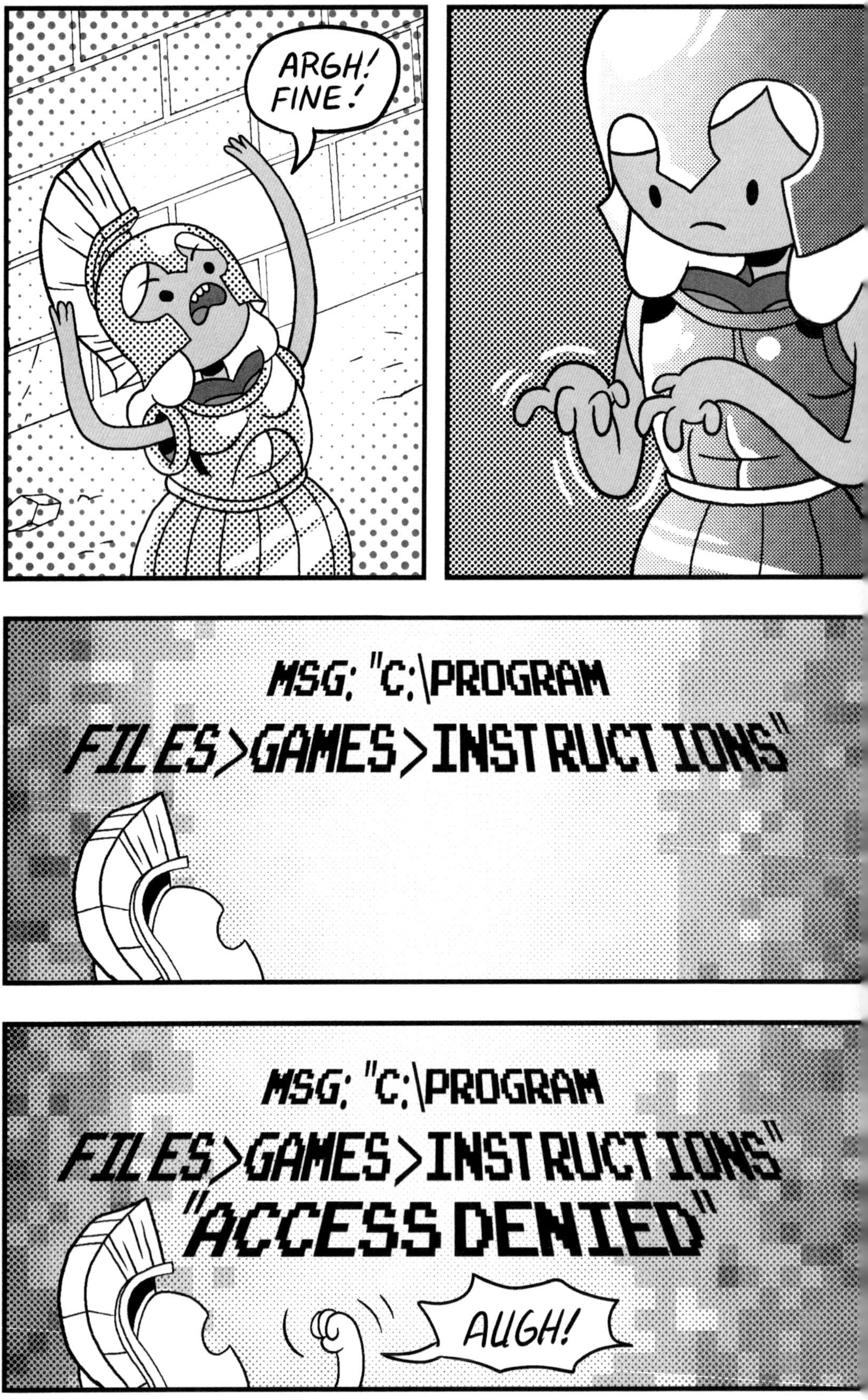
ARGH! FINE!
MSG: "C:\PROGRAM FILES>GAMES>INSTRUCTIONS"
MSG: "C:\PROGRAM FILES>GAMES>INSTRUCTIONS"
"ACCESS DENIED"
AUGH!

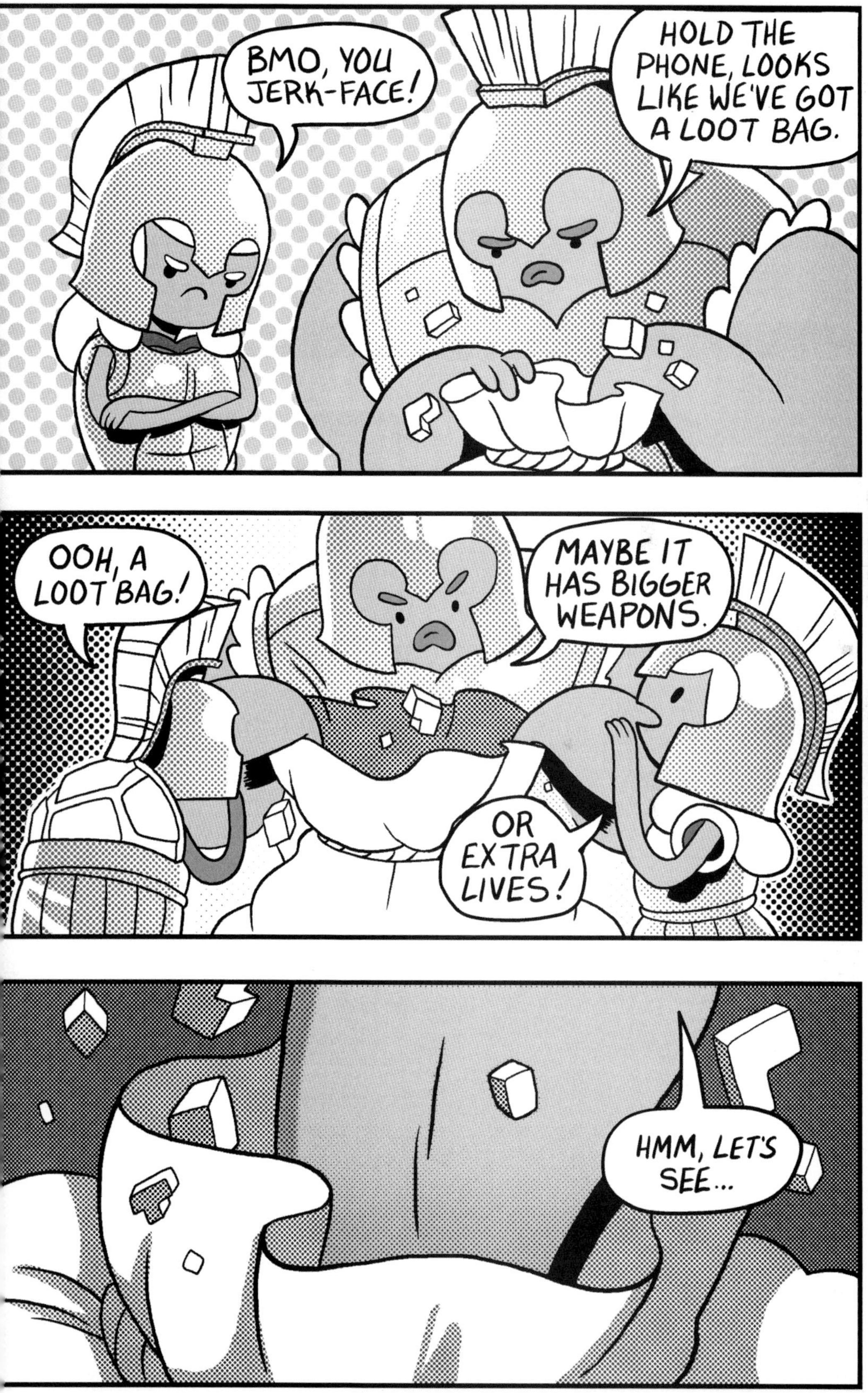
BMO, YOU JERK-FACE!
HOLD THE PHONE, LOOKS LIKE WE'VE GOT A LOOT BAG.
OOH, A LOOT BAG!
MAYBE IT HAS BIGGER WEAPONS.
OR EXTRA LIVES!
HMM, LET'S SEE...

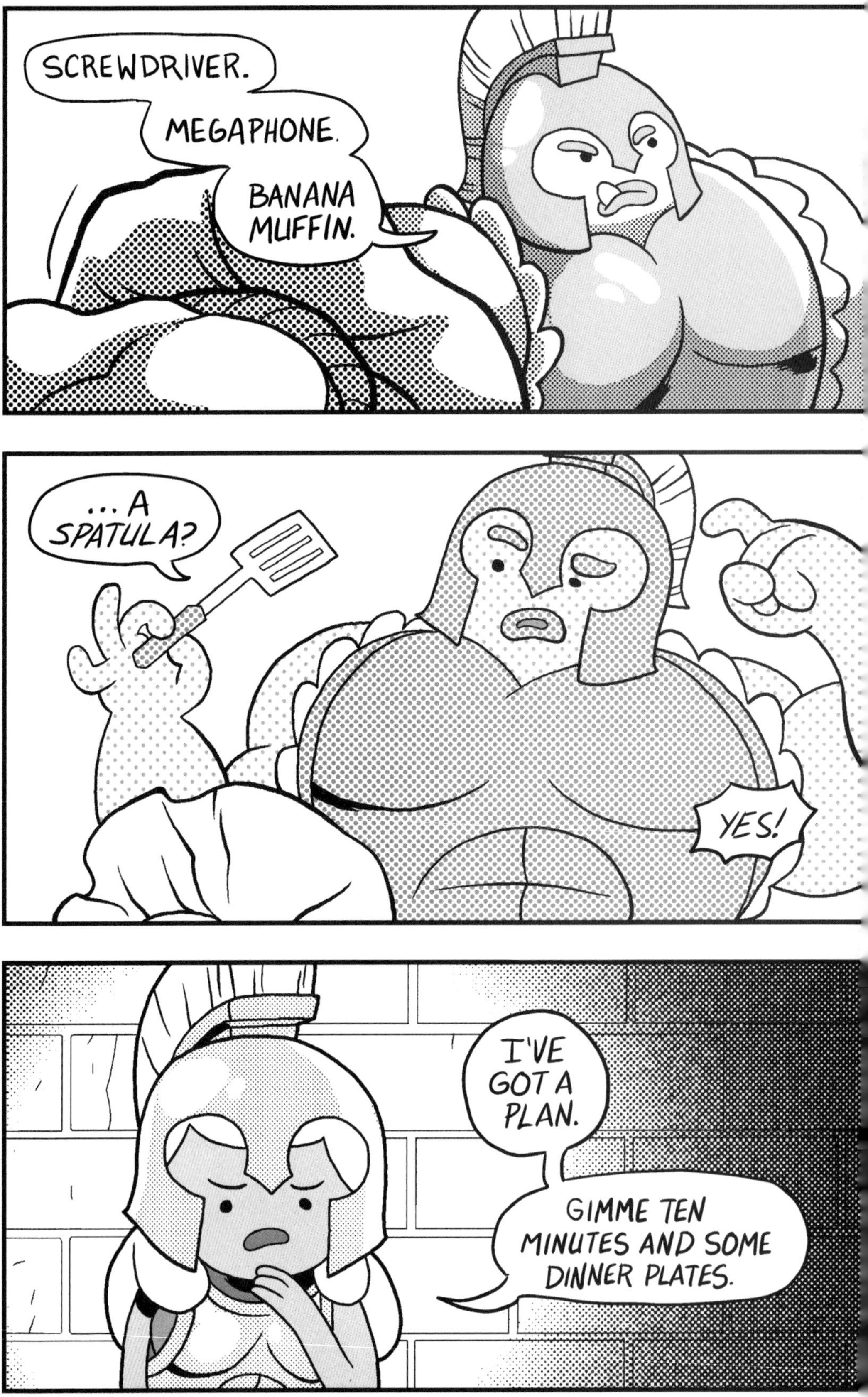
SCREWDRIVER.
MEGAPHONE.
BANANA MUFFIN.
...A SPATULA?
YES!
I'VE GOT A PLAN.
GIMME TEN MINUTES AND SOME DINNER PLATES.

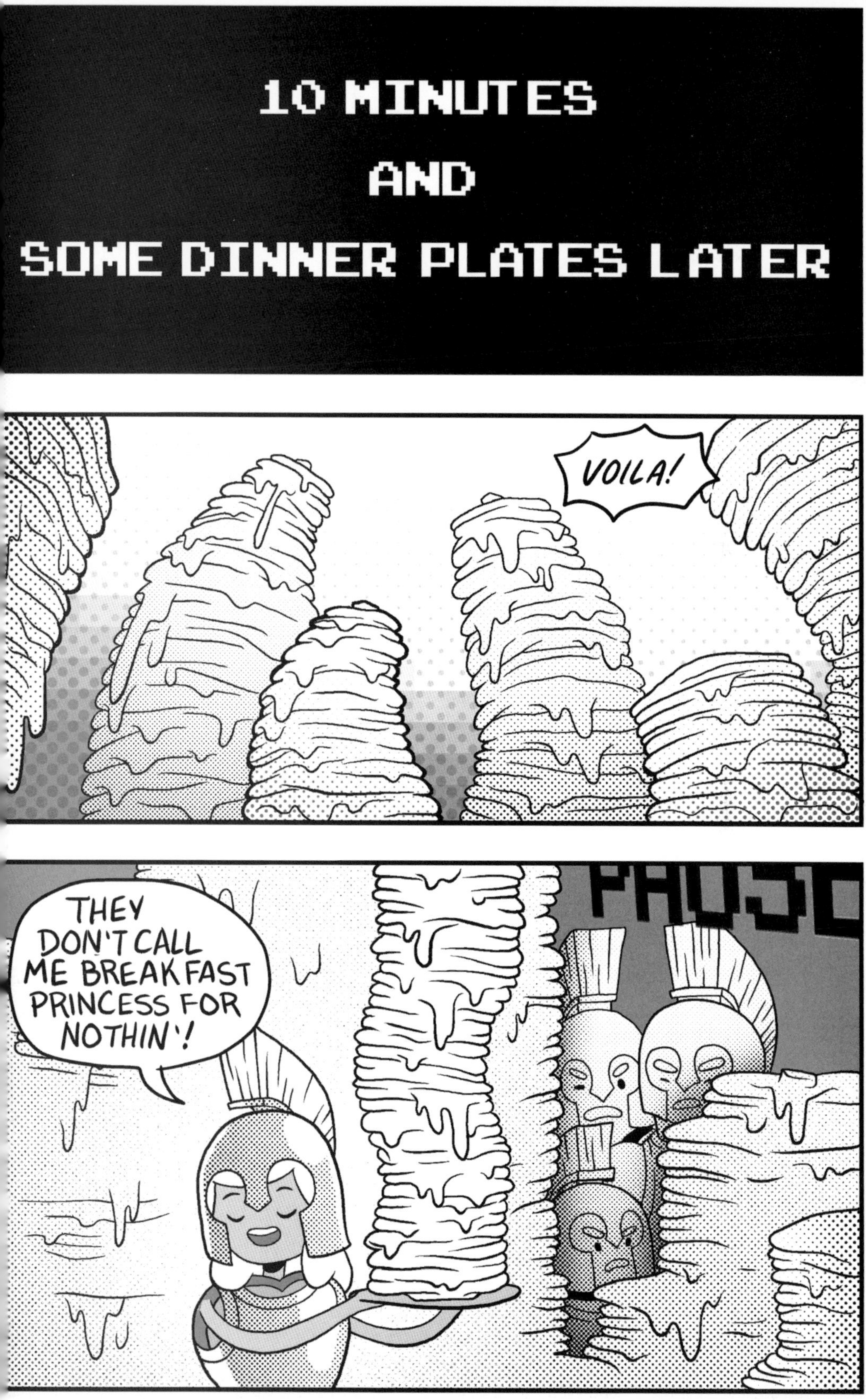
10 MINUTES AND SOME DINNER PLATES LATER
VOILA!
THEY DON'T CALL ME BREAKFAST PRINCESS FOR NOTHIN'!

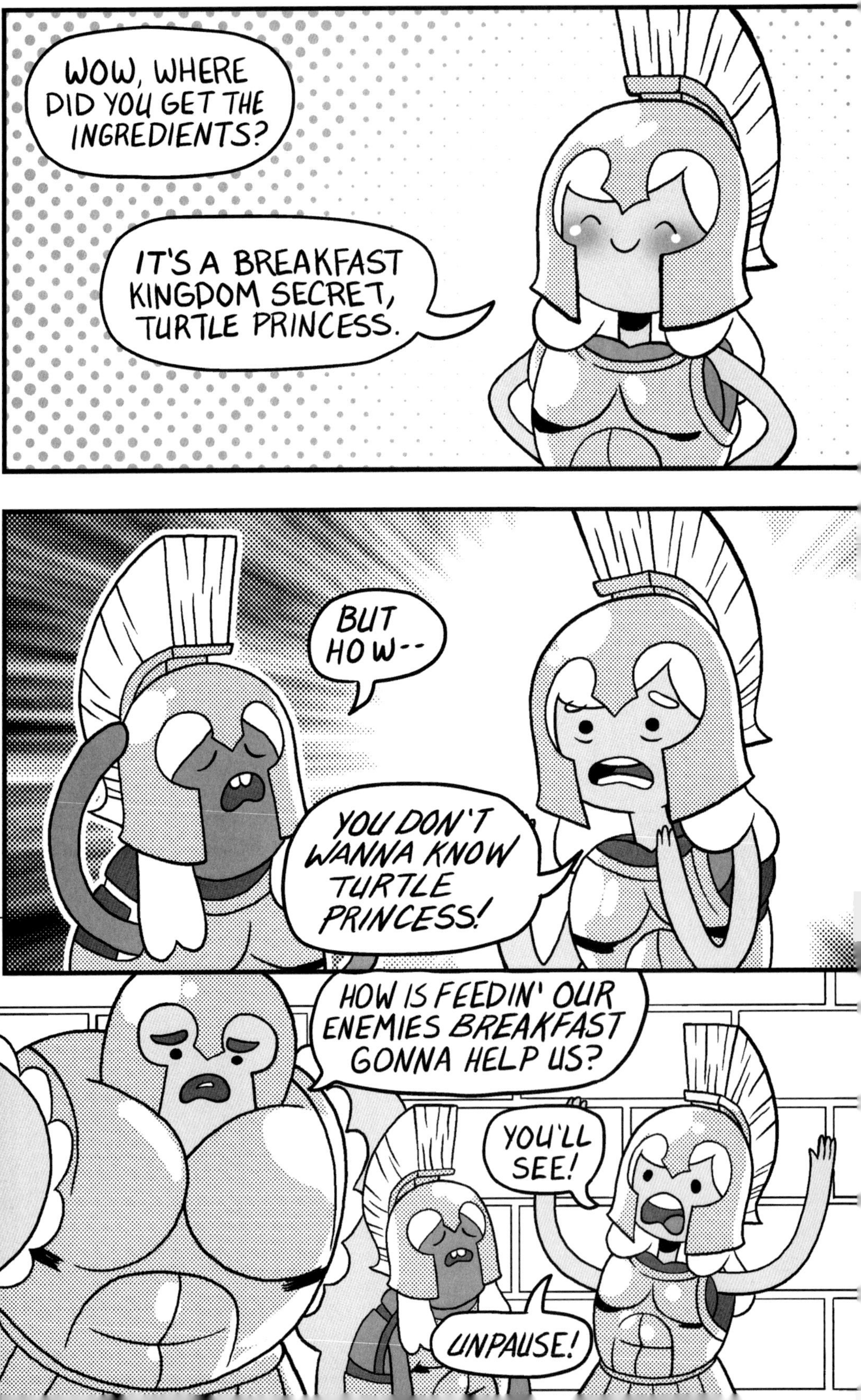
WOW, WHERE DID YOU GET THE INGREDIENTS?
IT'S A BREAKFAST KINGDOM SECRET, TURTLE PRINCESS.
BUT HOW--
YOU DON'T WANNA KNOW TURTLE PRINCESS!
HOW IS FEEDIN' OUR ENEMIES BREAKFAST GONNA HELP US?
YOU'LL SEE!
UNPAUSE!

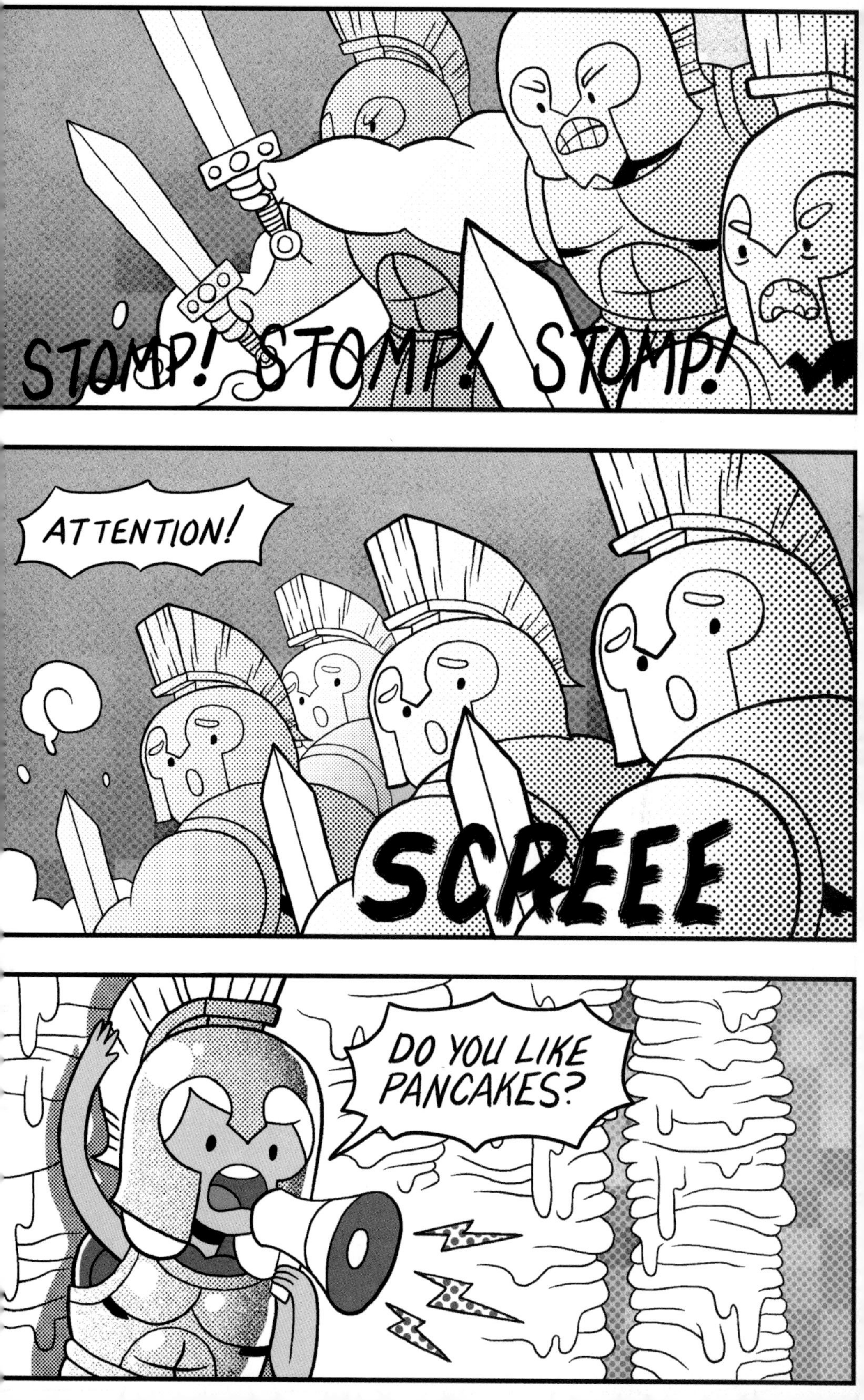
STOMP! STOMP! STOMP!
ATTENTION!
SCREEE
DO YOU LIKE PANCAKES?

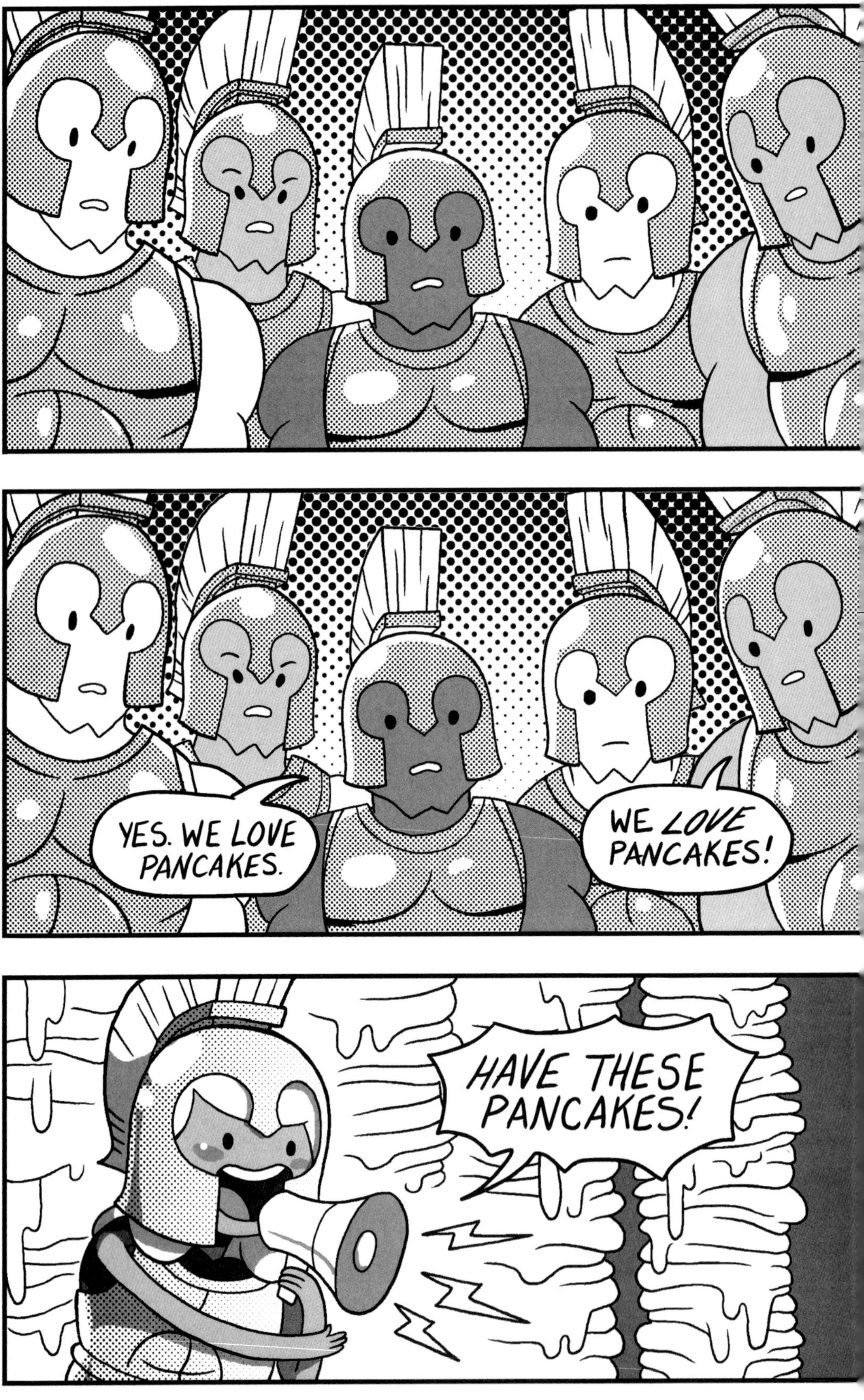
YES. WE LOVE PANCAKES.
WE LOVE PANCAKES!
HAVE THESE PANCAKES!

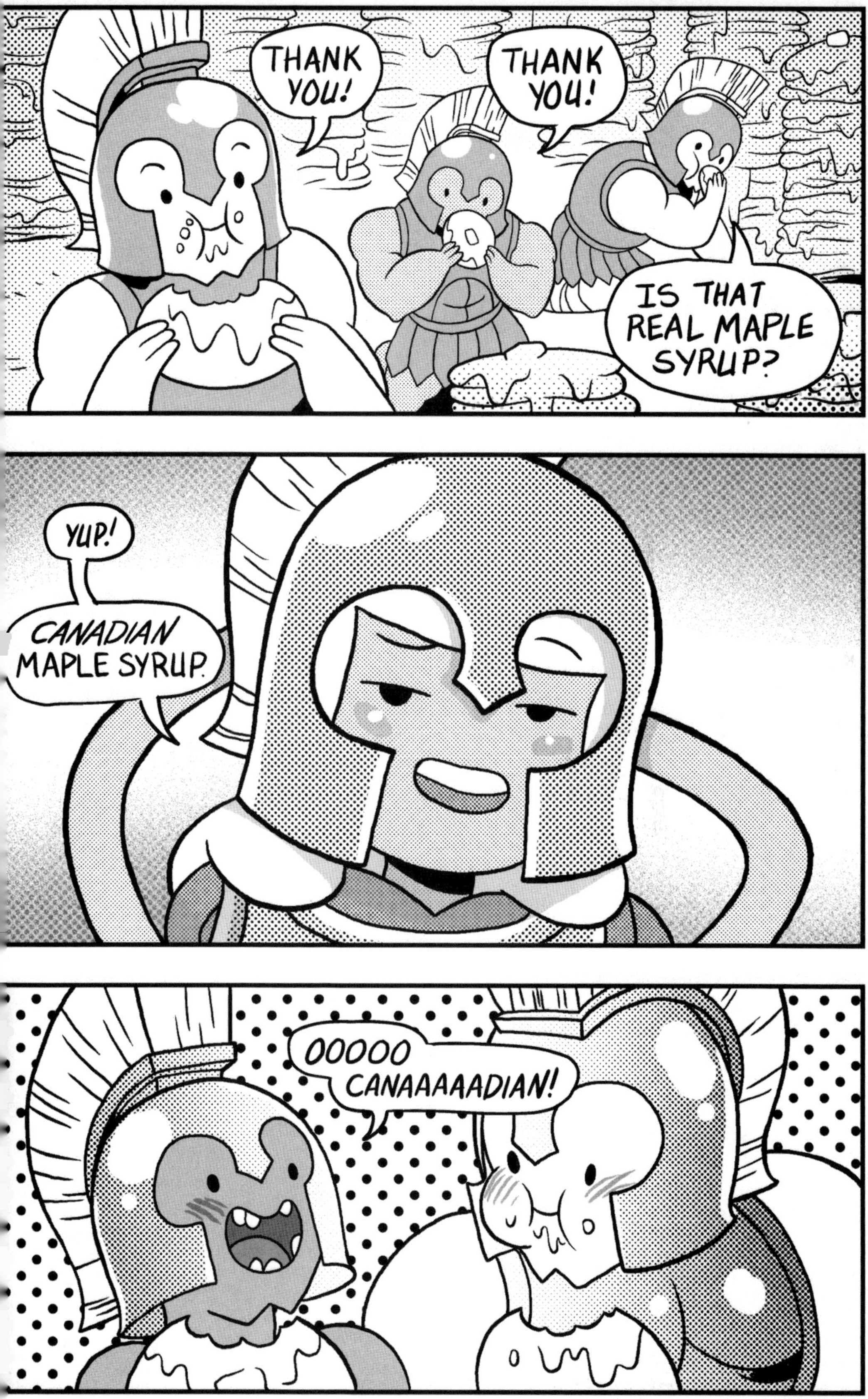
THANK YOU!
THANK YOU!
IS THAT REAL MAPLE SYRUP?
YUP!
CANADIAN MAPLE SYRUP.
OOOOO CANAAAAADIAN!

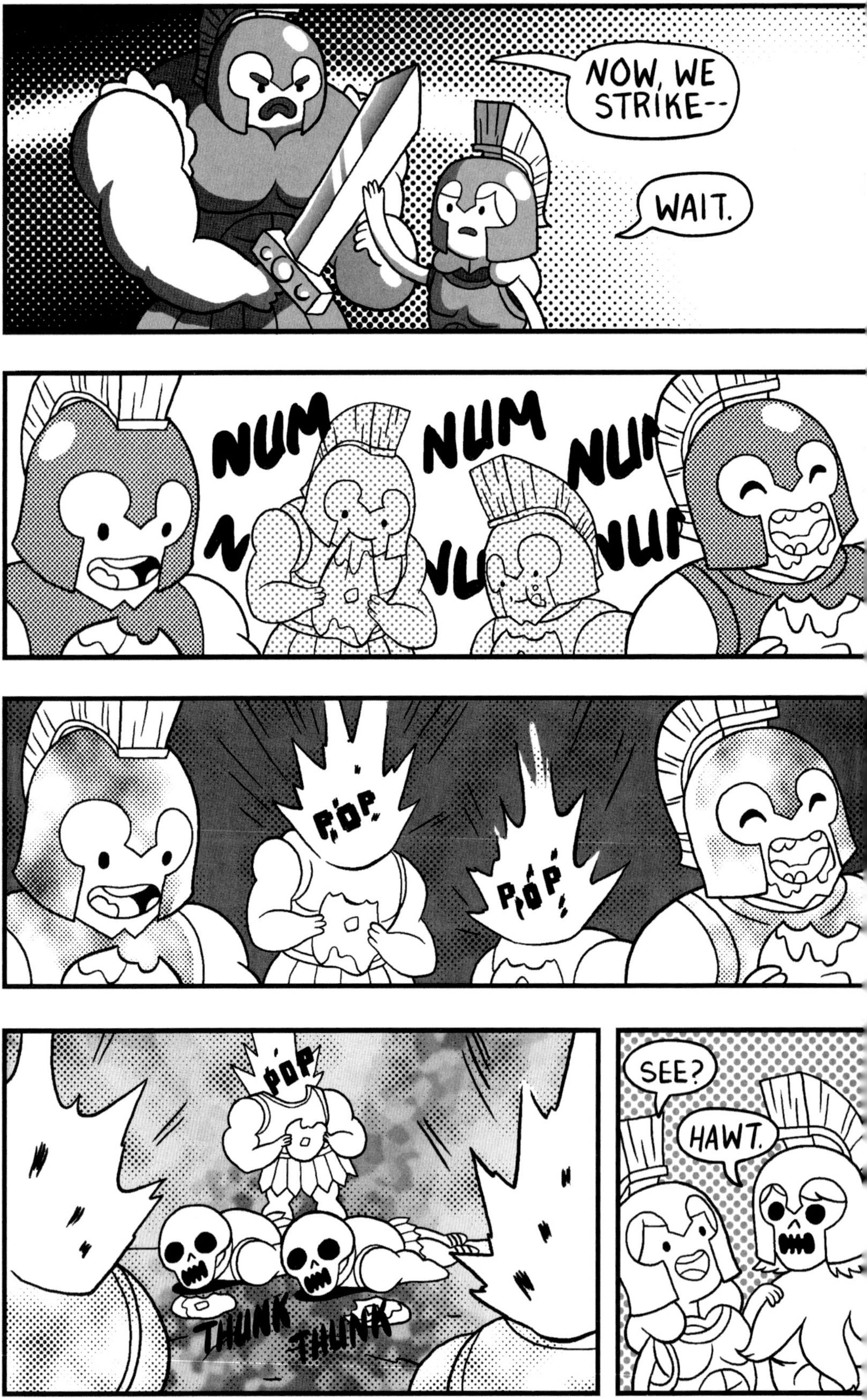

NOW, WE STRIKE--
WAIT.
NUM NUM NUM
NUM NUM NUM
POP
POP
POP
THUNK
THUNK
SEE?
HAWT.

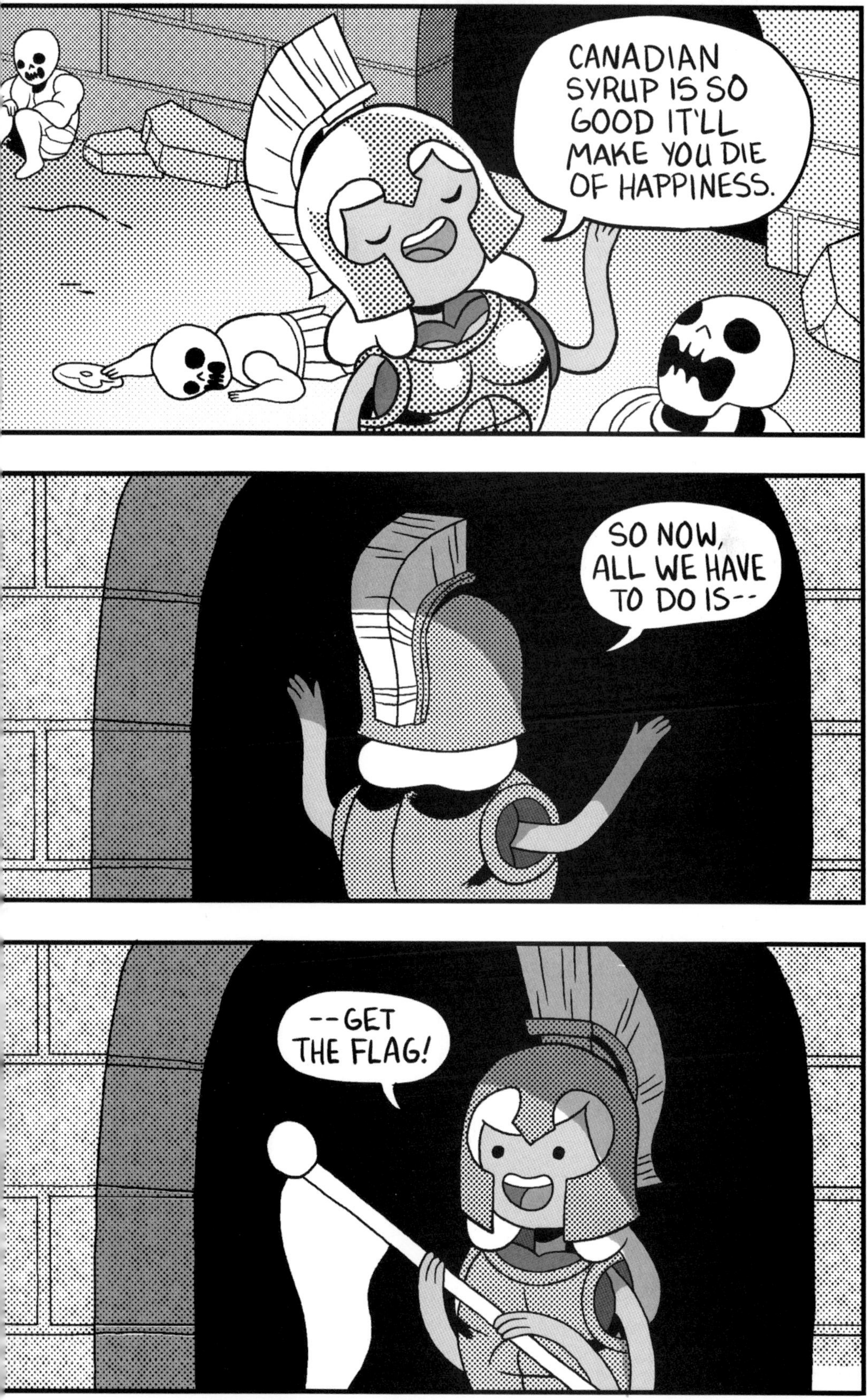
CANADIAN SYRUP IS SO GOOD IT'LL MAKE YOU DIE OF HAPPINESS.
SO NOW, ALL WE HAVE TO DO IS--
--GET THE FLAG!

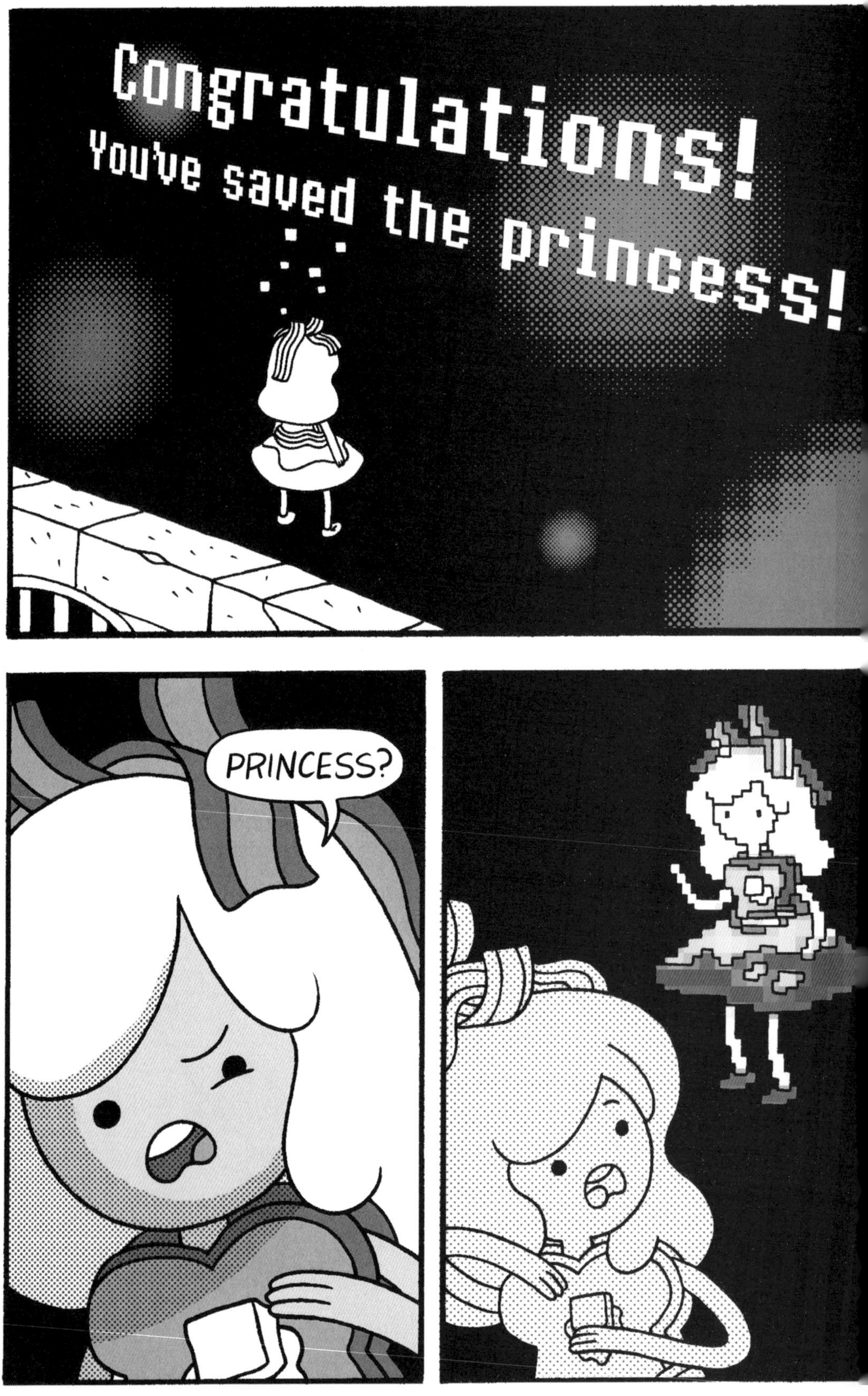
Congratulations!
You've saved the princess!
PRINCESS?

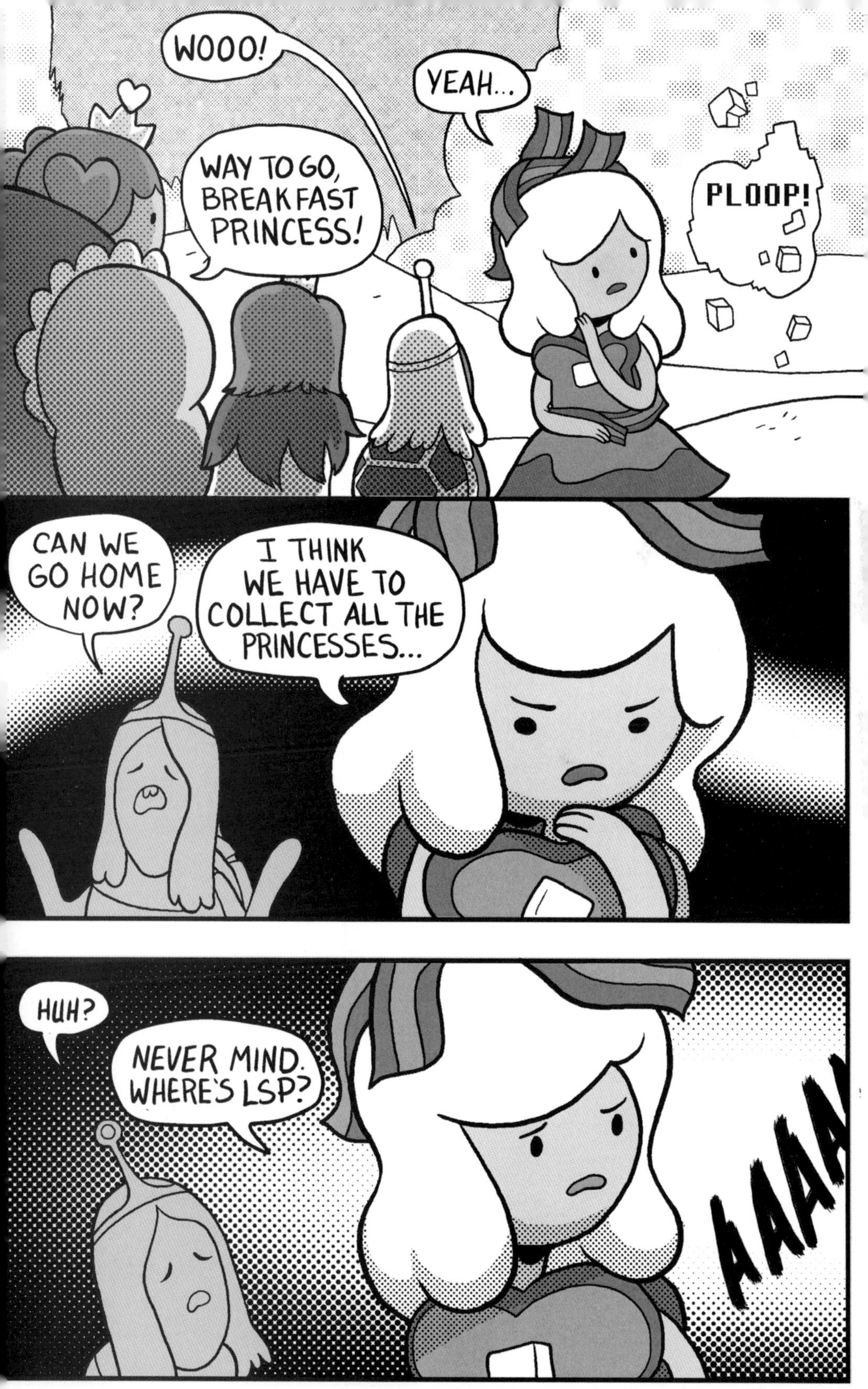
WOOO!
YEAH...
WAY TO GO, BREAKFAST PRINCESS!
PLOOP!
CAN WE GO HOME NOW?
I THINK WE HAVE TO COLLECT ALL THE PRINCESSES...
HUH?
NEVER MIND. WHERE'S LSP?
AAAA

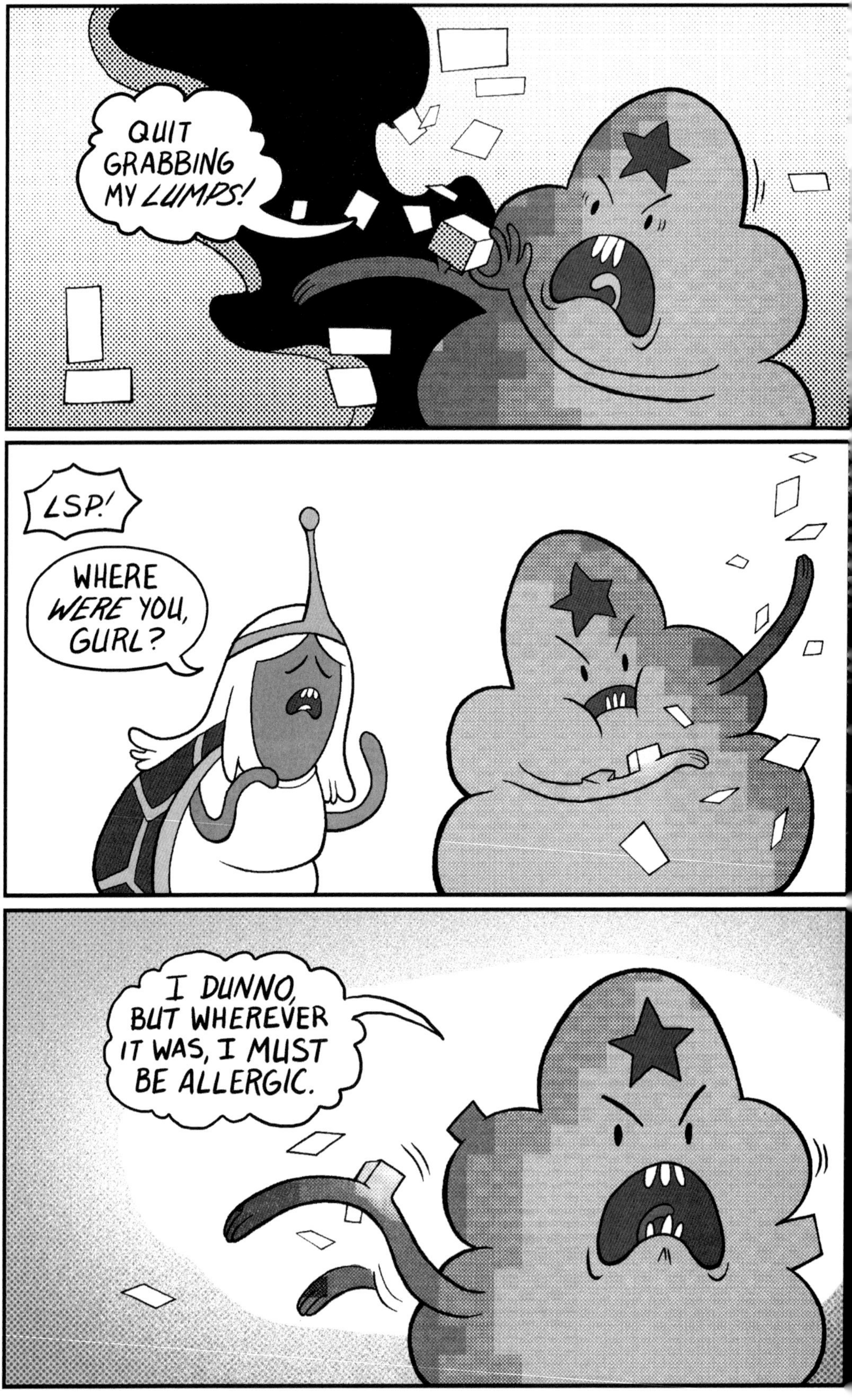
QUIT GRABBING MY LUMPS!
LSP!
WHERE WERE YOU, GURL?
I DUNNO, BUT WHEREVER IT WAS, I MUST BE ALLERGIC.

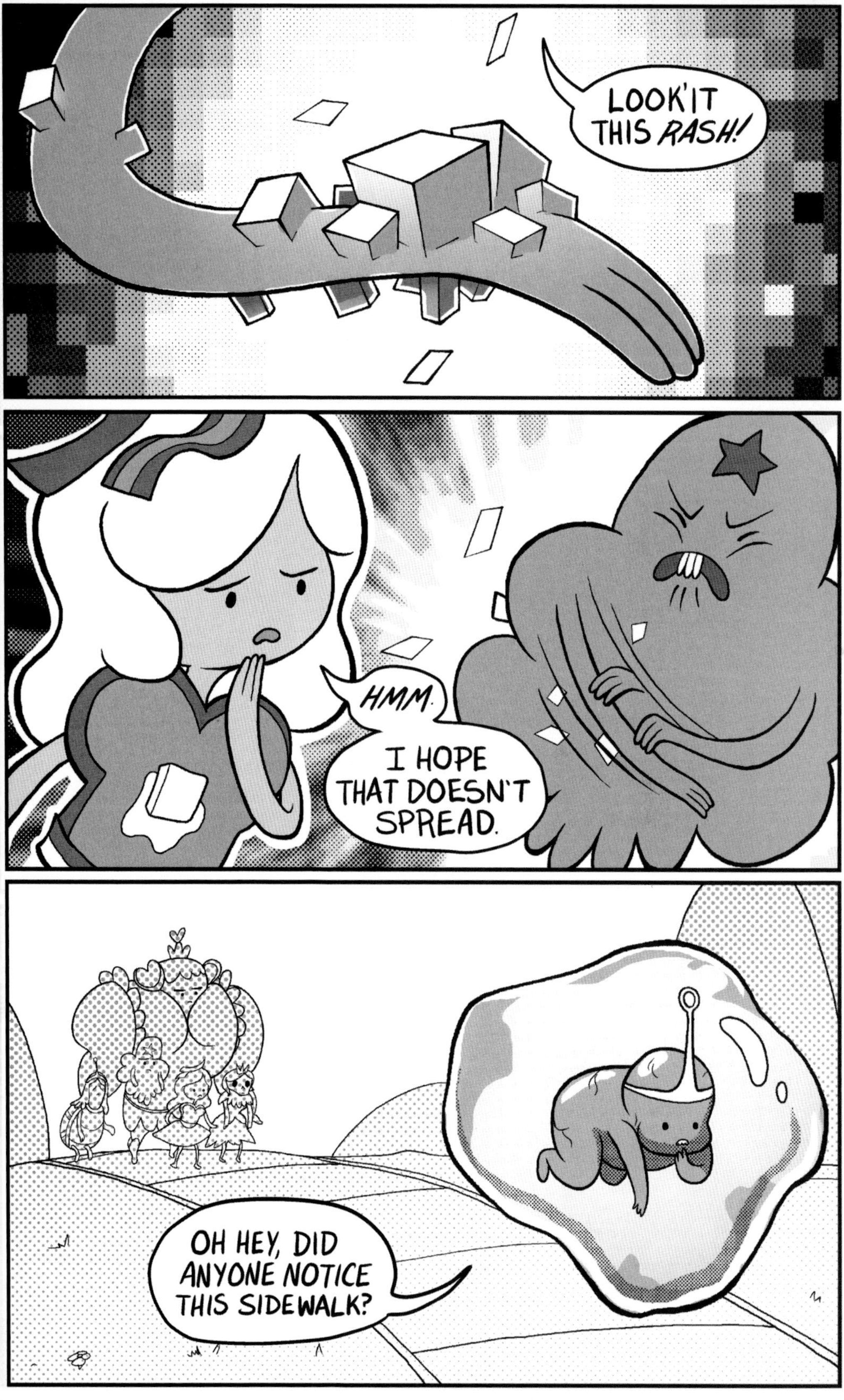
LOOK'IT THIS RASH!
HMM.
I HOPE THAT DOESN'T SPREAD.
OH HEY, DID ANYONE NOTICE THIS SIDEWALK?

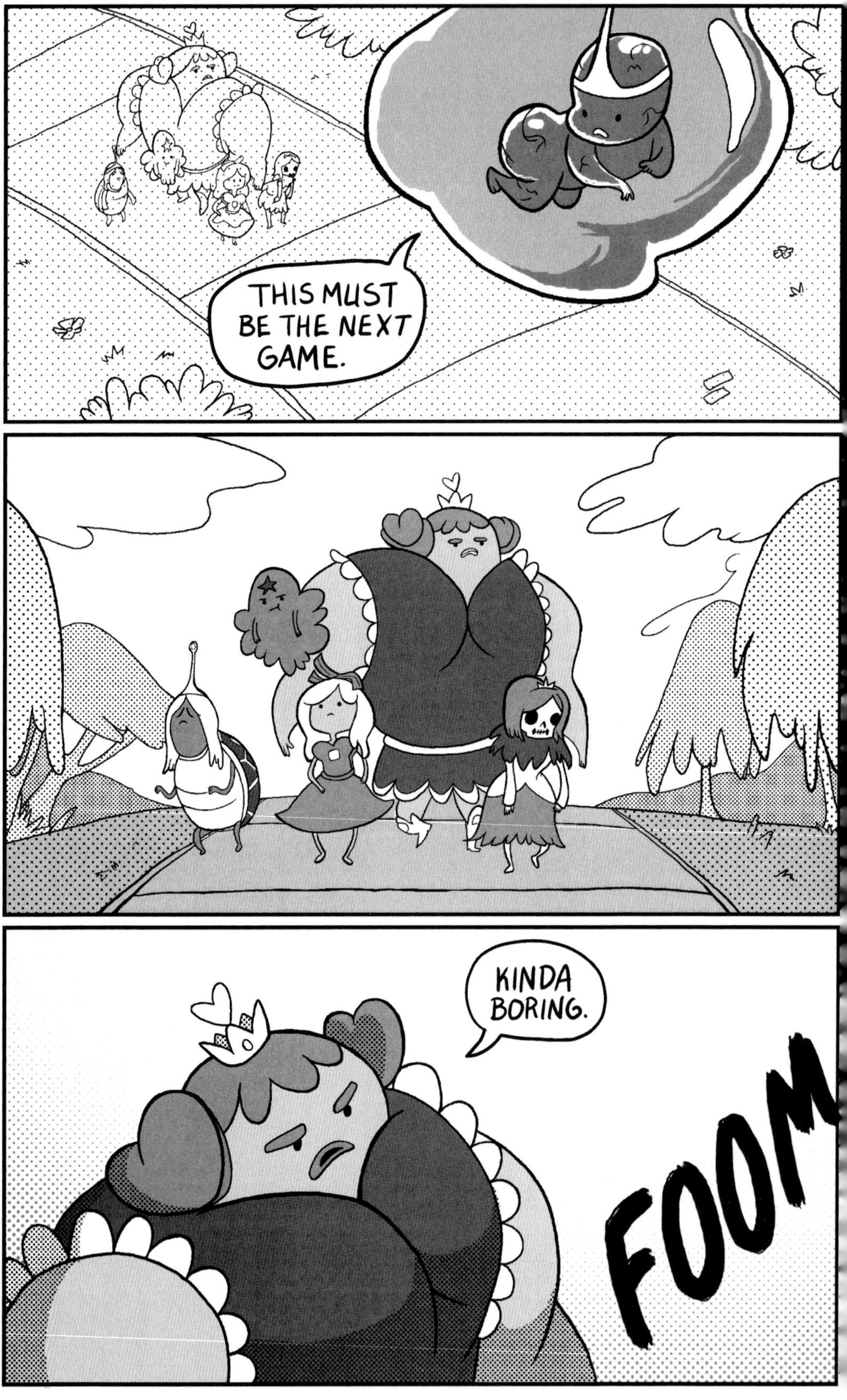
THIS MUST BE THE NEXT GAME.
KINDA BORING.
FOOM

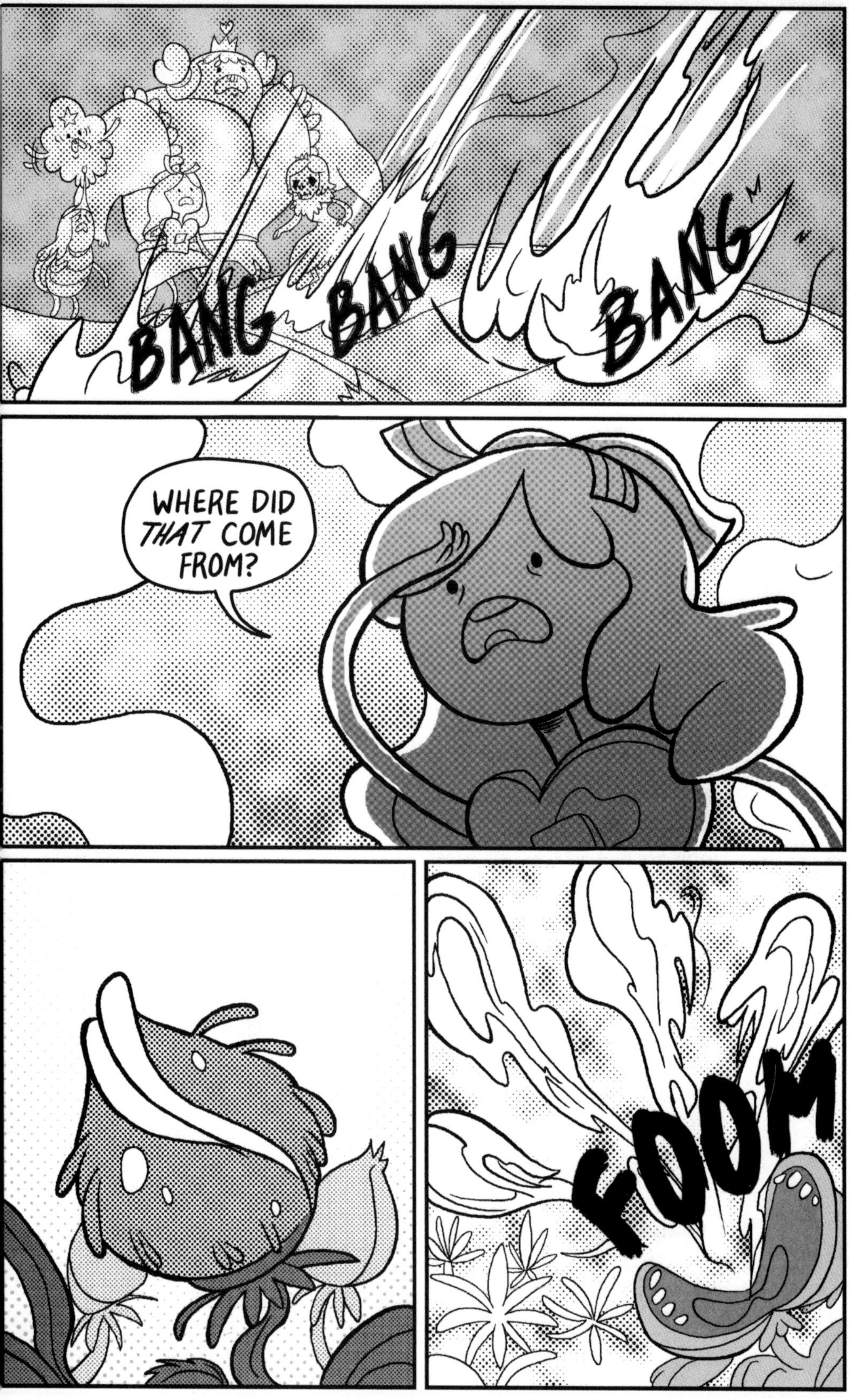
BANG BANG BANG
WHERE DID THAT COME FROM?
FOOM

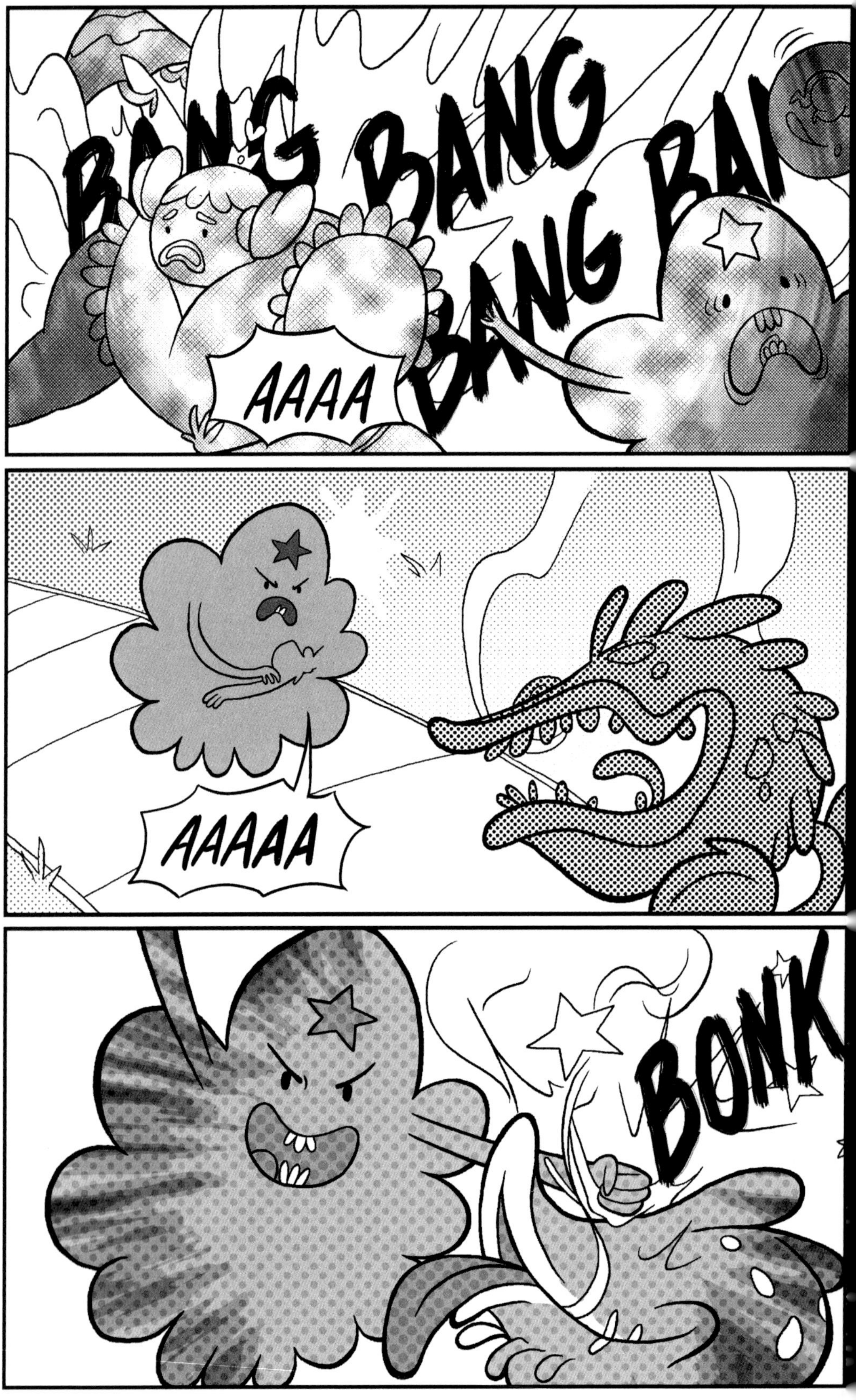
BANG BANG
BANG BA
AAAA
AAAAA
BONK

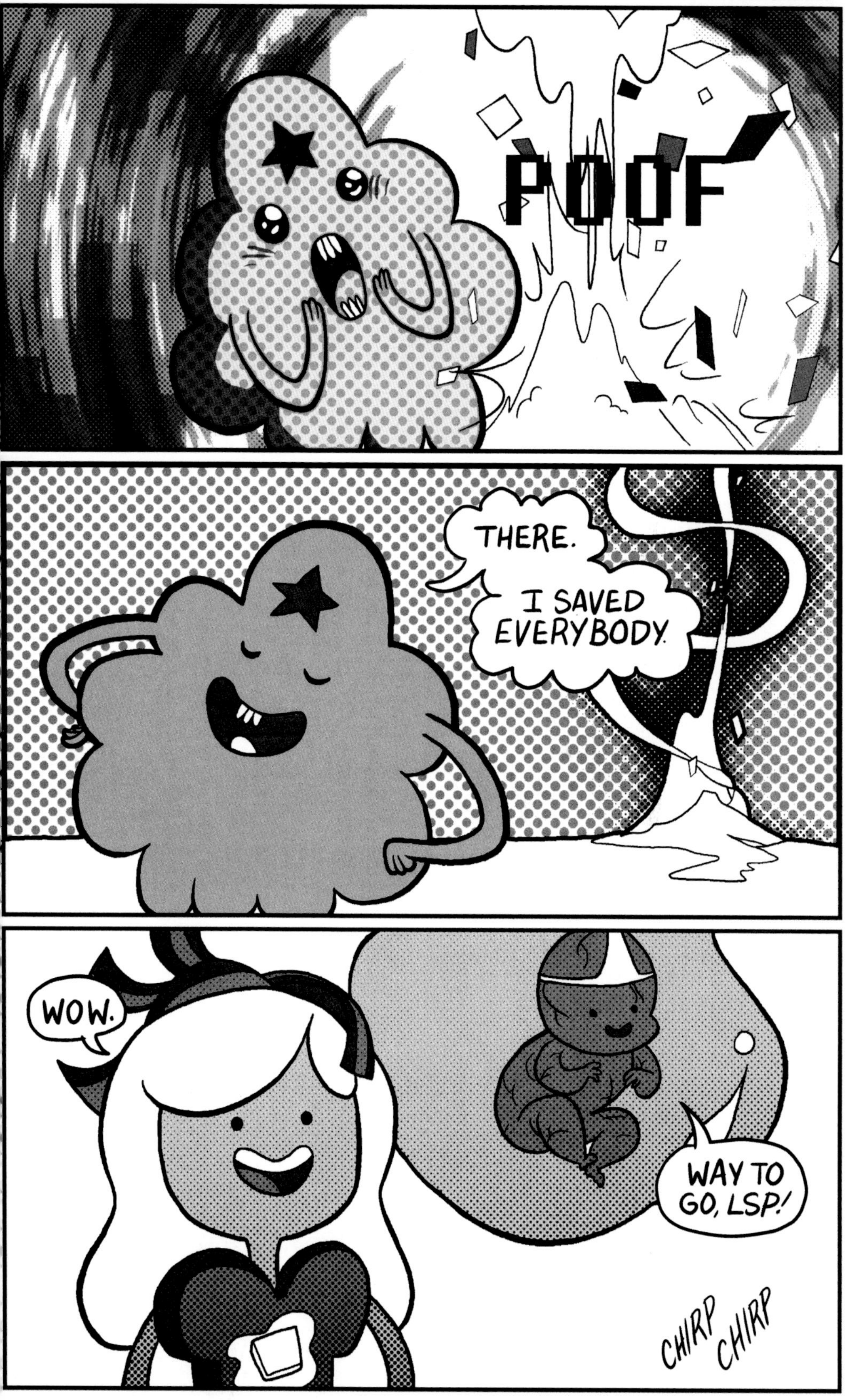
POOF
THERE.
I SAVED EVERYBODY.
WOW.
WAY TO GO, LSP!
CHIRP CHIRP

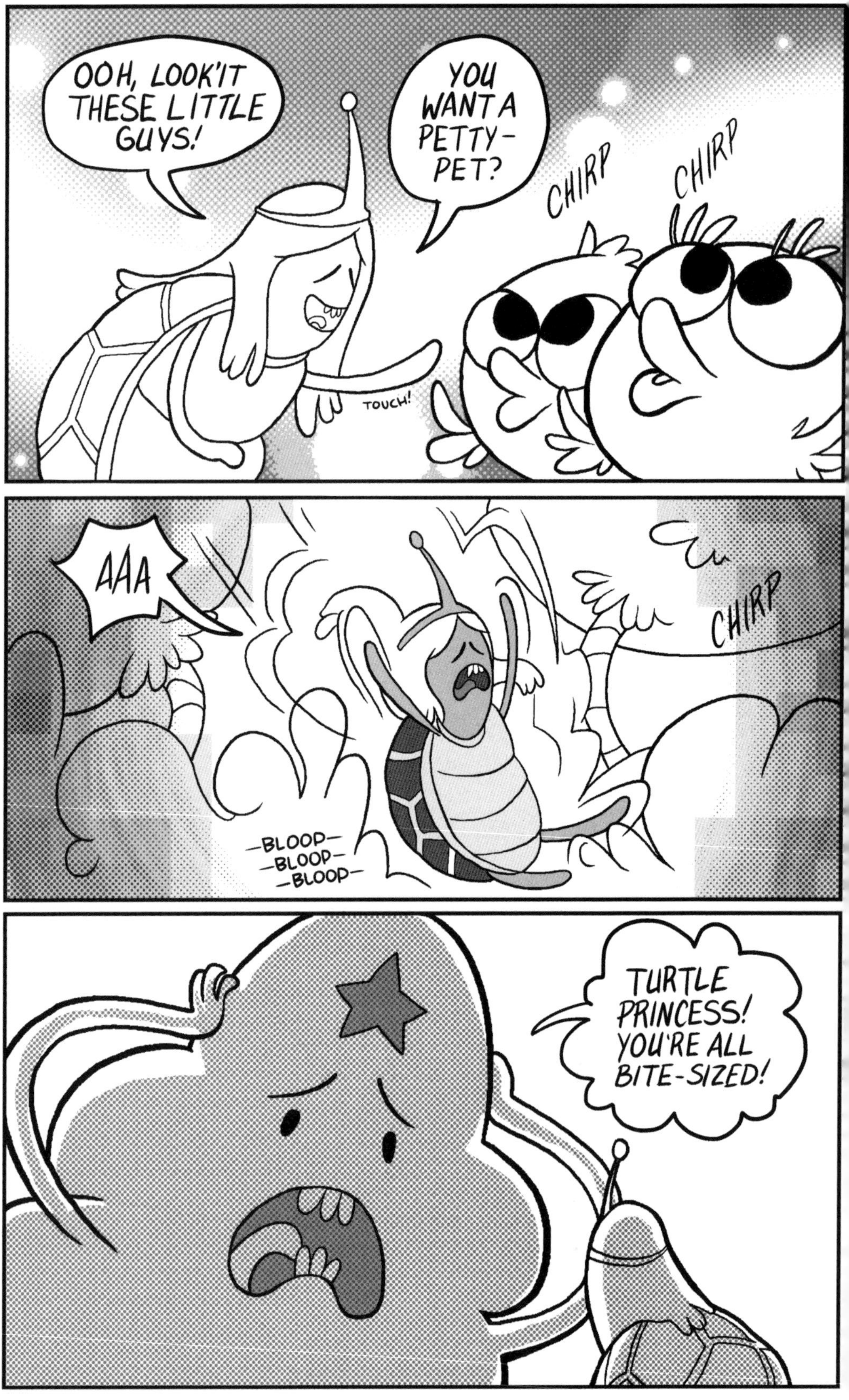
OOH, LOOK'IT THESE LITTLE GUYS!
YOU WANT A PETTY-PET?
CHIRP
CHIRP
TOUCH!
AAA
CHIRP
-BLOOP-
-BLOOP-
-BLOOP-
TURTLE PRINCESS! YOU'RE ALL BITE-SIZED!

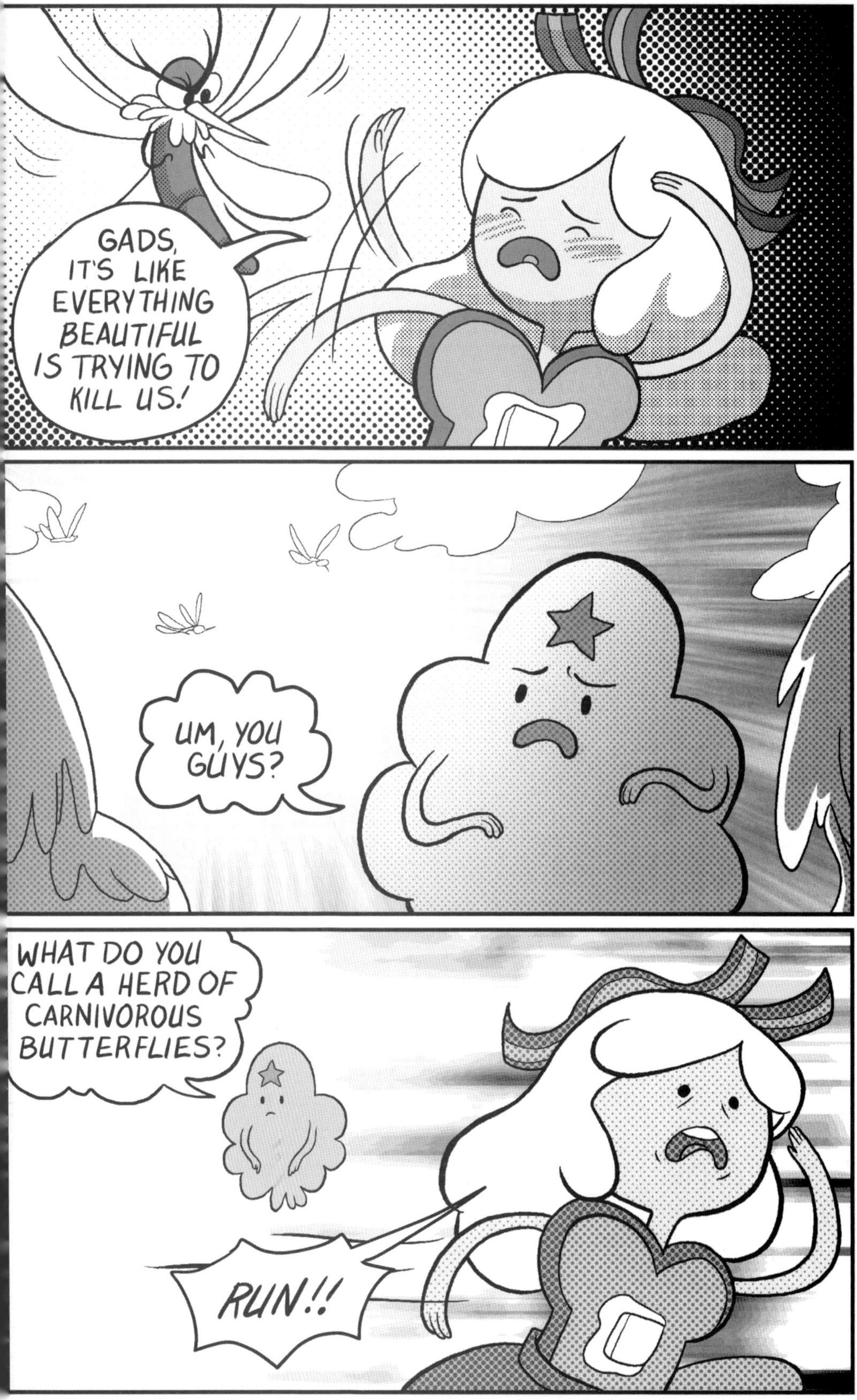
GADS, IT'S LIKE EVERYTHING BEAUTIFUL IS TRYING TO KILL US!
UM, YOU GUYS?
WHAT DO YOU CALL A HERD OF CARNIVOROUS BUTTERFLIES?
RUN!!

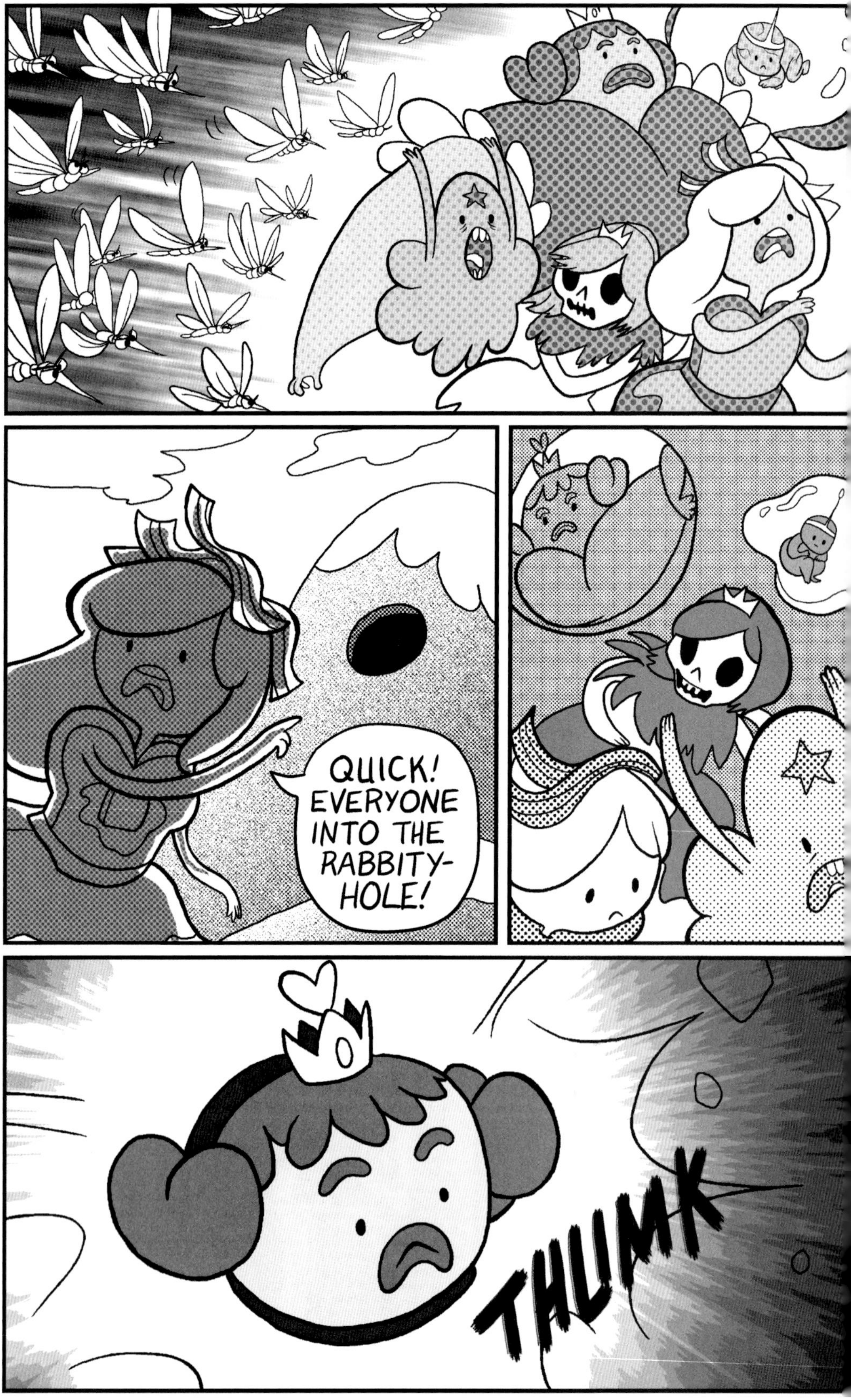
QUICK! EVERYONE INTO THE RABBITY-HOLE!
THUMK

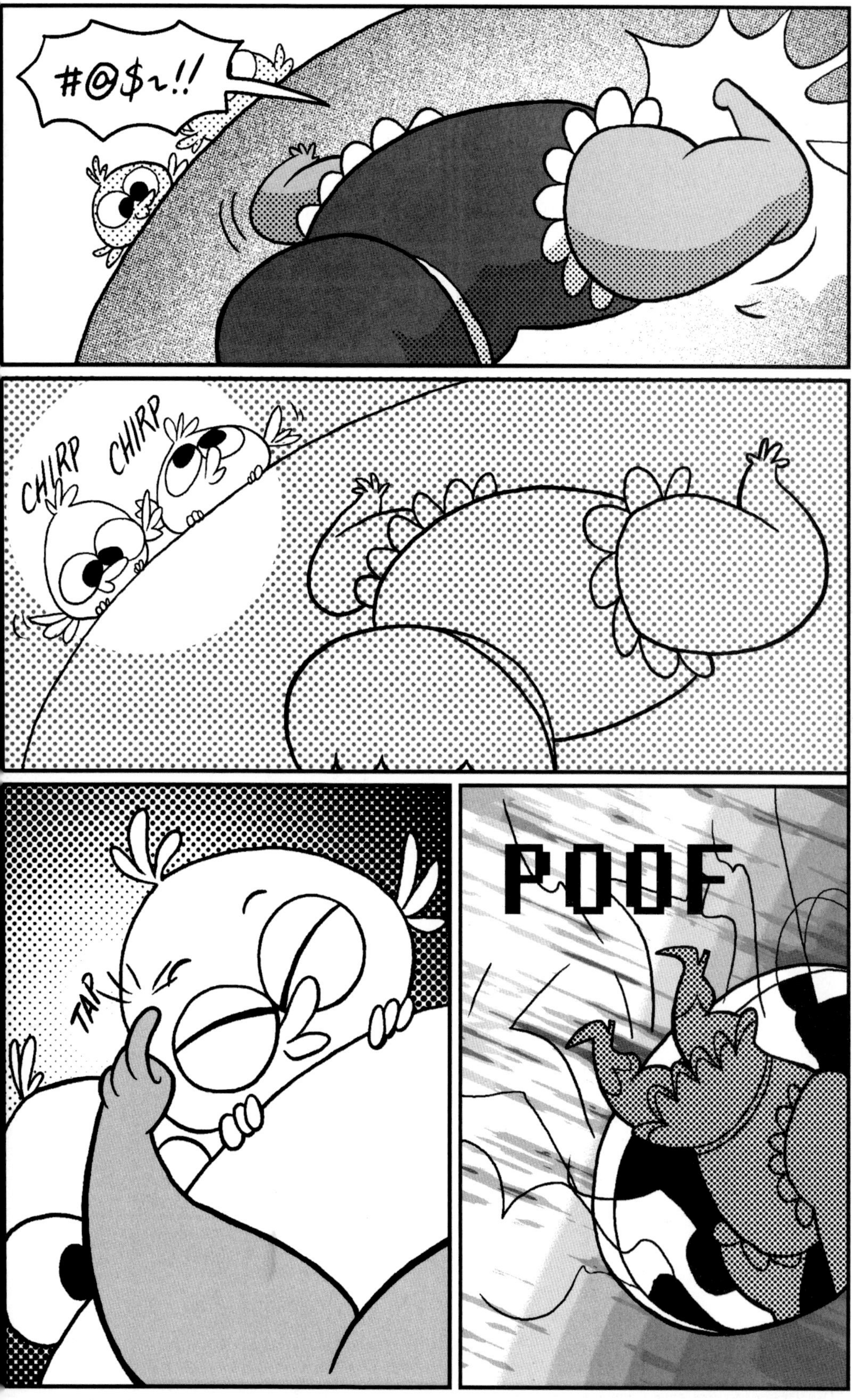
#@$₂!!
CHIRP CHIRP
TAP
POOF

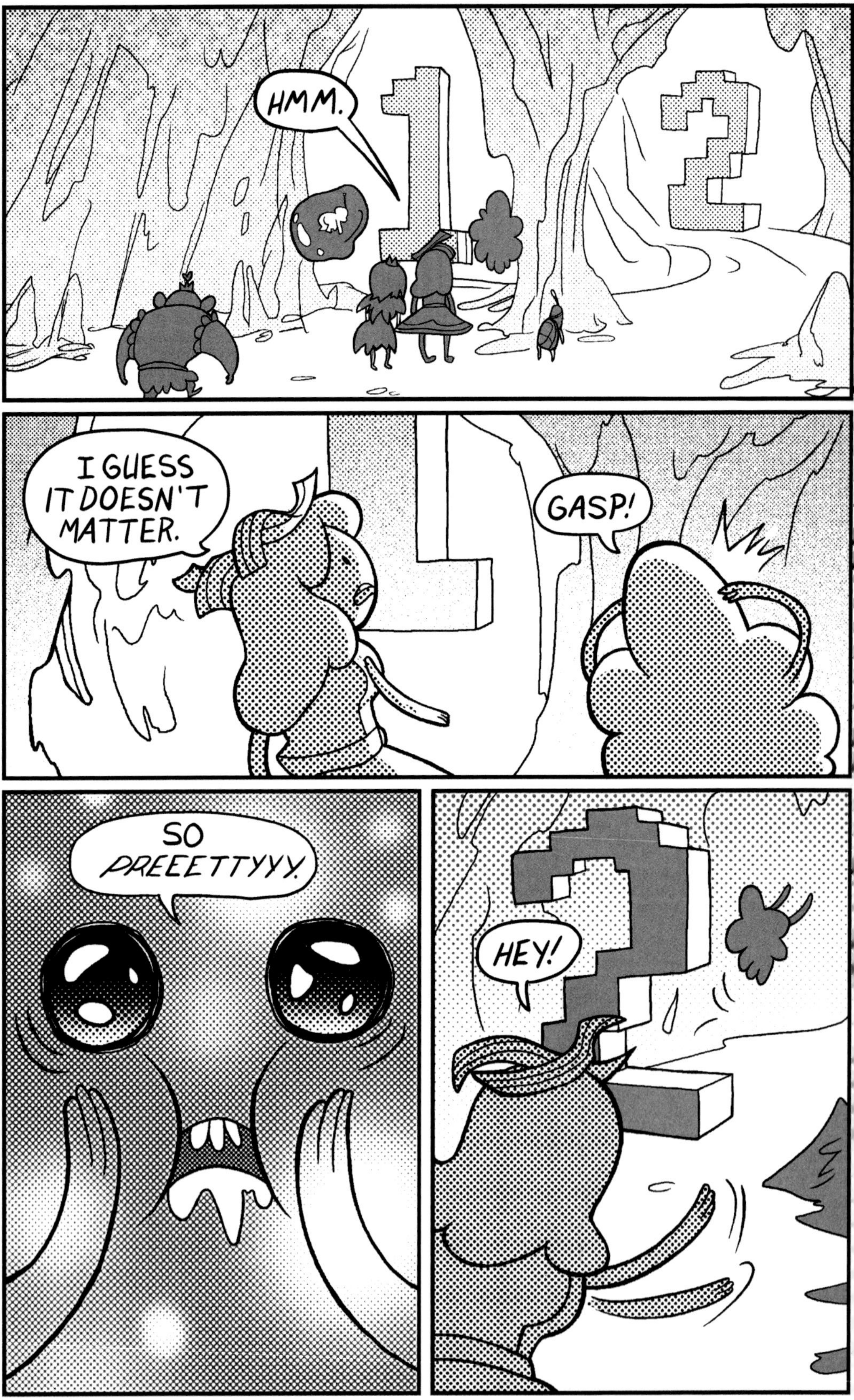
HMM.
I GUESS IT DOESN'T MATTER.
GASP!
SO PREEETTYYY.
HEY!

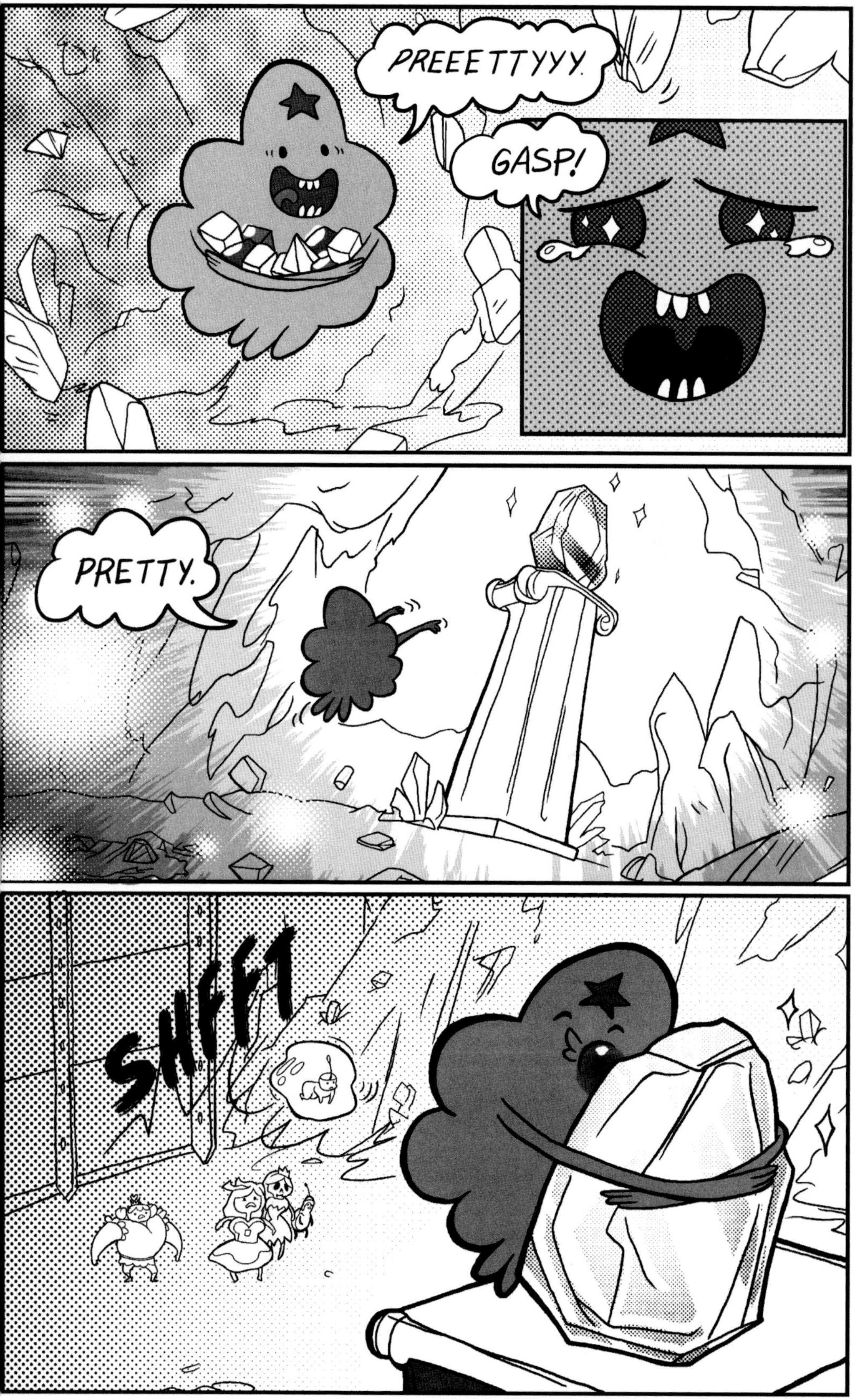
PREEETTYYY.
GASP!
PRETTY.
SHFFT

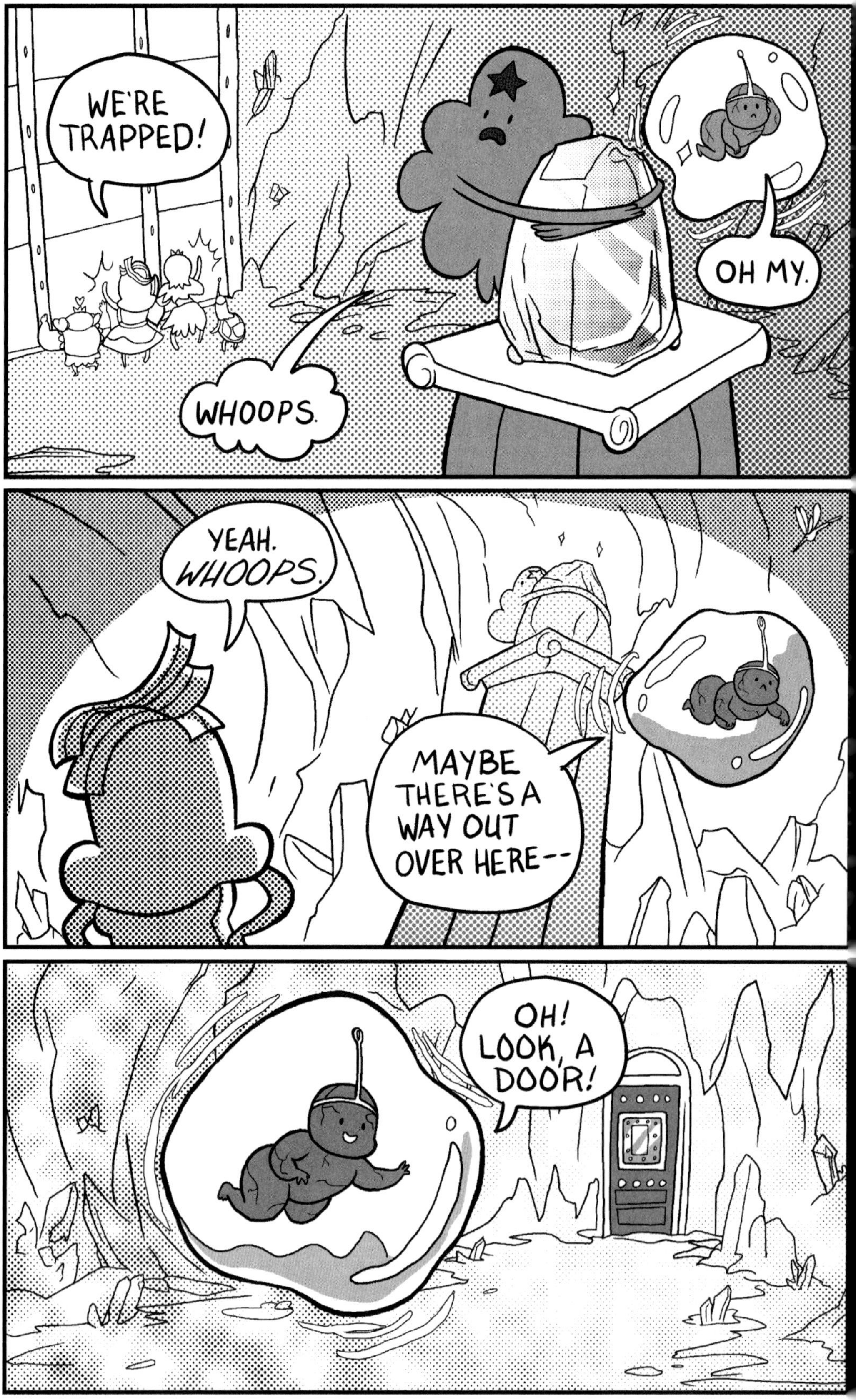
WE'RE TRAPPED!
OH MY.
WHOOPS.
YEAH. WHOOPS.
MAYBE THERE'S A WAY OUT OVER HERE--
OH! LOOK, A DOOR!

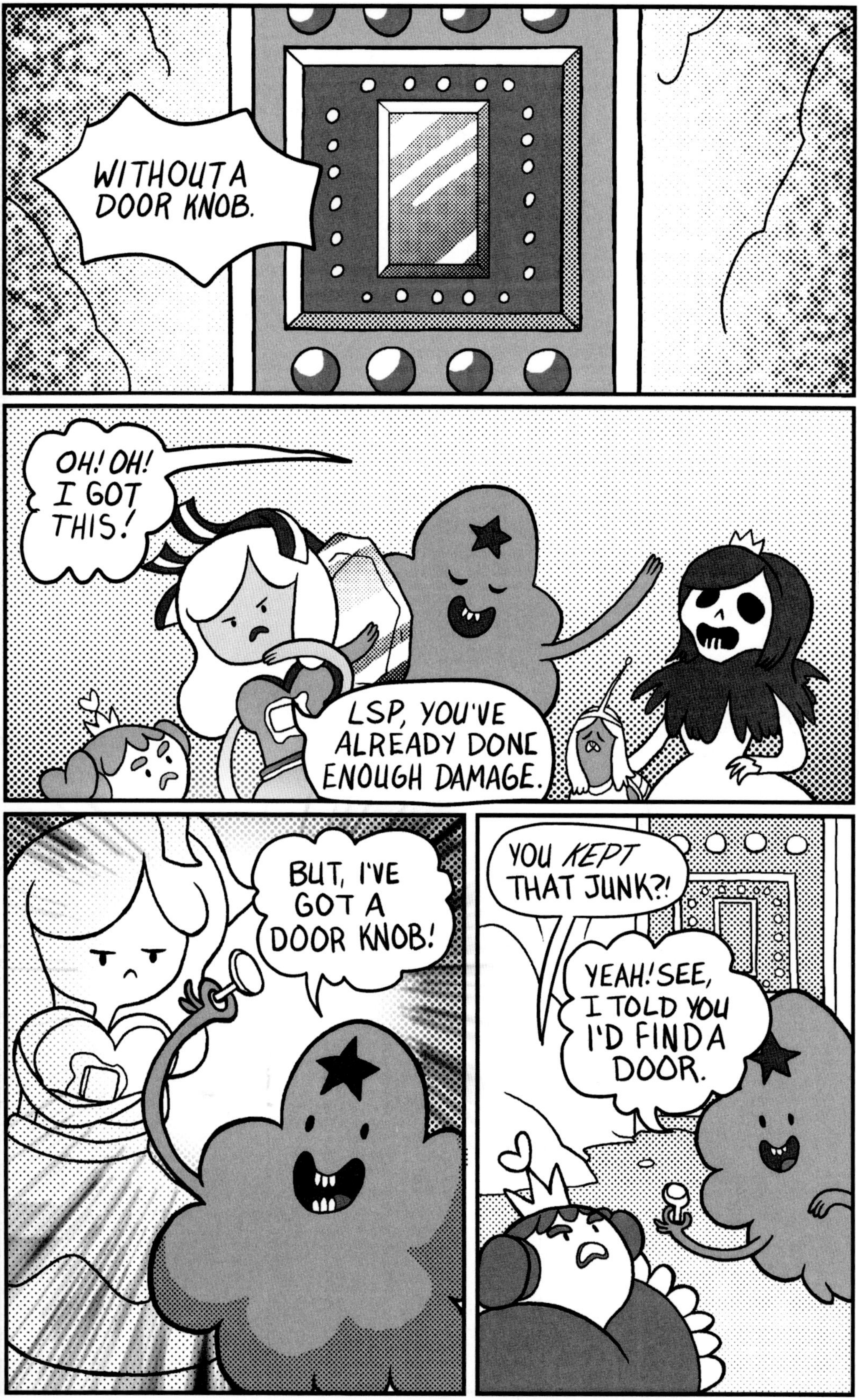

WITHOUT A DOOR KNOB.
OH! OH! I GOT THIS!
LSP, YOU'VE ALREADY DONE ENOUGH DAMAGE.
BUT, I'VE GOT A DOOR KNOB!
YOU KEPT THAT JUNK?!
YEAH! SEE, I TOLD YOU I'D FIND A DOOR.

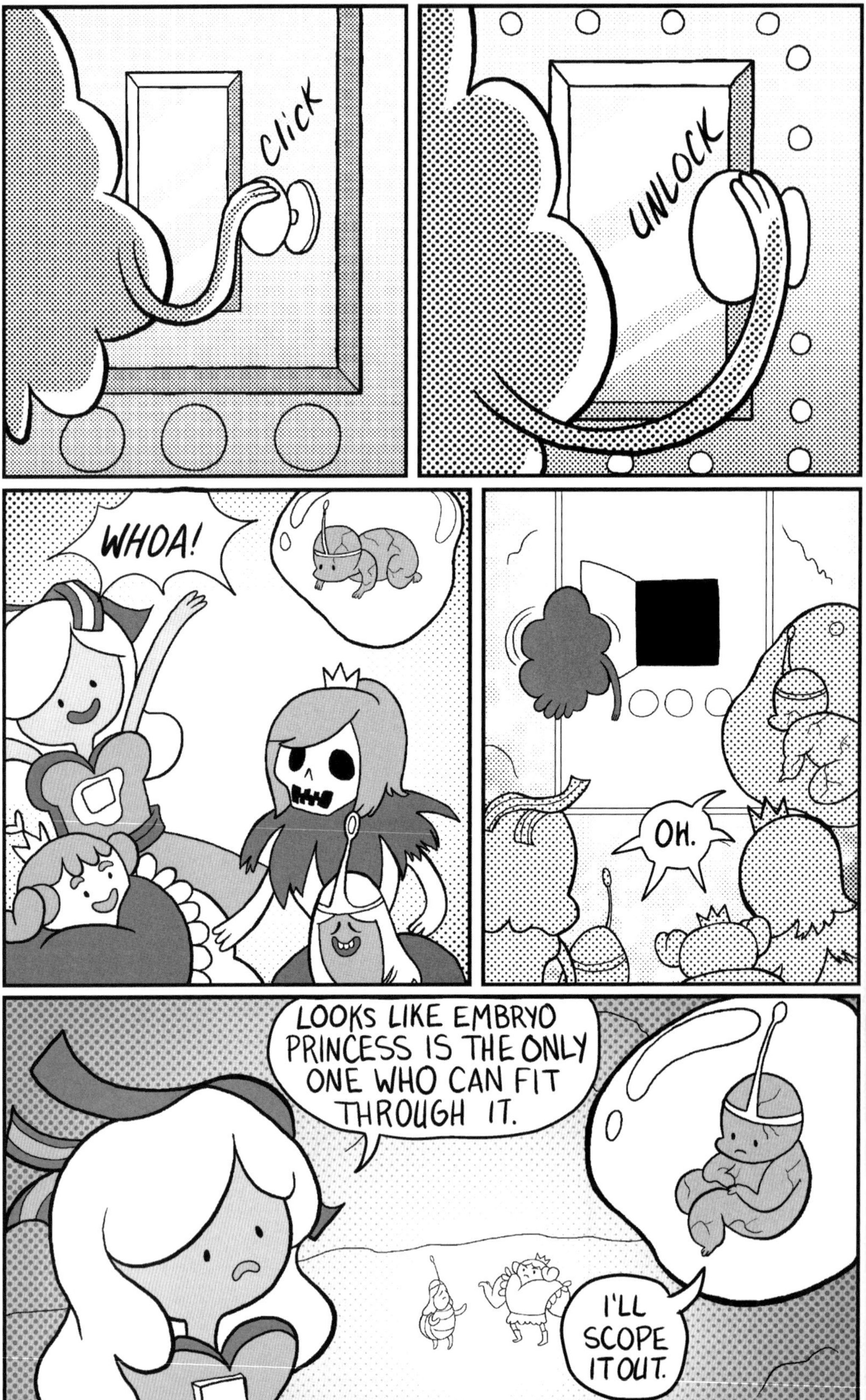
CLICK
UNLOCK
WHOA!
OH.
LOOKS LIKE EMBRYO PRINCESS IS THE ONLY ONE WHO CAN FIT THROUGH IT.
I'LL SCOPE IT OUT.

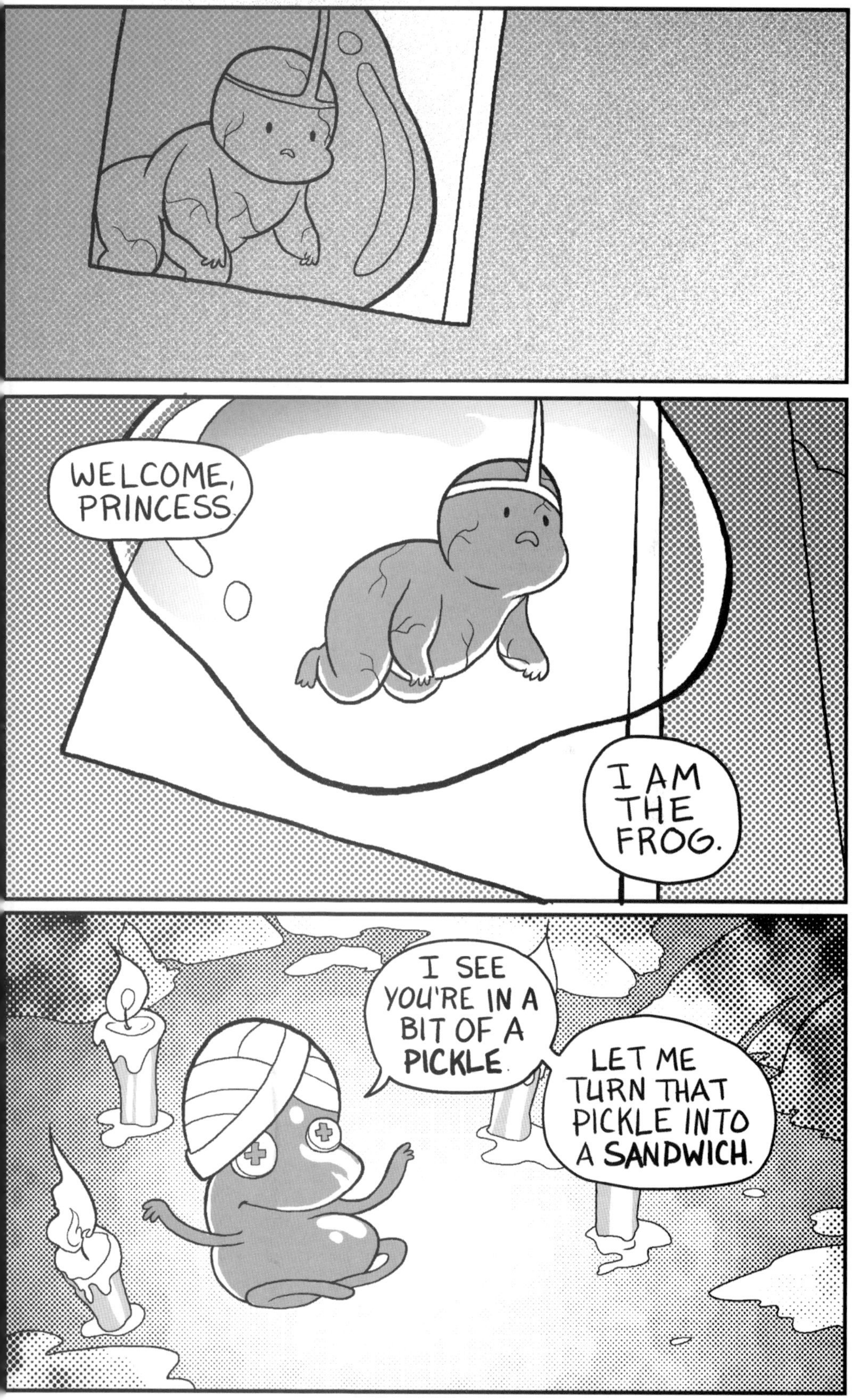
WELCOME, PRINCESS.
I AM THE FROG.
I SEE YOU'RE IN A BIT OF A **PICKLE**.
LET ME TURN THAT PICKLE INTO A **SANDWICH**.

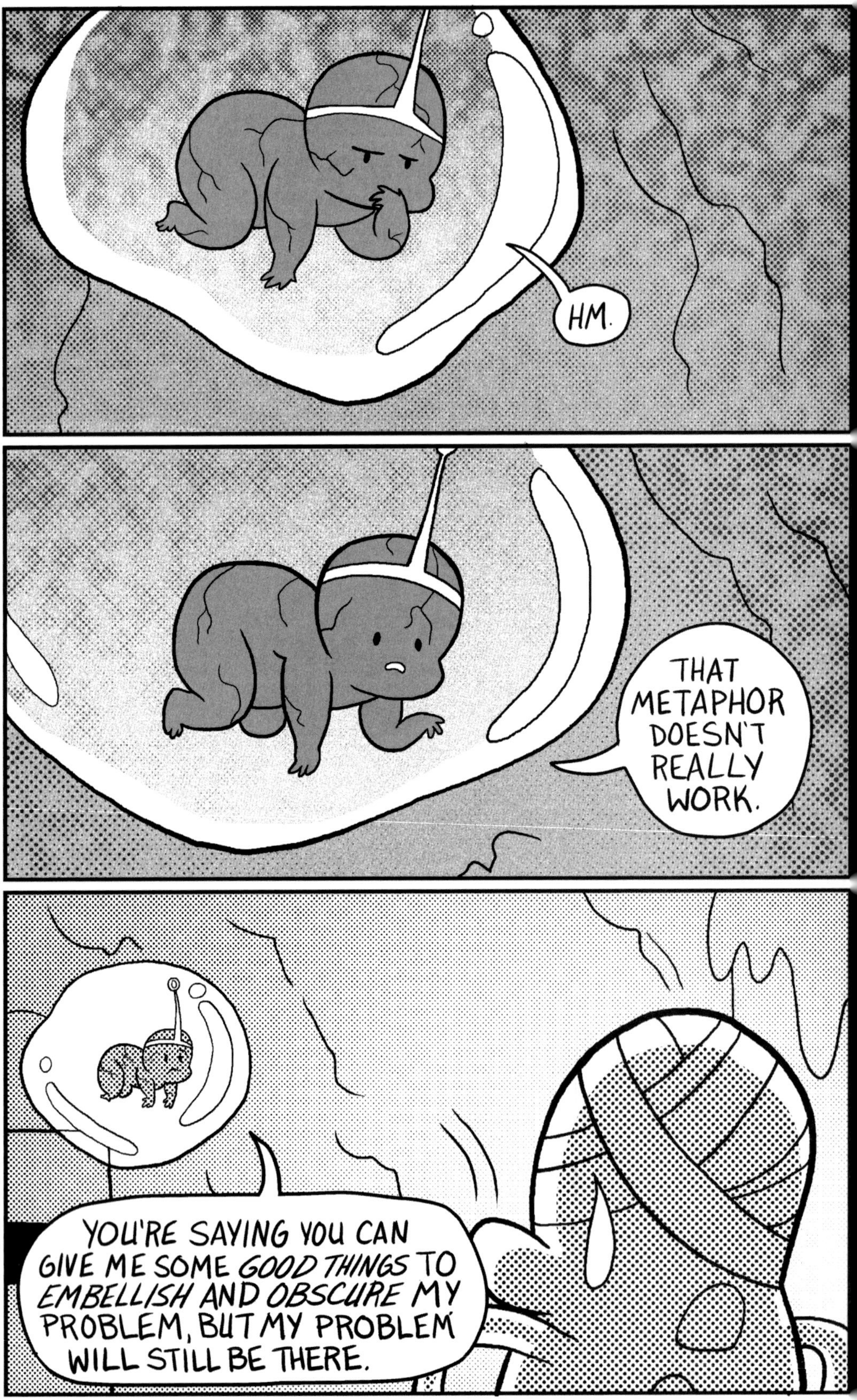
HM.
THAT METAPHOR DOESN'T REALLY WORK.
YOU'RE SAYING YOU CAN GIVE ME SOME *GOOD THINGS* TO *EMBELLISH* AND *OBSCURE* MY PROBLEM, BUT MY PROBLEM WILL STILL BE THERE.

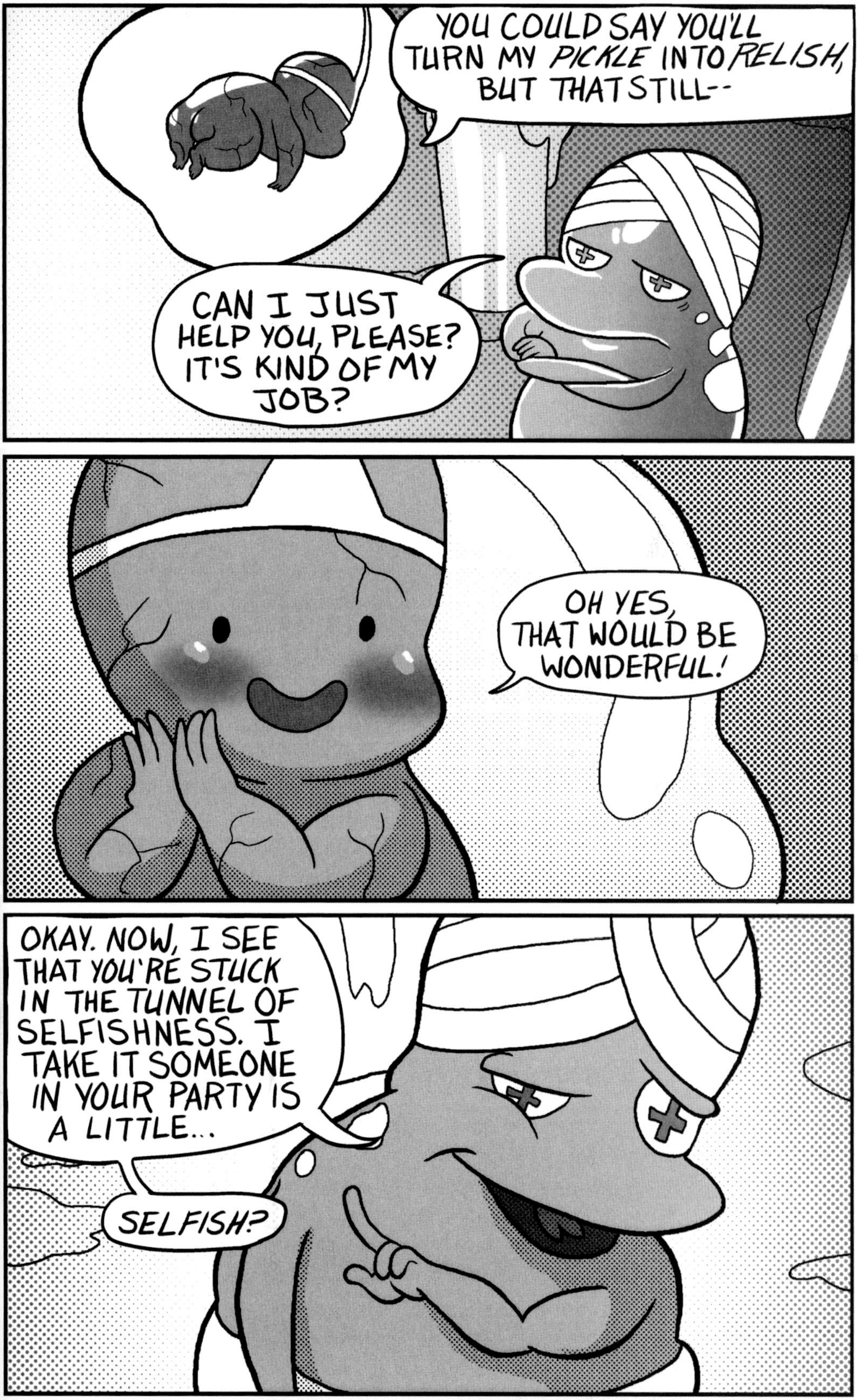
YOU COULD SAY YOU'LL TURN MY *PICKLE* INTO *RELISH*, BUT THAT STILL--
CAN I JUST HELP YOU, PLEASE? IT'S KIND OF MY JOB?
OH YES, THAT WOULD BE WONDERFUL!
OKAY. NOW, I SEE THAT YOU'RE STUCK IN THE TUNNEL OF SELFISHNESS. I TAKE IT SOMEONE IN YOUR PARTY IS A LITTLE...
SELFISH?

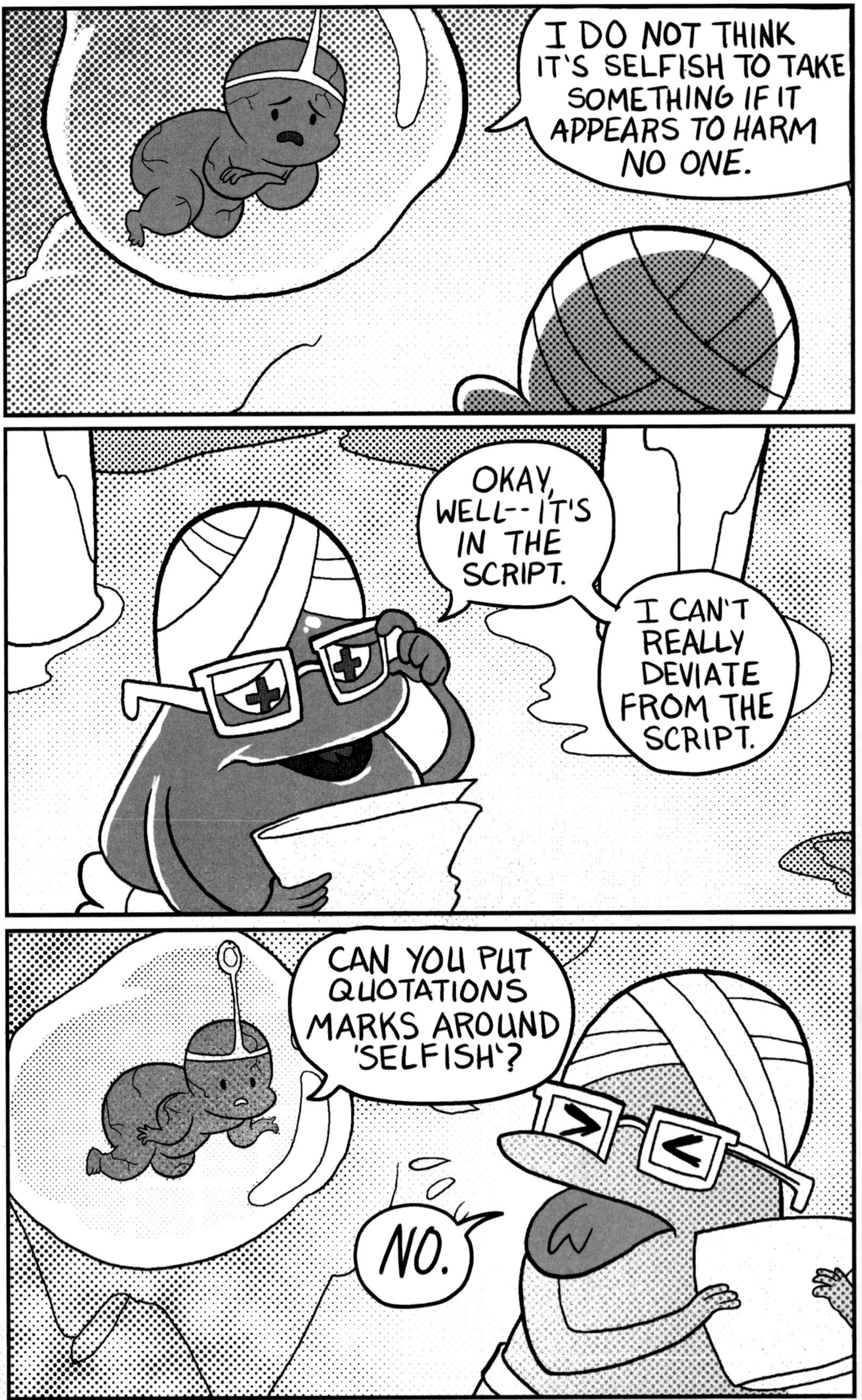
I DO NOT THINK IT'S SELFISH TO TAKE SOMETHING IF IT APPEARS TO HARM NO ONE.
OKAY, WELL-- IT'S IN THE SCRIPT.
I CAN'T REALLY DEVIATE FROM THE SCRIPT.
CAN YOU PUT QUOTATIONS MARKS AROUND 'SELFISH'?
NO.

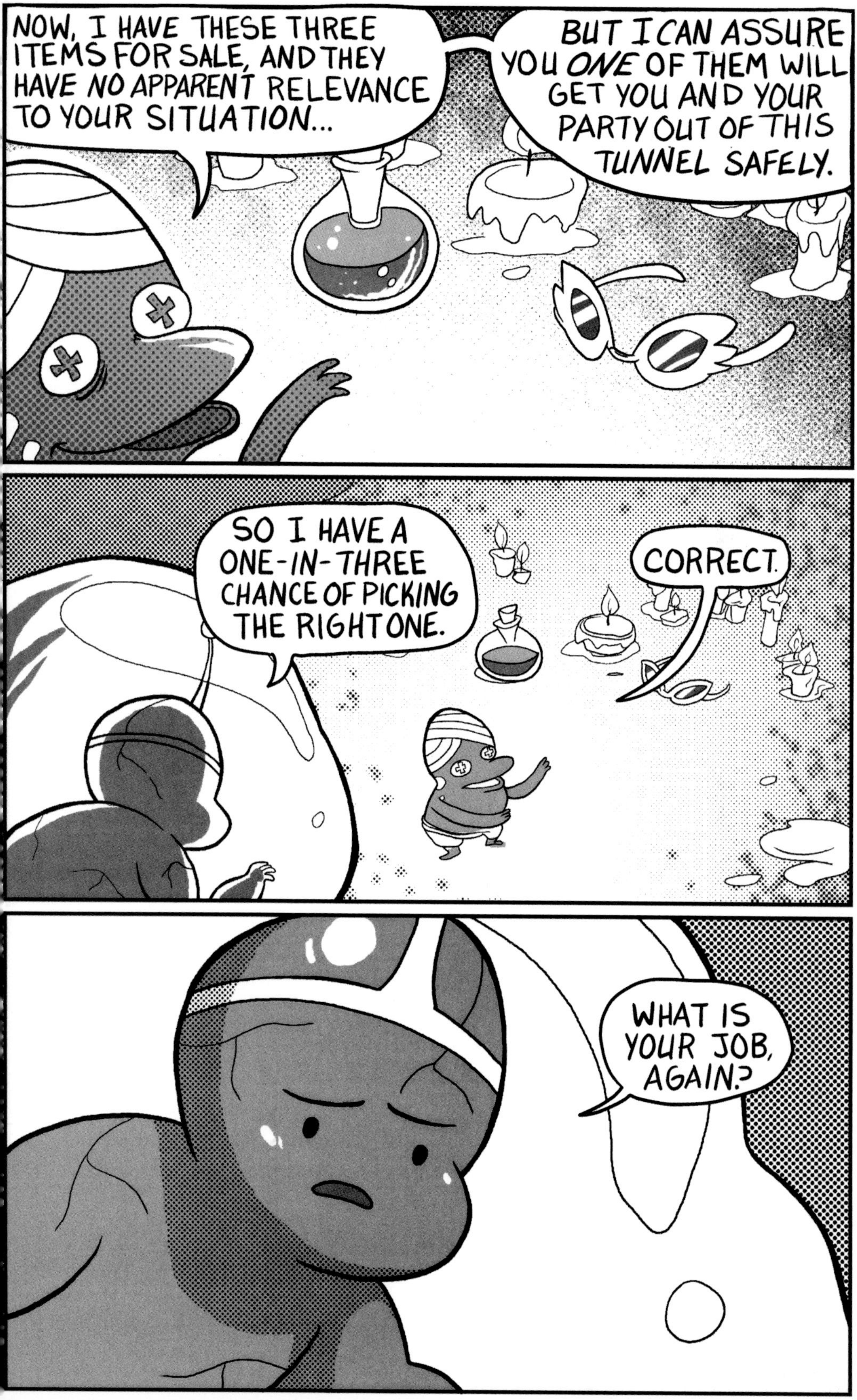
NOW, I HAVE THESE THREE ITEMS FOR SALE, AND THEY HAVE NO APPARENT RELEVANCE TO YOUR SITUATION...
BUT I CAN ASSURE YOU ONE OF THEM WILL GET YOU AND YOUR PARTY OUT OF THIS TUNNEL SAFELY.
SO I HAVE A ONE-IN-THREE CHANCE OF PICKING THE RIGHT ONE.
CORRECT.
WHAT IS YOUR JOB, AGAIN?

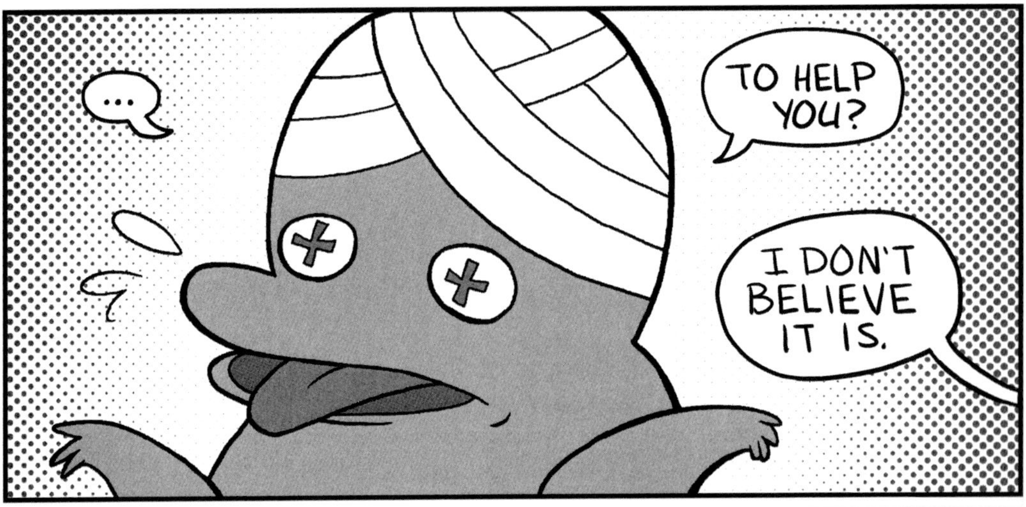
...
TO HELP YOU?
I DON'T BELIEVE IT IS.

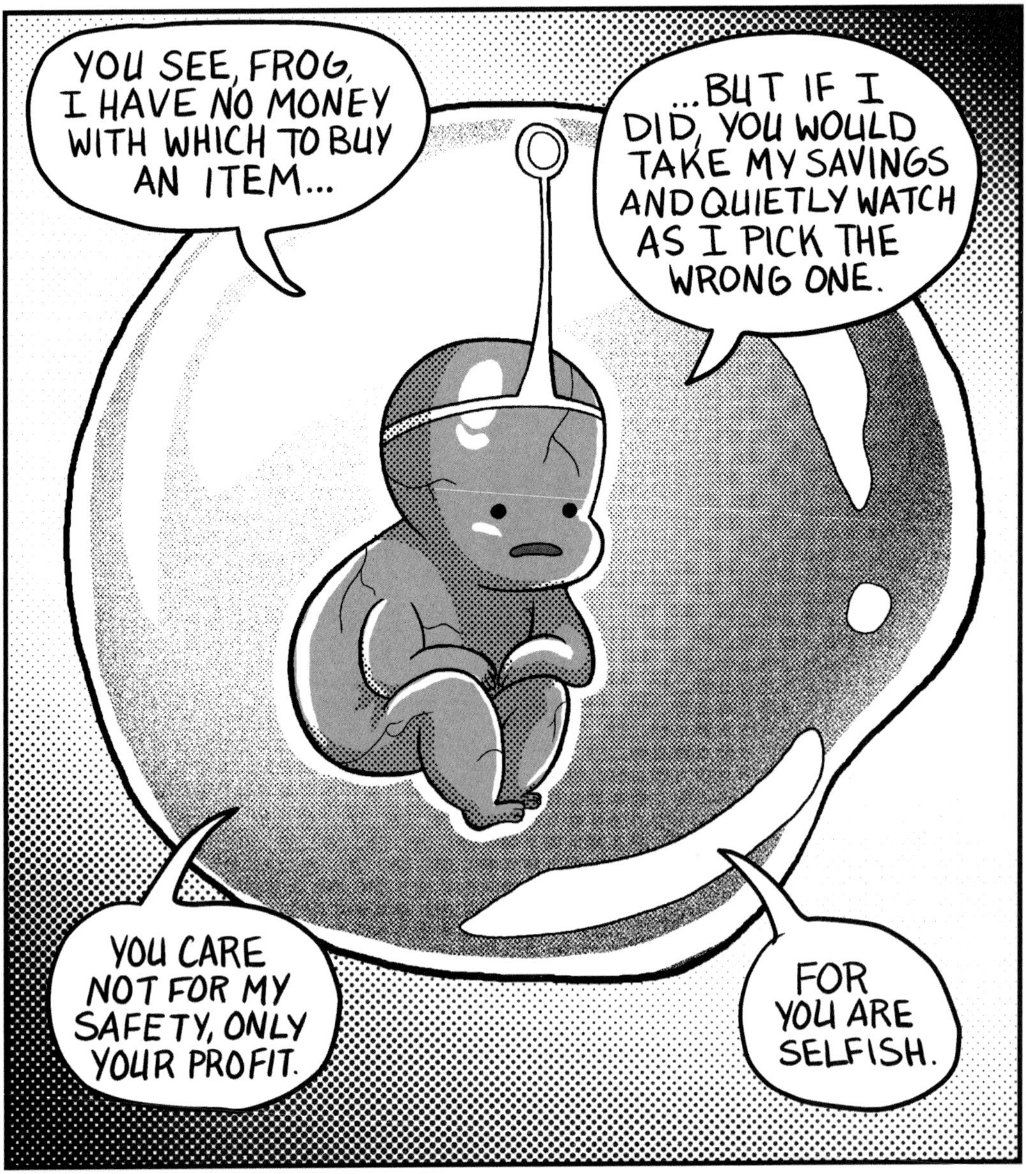
YOU SEE, FROG, I HAVE NO MONEY WITH WHICH TO BUY AN ITEM...
...BUT IF I DID, YOU WOULD TAKE MY SAVINGS AND QUIETLY WATCH AS I PICK THE WRONG ONE.
YOU CARE NOT FOR MY SAFETY, ONLY YOUR PROFIT.
FOR YOU ARE SELFISH.

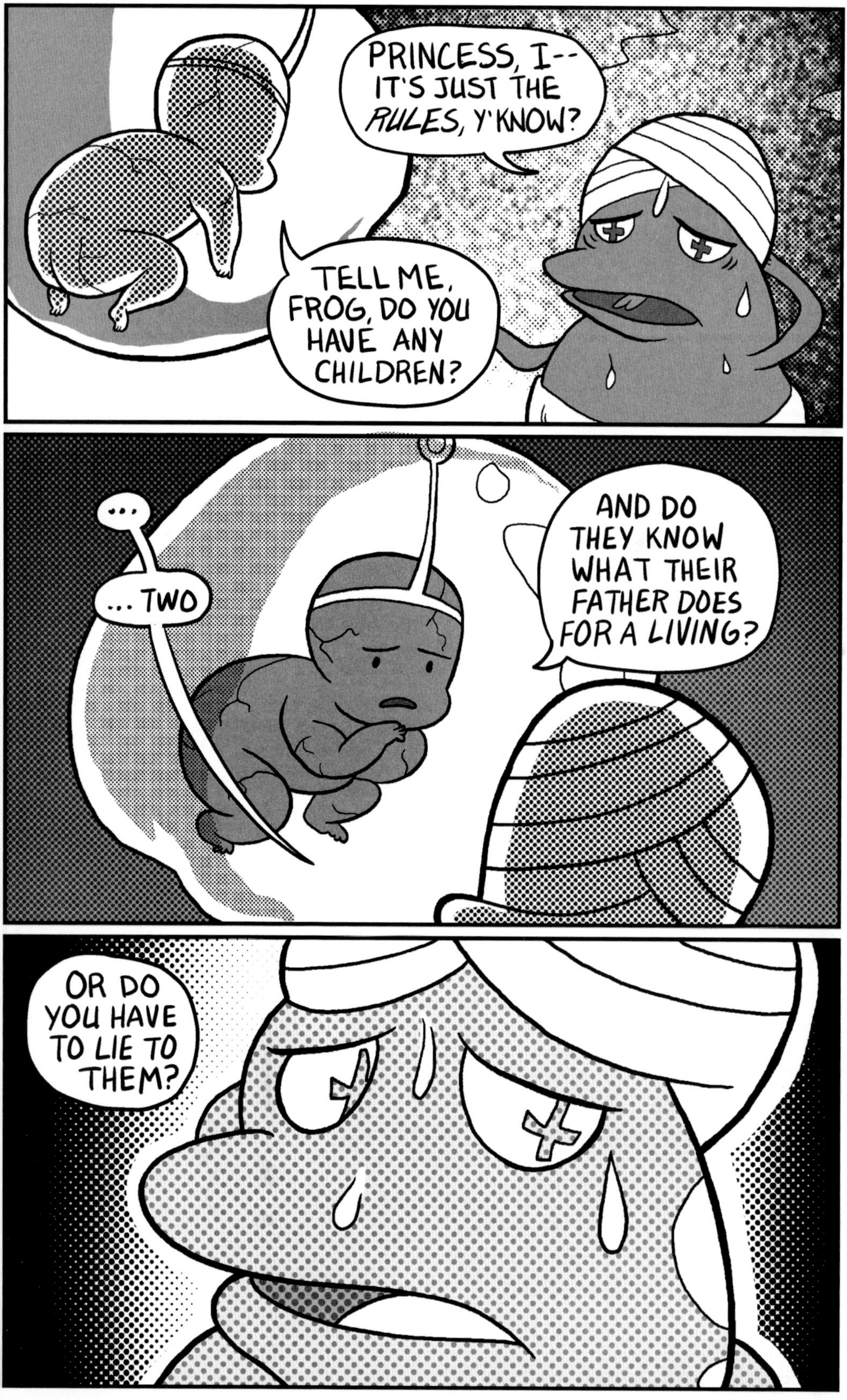
PRINCESS, I-- IT'S JUST THE RULES, Y'KNOW?
TELL ME, FROG, DO YOU HAVE ANY CHILDREN?
...
... TWO
AND DO THEY KNOW WHAT THEIR FATHER DOES FOR A LIVING?
OR DO YOU HAVE TO LIE TO THEM?

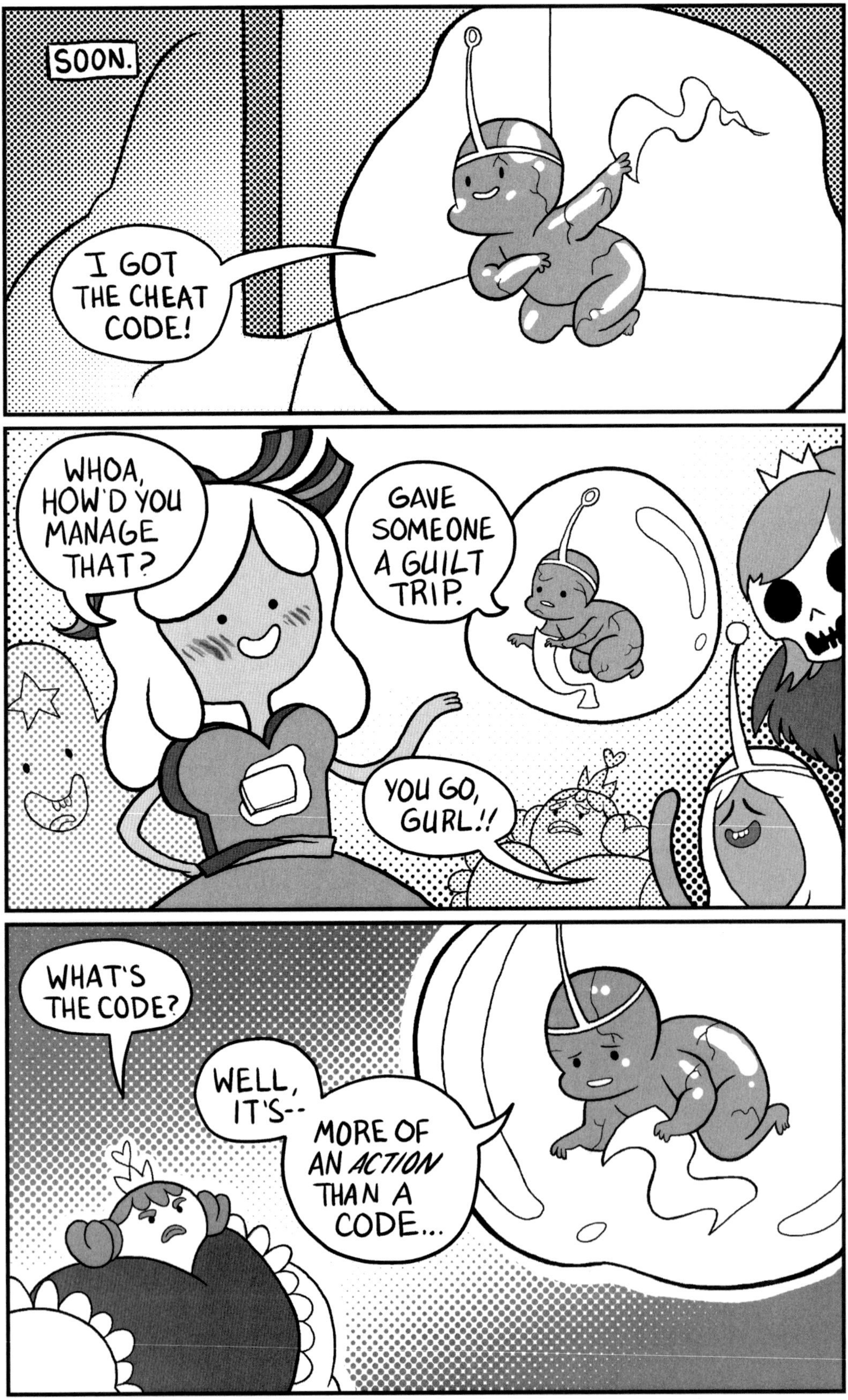
SOON.
I GOT THE CHEAT CODE!
WHOA, HOW'D YOU MANAGE THAT?
GAVE SOMEONE A GUILT TRIP.
YOU GO, GURL!!
WHAT'S THE CODE?
WELL, IT'S--
MORE OF AN *ACTION* THAN A CODE...

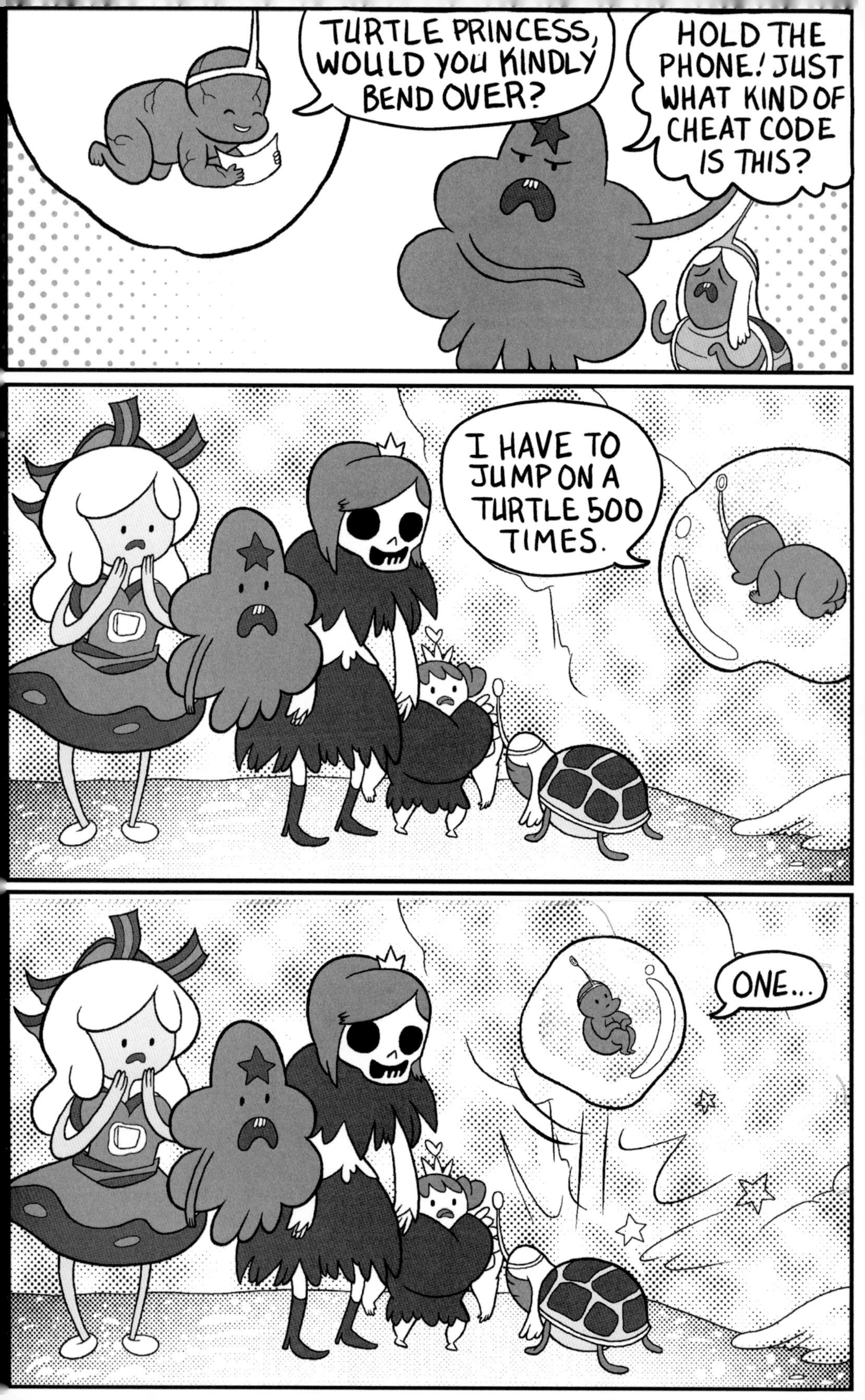
TURTLE PRINCESS, WOULD YOU KINDLY BEND OVER?
HOLD THE PHONE! JUST WHAT KIND OF CHEAT CODE IS THIS?
I HAVE TO JUMP ON A TURTLE 500 TIMES.
ONE...

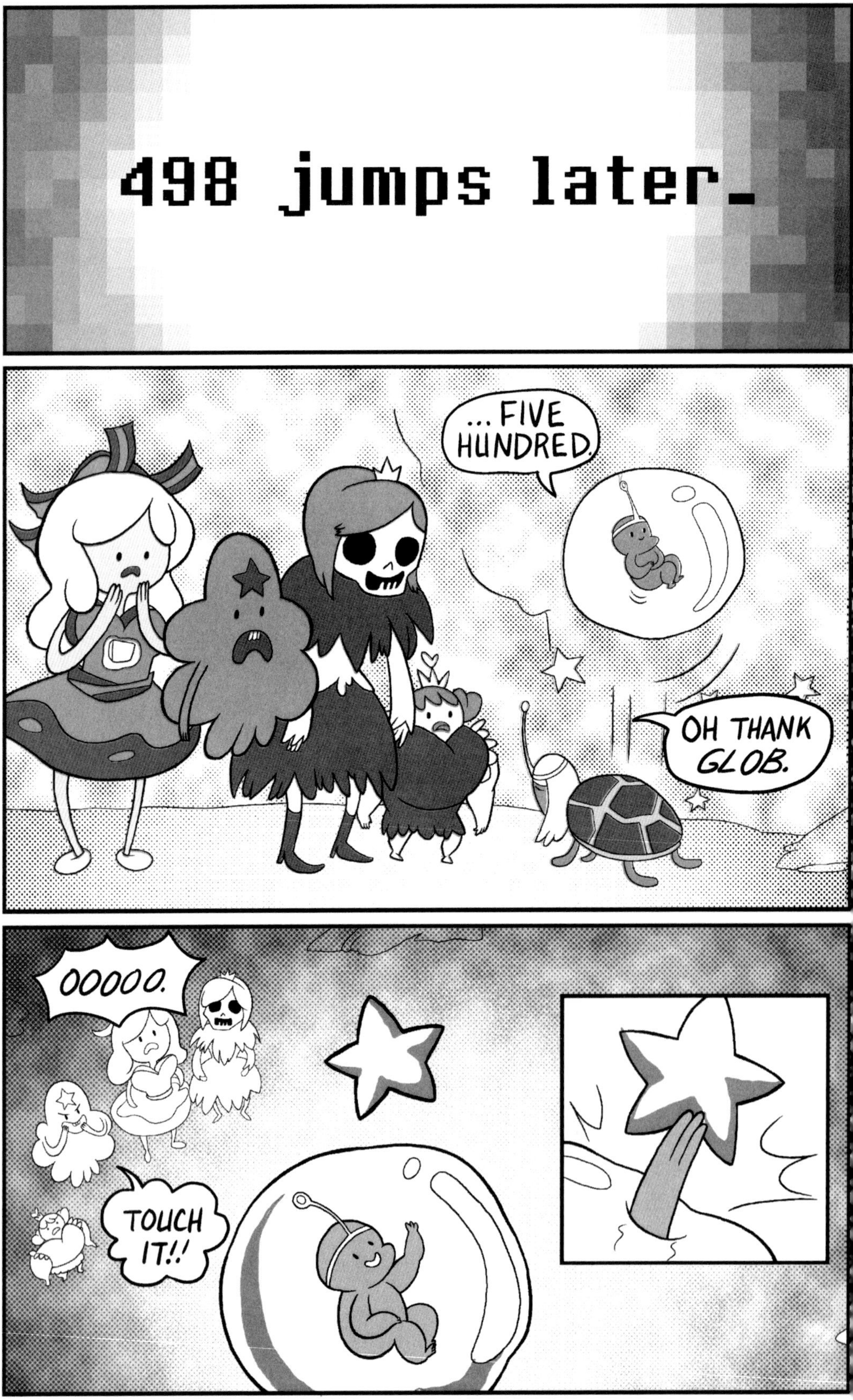
498 jumps later_
...FIVE HUNDRED.
OH THANK GLOB.
OOOOO.
TOUCH IT!!

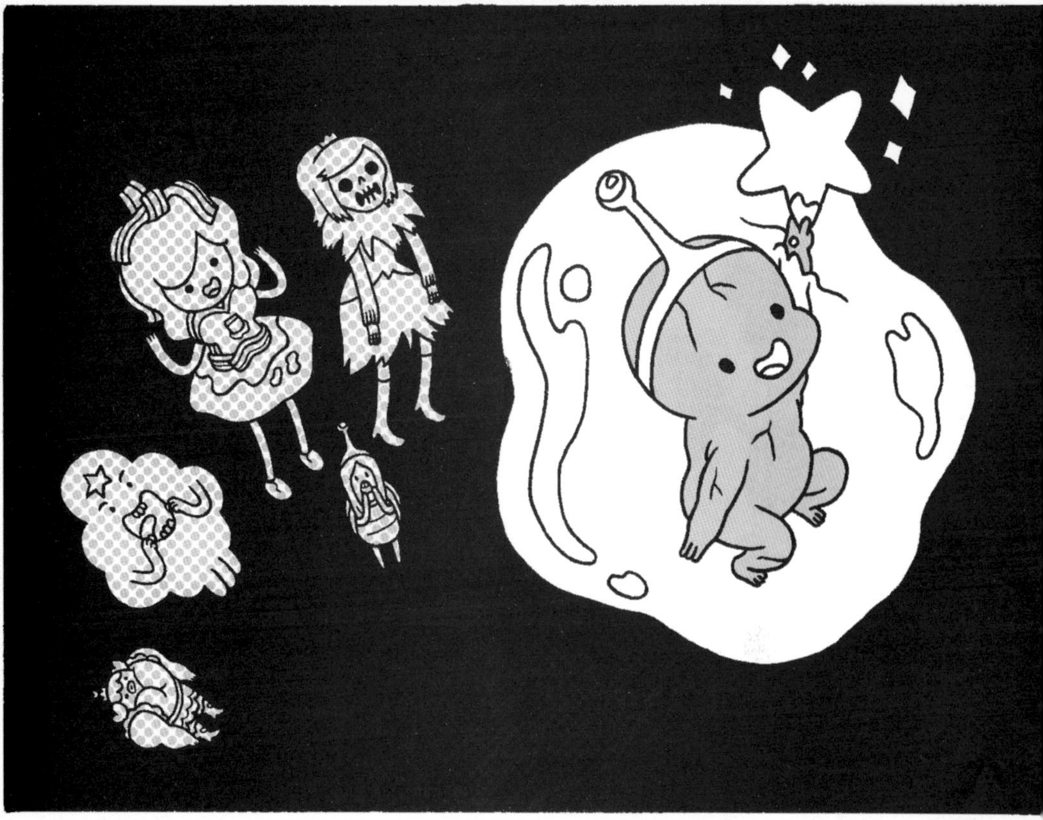

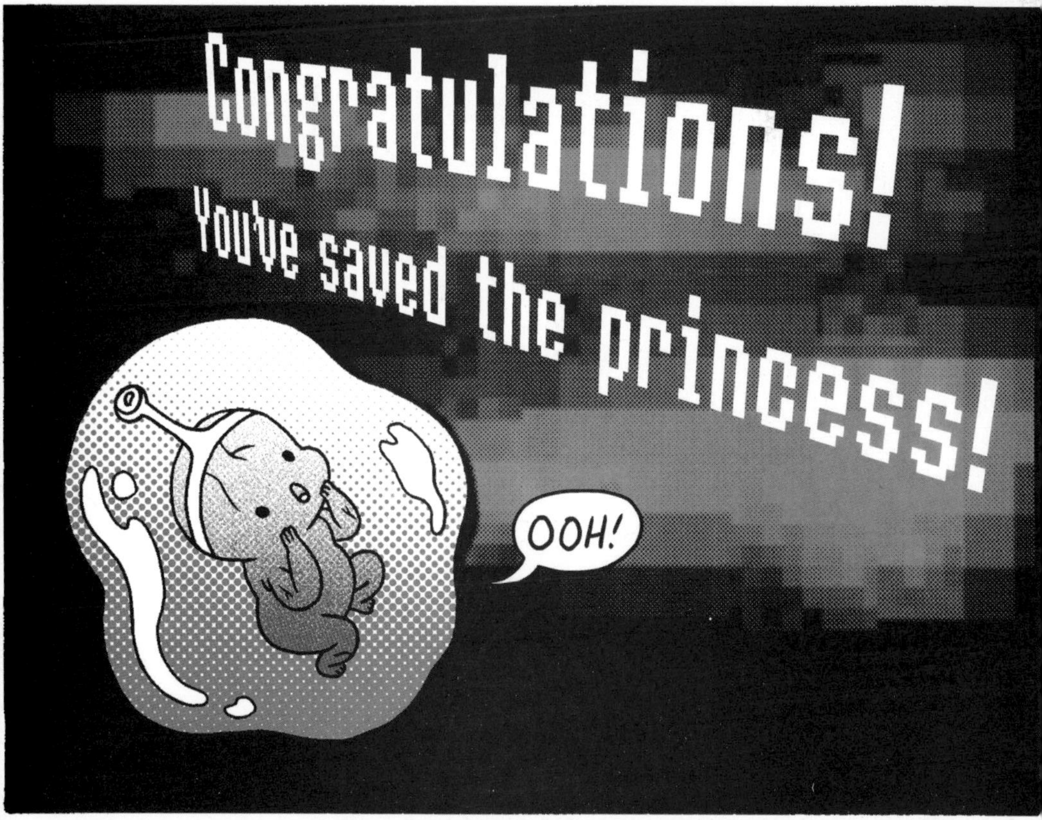
Congratulations!
You've saved the princess!
OOH!

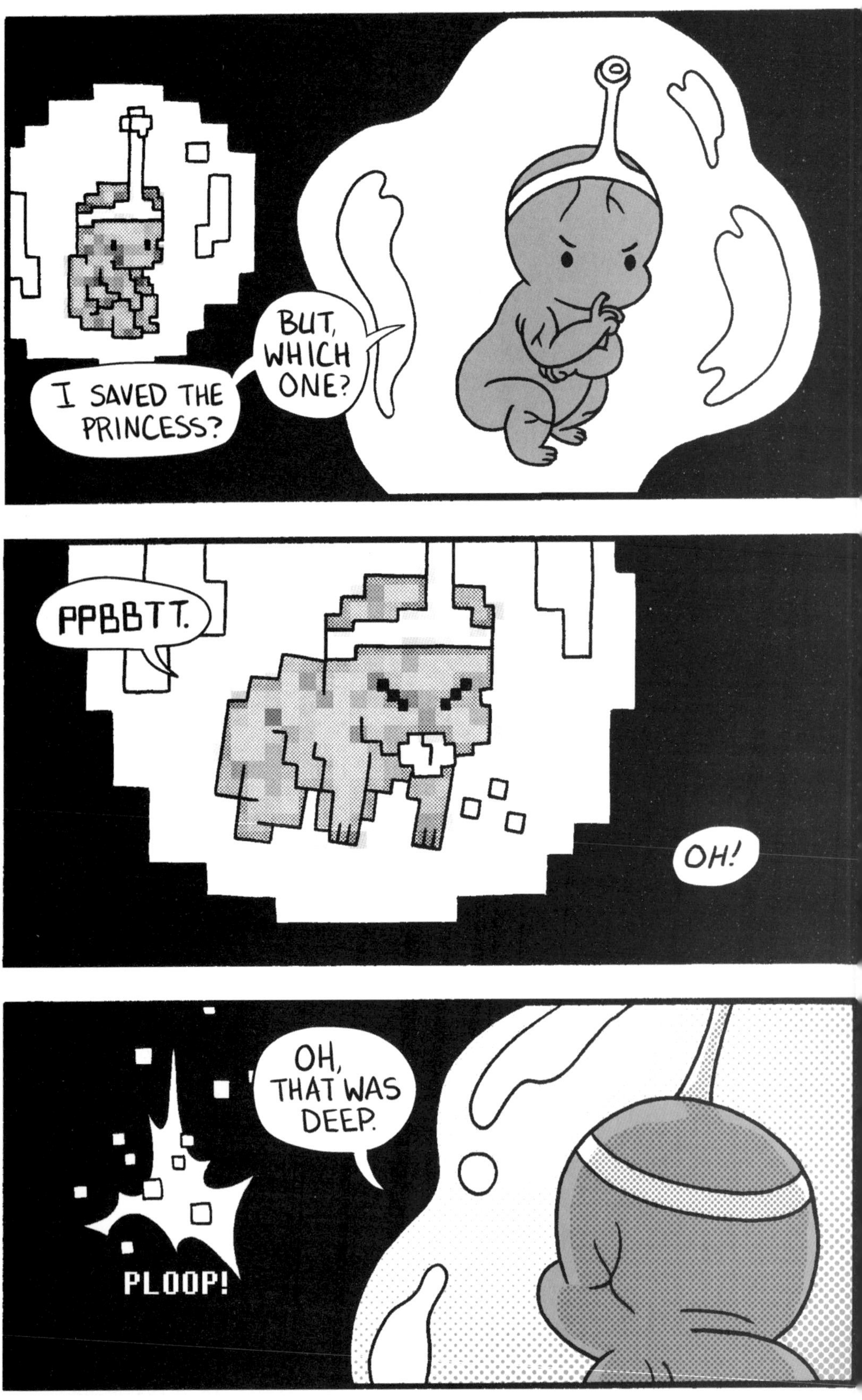
I SAVED THE PRINCESS?
BUT, WHICH ONE?
PPBBTT.
OH!
PLOOP!
OH, THAT WAS DEEP.

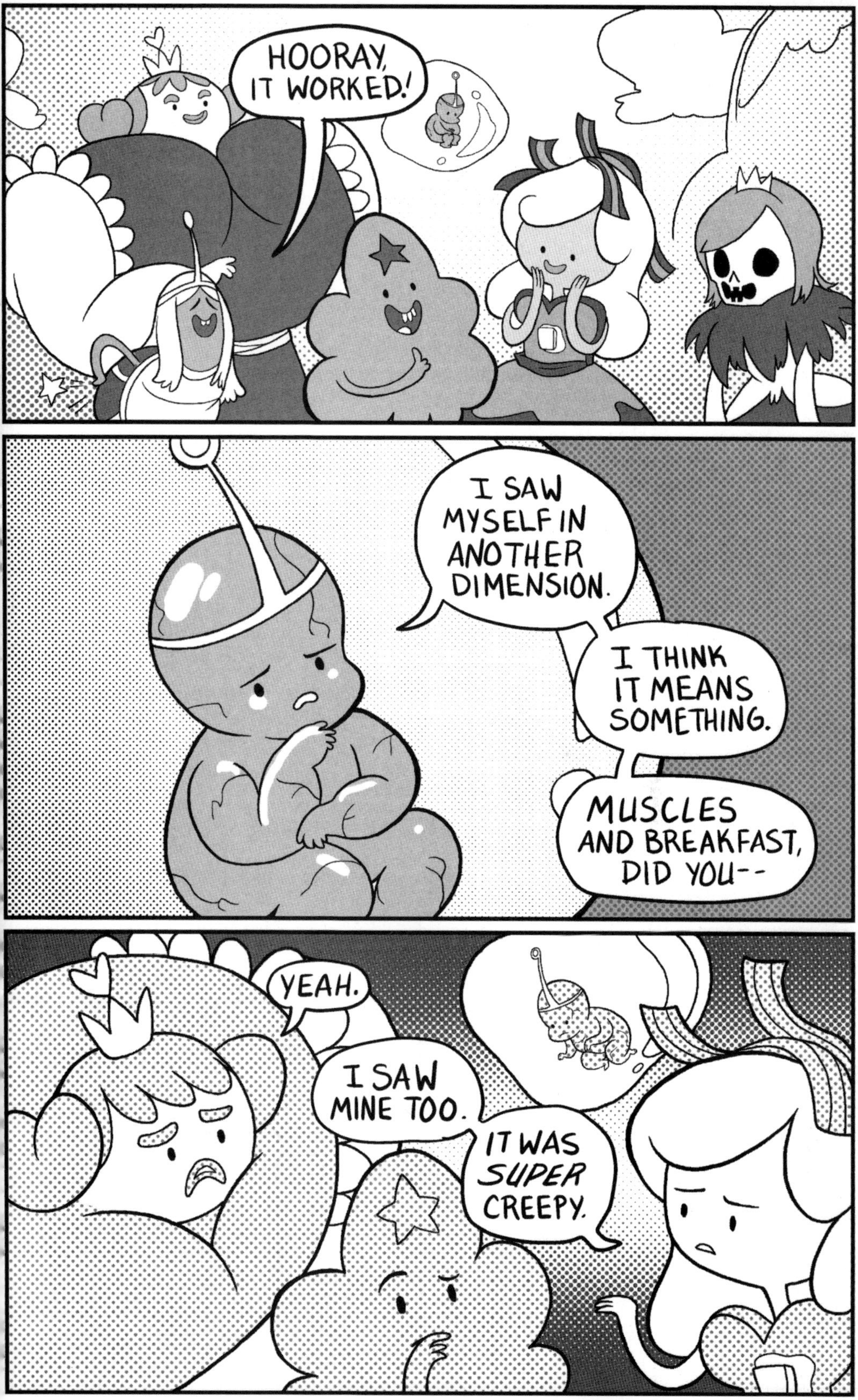
HOORAY, IT WORKED!
I SAW MYSELF IN ANOTHER DIMENSION.
I THINK IT MEANS SOMETHING.
MUSCLES AND BREAKFAST, DID YOU--
YEAH.
I SAW MINE TOO.
IT WAS *SUPER* CREEPY.

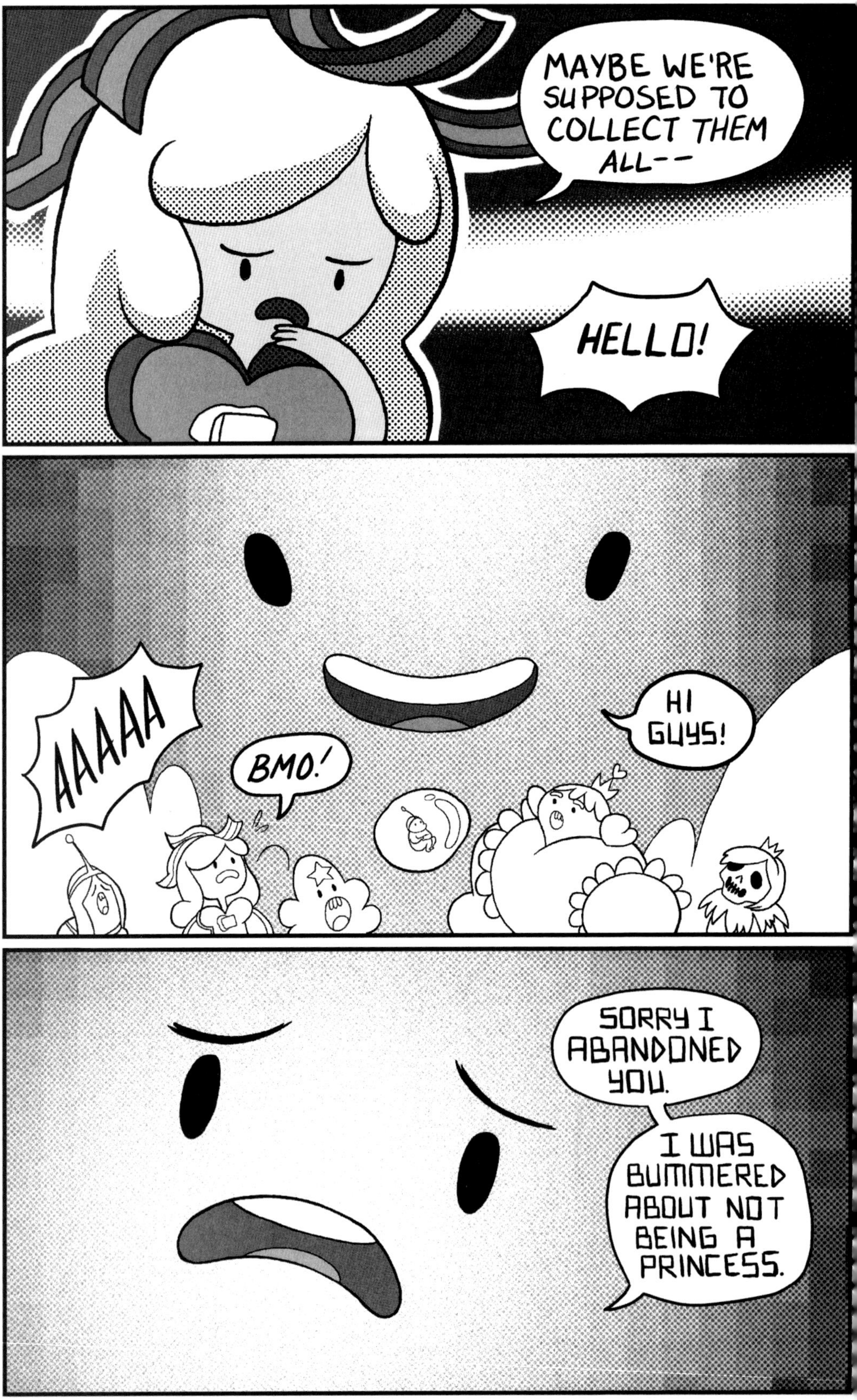
MAYBE WE'RE SUPPOSED TO COLLECT THEM ALL--
HELLO!
HI GUYS!
AAAAA
BMO!
SORRY I ABANDONED YOU.
I WAS BUMMERED ABOUT NOT BEING A PRINCESS.

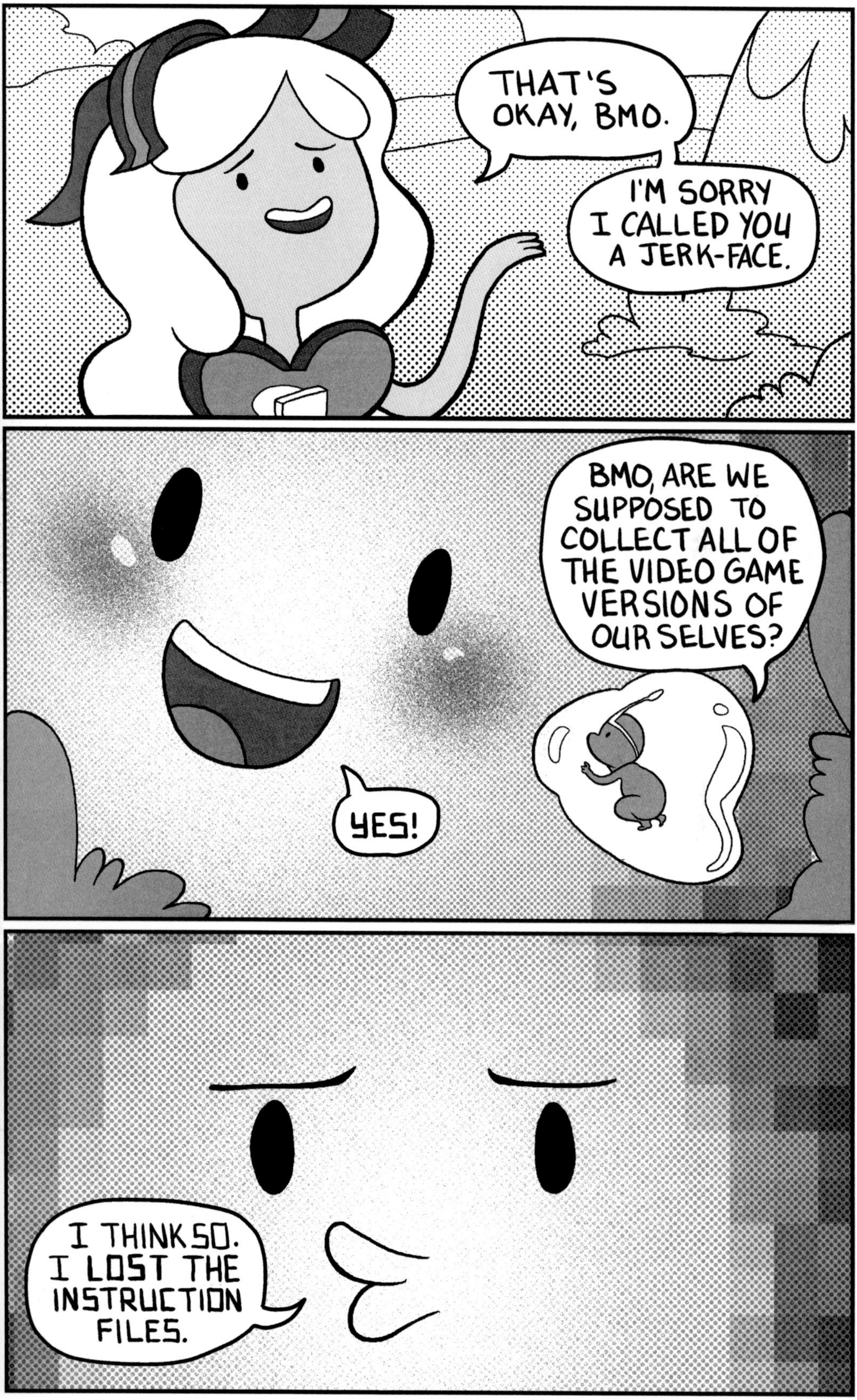
THAT'S OKAY, BMO.
I'M SORRY I CALLED YOU A JERK-FACE.
BMO, ARE WE SUPPOSED TO COLLECT ALL OF THE VIDEO GAME VERSIONS OF OURSELVES?
YES!
I THINK SO. I LOST THE INSTRUCTION FILES.

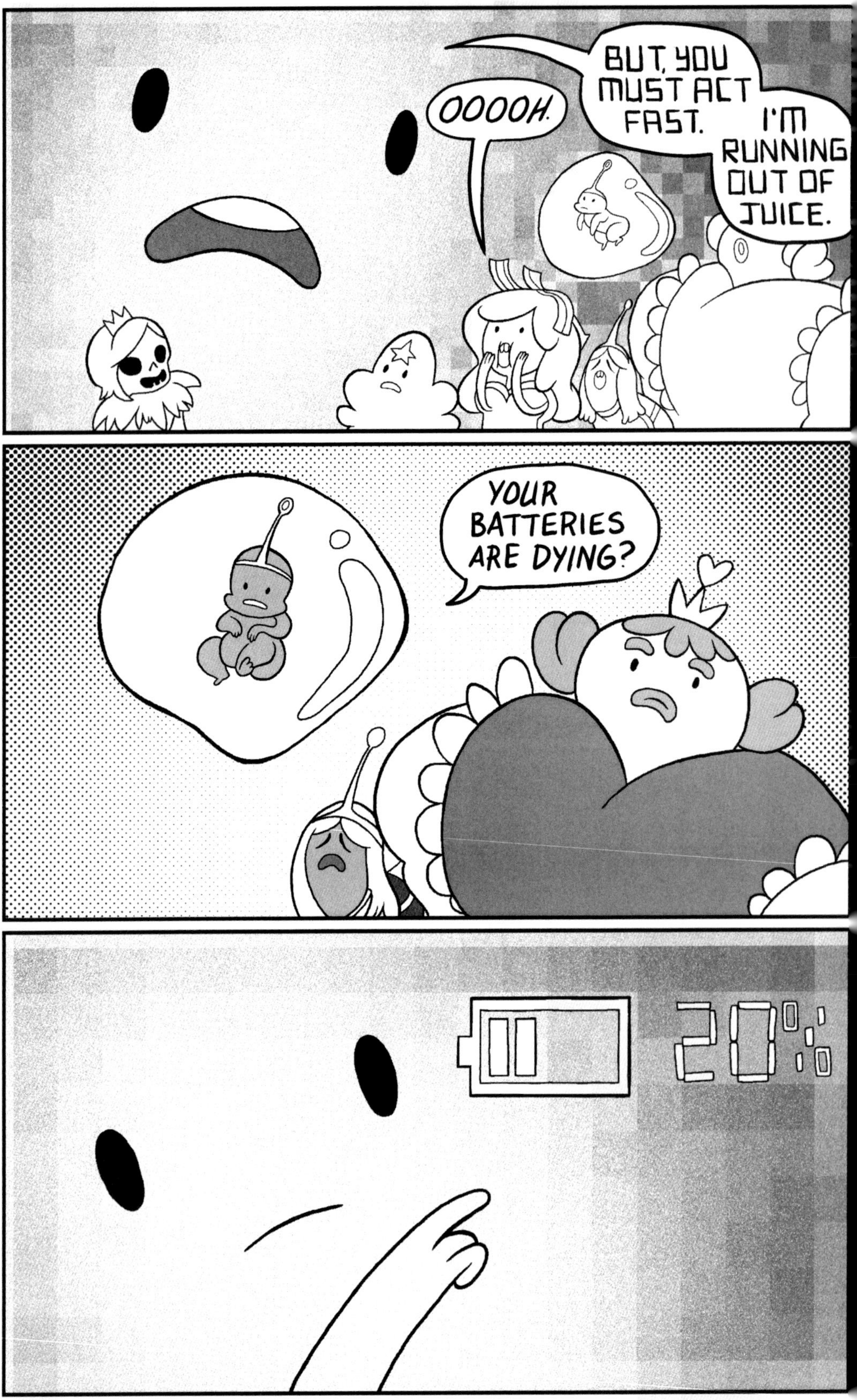
OOOOH.
BUT, YOU MUST ACT FAST.
I'M RUNNING OUT OF JUICE.
YOUR BATTERIES ARE DYING?
20%

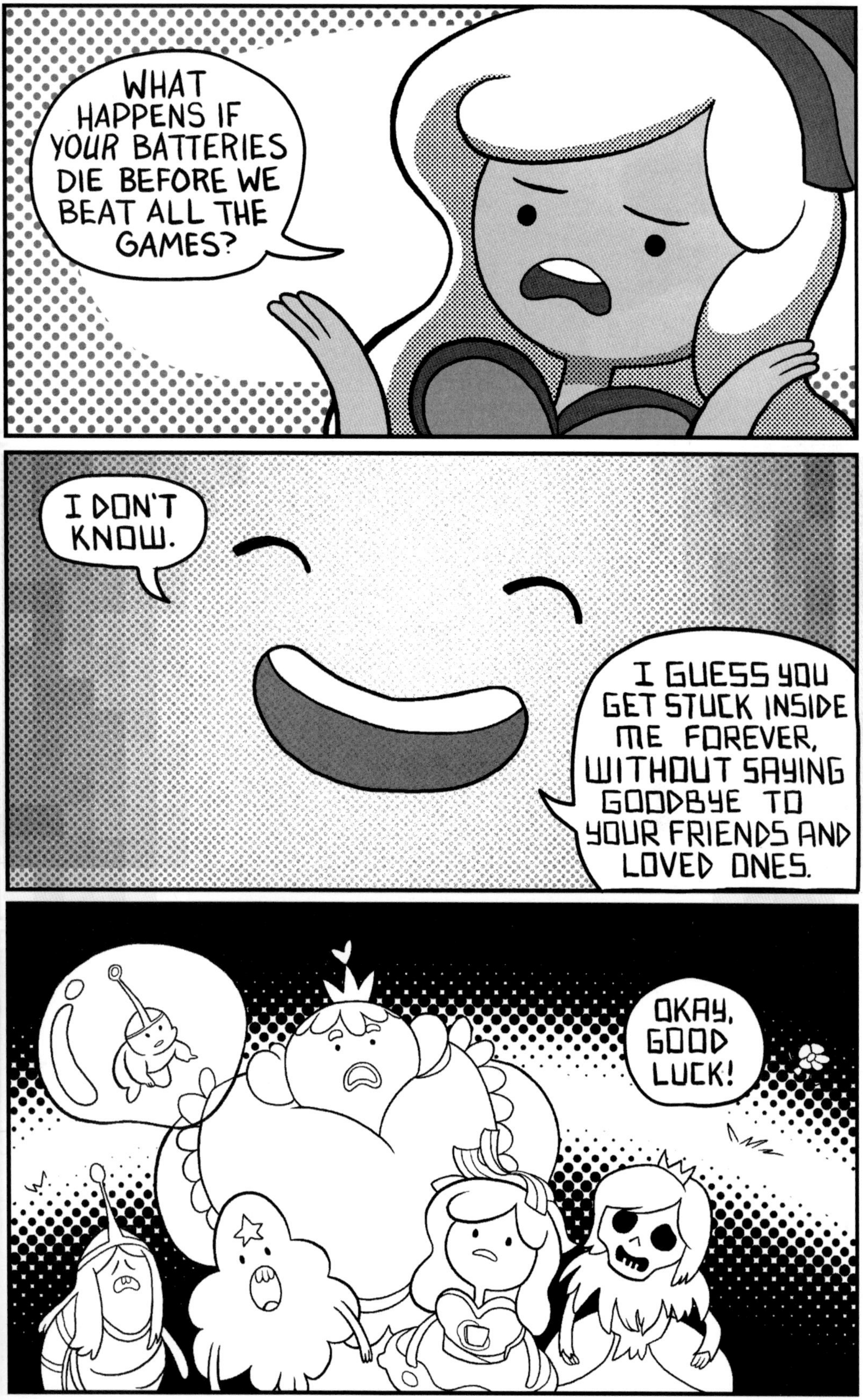
WHAT HAPPENS IF YOUR BATTERIES DIE BEFORE WE BEAT ALL THE GAMES?
I DON'T KNOW.
I GUESS YOU GET STUCK INSIDE ME FOREVER, WITHOUT SAYING GOODBYE TO YOUR FRIENDS AND LOVED ONES.
OKAY, GOOD LUCK!

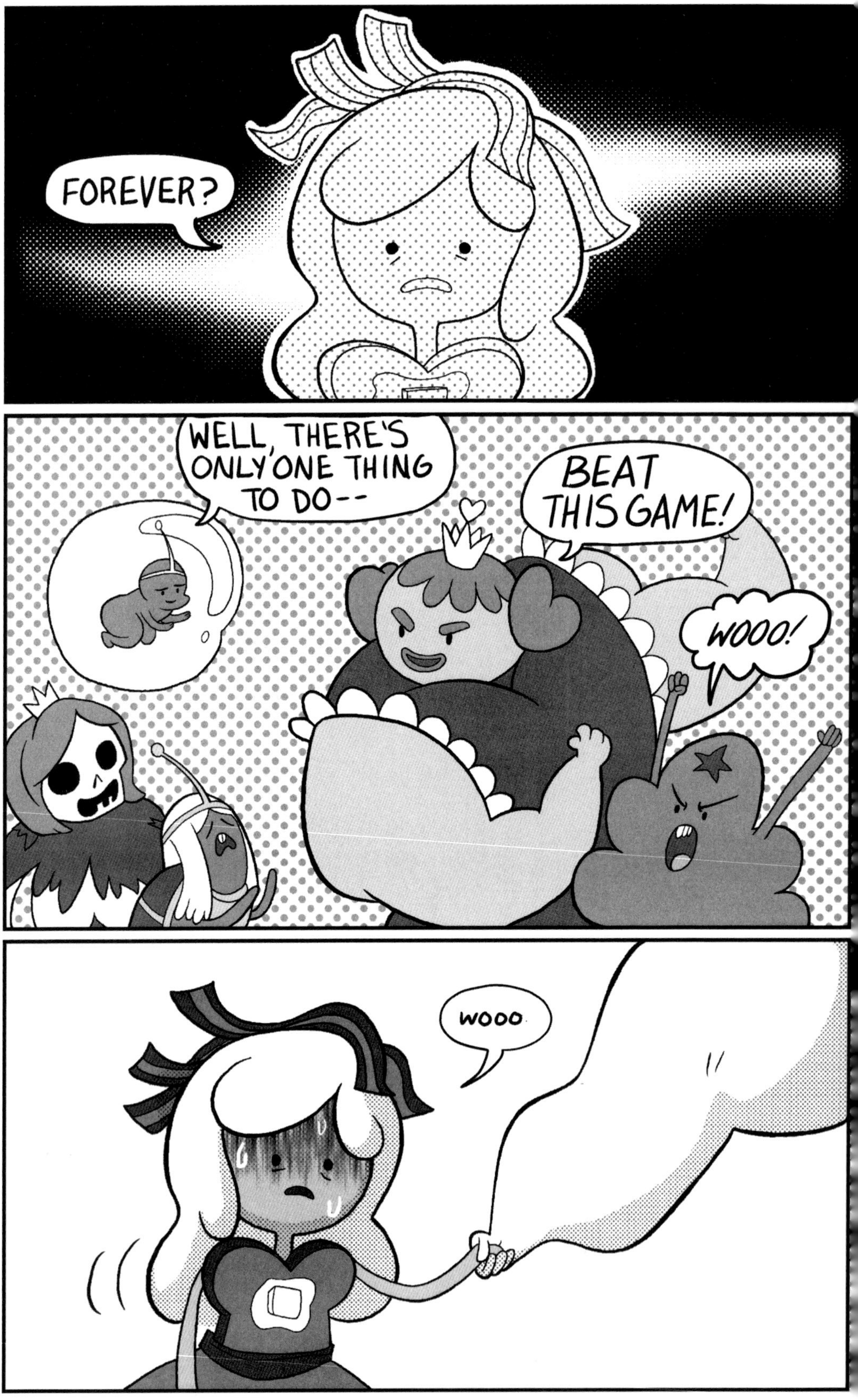
FOREVER?
WELL, THERE'S ONLY ONE THING TO DO--
BEAT THIS GAME!
WOOO!
WOOO

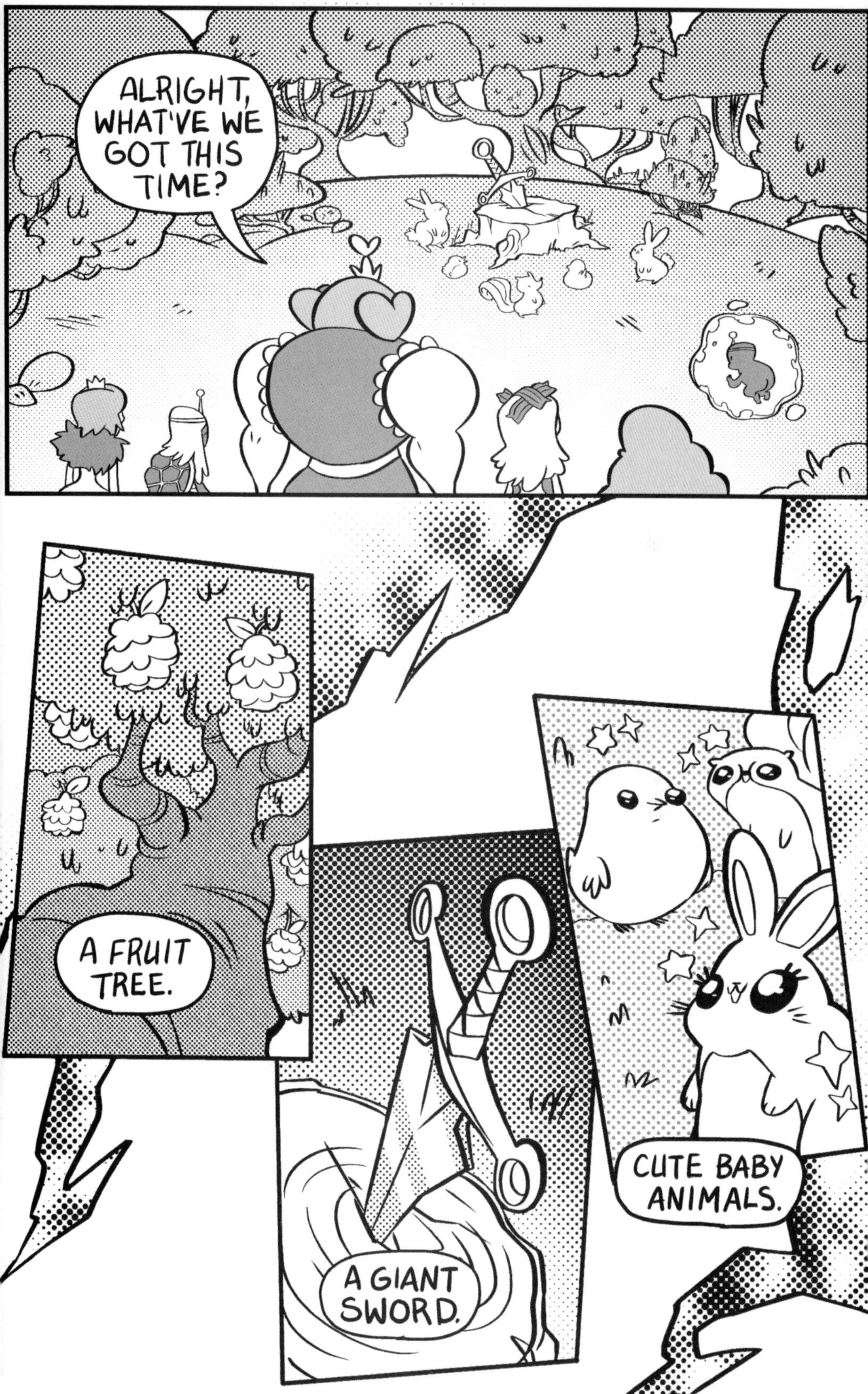
ALRIGHT, WHAT'VE WE GOT THIS TIME?
A FRUIT TREE.
A GIANT SWORD.
CUTE BABY ANIMALS.

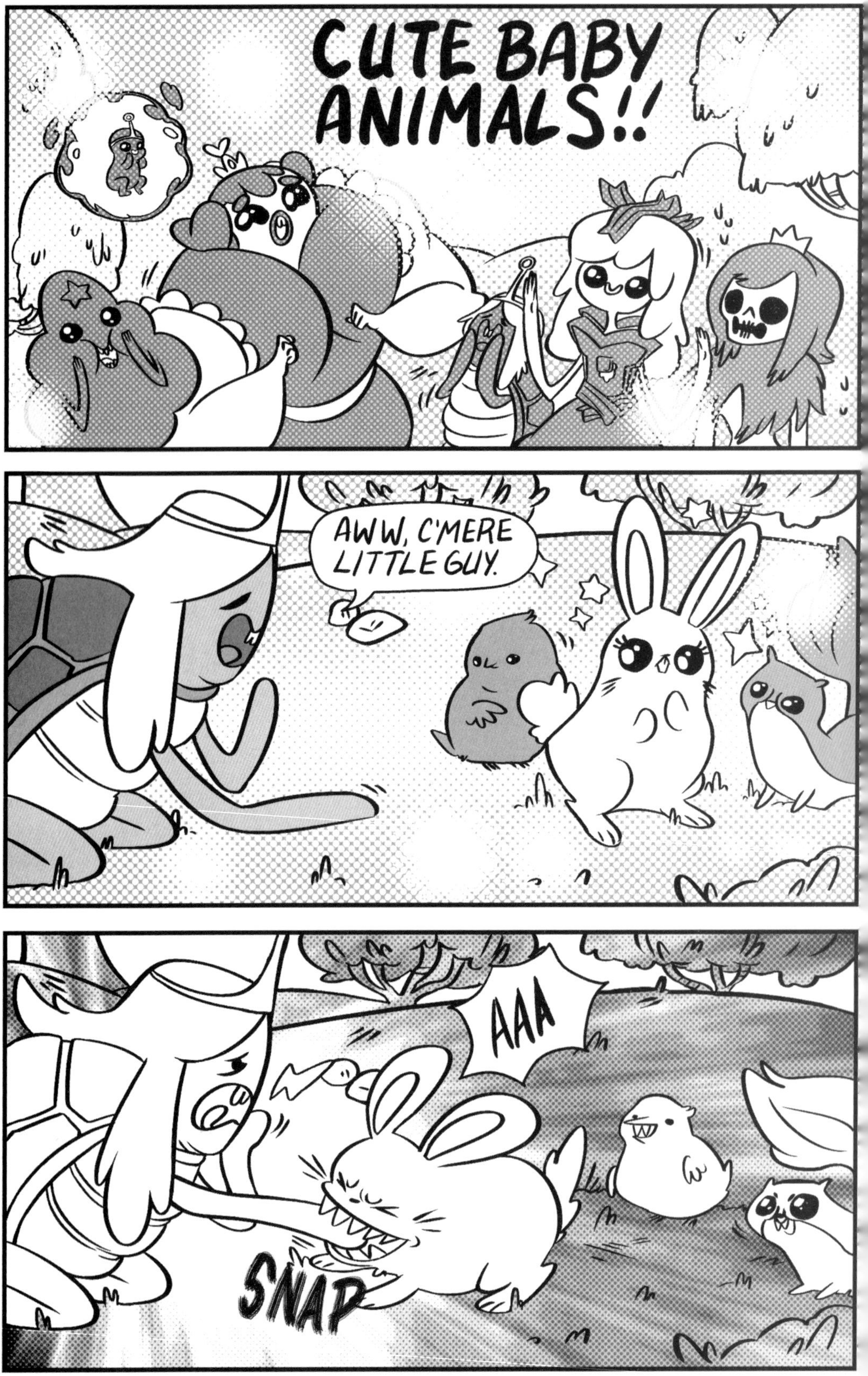
CUTE BABY ANIMALS!!
AWW, C'MERE LITTLE GUY.
AAA
SNAP

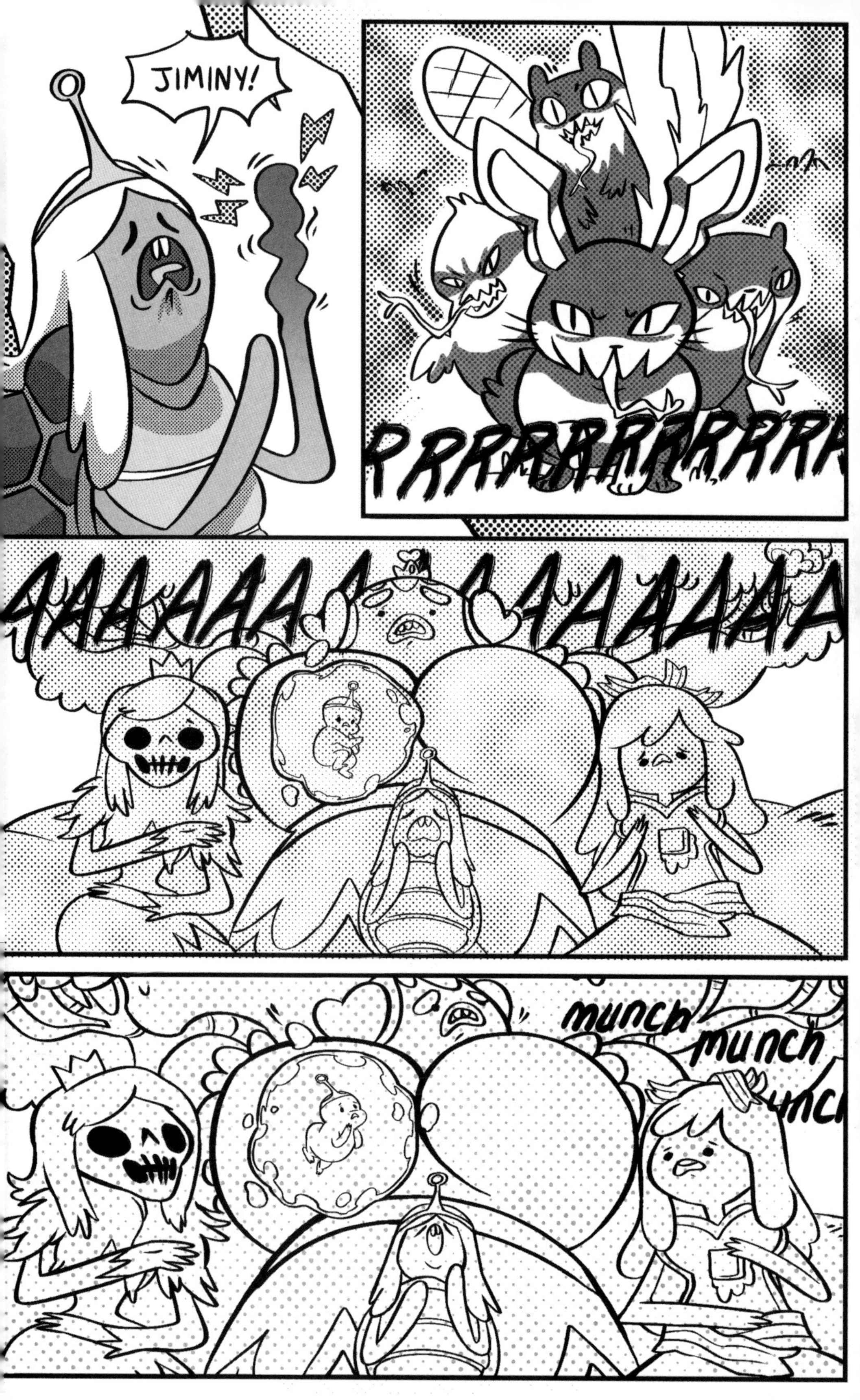
JIMINY!
RRRRRRRRRRRRRR
AAAAAAAAAAAAAAAA
munch
munch

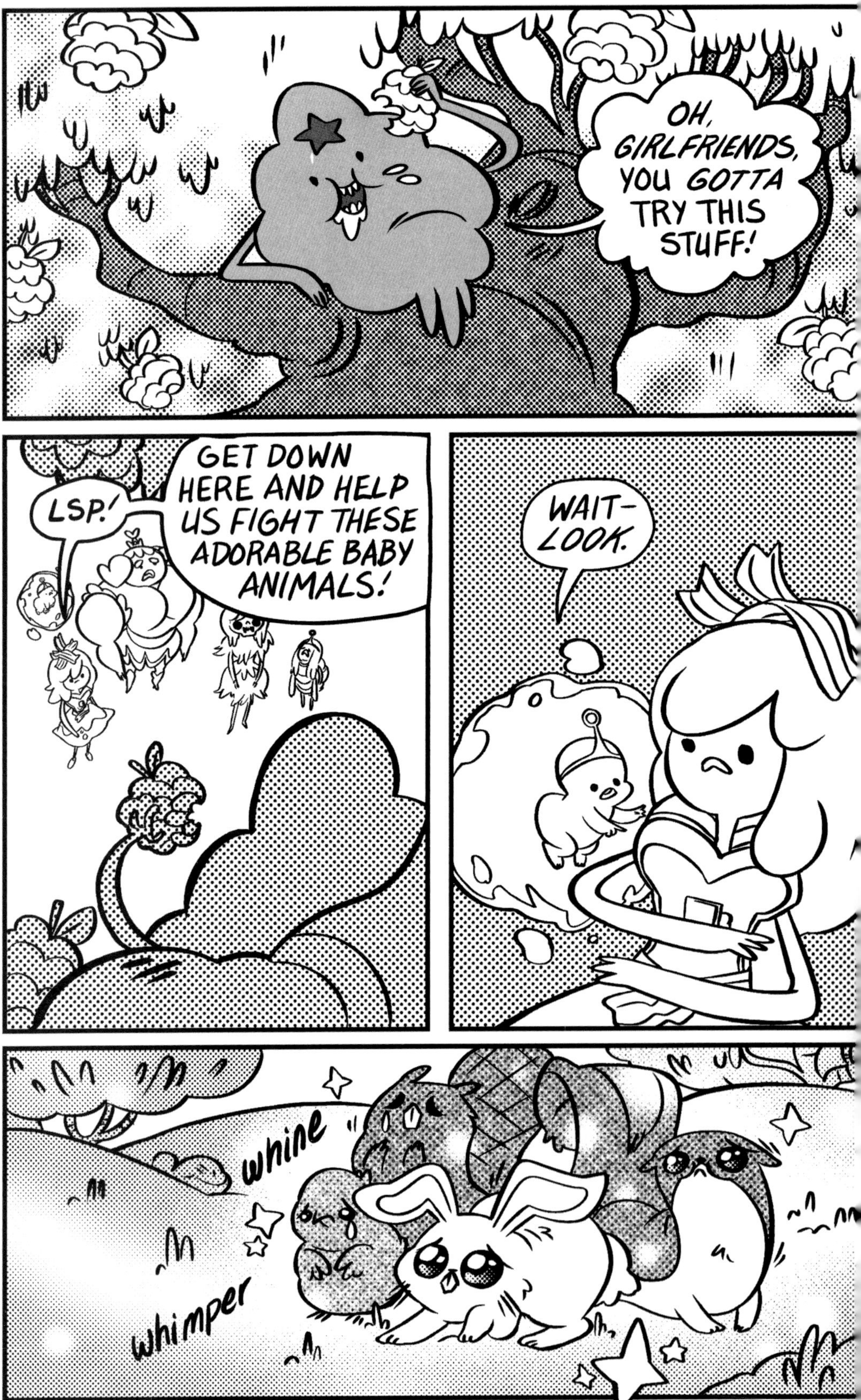
OH, GIRLFRIENDS, YOU GOTTA TRY THIS STUFF!
LSP!
GET DOWN HERE AND HELP US FIGHT THESE ADORABLE BABY ANIMALS!
WAIT- LOOK.
whine
whimper

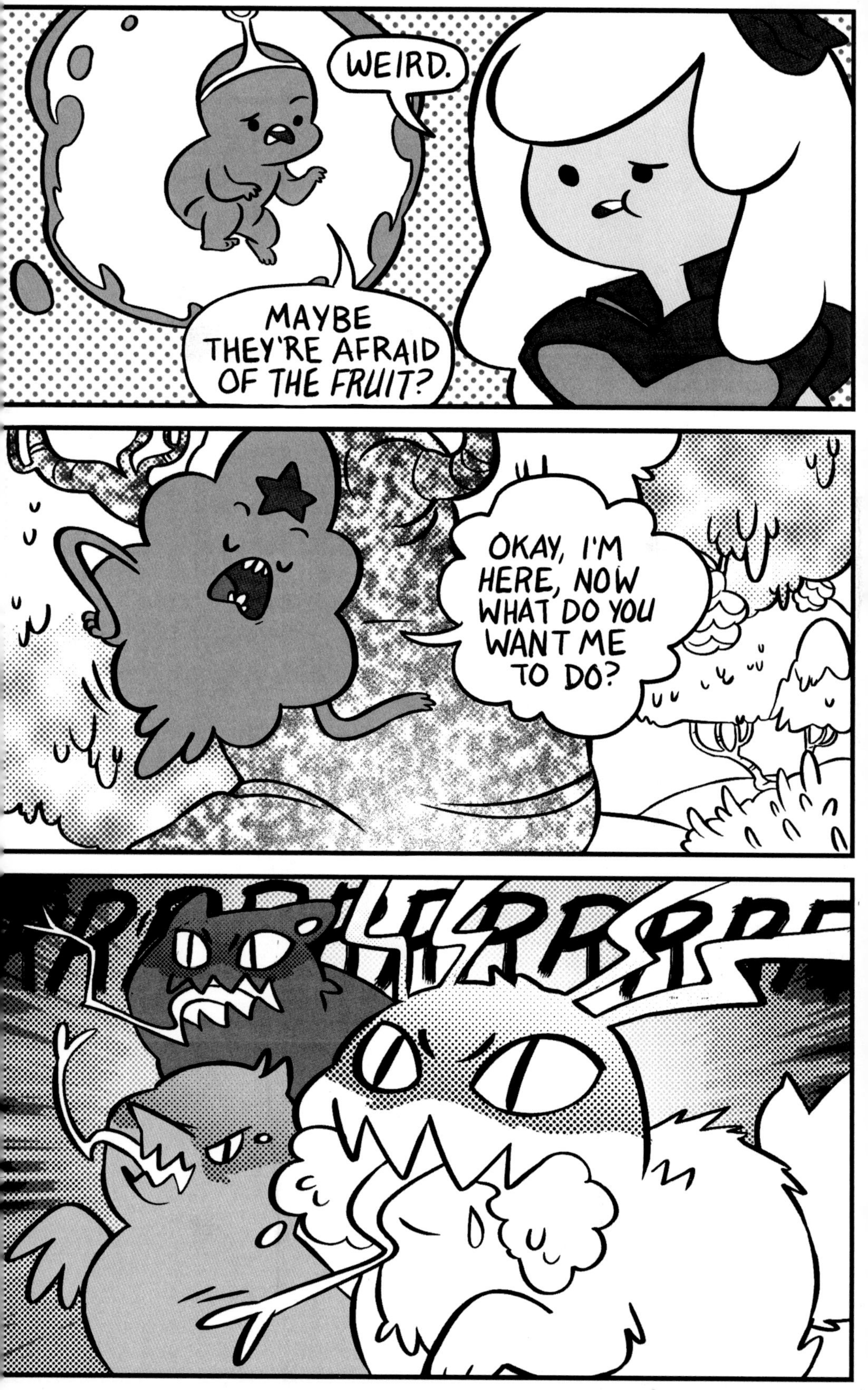
WEIRD.
MAYBE THEY'RE AFRAID OF THE FRUIT?
OKAY, I'M HERE, NOW WHAT DO YOU WANT ME TO DO?

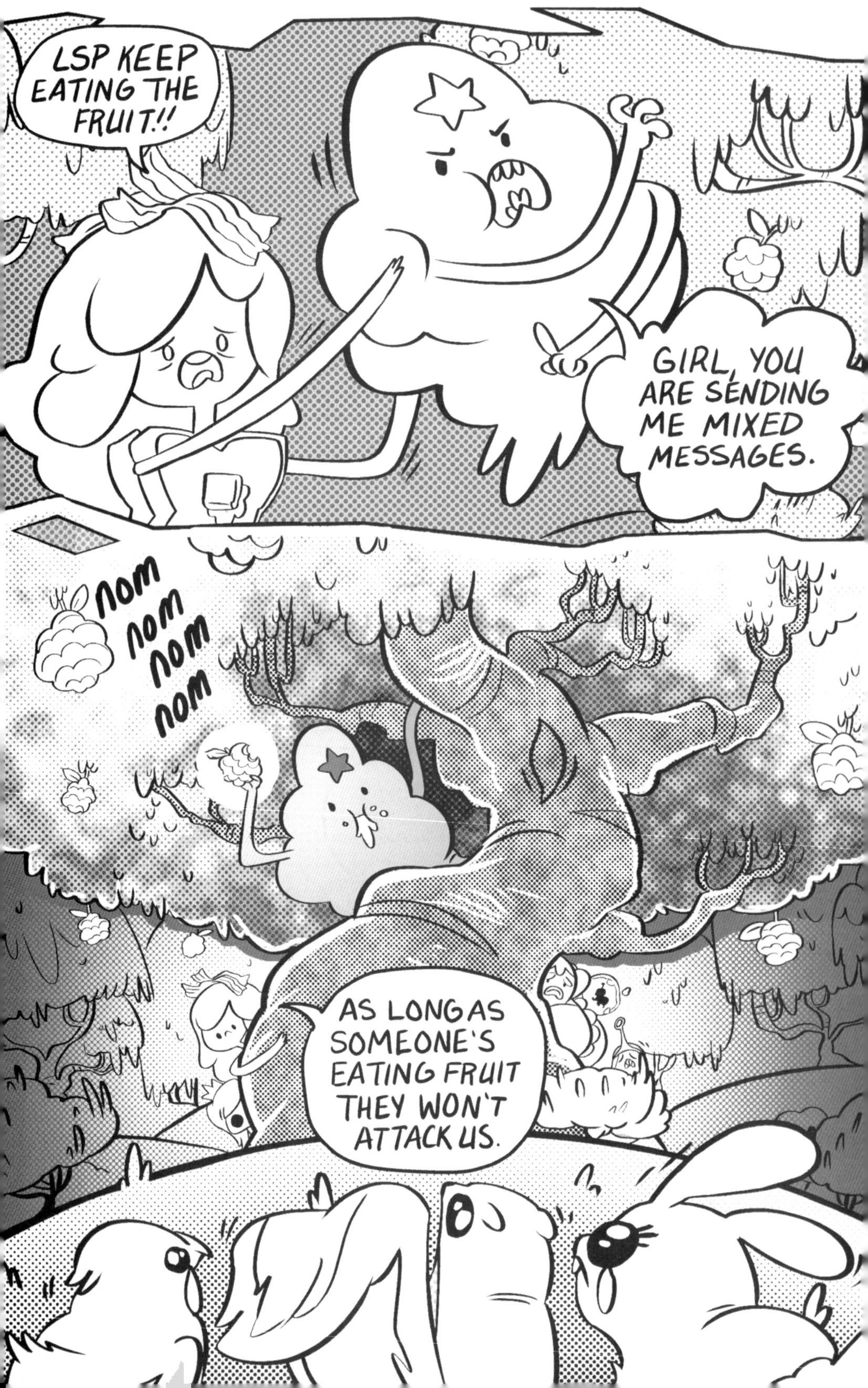
LSP KEEP EATING THE FRUIT!!
GIRL, YOU ARE SENDING ME MIXED MESSAGES.
nom nom nom nom
AS LONG AS SOMEONE'S EATING FRUIT THEY WON'T ATTACK US.

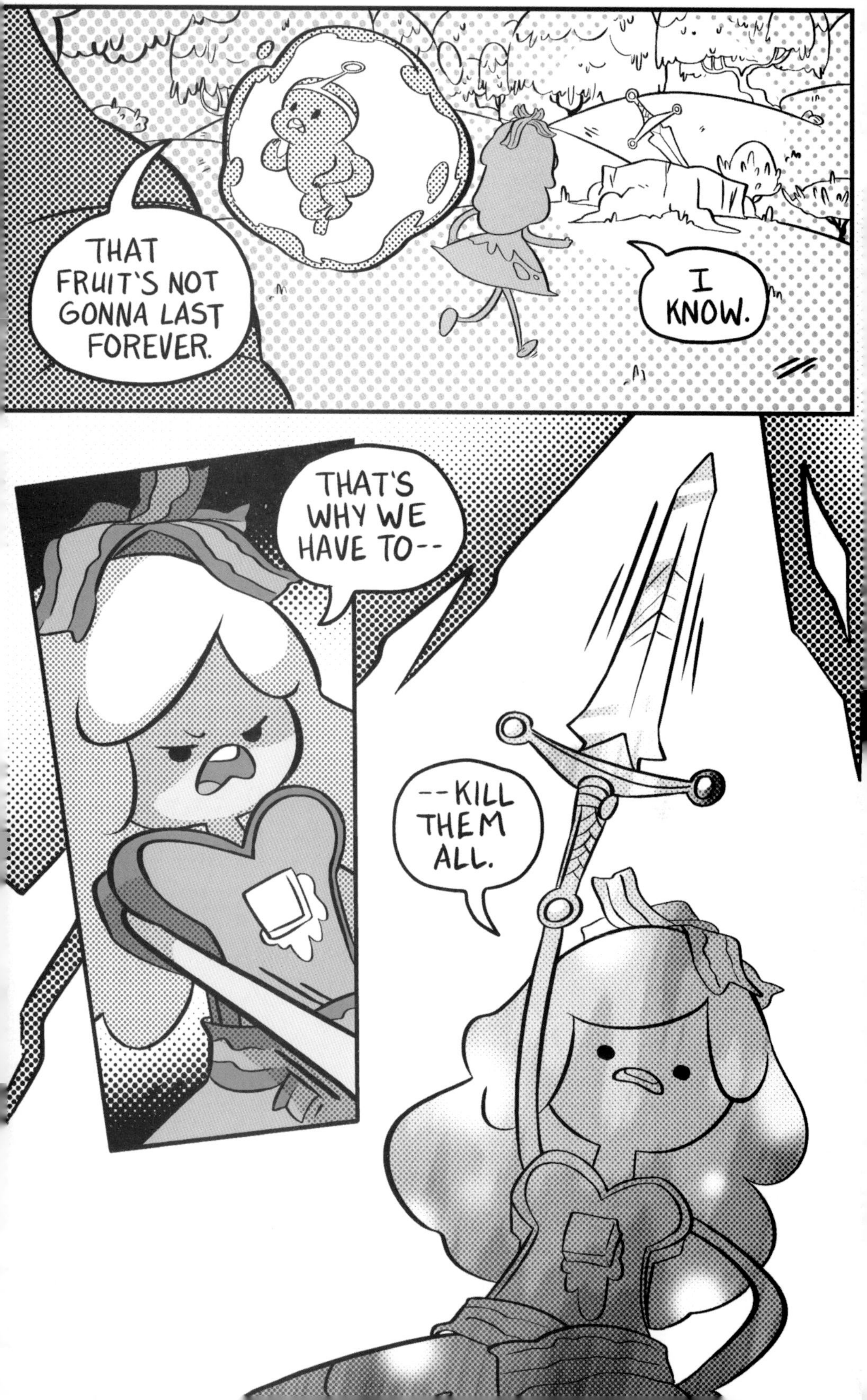
THAT FRUIT'S NOT GONNA LAST FOREVER.
I KNOW.
THAT'S WHY WE HAVE TO--
--KILL THEM ALL.

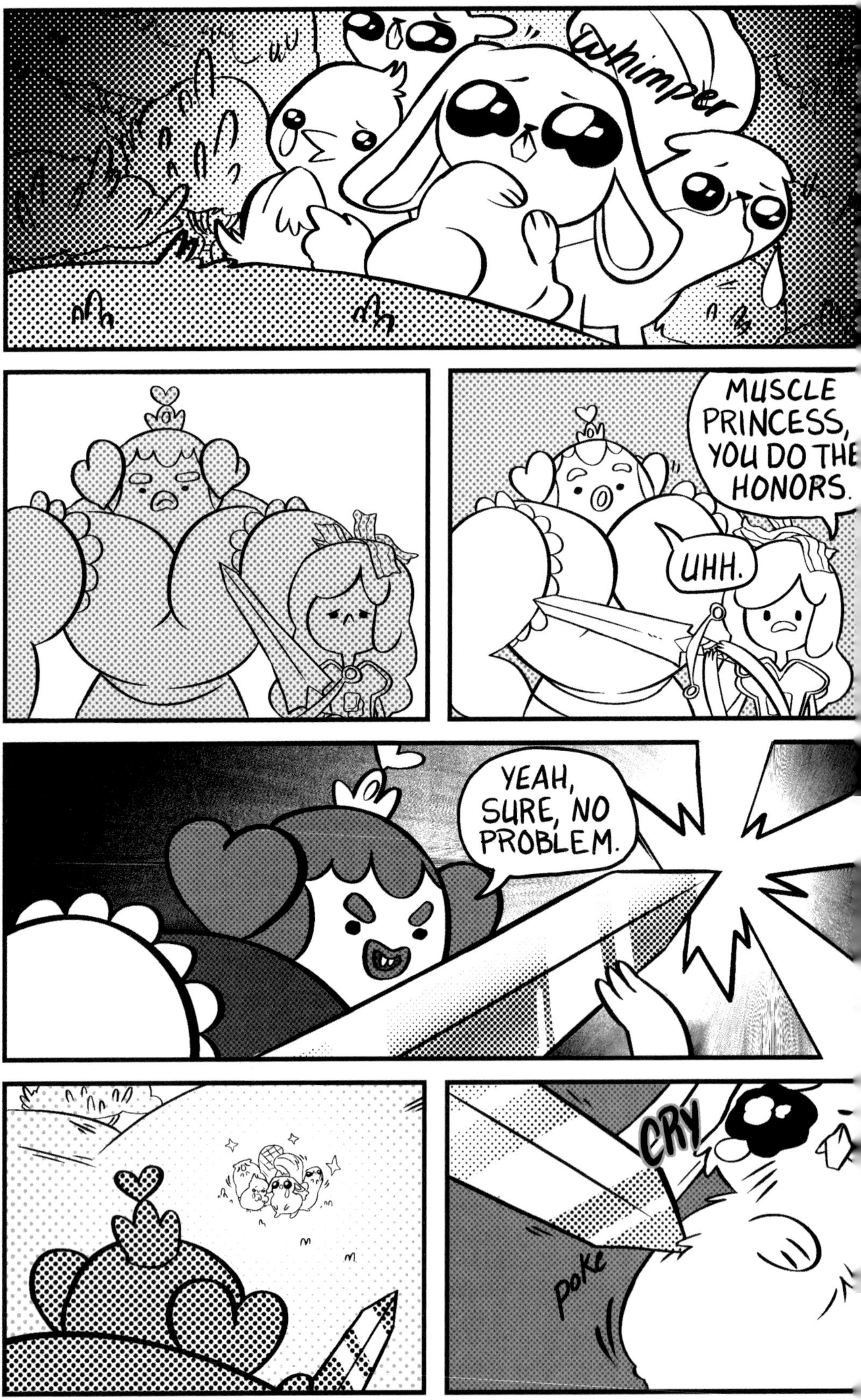
whimper
MUSCLE PRINCESS, YOU DO THE HONORS.
UHH.
YEAH, SURE, NO PROBLEM.
CRY
poke

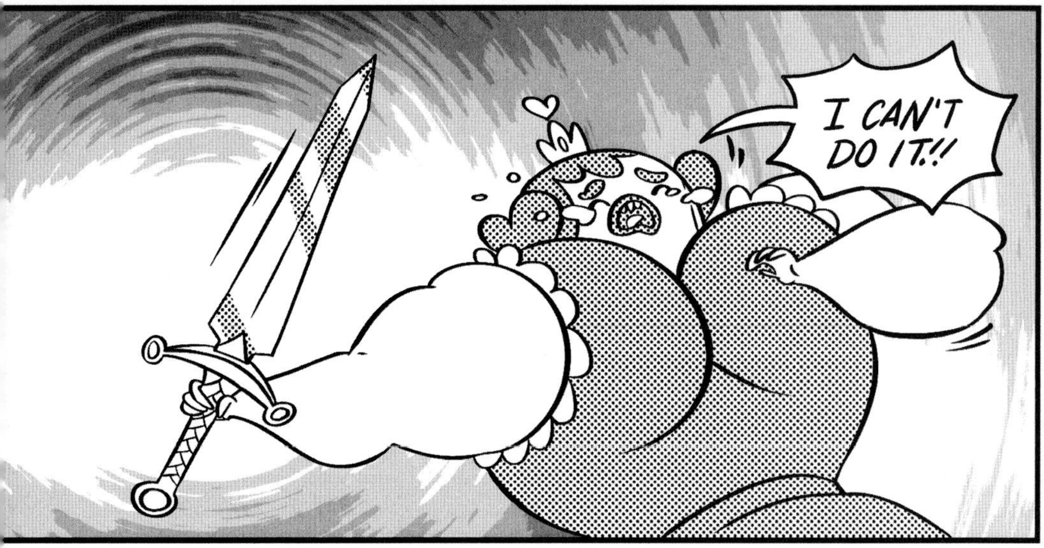
I CAN'T DO IT!!

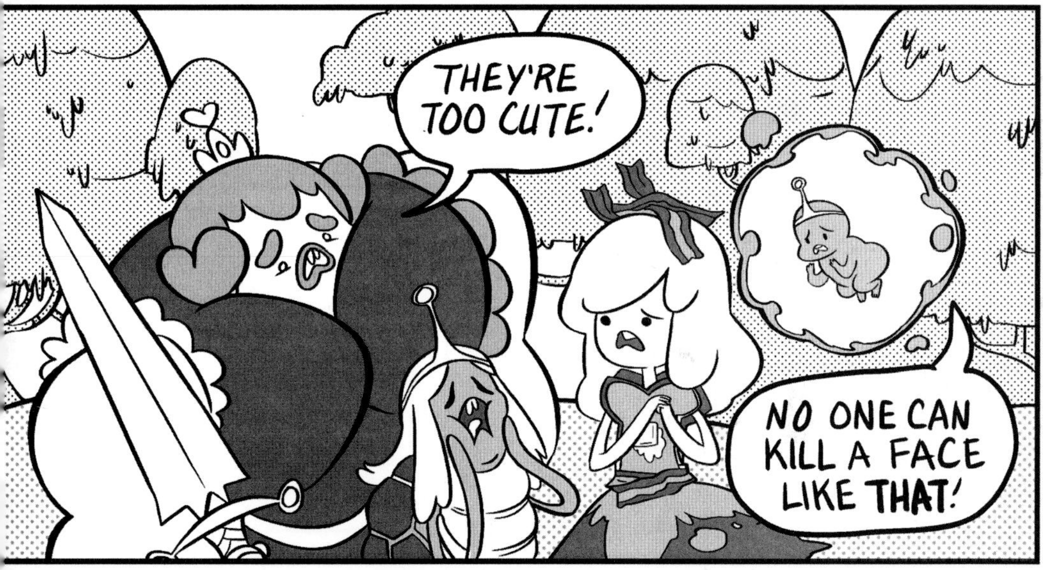
THEY'RE TOO CUTE!
NO ONE CAN KILL A FACE LIKE THAT!

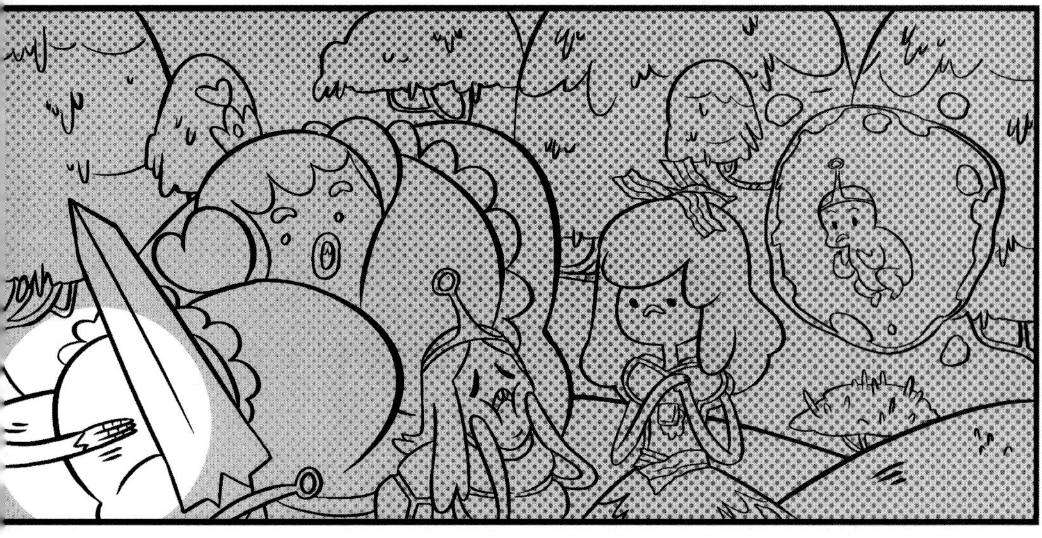

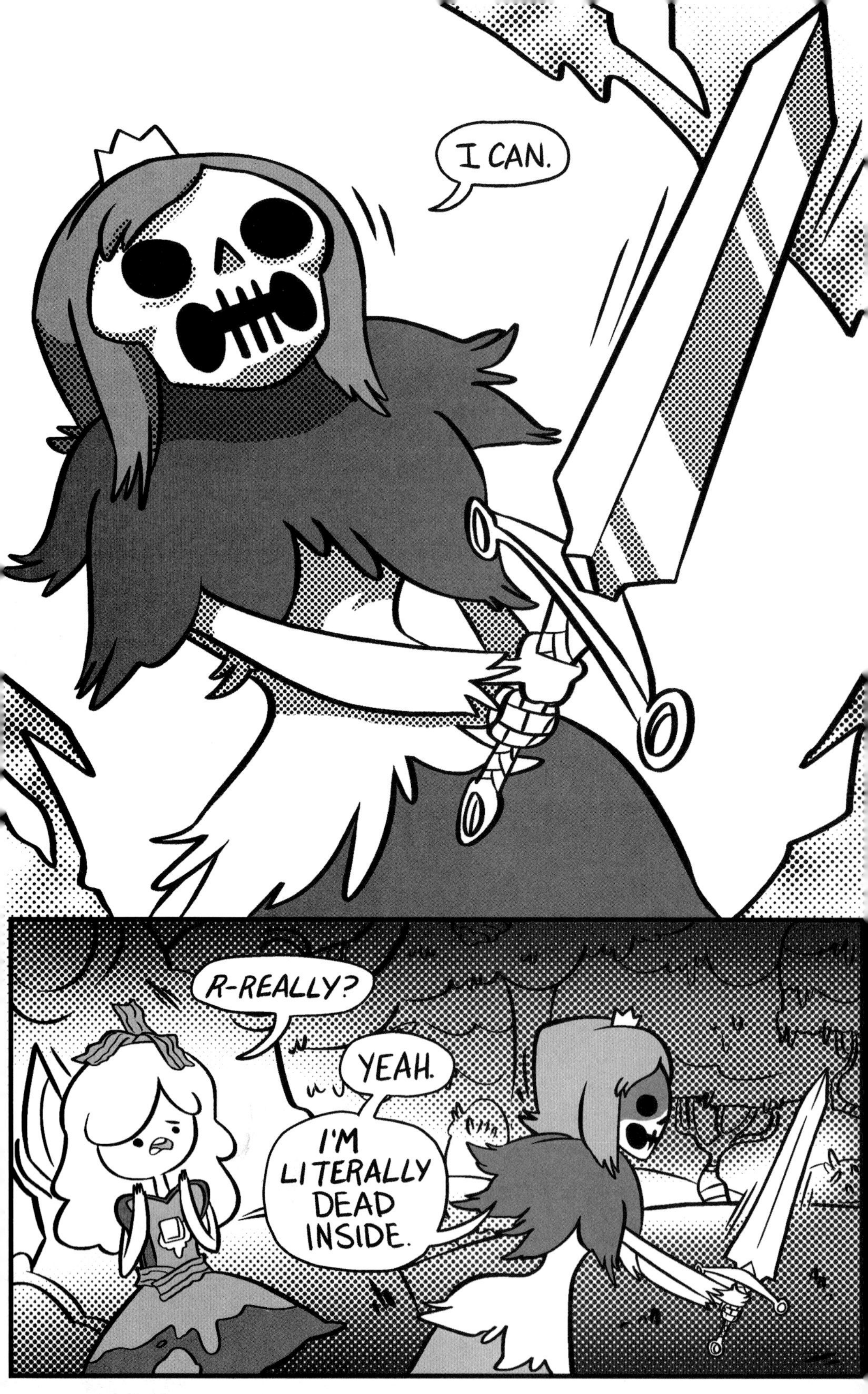
I CAN.
R-REALLY?
YEAH.
I'M LITERALLY DEAD INSIDE.

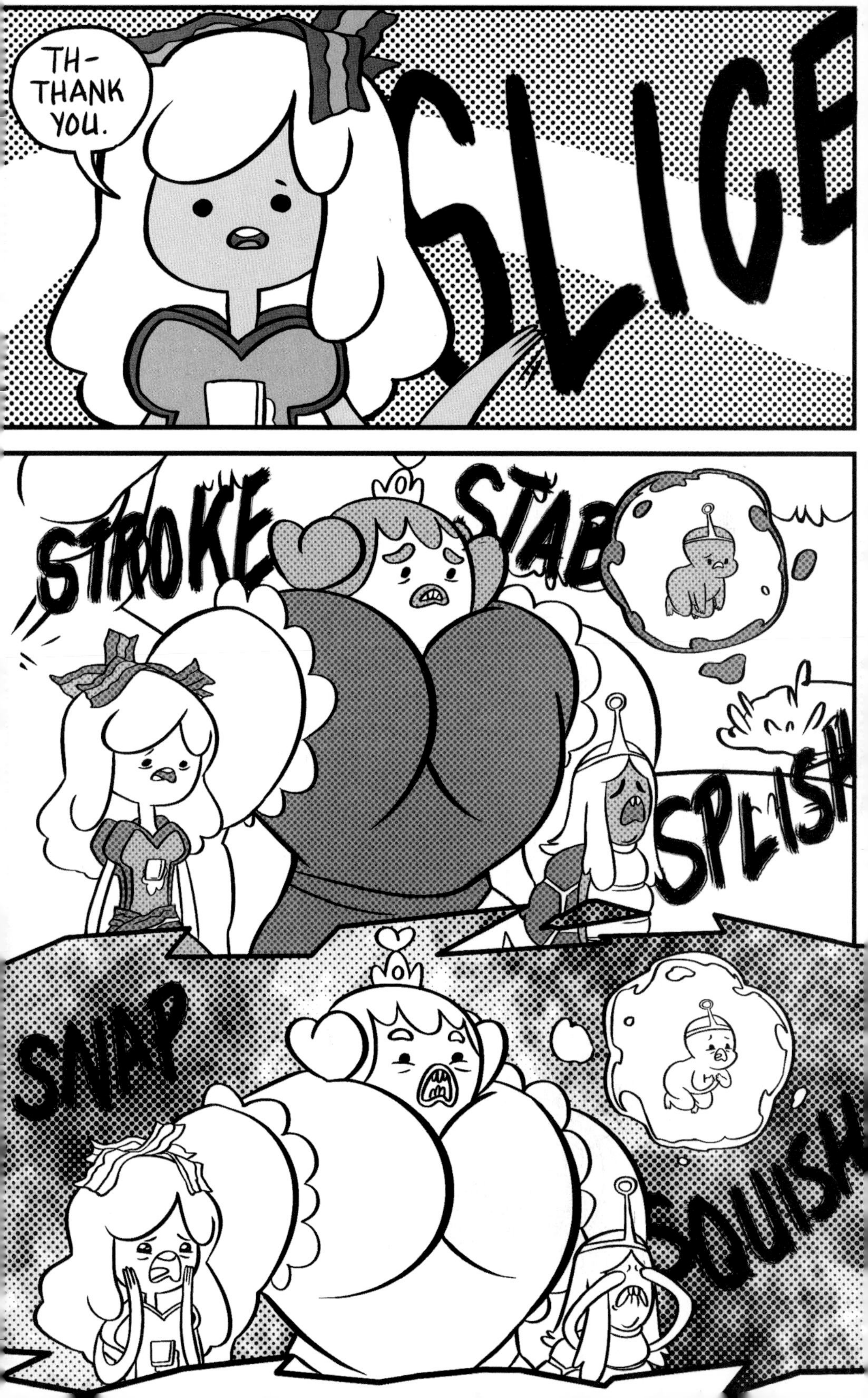

TH- THANK YOU.
SLICE
STROKE
STAB
SPLISH
SNAP
SQUISH

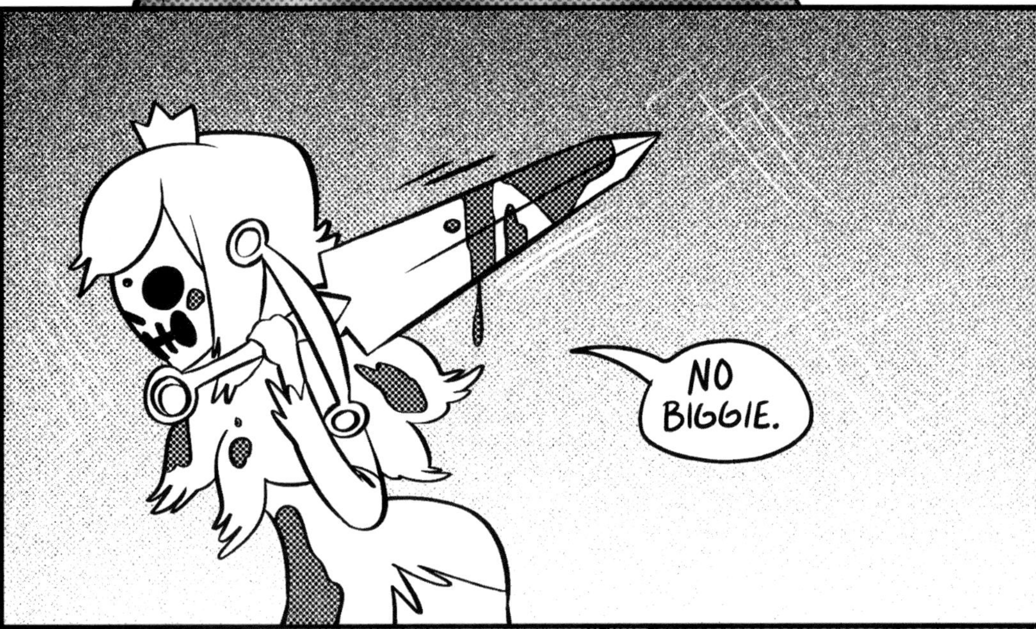
NO BIGGIE.

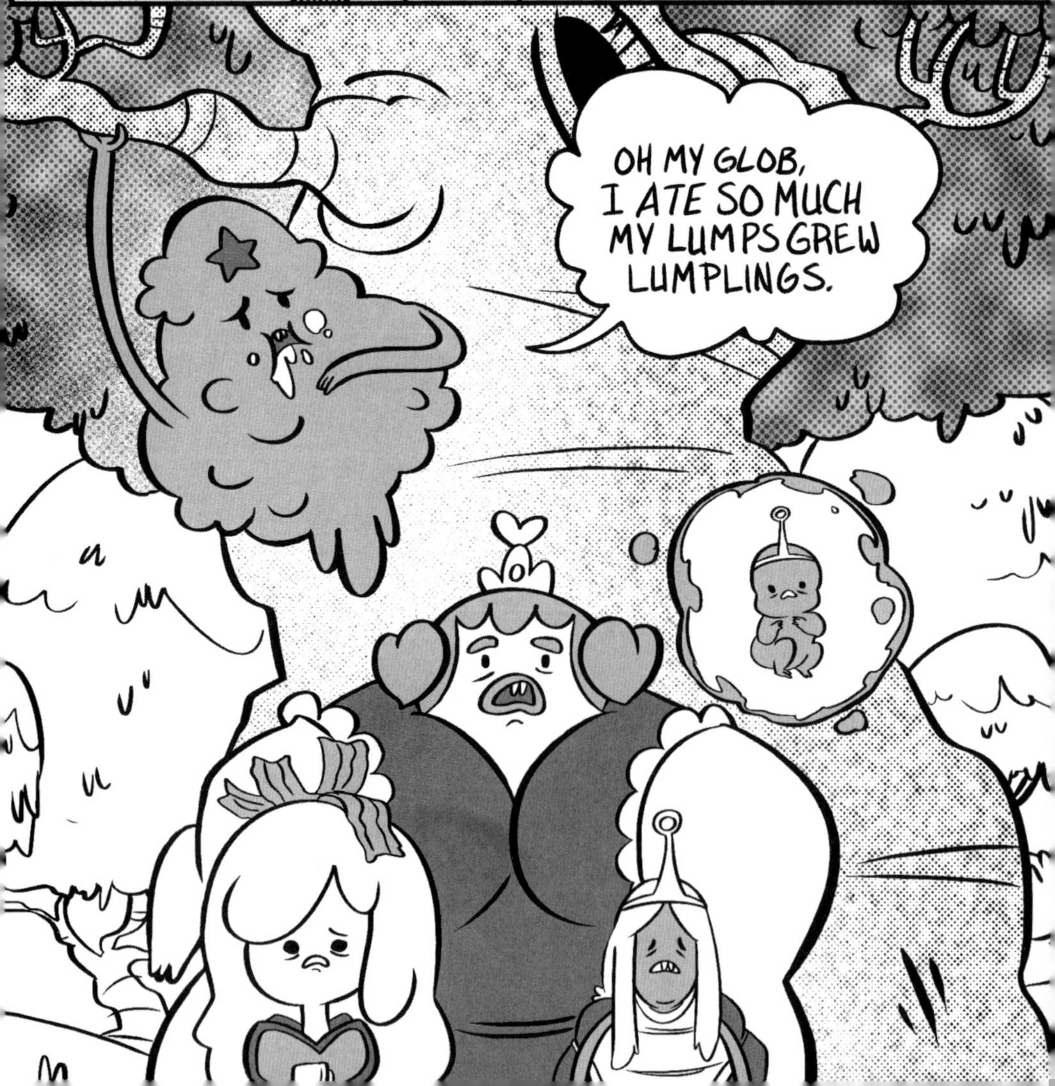
OH MY GLOB, I ATE SO MUCH MY LUMPS GREW LUMPLINGS.

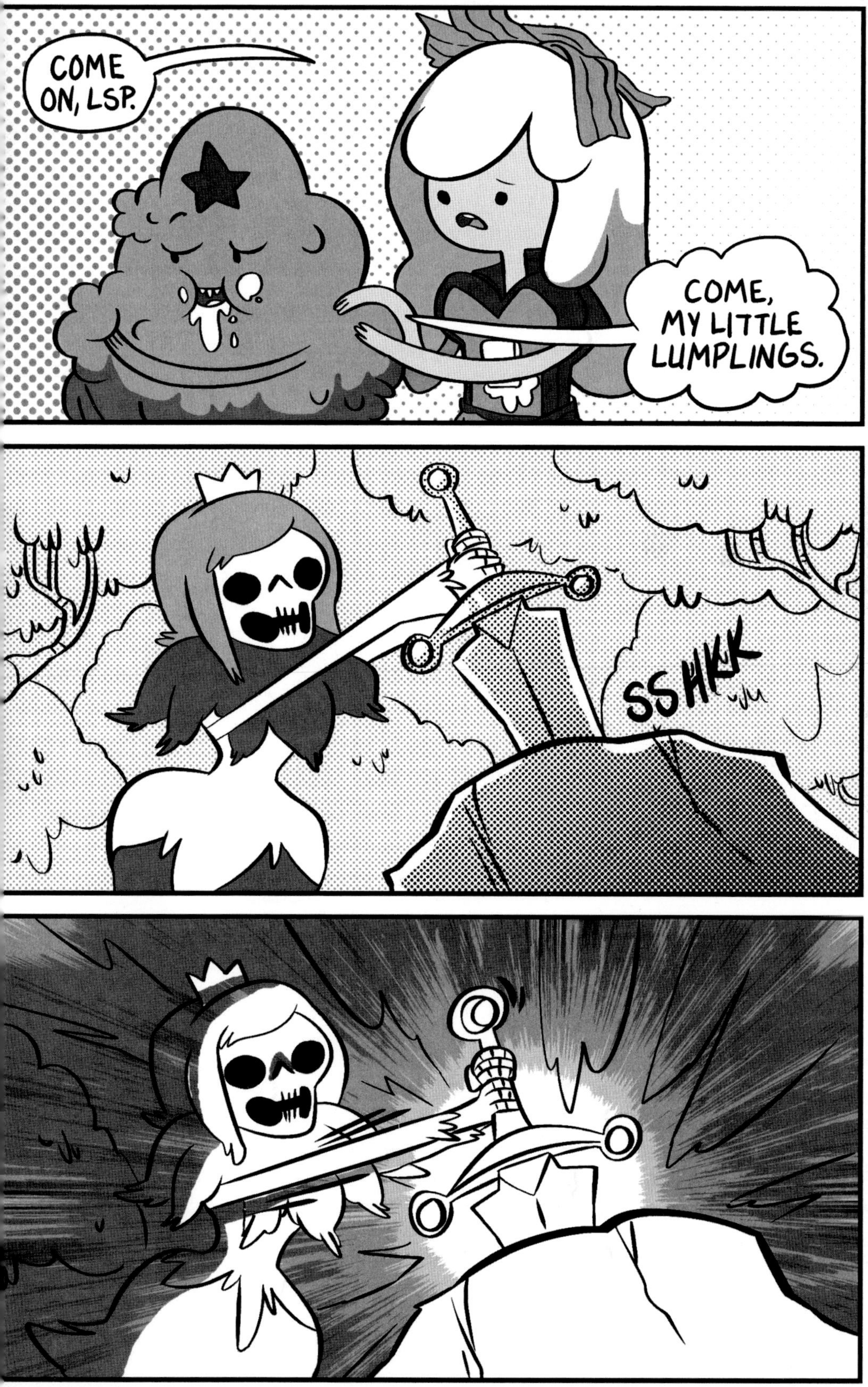
COME ON, LSP.
COME, MY LITTLE LUMPLINGS.
SSHKK

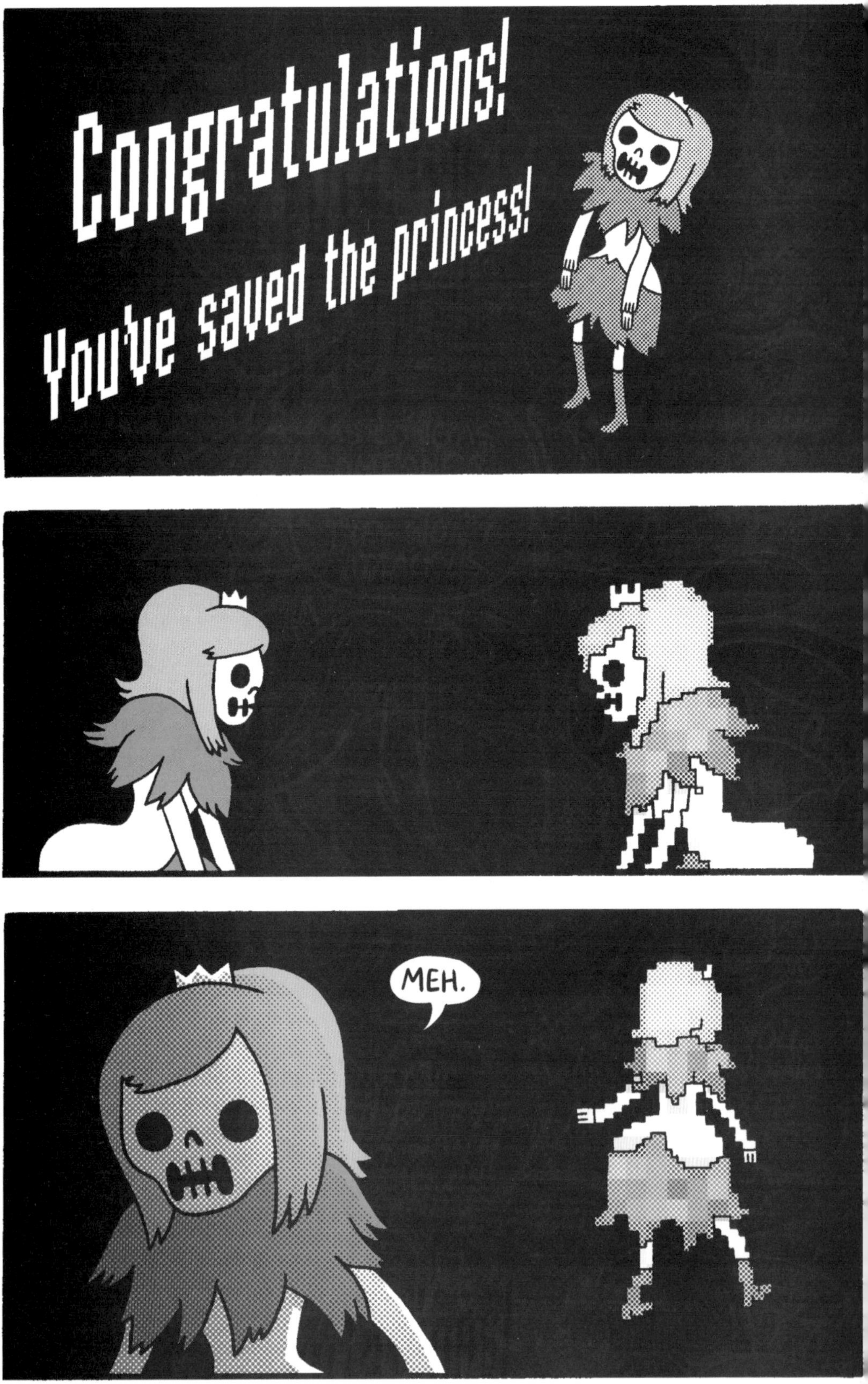
Congratulations!
You've saved the princess!
MEH.

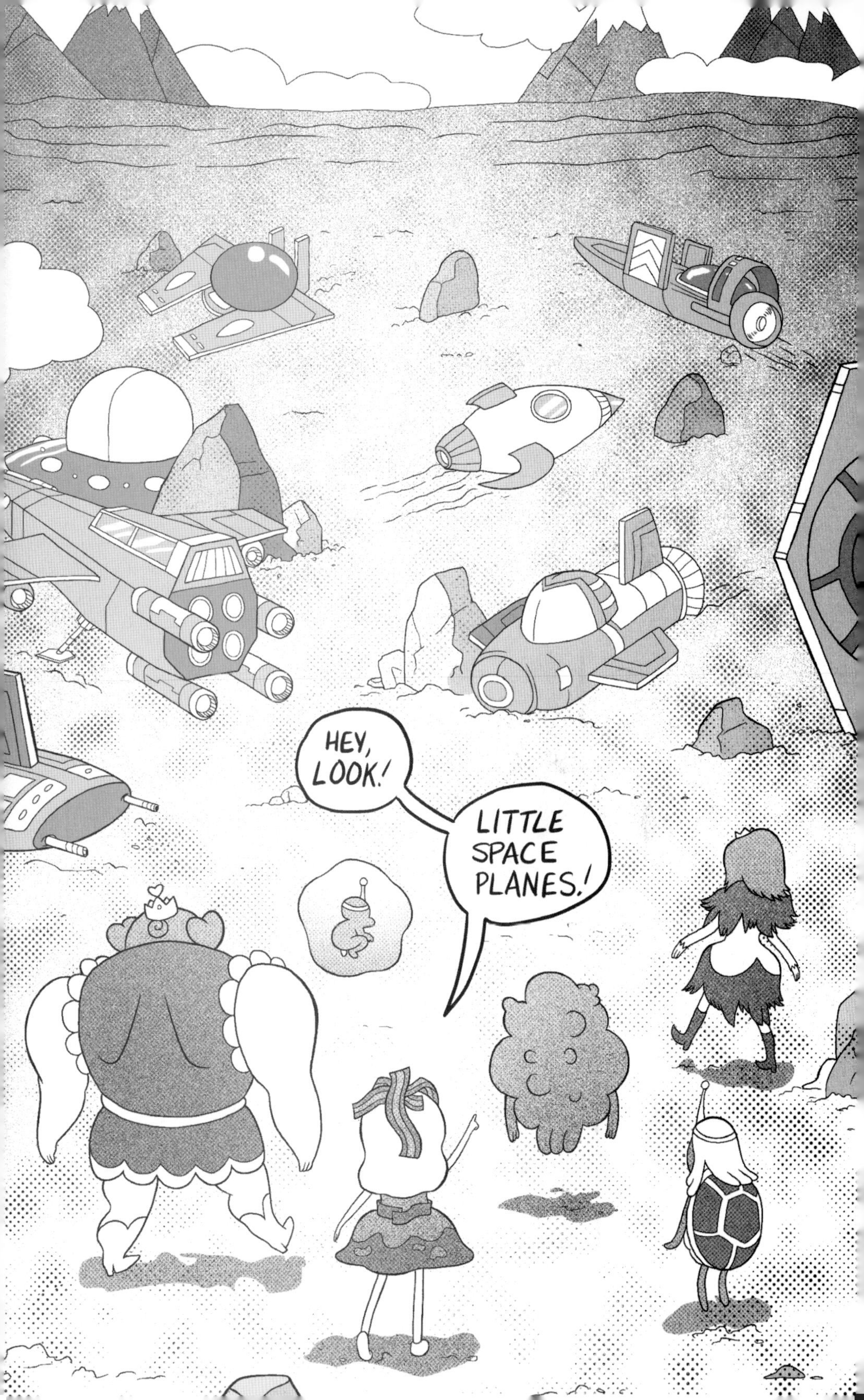
HEY, LOOK!
LITTLE SPACE PLANES!

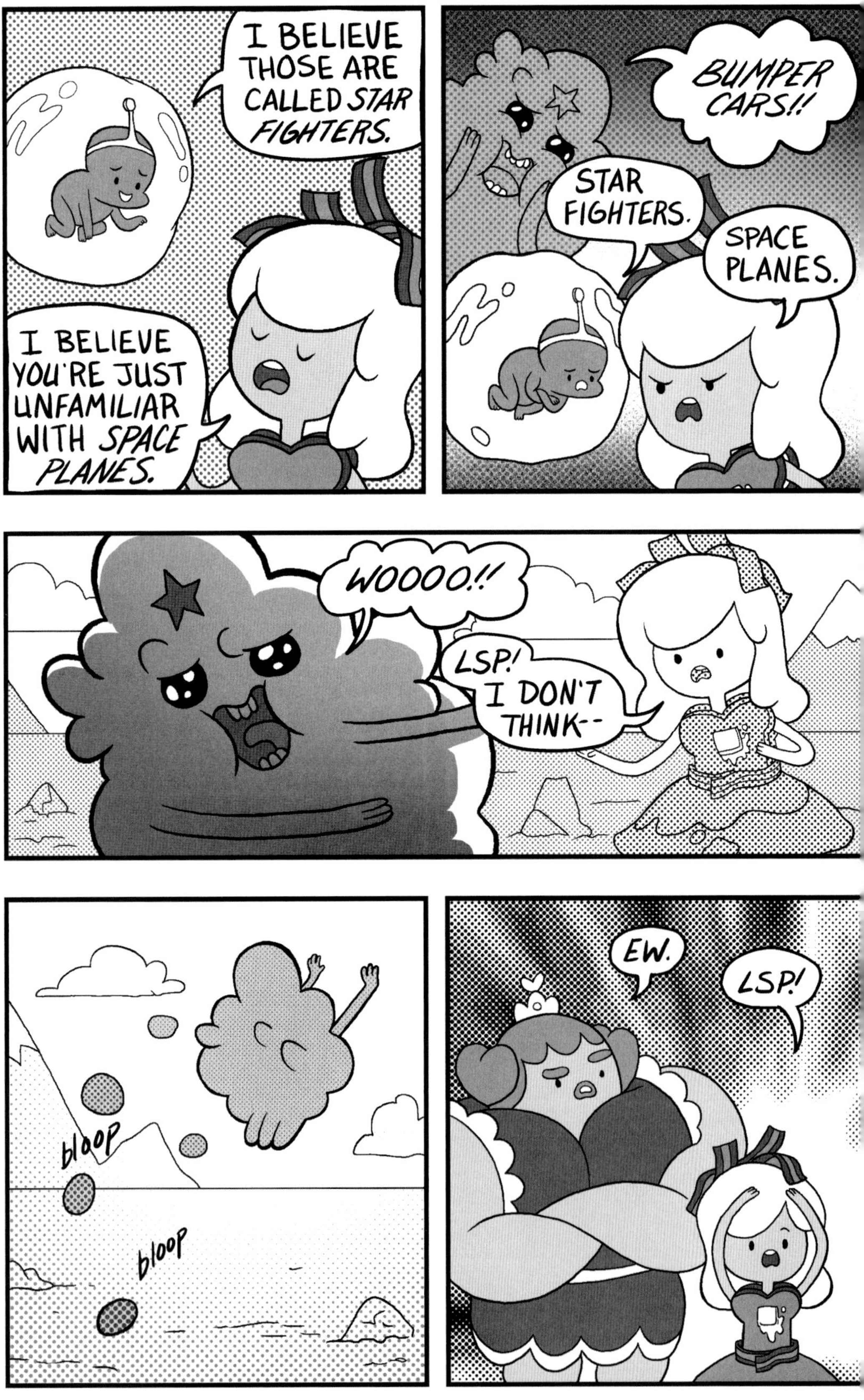
I BELIEVE THOSE ARE CALLED STAR FIGHTERS.
I BELIEVE YOU'RE JUST UNFAMILIAR WITH SPACE PLANES.
BUMPER CARS!!
STAR FIGHTERS.
SPACE PLANES.
WOOOO!!
LSP! I DON'T THINK--
bloop
bloop
EW.
LSP!

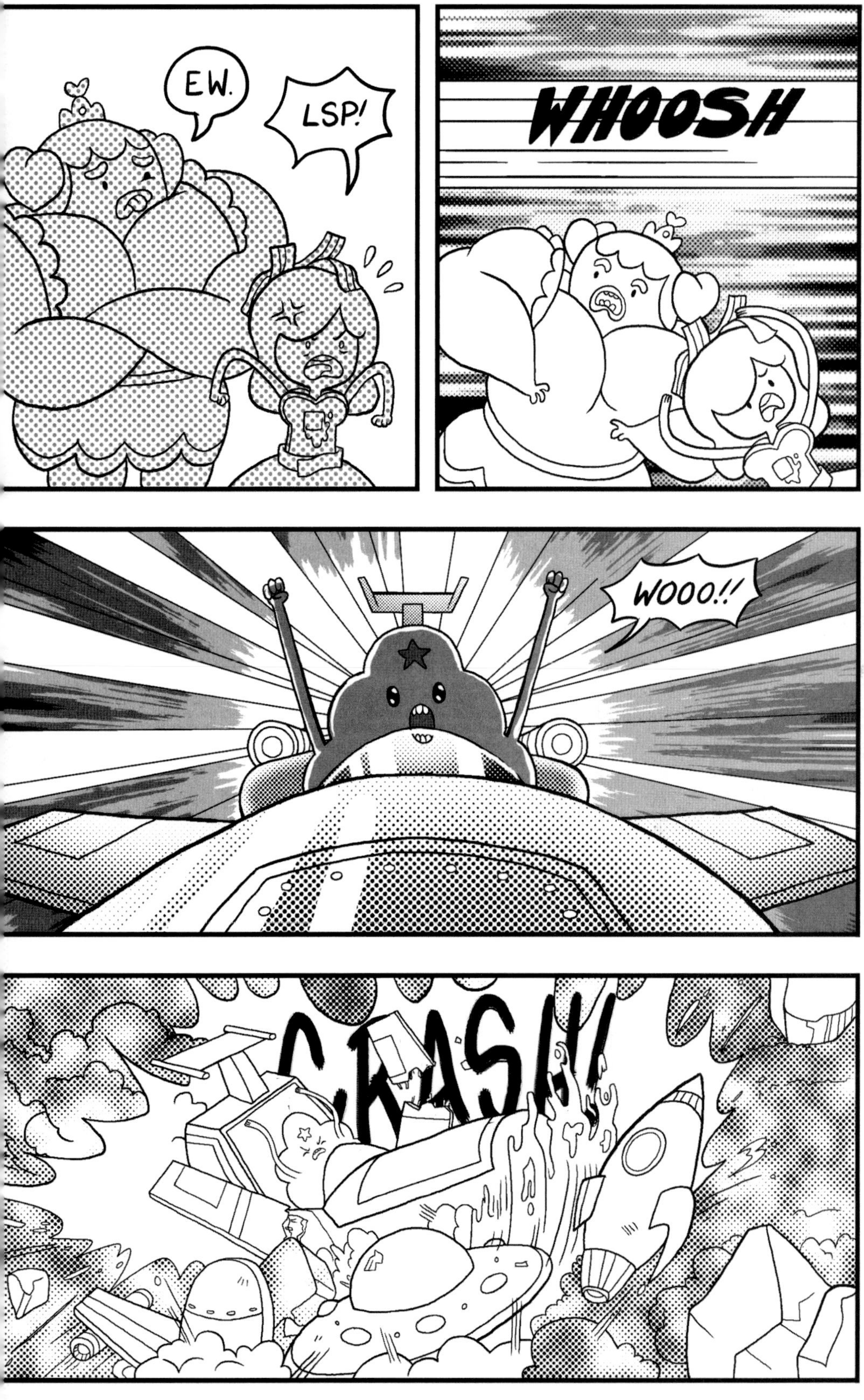
EW.
LSP!
WHOOSH
WOOO!!
CRASH!!

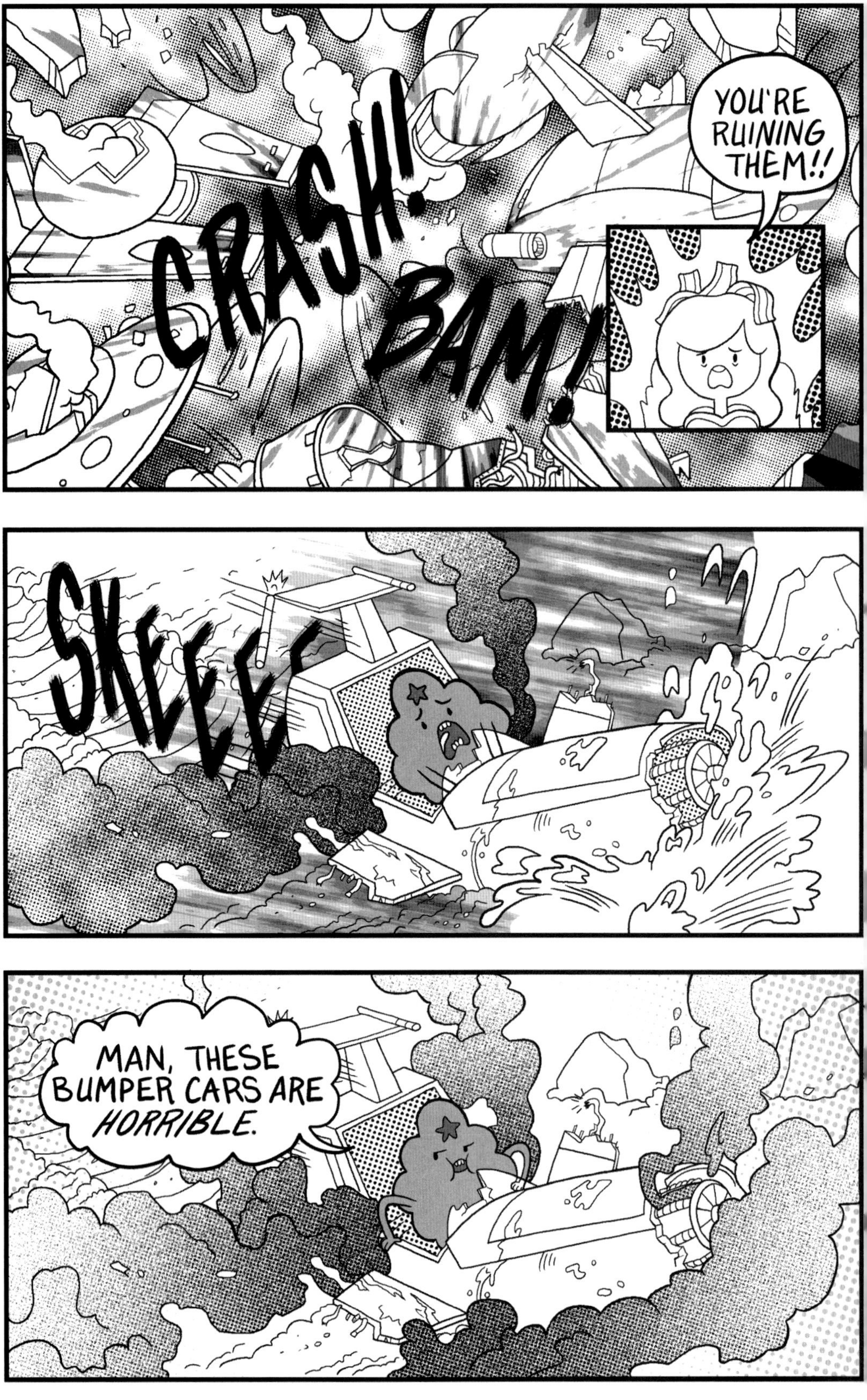
CRASH!
BAM!
YOU'RE RUINING THEM!!
SKEEEE
MAN, THESE BUMPER CARS ARE *HORRIBLE*.

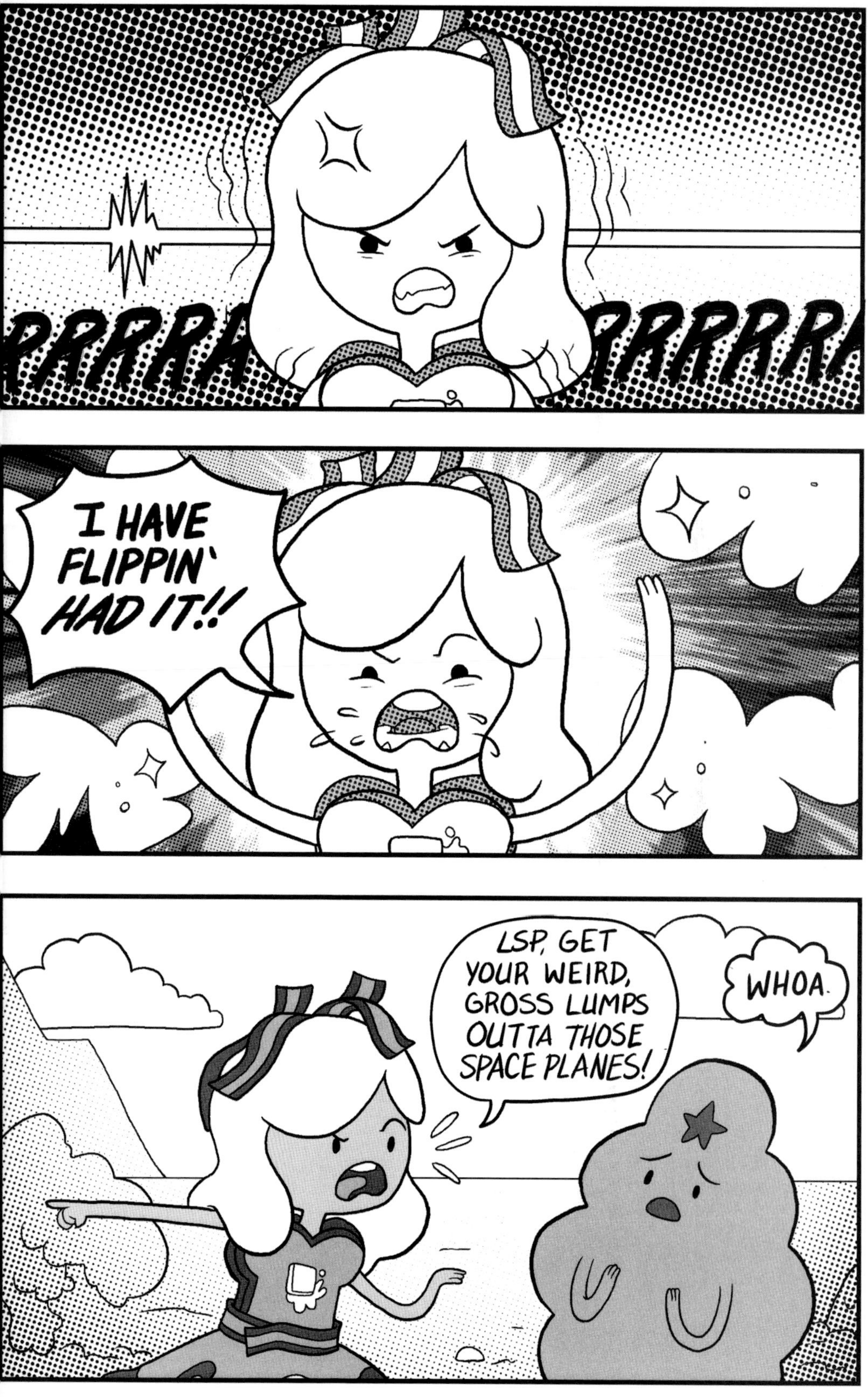
RRRRA RRRRRA
I HAVE FLIPPIN' HAD IT!!
LSP, GET YOUR WEIRD, GROSS LUMPS OUTTA THOSE SPACE PLANES!
WHOA.

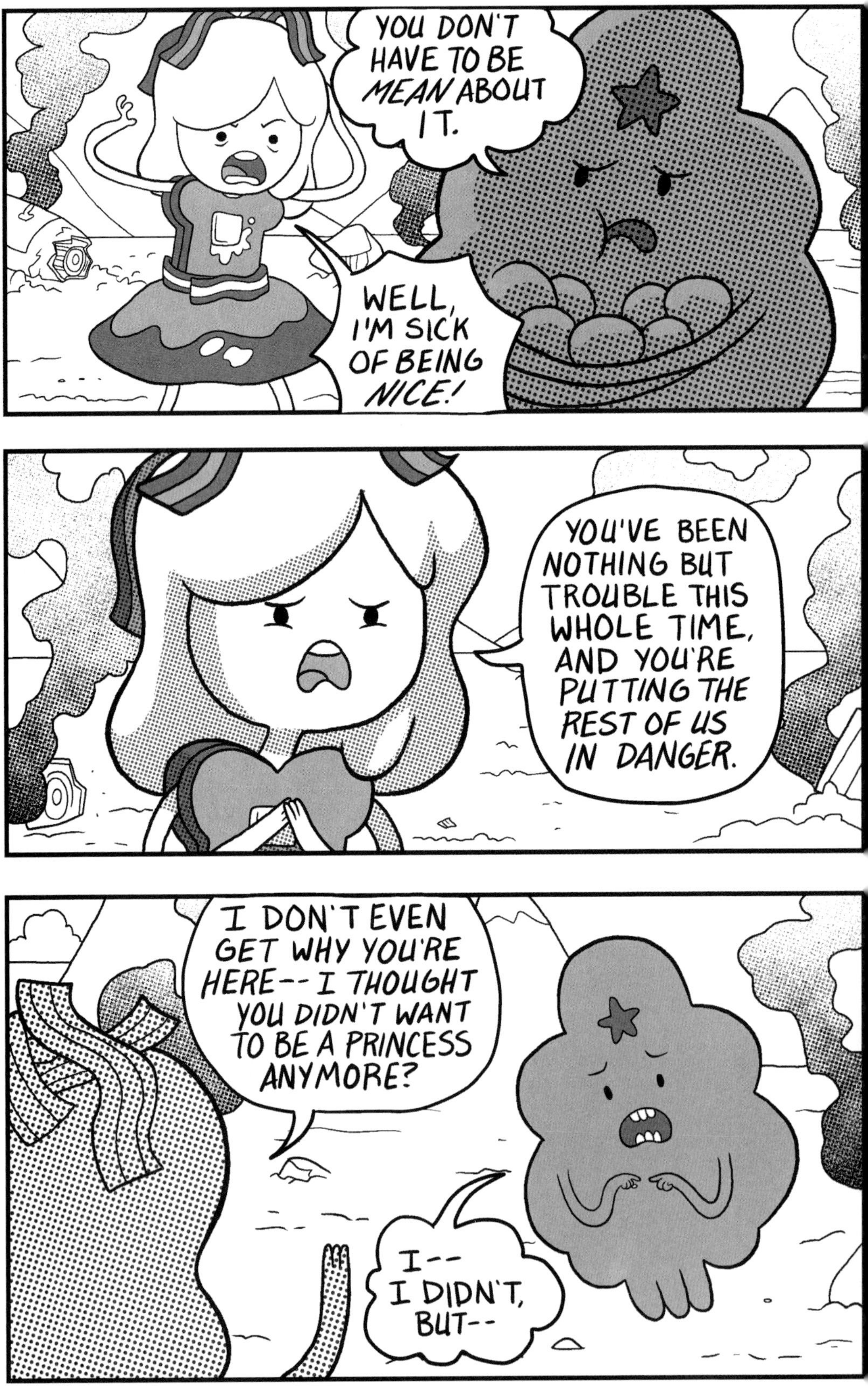
YOU DON'T HAVE TO BE MEAN ABOUT IT.
WELL, I'M SICK OF BEING NICE!
YOU'VE BEEN NOTHING BUT TROUBLE THIS WHOLE TIME, AND YOU'RE PUTTING THE REST OF US IN DANGER.
I DON'T EVEN GET WHY YOU'RE HERE-- I THOUGHT YOU DIDN'T WANT TO BE A PRINCESS ANYMORE?
I-- I DIDN'T, BUT--

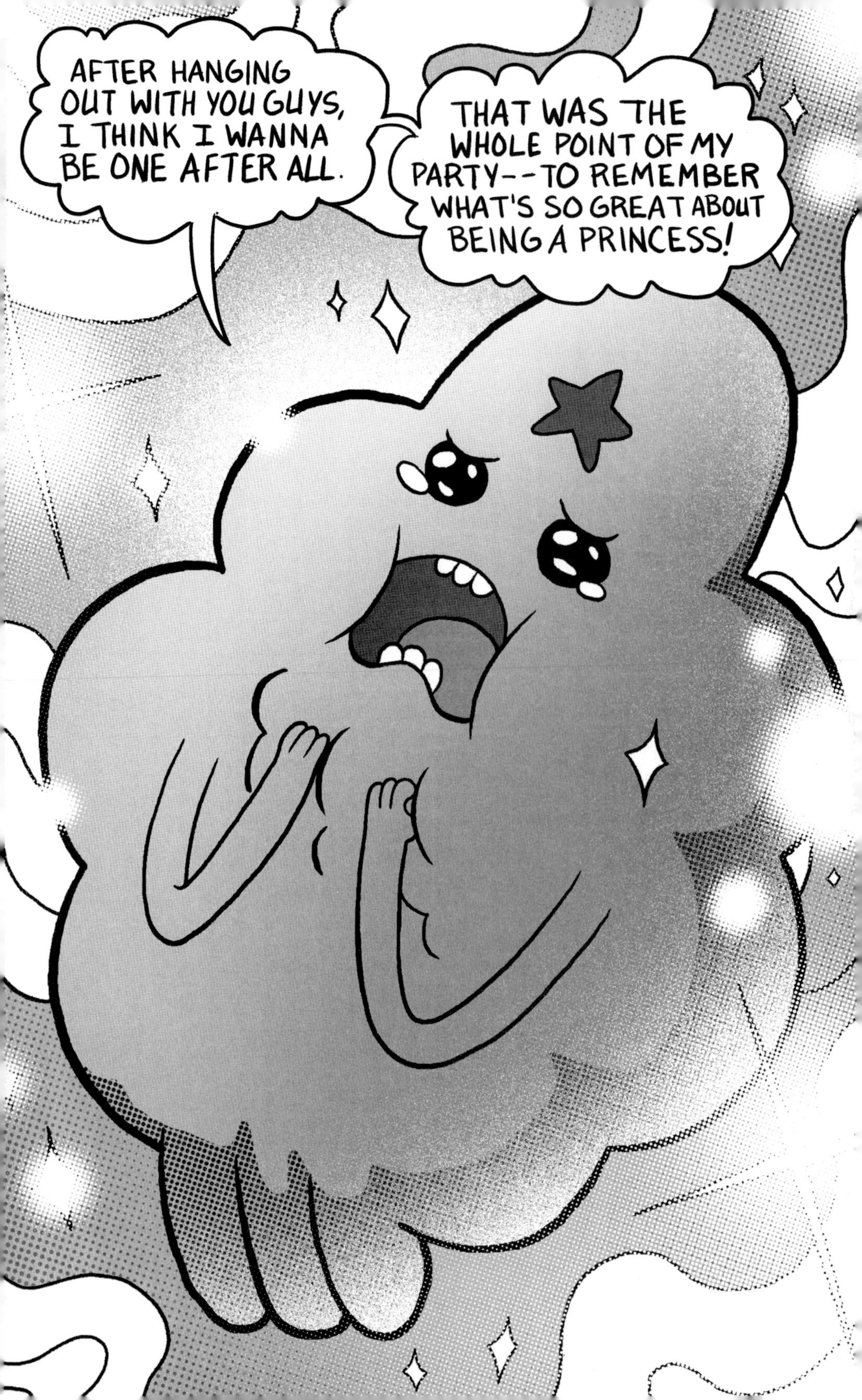
AFTER HANGING OUT WITH YOU GUYS, I THINK I WANNA BE ONE AFTER ALL.
THAT WAS THE WHOLE POINT OF MY PARTY--TO REMEMBER WHAT'S SO GREAT ABOUT BEING A PRINCESS!

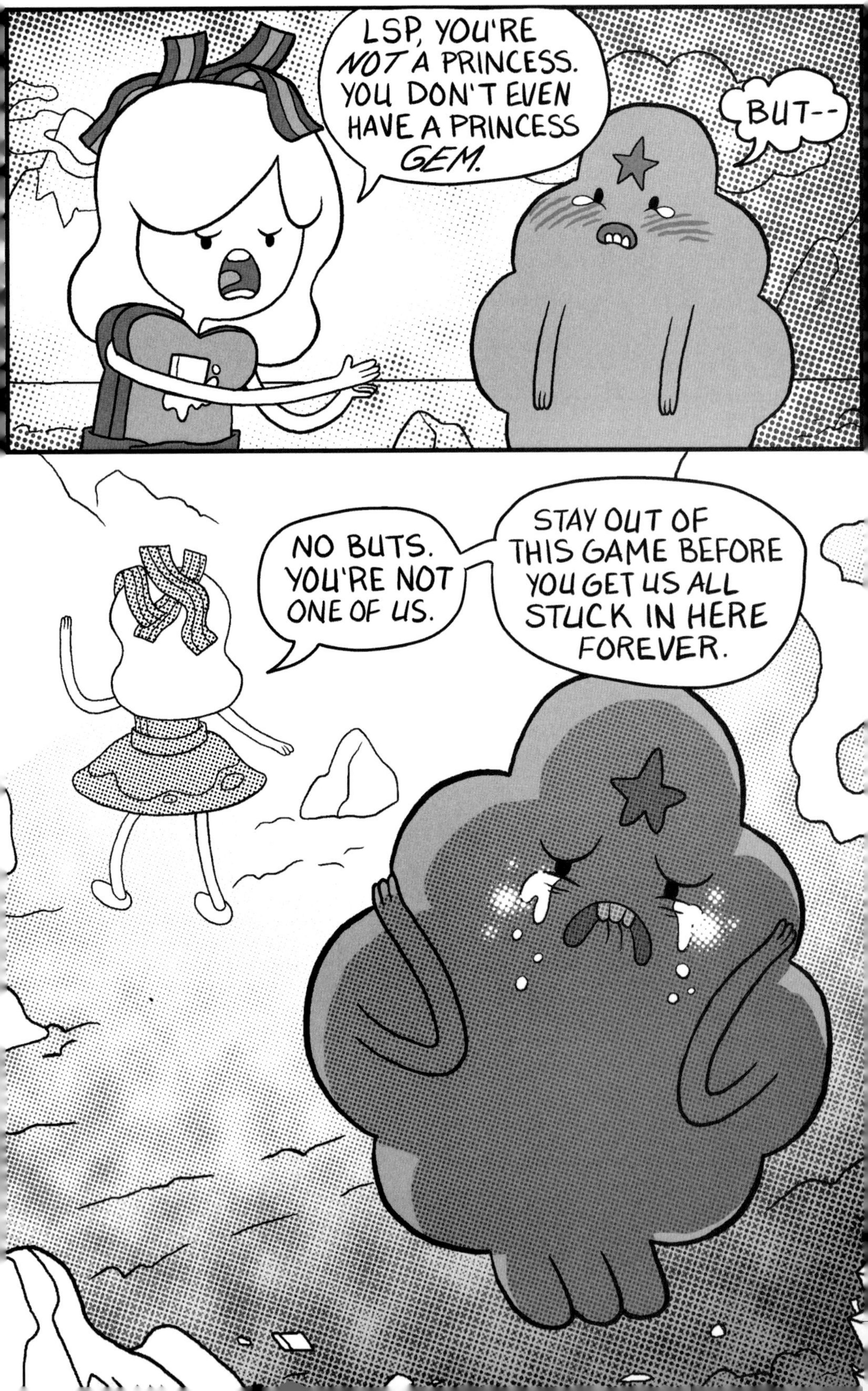
LSP, YOU'RE *NOT* A PRINCESS. YOU DON'T EVEN HAVE A PRINCESS *GEM*.
BUT--
NO BUTS. YOU'RE NOT ONE OF US.
STAY OUT OF THIS GAME BEFORE YOU GET US ALL STUCK IN HERE FOREVER.

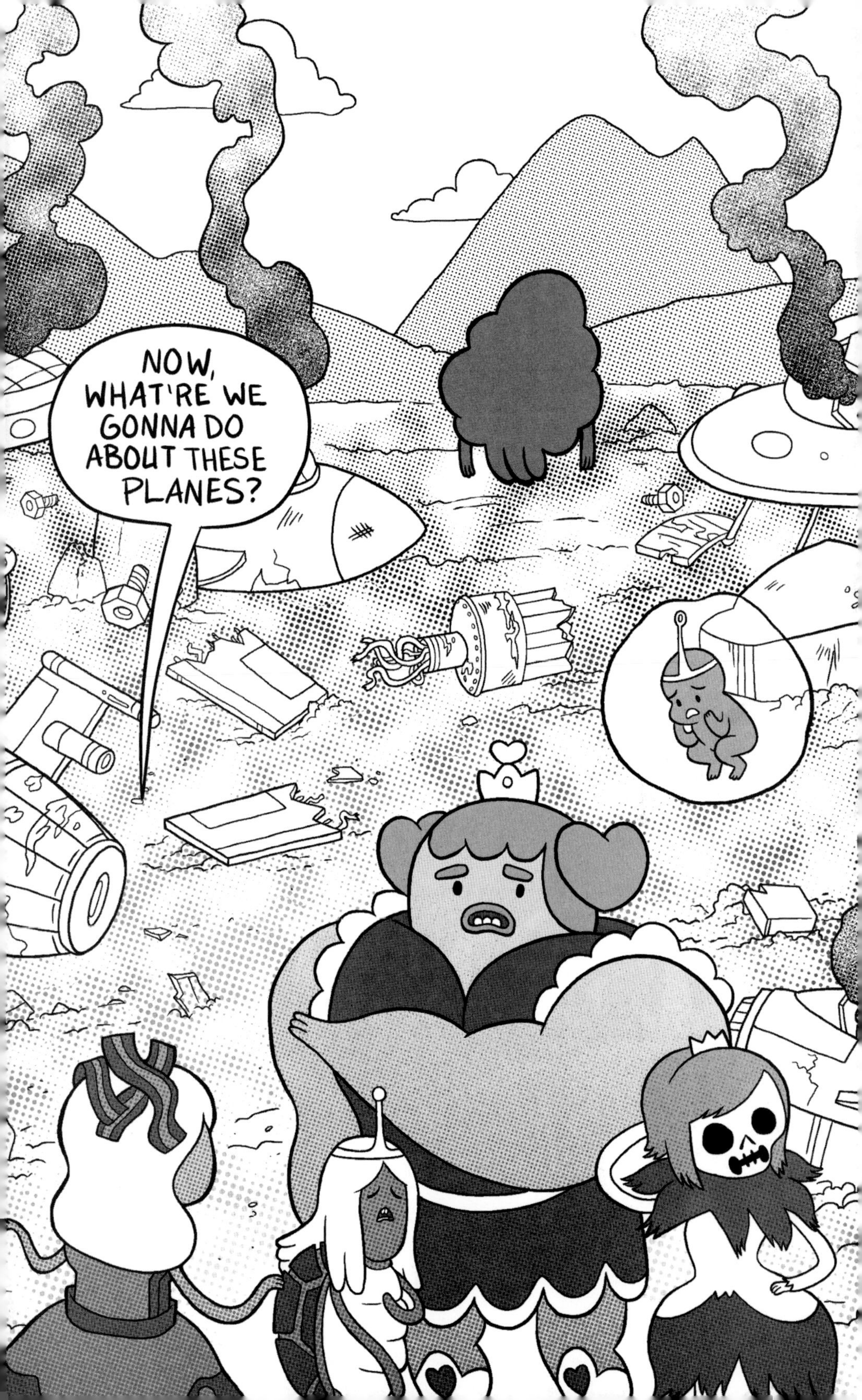
NOW, WHAT'RE WE GONNA DO ABOUT THESE PLANES?

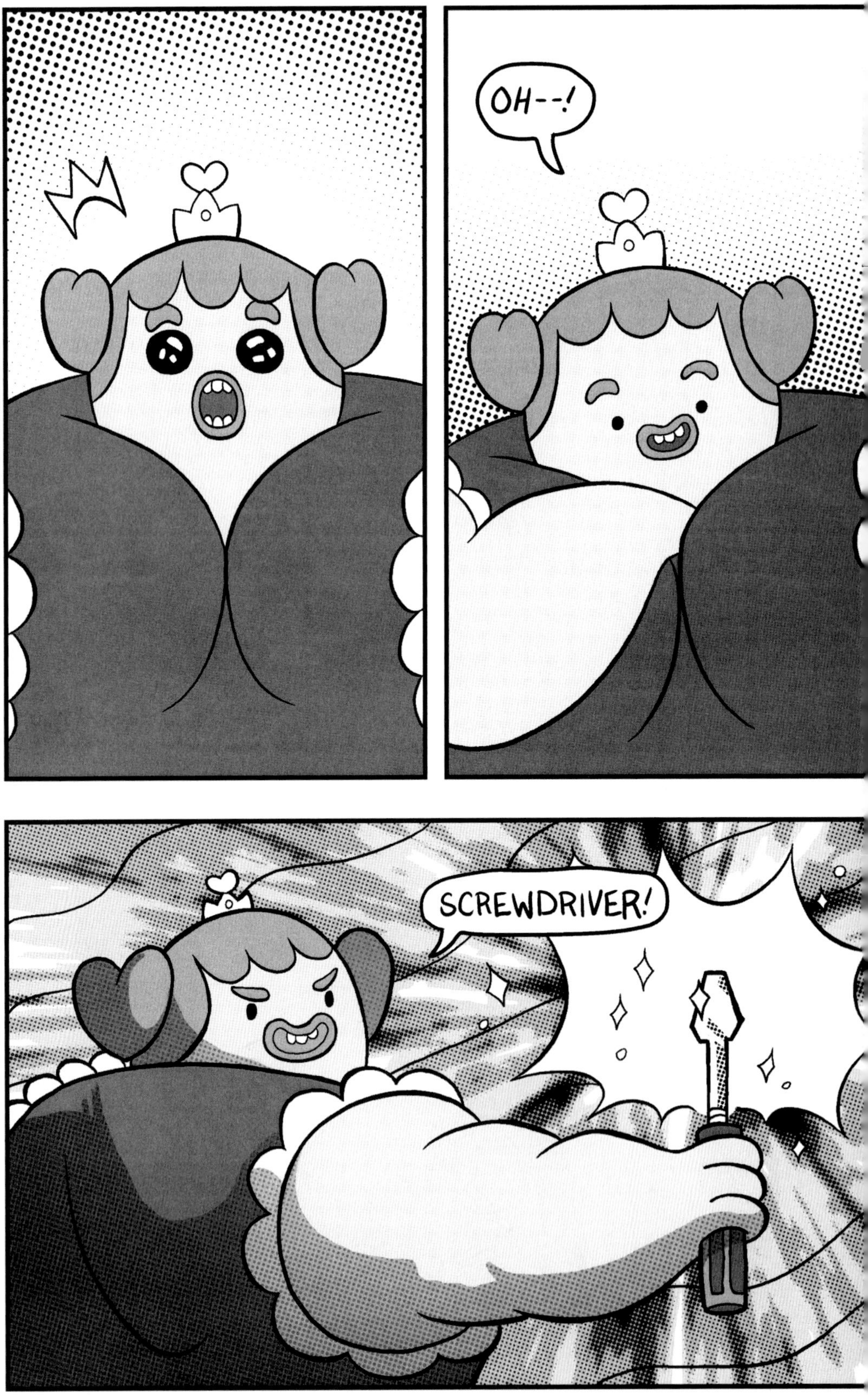
OH--!
SCREWDRIVER!

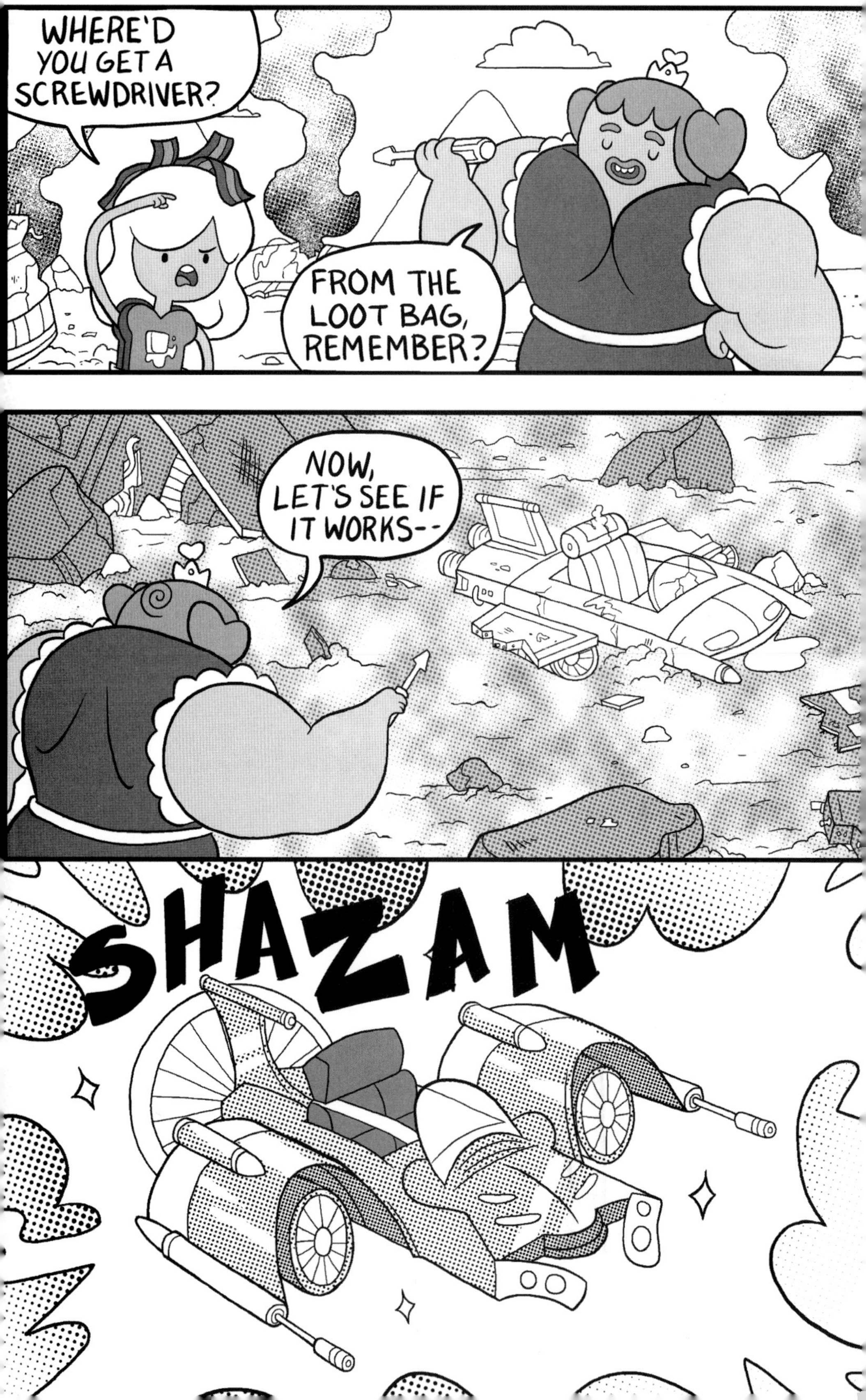
WHERE'D YOU GET A SCREWDRIVER?
FROM THE LOOT BAG, REMEMBER?
NOW, LET'S SEE IF IT WORKS--
SHAZAM

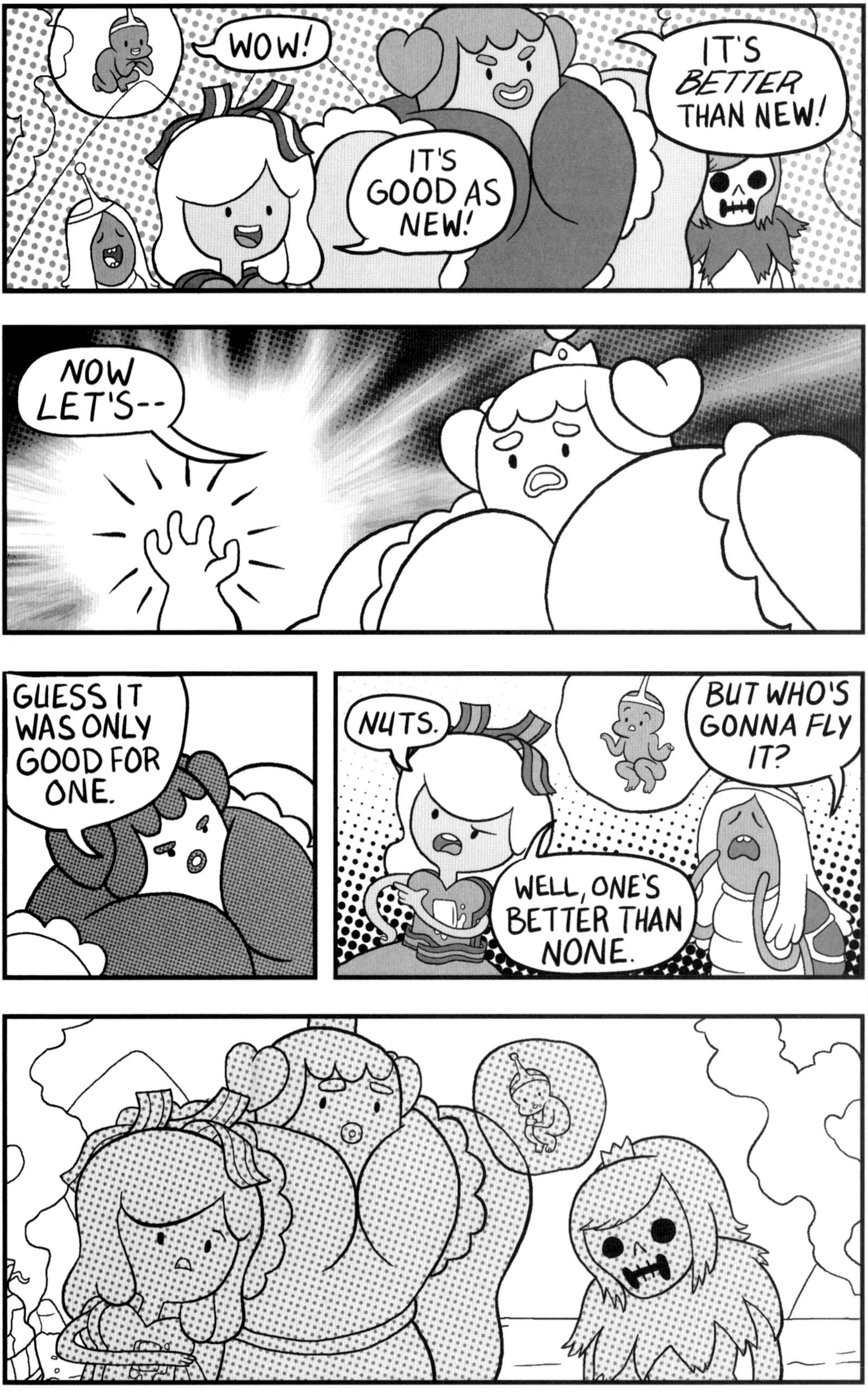
WOW!
IT'S BETTER THAN NEW!
IT'S GOOD AS NEW!
NOW LET'S--
GUESS IT WAS ONLY GOOD FOR ONE.
NUTS.
BUT WHO'S GONNA FLY IT?
WELL, ONE'S BETTER THAN NONE.

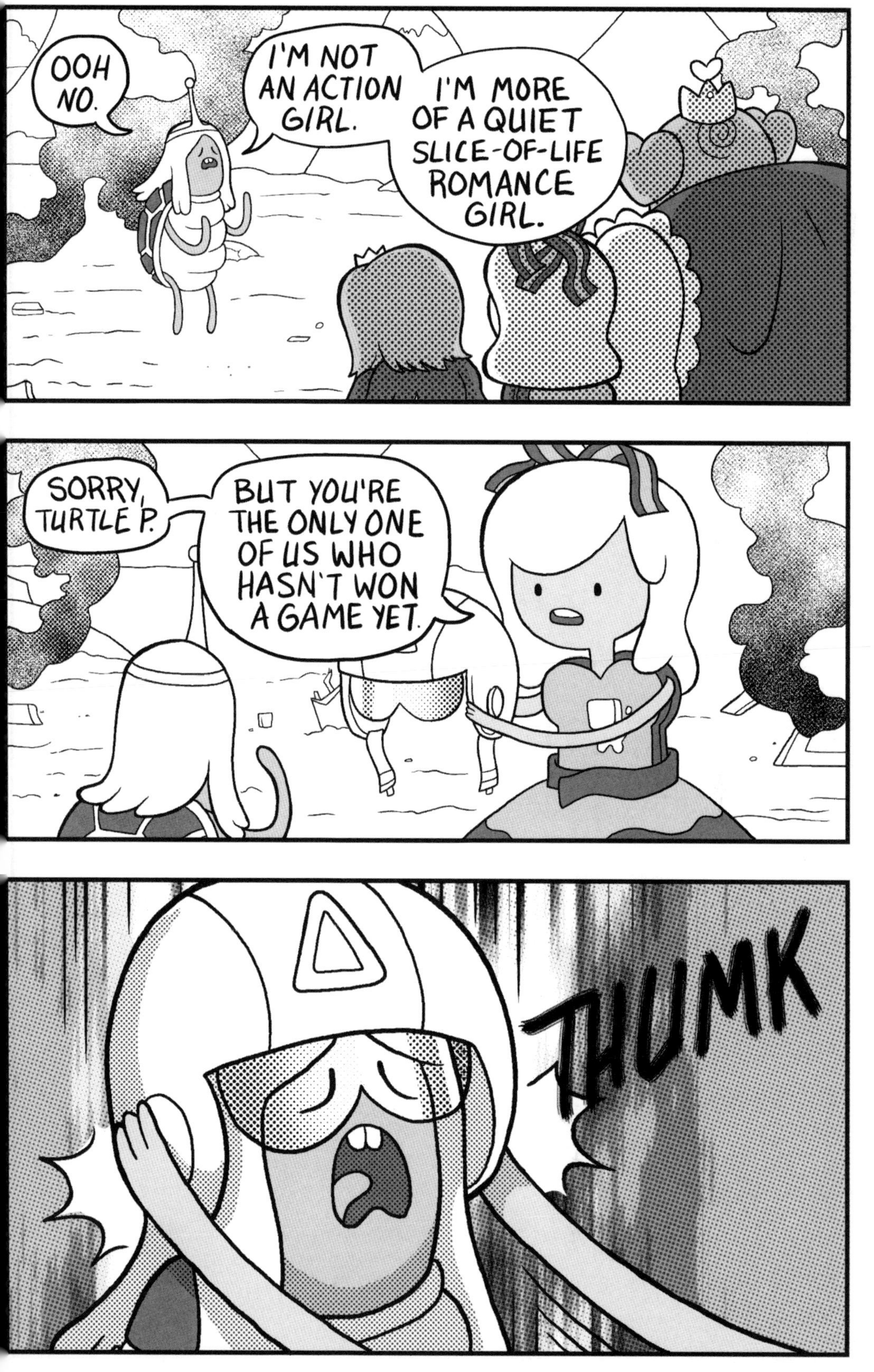
OOH NO.
I'M NOT AN ACTION GIRL.
I'M MORE OF A QUIET SLICE-OF-LIFE ROMANCE GIRL.
SORRY, TURTLE P.
BUT YOU'RE THE ONLY ONE OF US WHO HASN'T WON A GAME YET.
THUMK

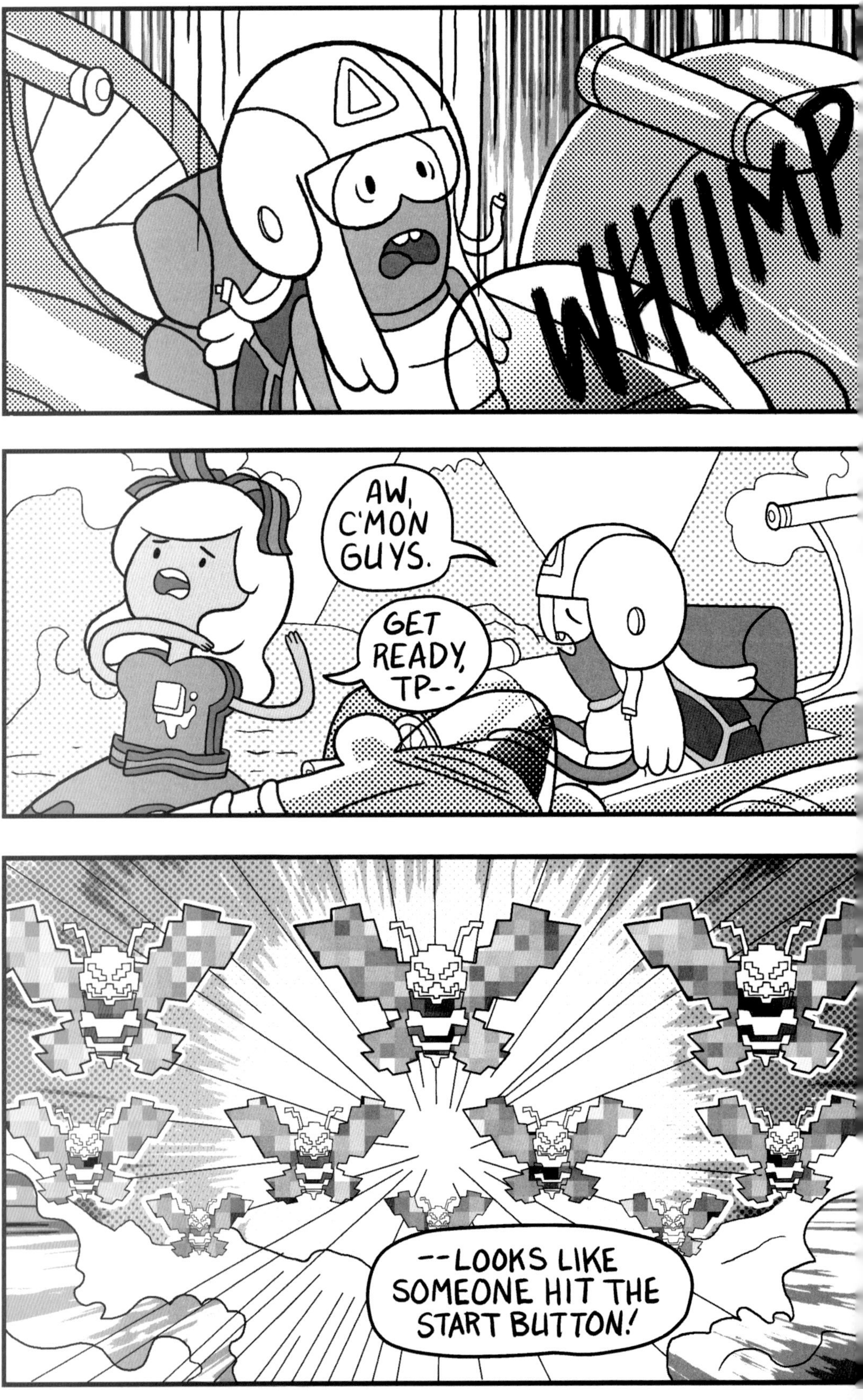
WHUMP
AW, C'MON GUYS.
GET READY, TP--
--LOOKS LIKE SOMEONE HIT THE START BUTTON!

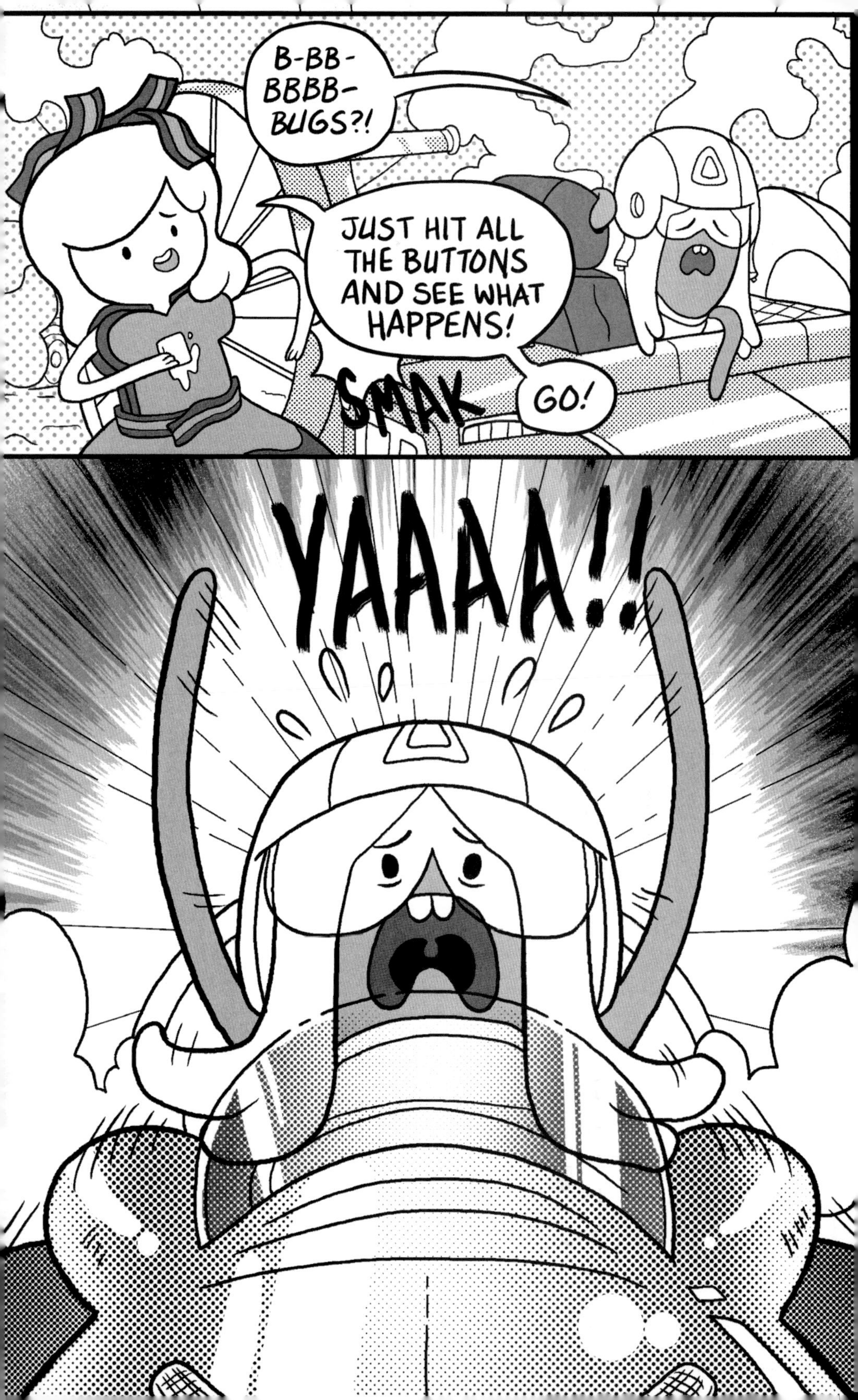
B-BB-
BBBB-
BUGS?!
JUST HIT ALL THE BUTTONS AND SEE WHAT HAPPENS!
SMAK
GO!
YAAAA!!

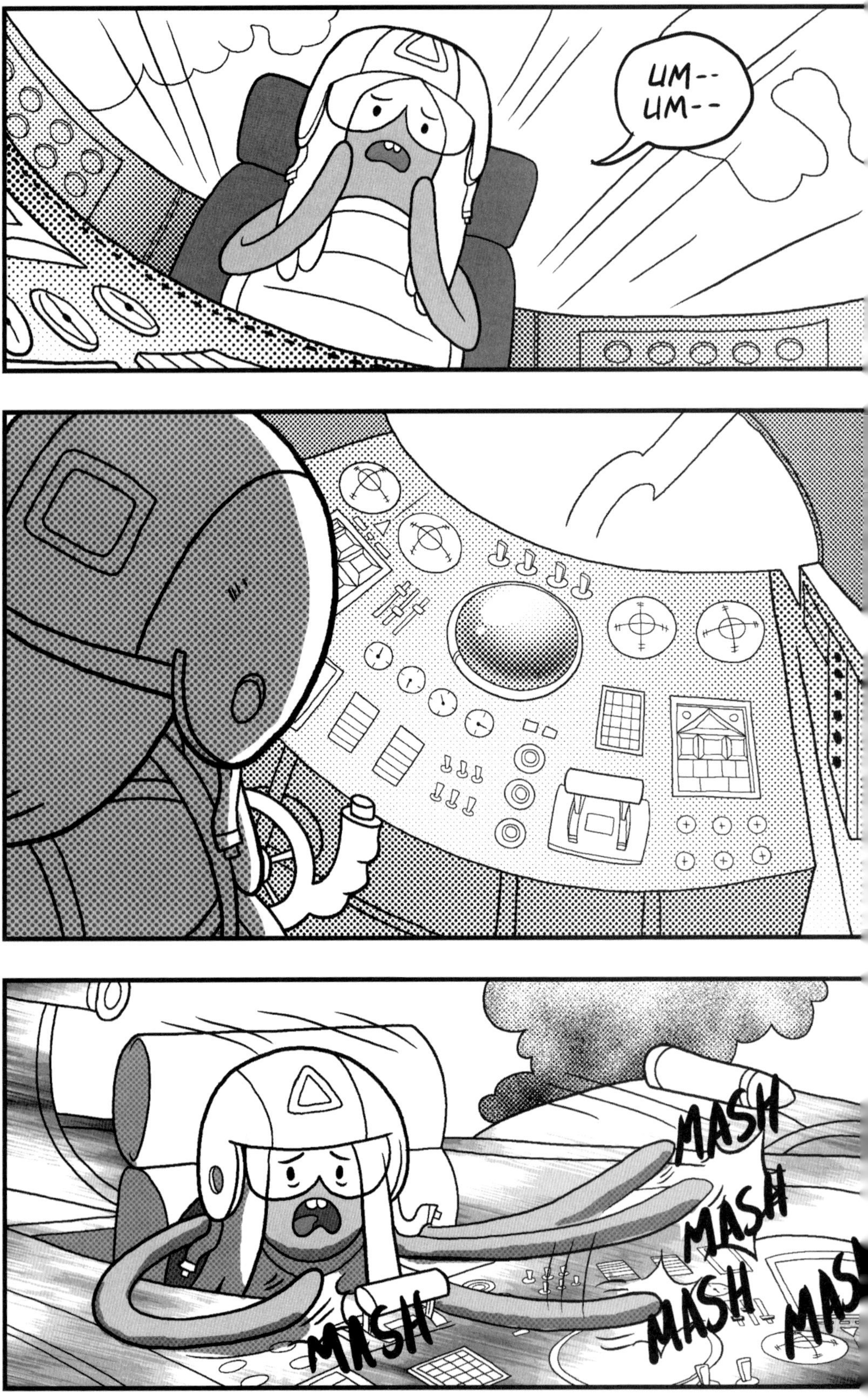
UM--
UM--
MASH
MASH
MASH
MASH

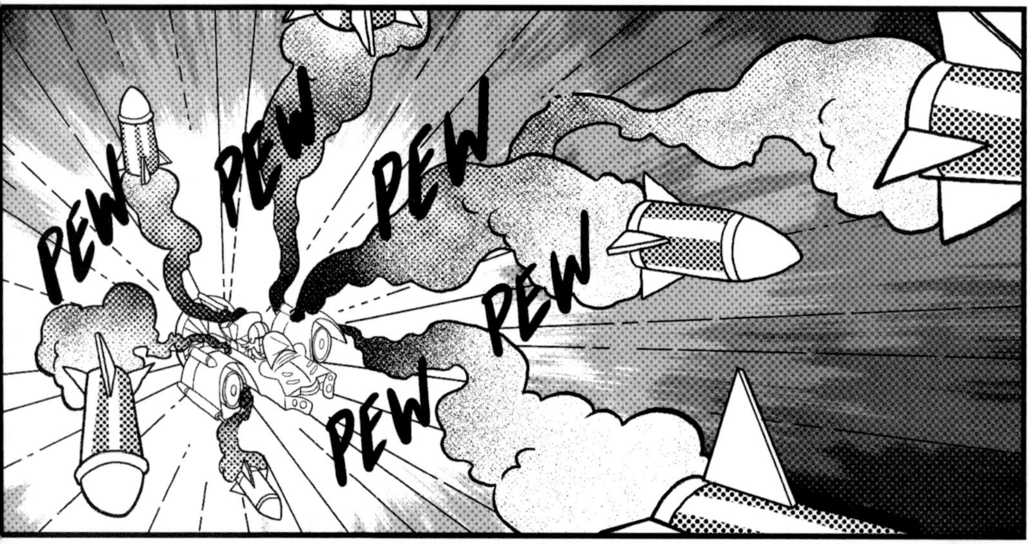
PEW
PEW
PEW
PEW
PEW
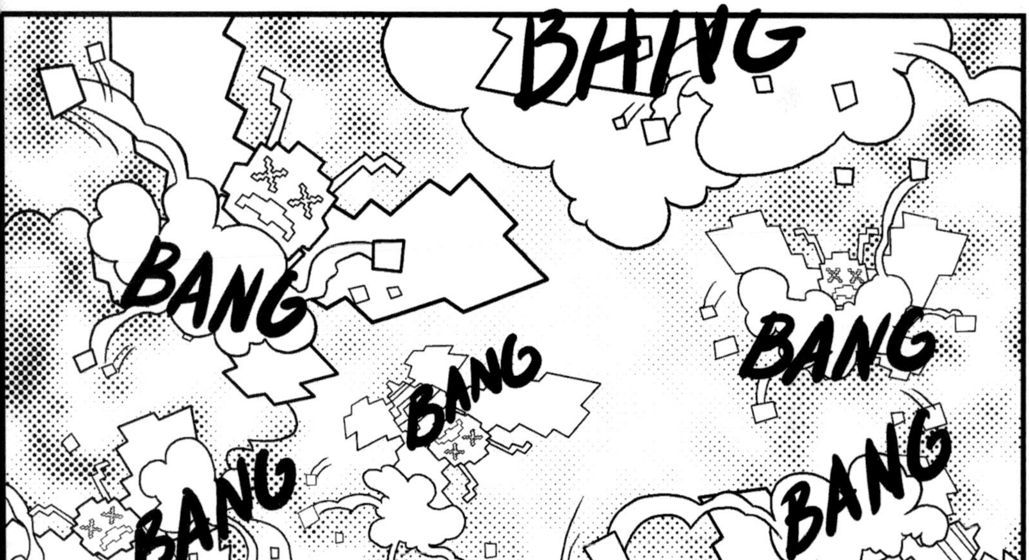
BANG
BANG
BANG
BANG
BANG
BANG
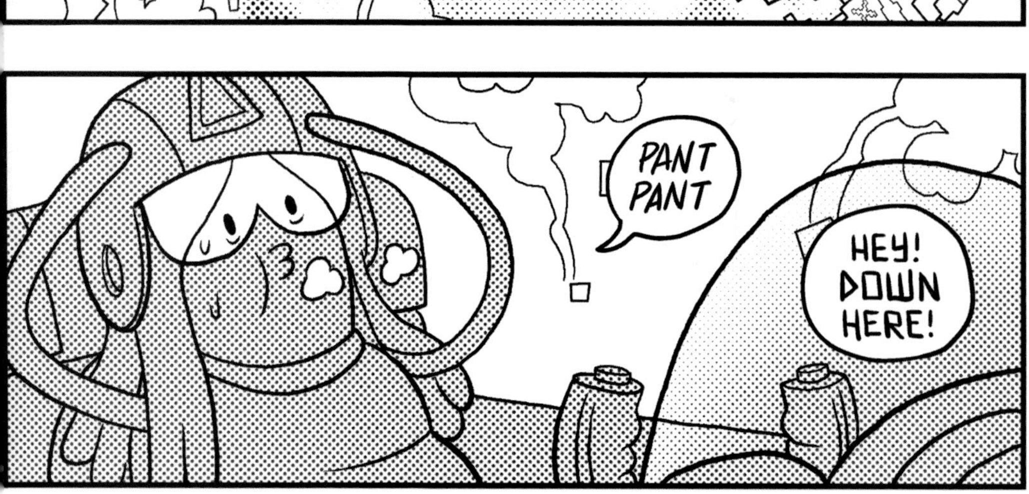
PANT PANT
HEY! DOWN HERE!

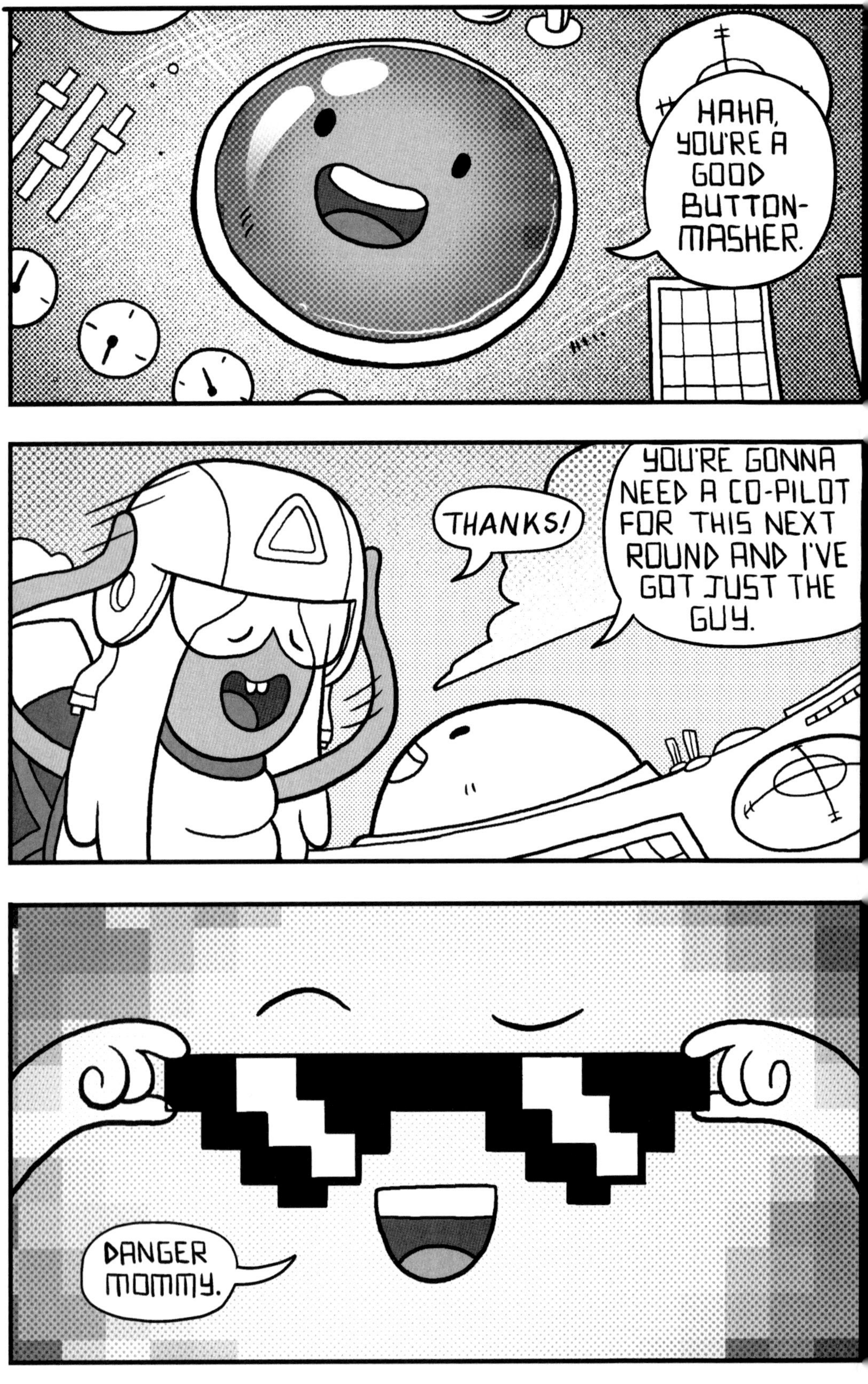
HAHA, YOU'RE A GOOD BUTTON-MASHER.
THANKS!
YOU'RE GONNA NEED A CO-PILOT FOR THIS NEXT ROUND AND I'VE GOT JUST THE GUY.
DANGER MOMMY.

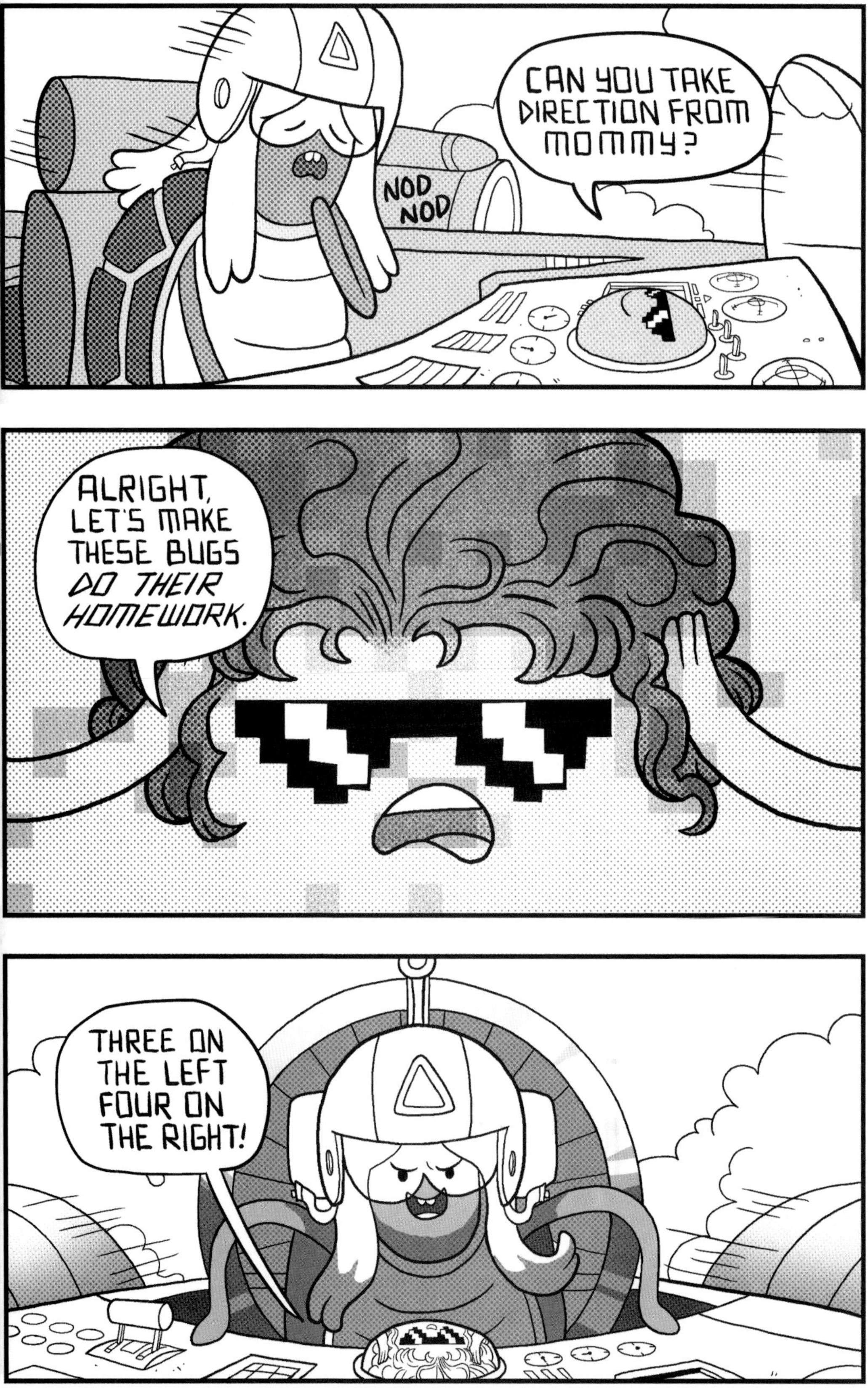
NOD NOD
CAN YOU TAKE DIRECTION FROM MOMMY?
ALRIGHT, LET'S MAKE THESE BUGS *DO THEIR HOMEWORK.*
THREE ON THE LEFT FOUR ON THE RIGHT!

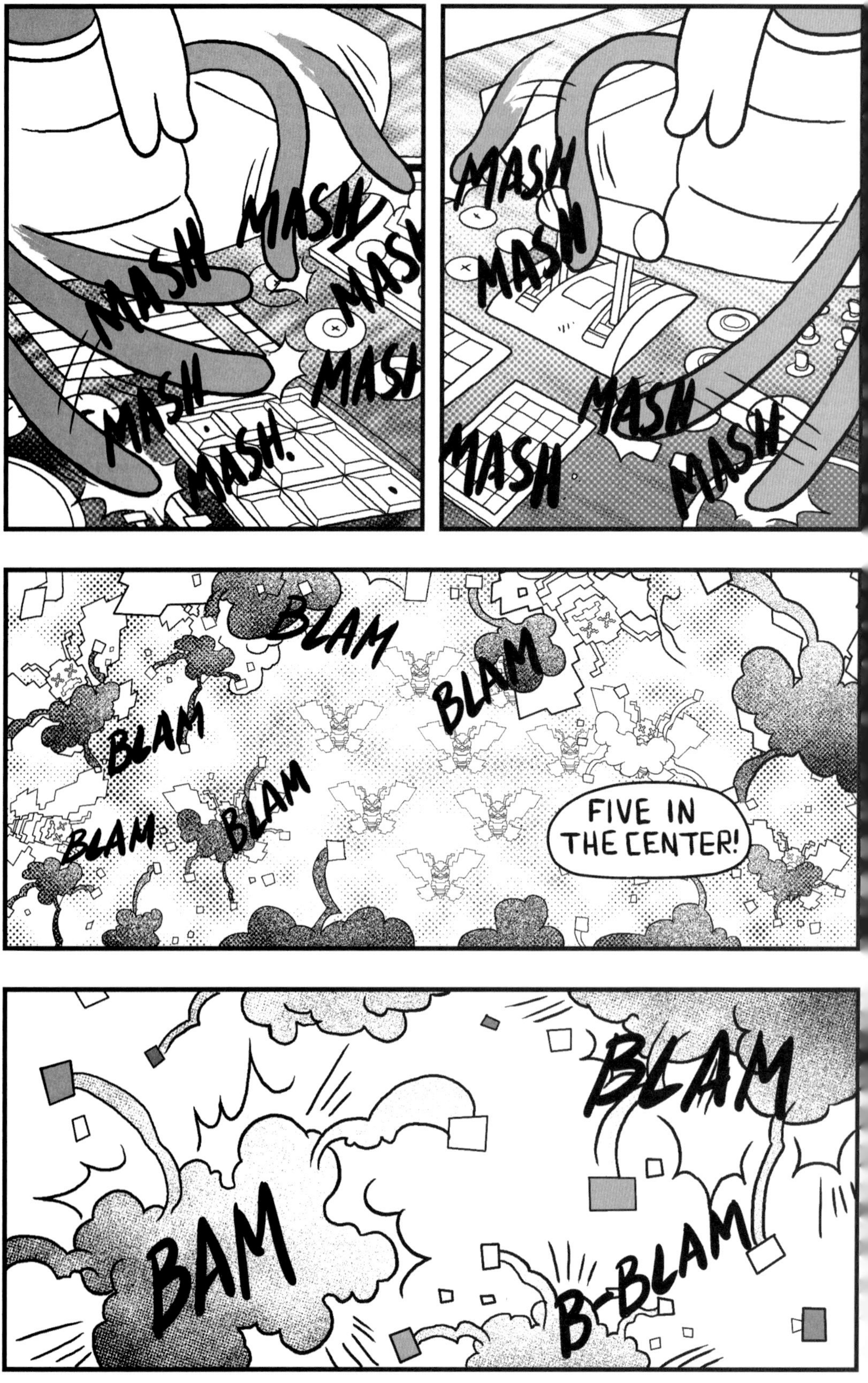
MASH
MASH
MASH
MASH
MASH
MASH
MASH.
MASH
MASH
MASH
MASH
MASH
BLAM
BLAM
BLAM
BLAM
BLAM
FIVE IN THE CENTER!
BLAM
BAM
B-BLAM

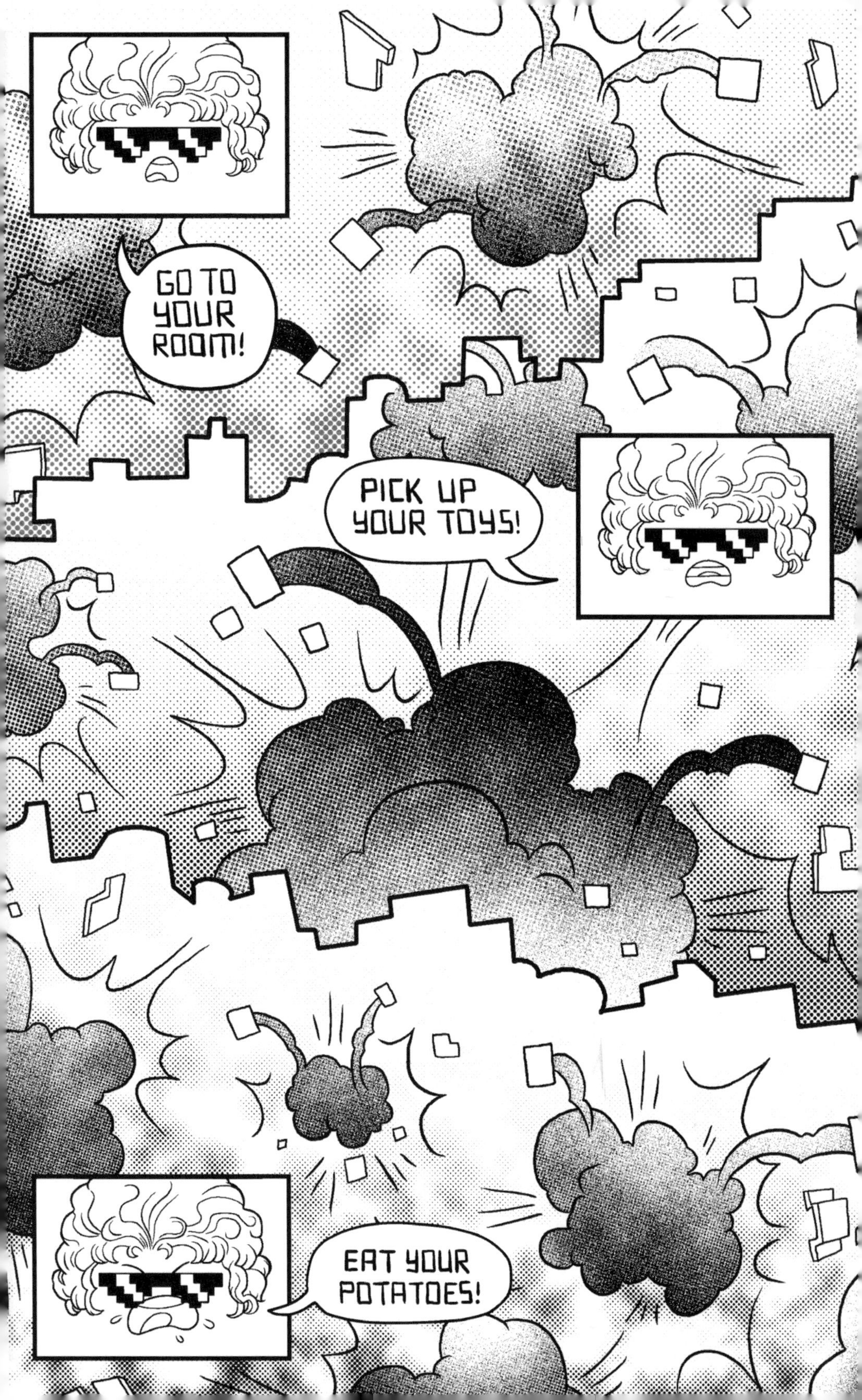
GO TO YOUR ROOM!
PICK UP YOUR TOYS!
EAT YOUR POTATOES!

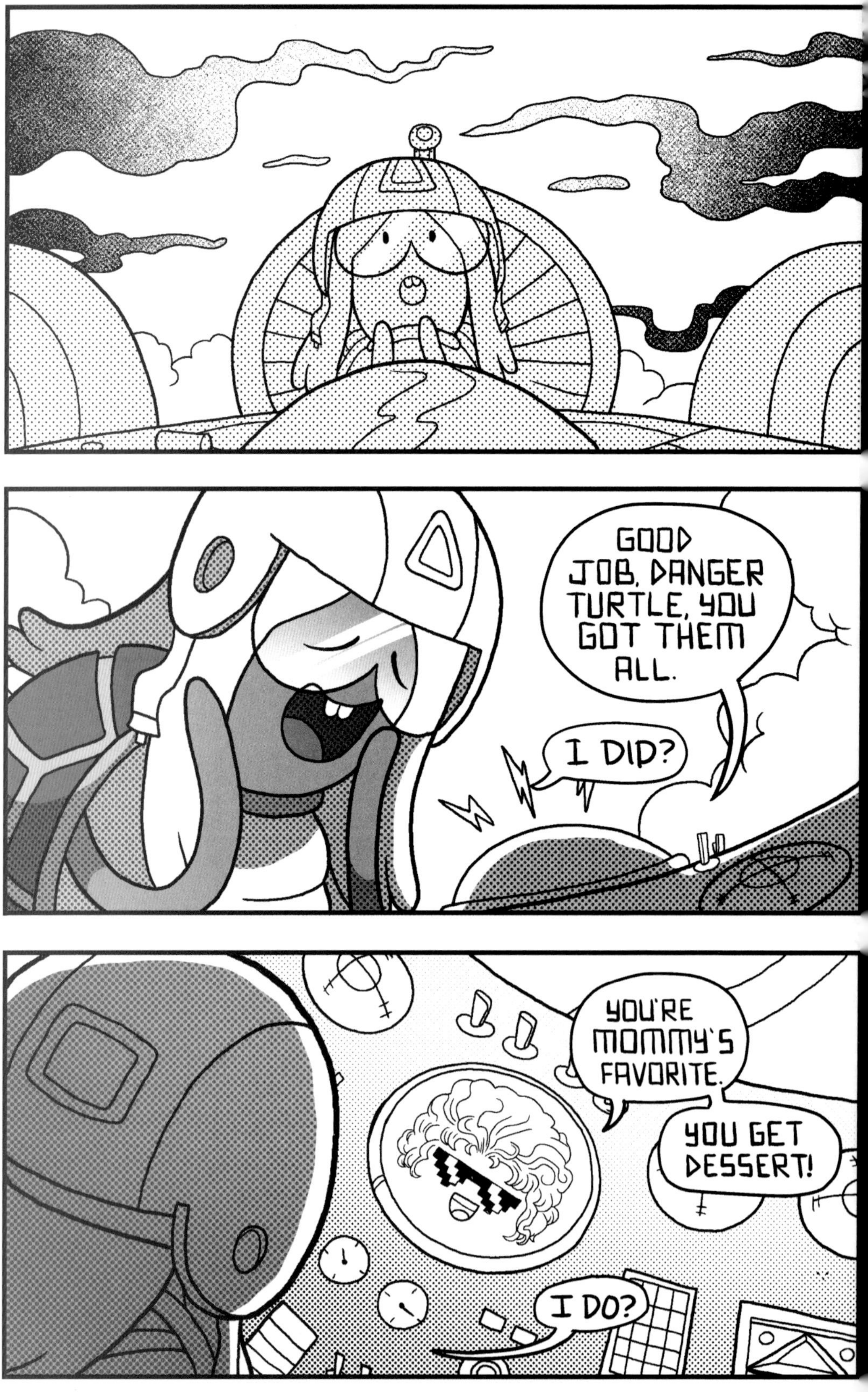
GOOD JOB, DANGER TURTLE, YOU GOT THEM ALL.
I DID?
YOU'RE MOMMY'S FAVORITE.
YOU GET DESSERT!
I DO?

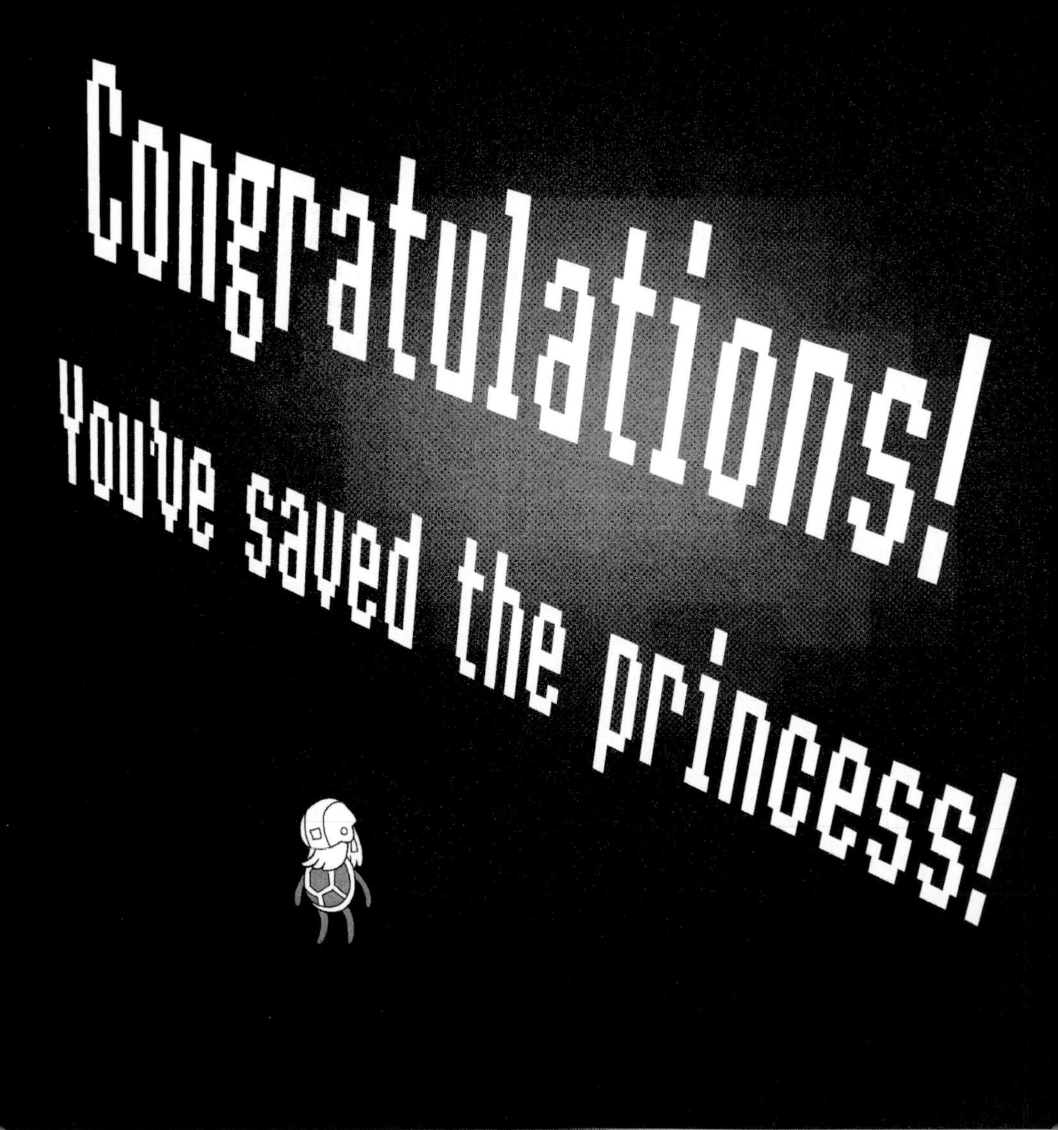
Congratulations!
You've saved the princess!

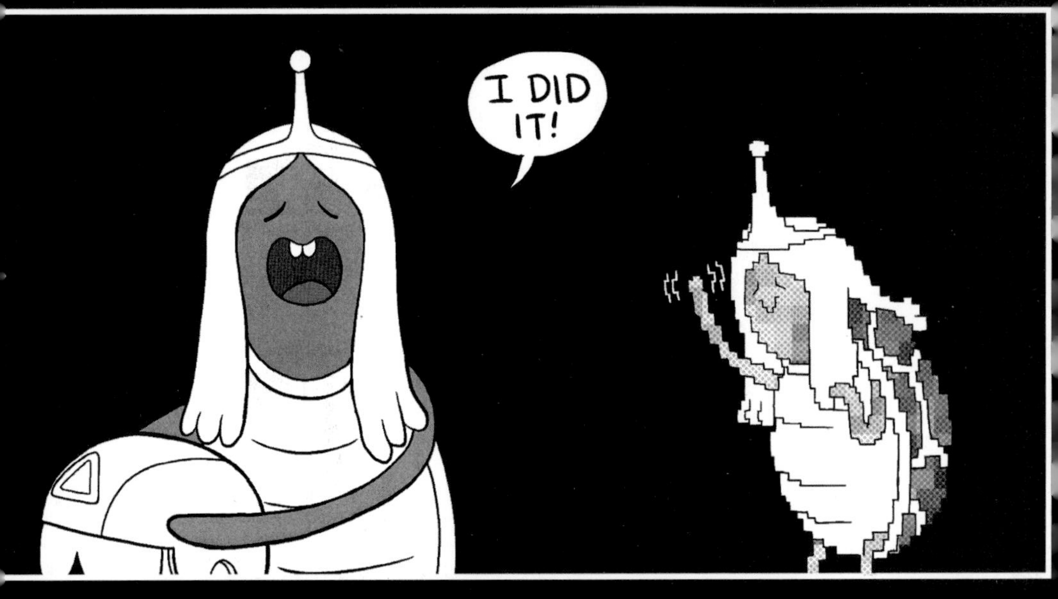
I DID IT!

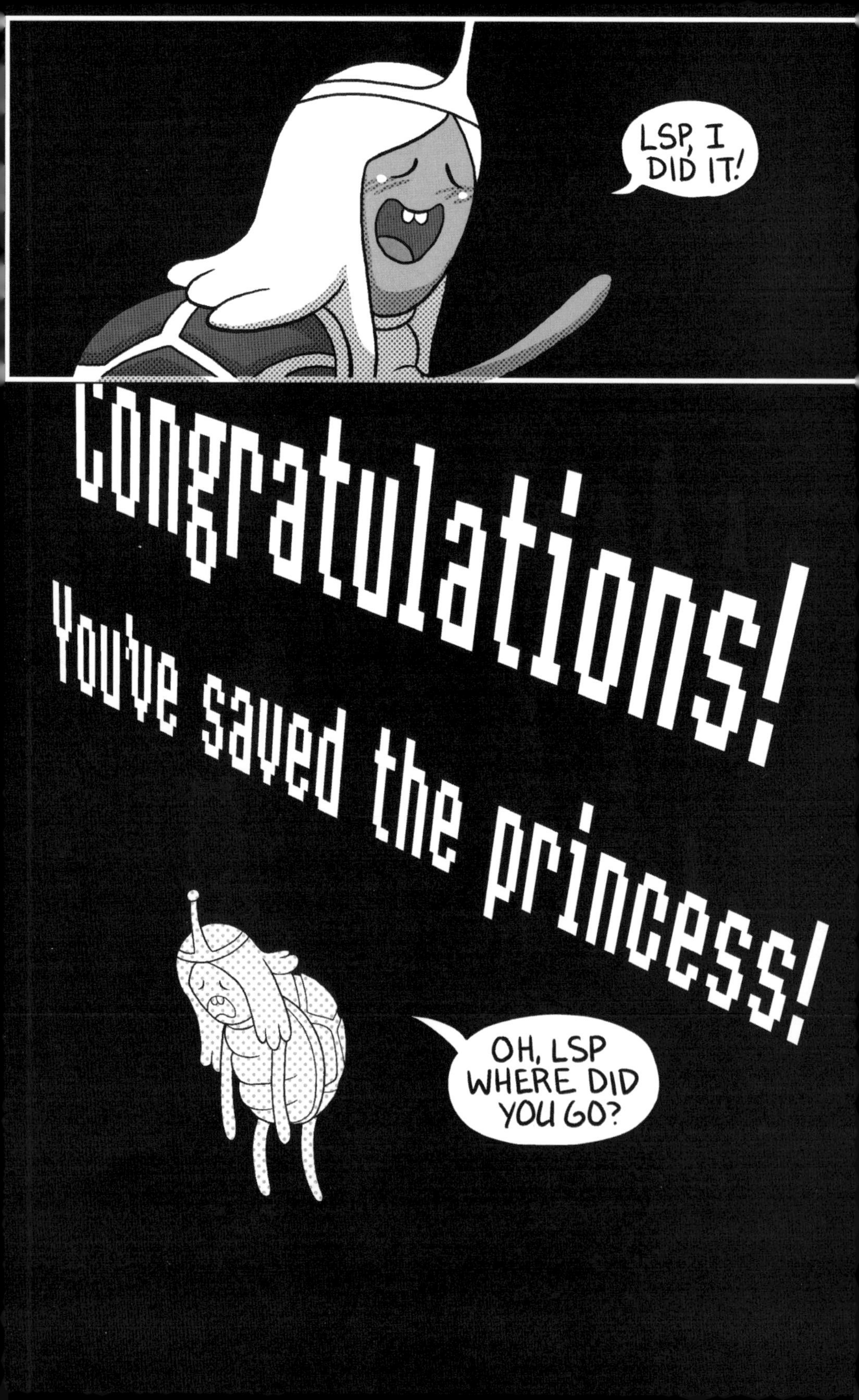
LSP, I DID IT!
Congratulations! You've saved the princess!
OH, LSP WHERE DID YOU GO?

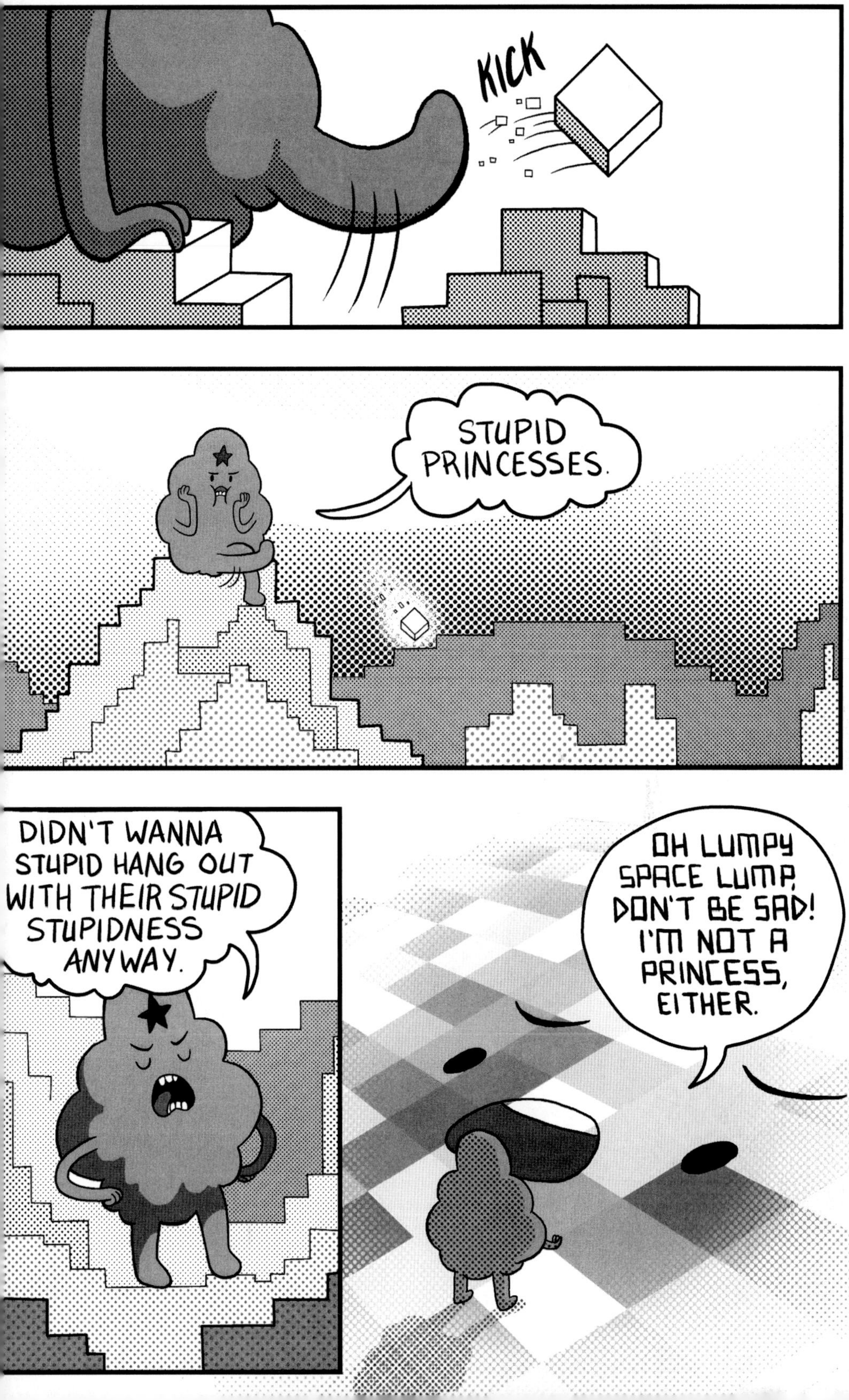
KICK
STUPID PRINCESSES.
DIDN'T WANNA STUPID HANG OUT WITH THEIR STUPID STUPIDNESS ANYWAY.
OH LUMPY SPACE LUMP, DON'T BE SAD! I'M NOT A PRINCESS, EITHER.

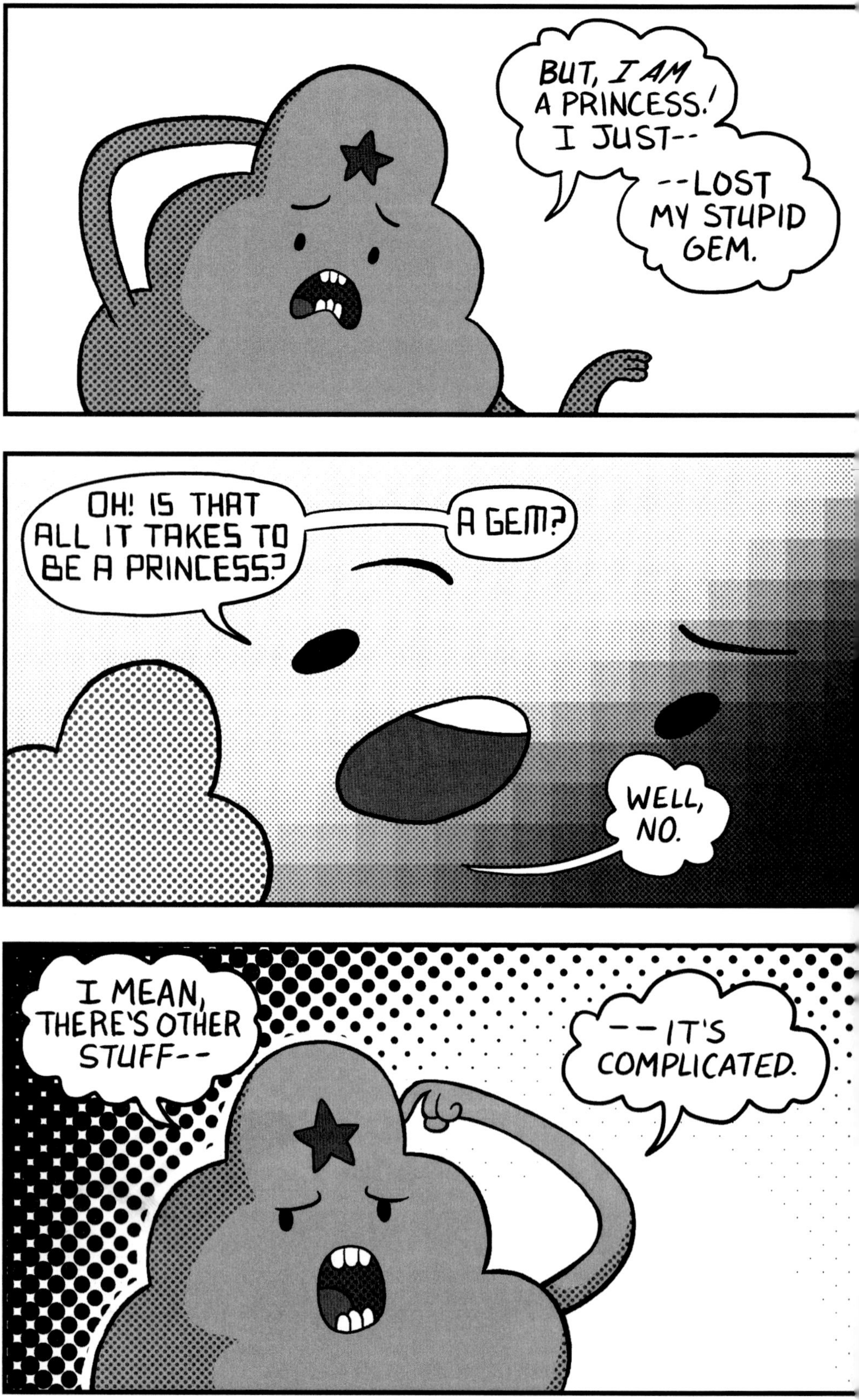
BUT, I AM A PRINCESS! I JUST--
--LOST MY STUPID GEM.
OH! IS THAT ALL IT TAKES TO BE A PRINCESS?
A GEM?
WELL, NO.
I MEAN, THERE'S OTHER STUFF--
--IT'S COMPLICATED.

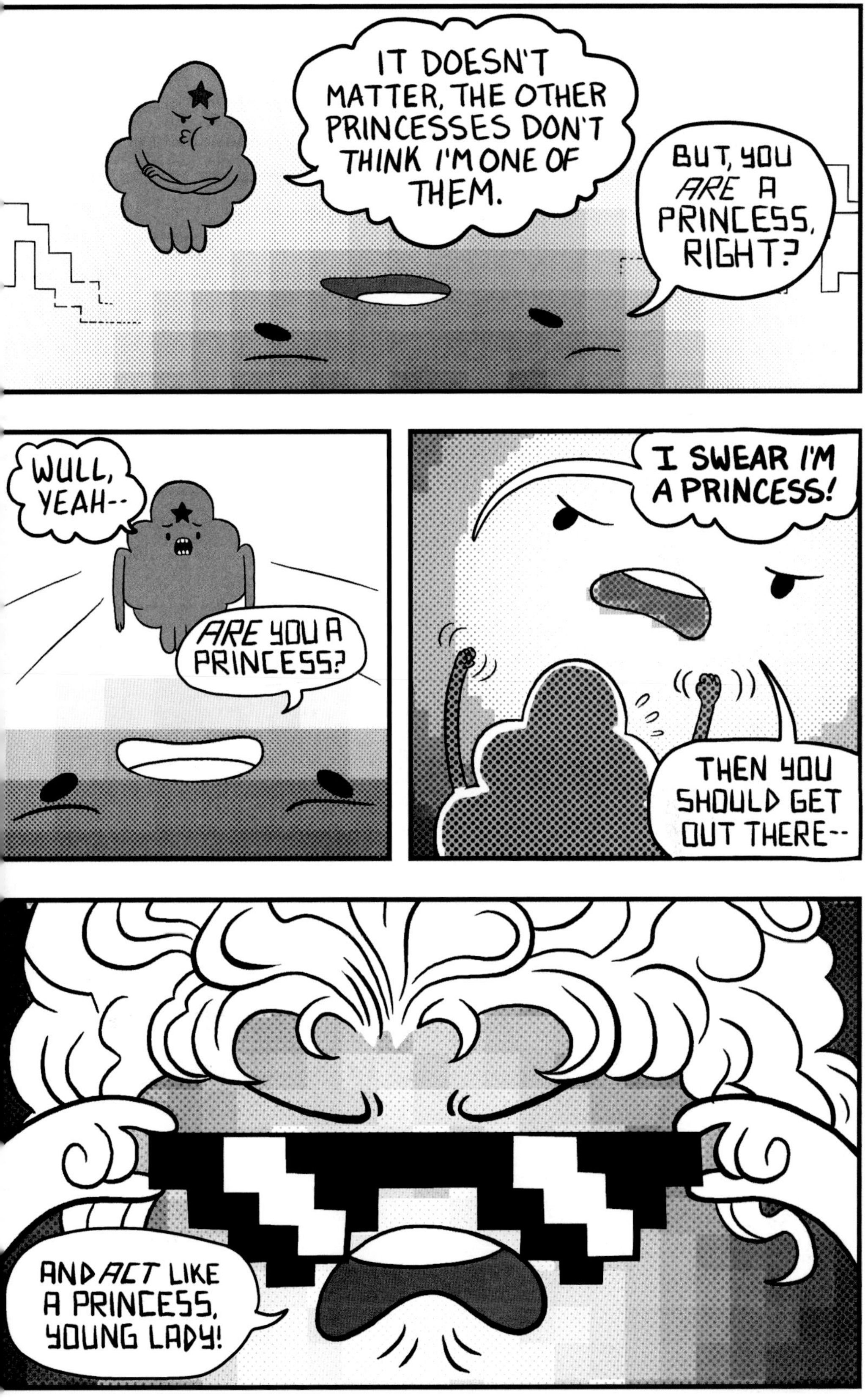
IT DOESN'T MATTER, THE OTHER PRINCESSES DON'T THINK I'M ONE OF THEM.
BUT, YOU ARE A PRINCESS, RIGHT?
WULL, YEAH--
ARE YOU A PRINCESS?
I SWEAR I'M A PRINCESS!
THEN YOU SHOULD GET OUT THERE--
AND ACT LIKE A PRINCESS, YOUNG LADY!

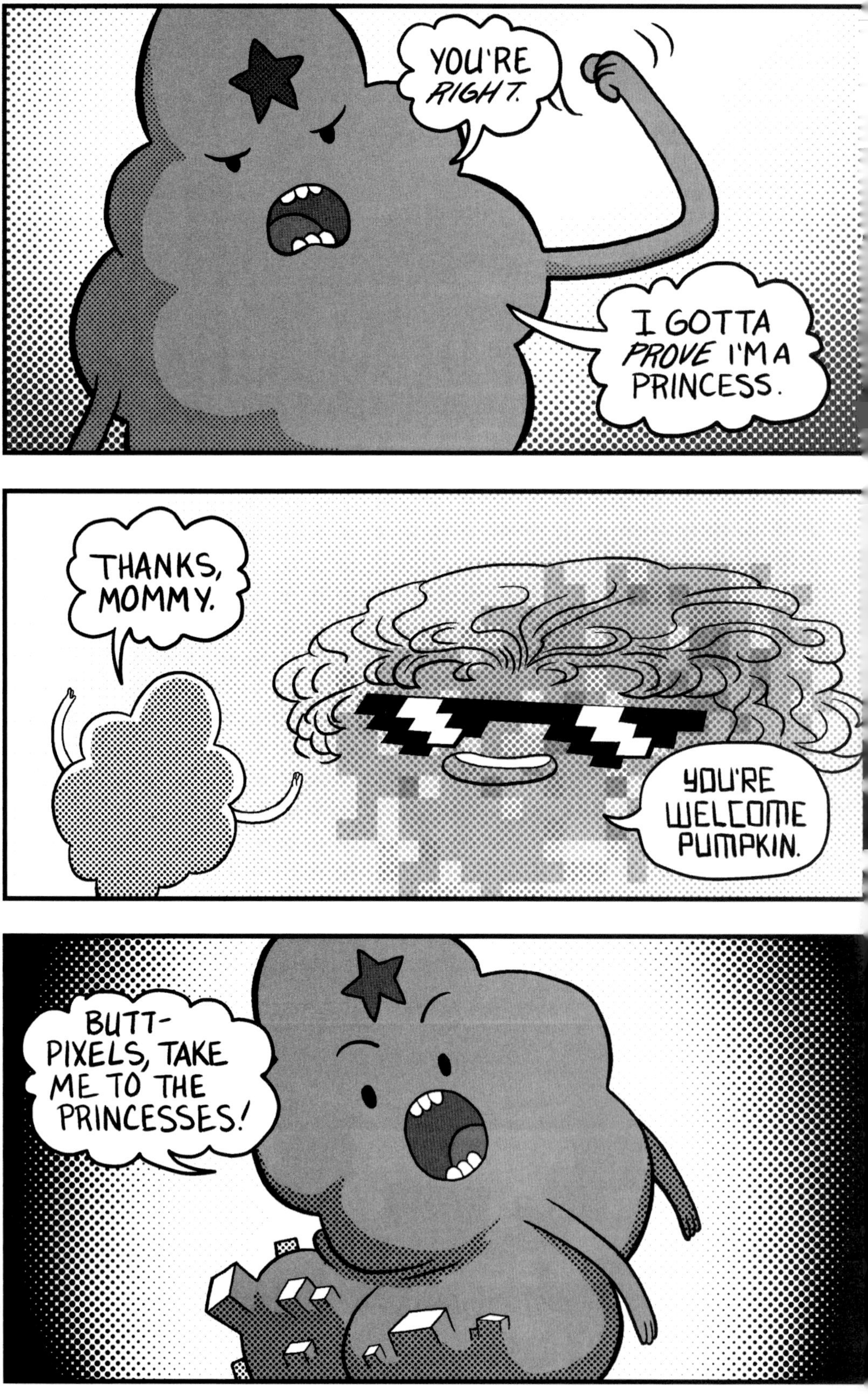
YOU'RE RIGHT.
I GOTTA PROVE I'M A PRINCESS.
THANKS, MOMMY.
YOU'RE WELCOME PUMPKIN.
BUTT-PIXELS, TAKE ME TO THE PRINCESSES!

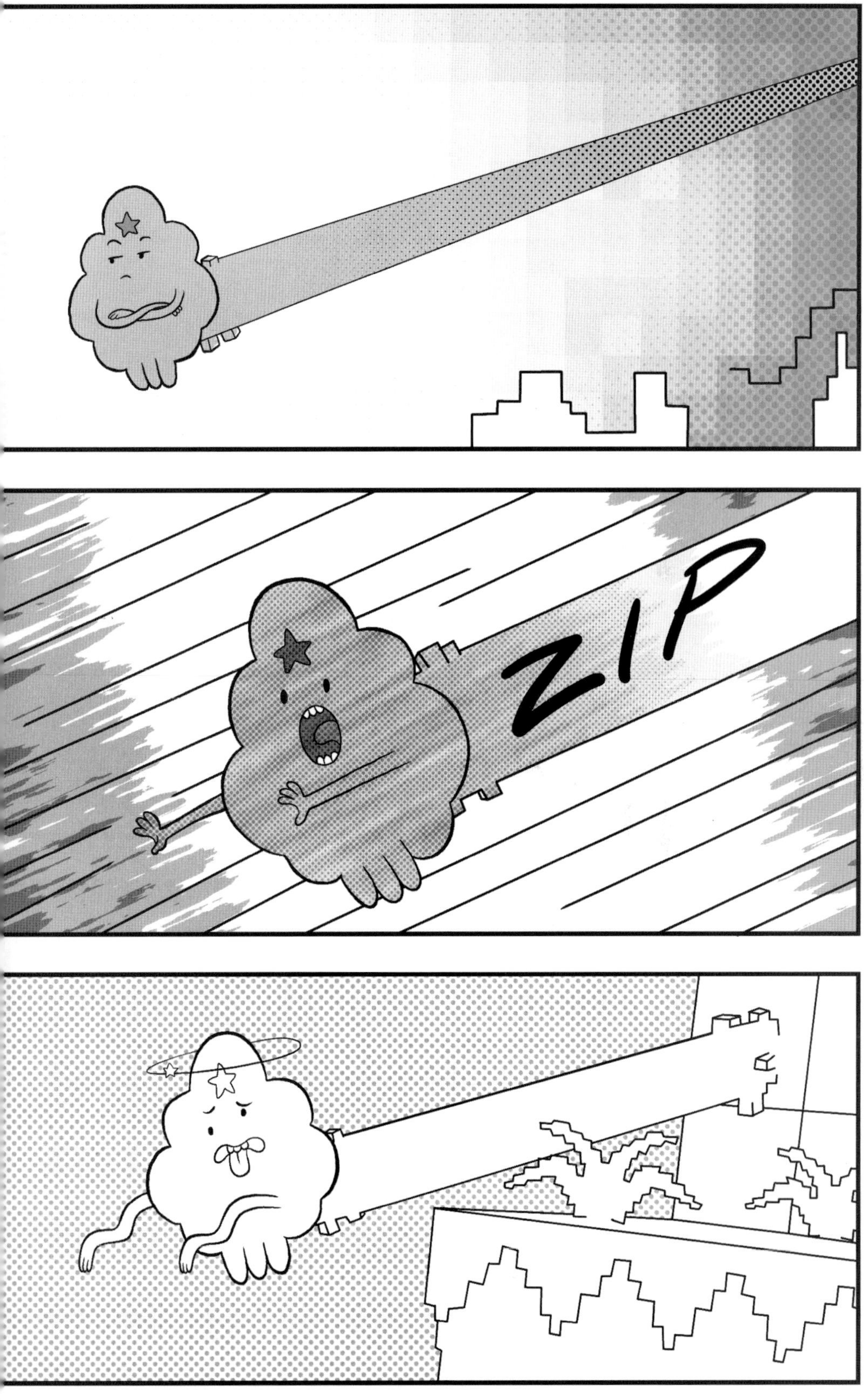
ZIP

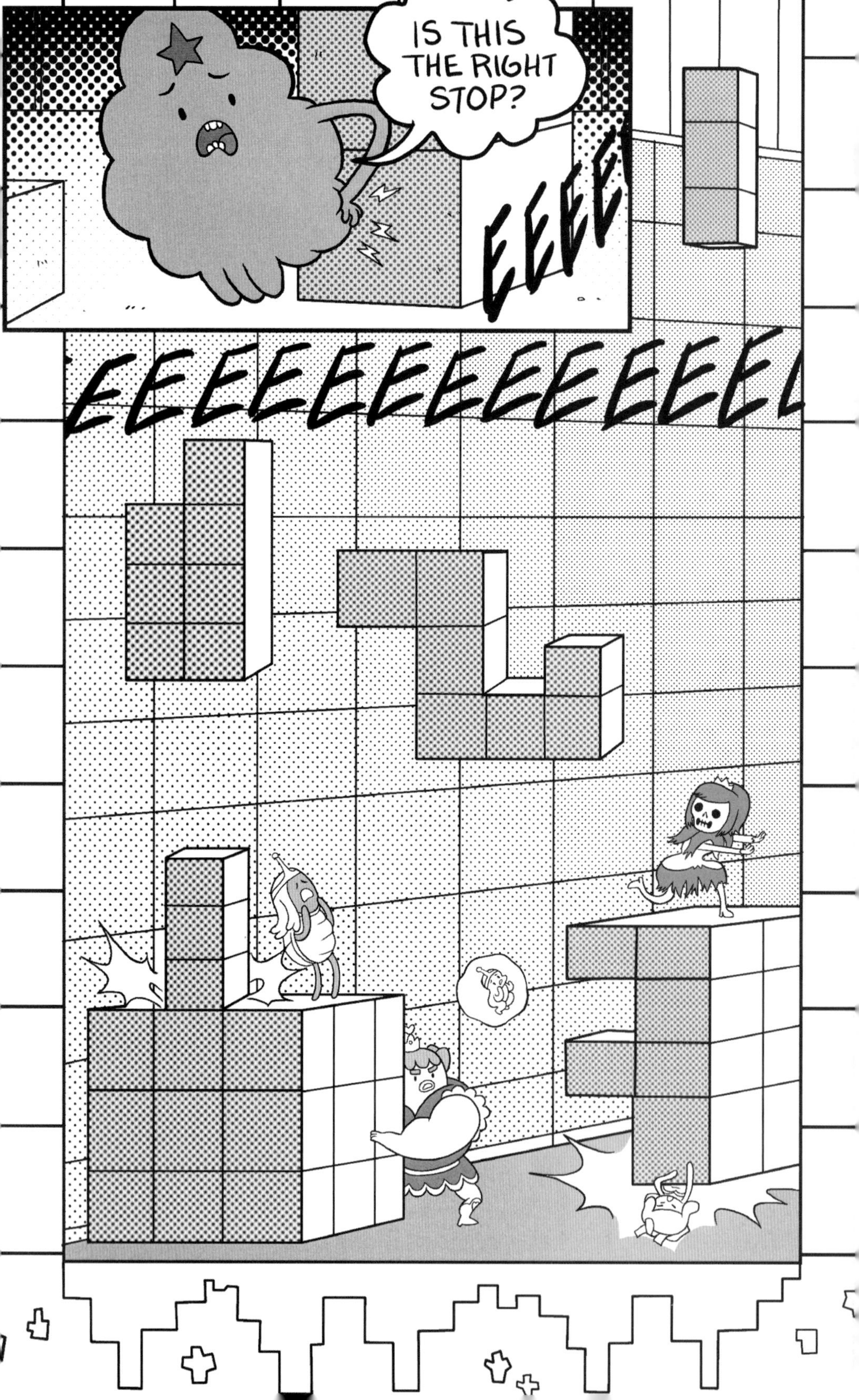
IS THIS THE RIGHT STOP?
EEEE
EEEEEEEEEEEEE

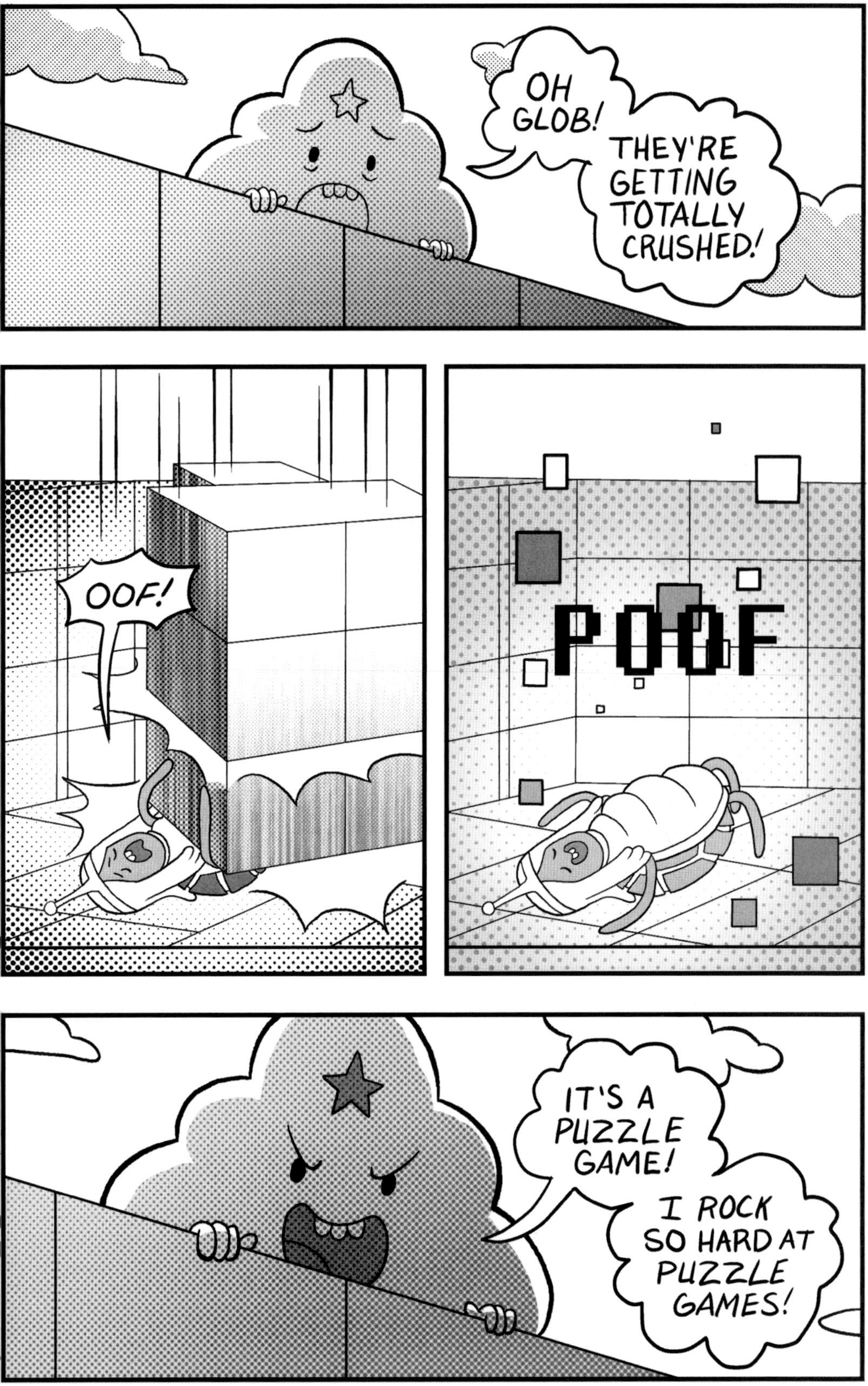
OH GLOB!
THEY'RE GETTING TOTALLY CRUSHED!
OOF!
POOF
IT'S A PUZZLE GAME!
I ROCK SO HARD AT PUZZLE GAMES!

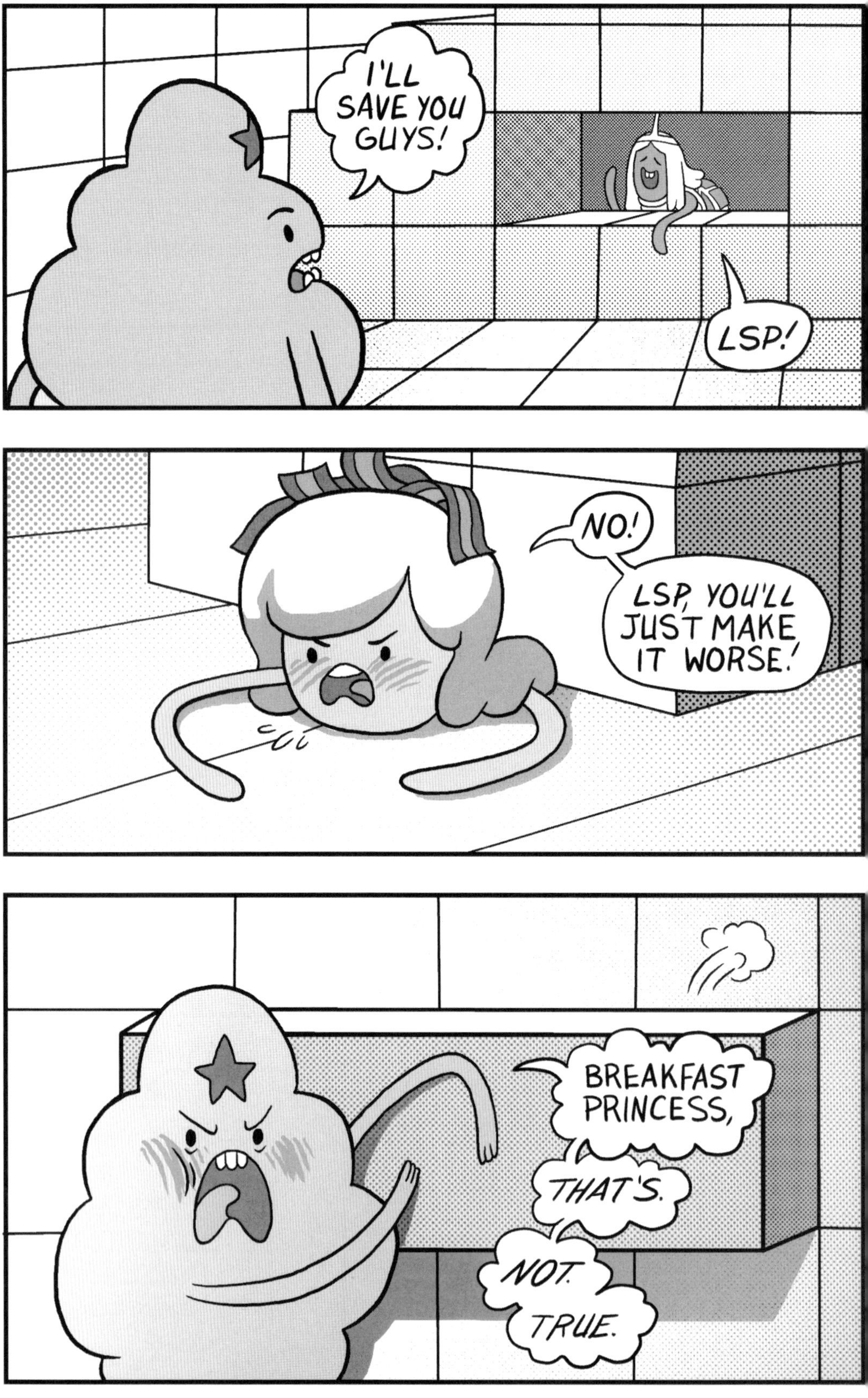
I'LL SAVE YOU GUYS!
LSP!
NO!
LSP, YOU'LL JUST MAKE IT WORSE!
BREAKFAST PRINCESS,
THAT'S.
NOT.
TRUE.

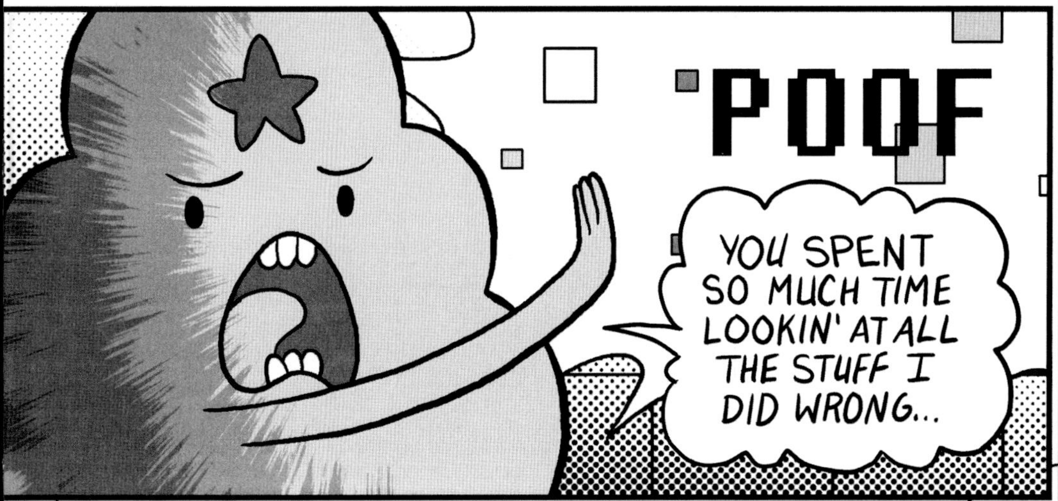
POOF
YOU SPENT SO MUCH TIME LOOKIN' AT ALL THE STUFF I DID WRONG...

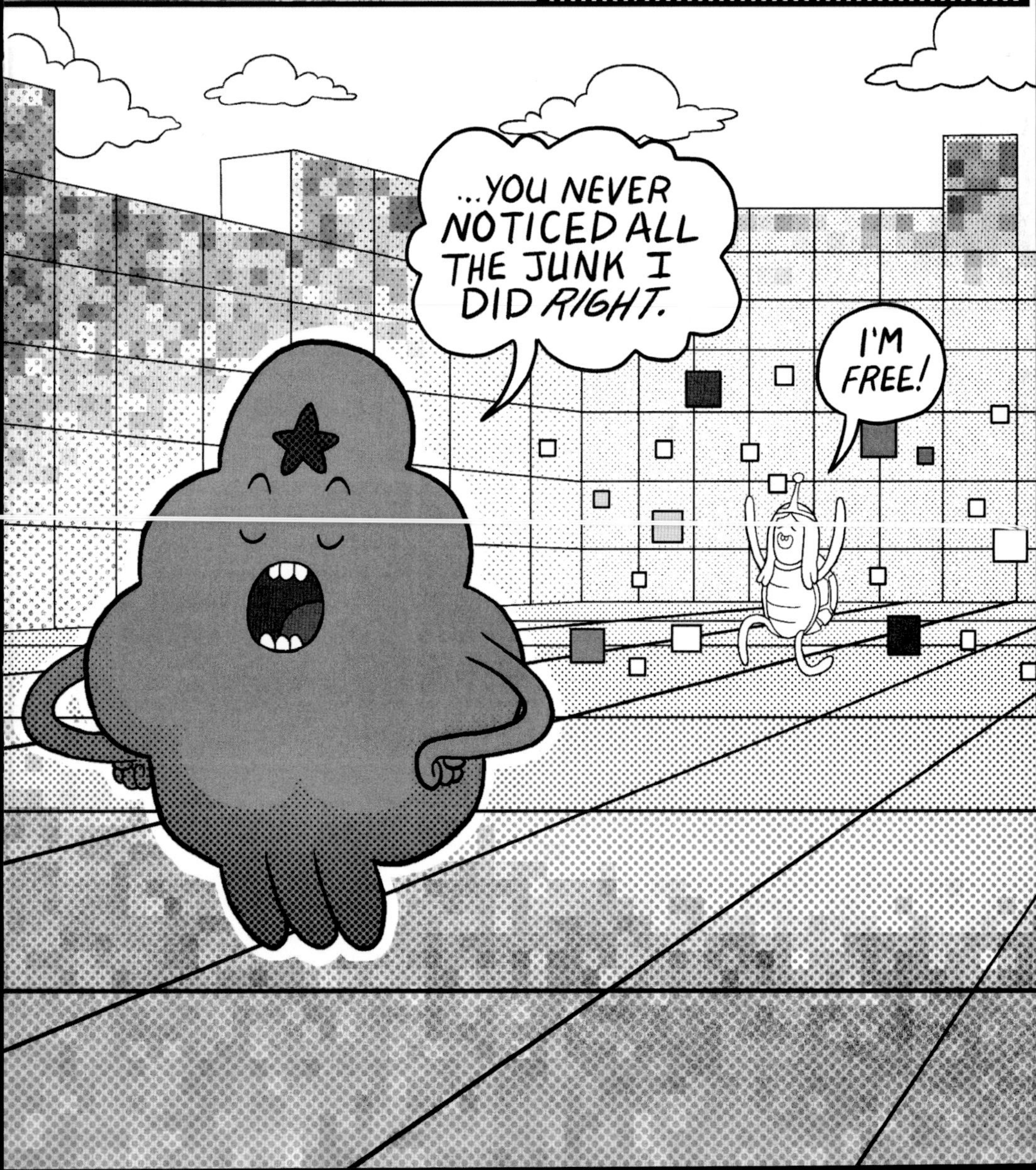
...YOU NEVER NOTICED ALL THE JUNK I DID RIGHT.
I'M FREE!

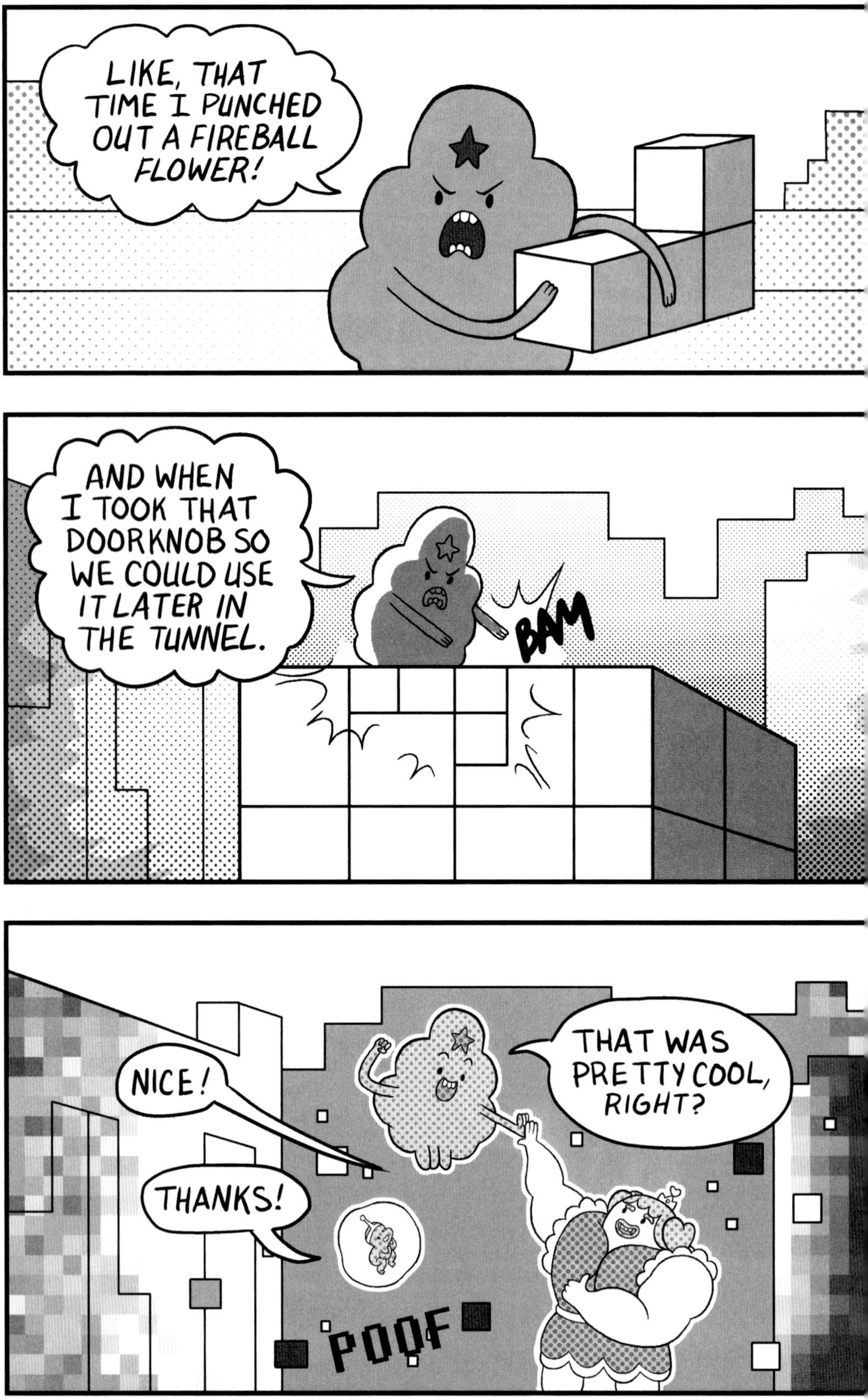
LIKE, THAT TIME I PUNCHED OUT A FIREBALL FLOWER!
AND WHEN I TOOK THAT DOORKNOB SO WE COULD USE IT LATER IN THE TUNNEL.
BAM
NICE!
THAT WAS PRETTY COOL, RIGHT?
THANKS!
POOF

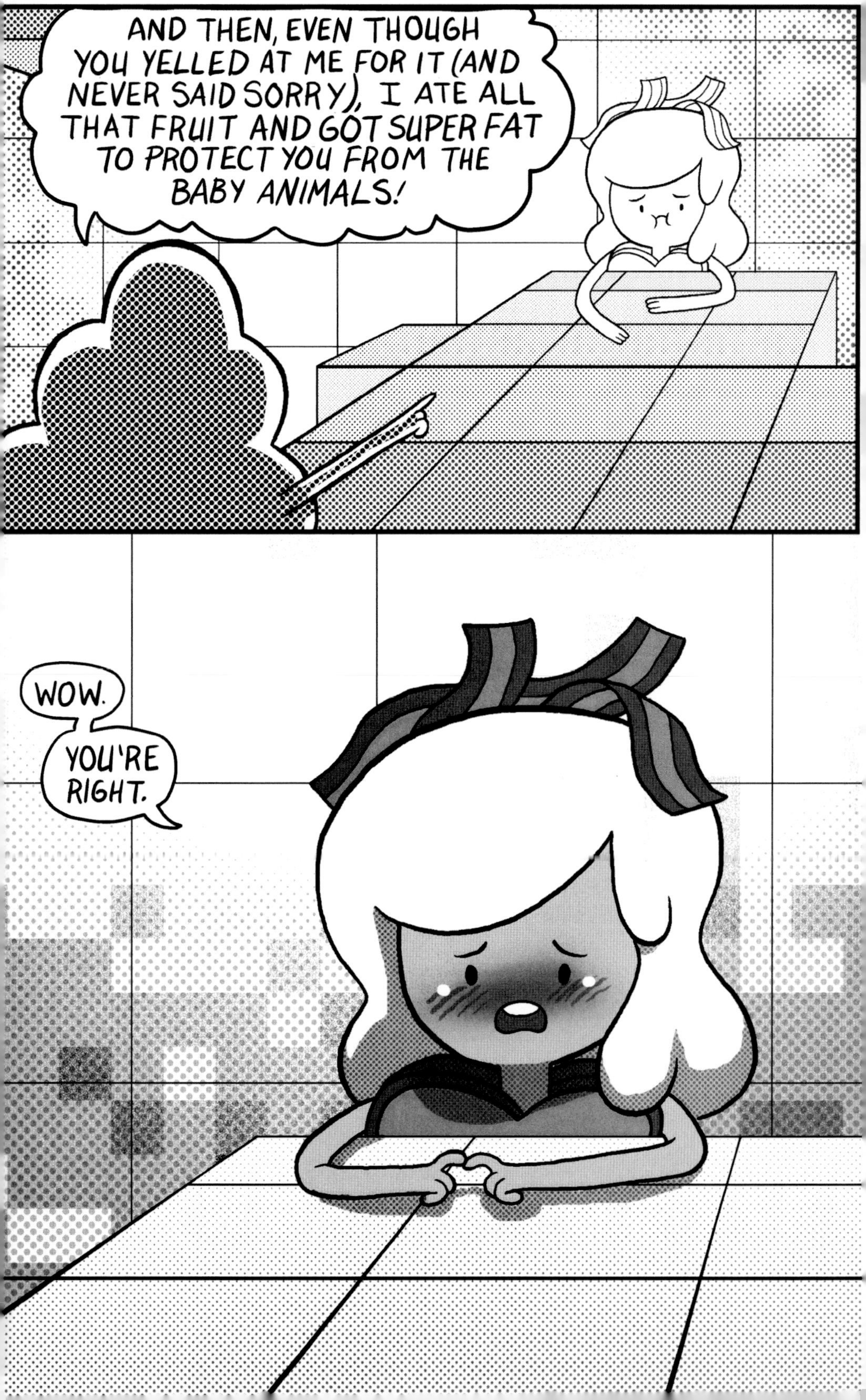
AND THEN, EVEN THOUGH YOU YELLED AT ME FOR IT (AND NEVER SAID SORRY), I ATE ALL THAT FRUIT AND GOT SUPER FAT TO PROTECT YOU FROM THE BABY ANIMALS!
WOW.
YOU'RE RIGHT.

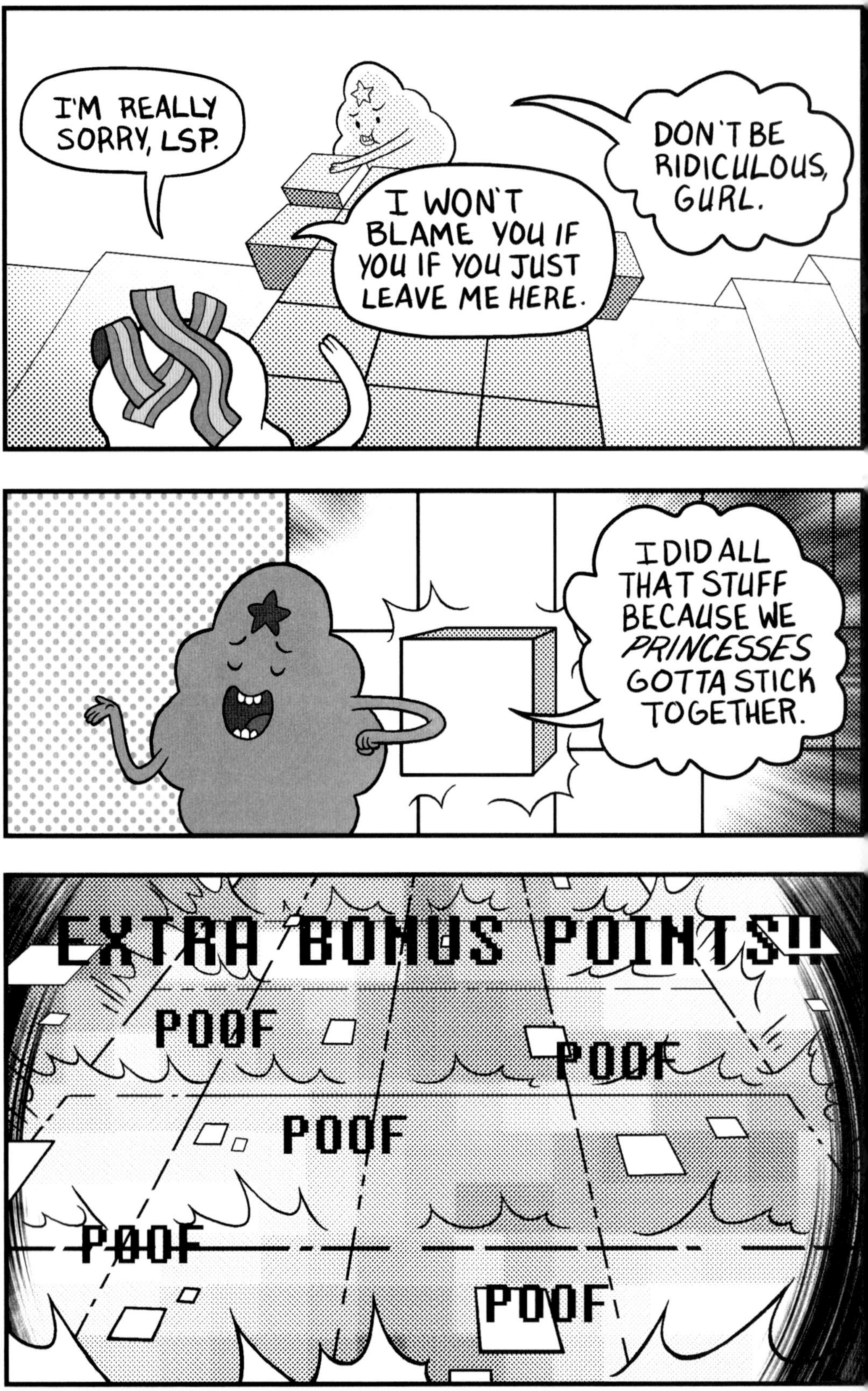
I'M REALLY SORRY, LSP.
I WON'T BLAME YOU IF YOU IF YOU JUST LEAVE ME HERE.
DON'T BE RIDICULOUS, GURL.
I DID ALL THAT STUFF BECAUSE WE *PRINCESSES* GOTTA STICK TOGETHER.
EXTRA BONUS POINTS!!
POOF
POOF
POOF
POOF
POOF

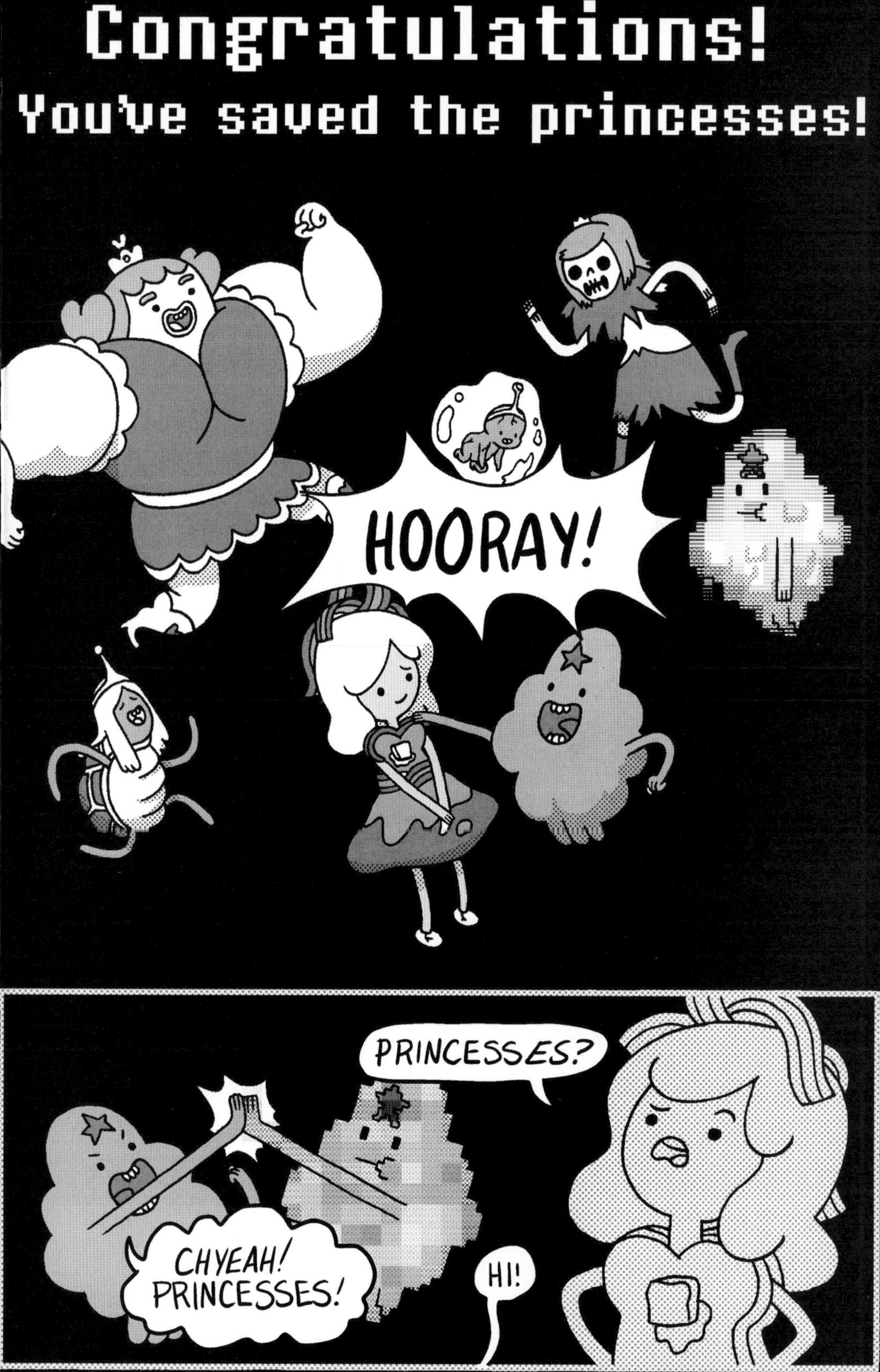
Congratulations!
You've saved the princesses!
HOORAY!
PRINCESSES?
CHYEAH! PRINCESSES!
HI!

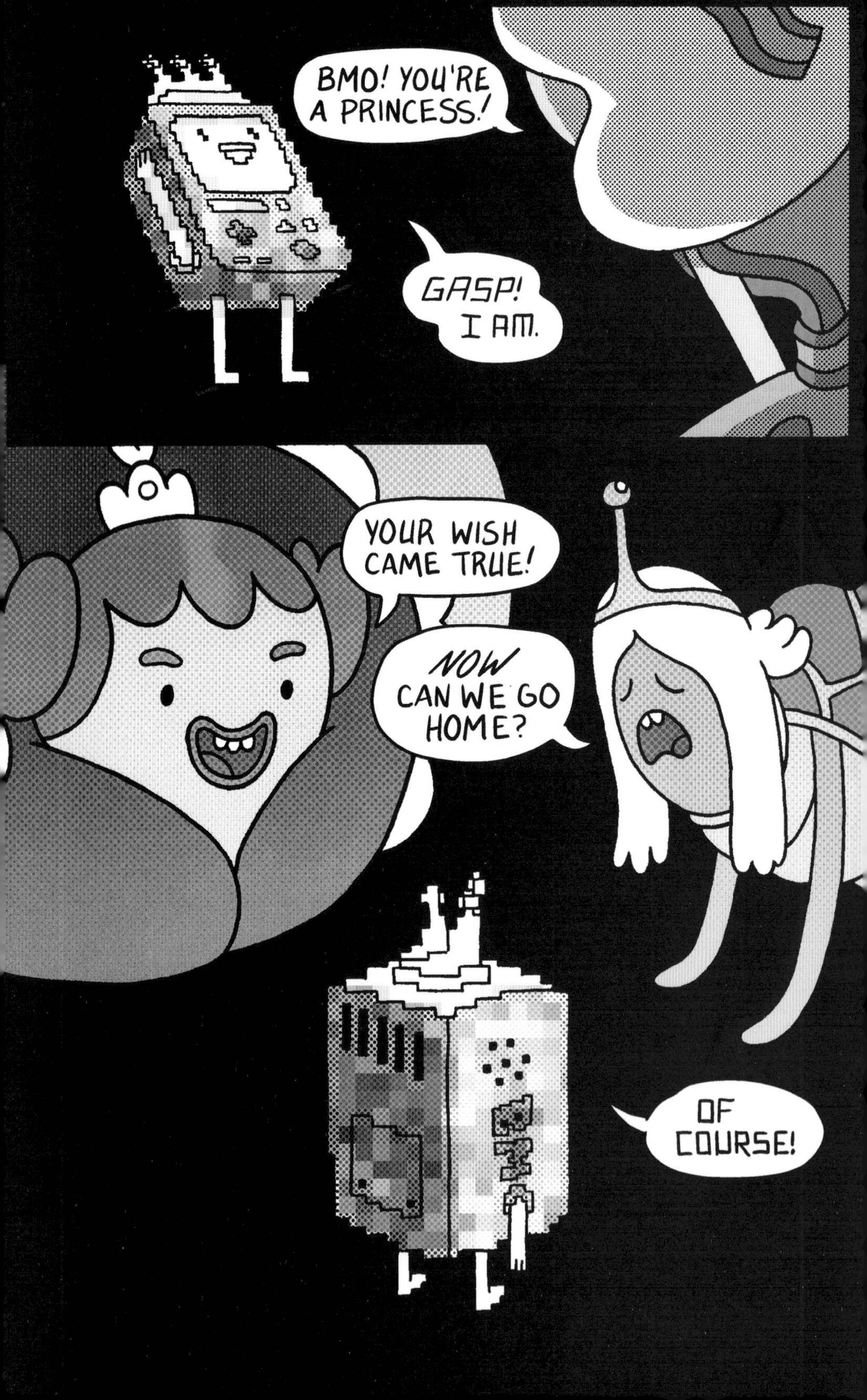
BMO! YOU'RE A PRINCESS!
GASP! I AM.
YOUR WISH CAME TRUE!
NOW CAN WE GO HOME?
OF COURSE!

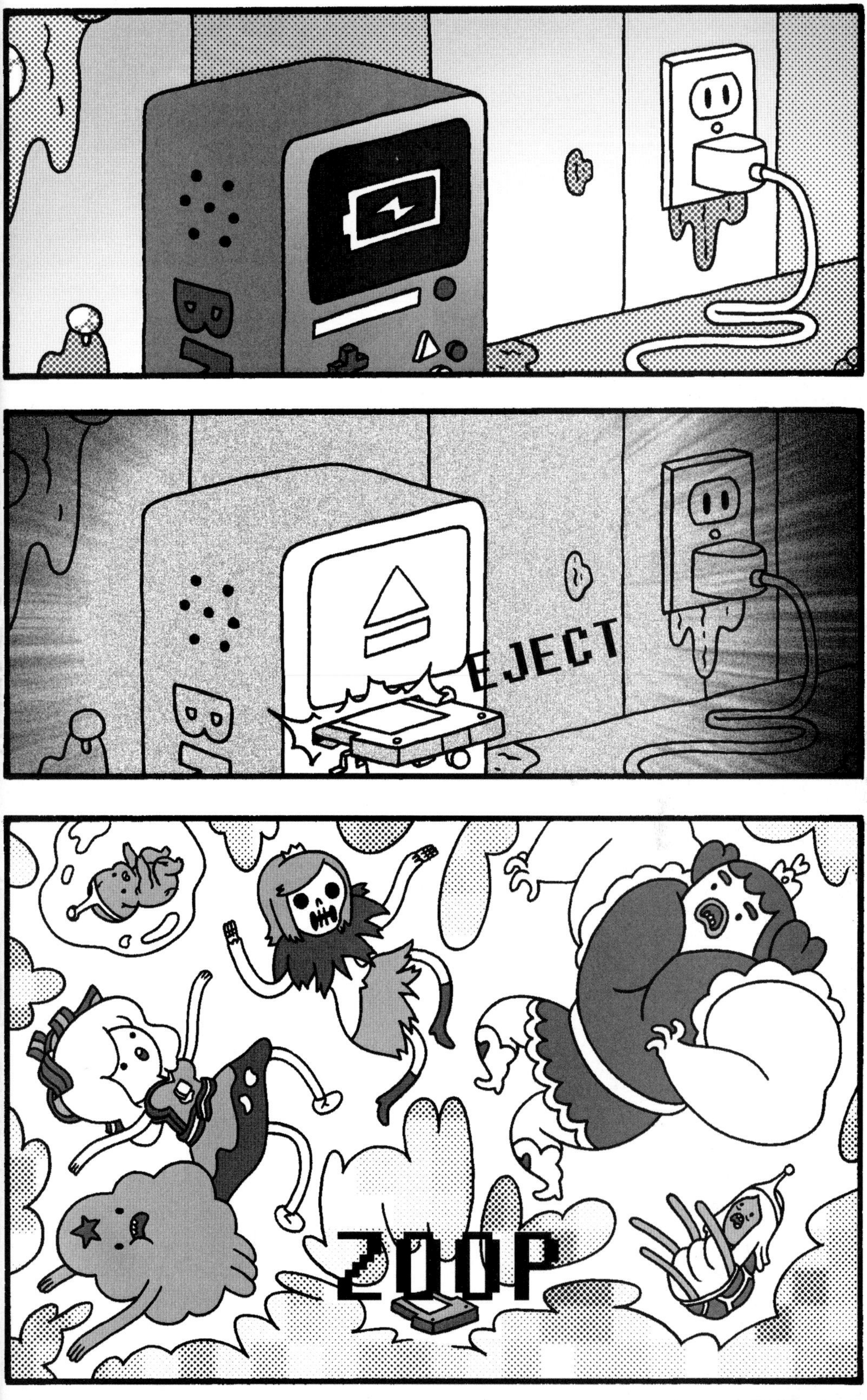
EJECT
ZOOP

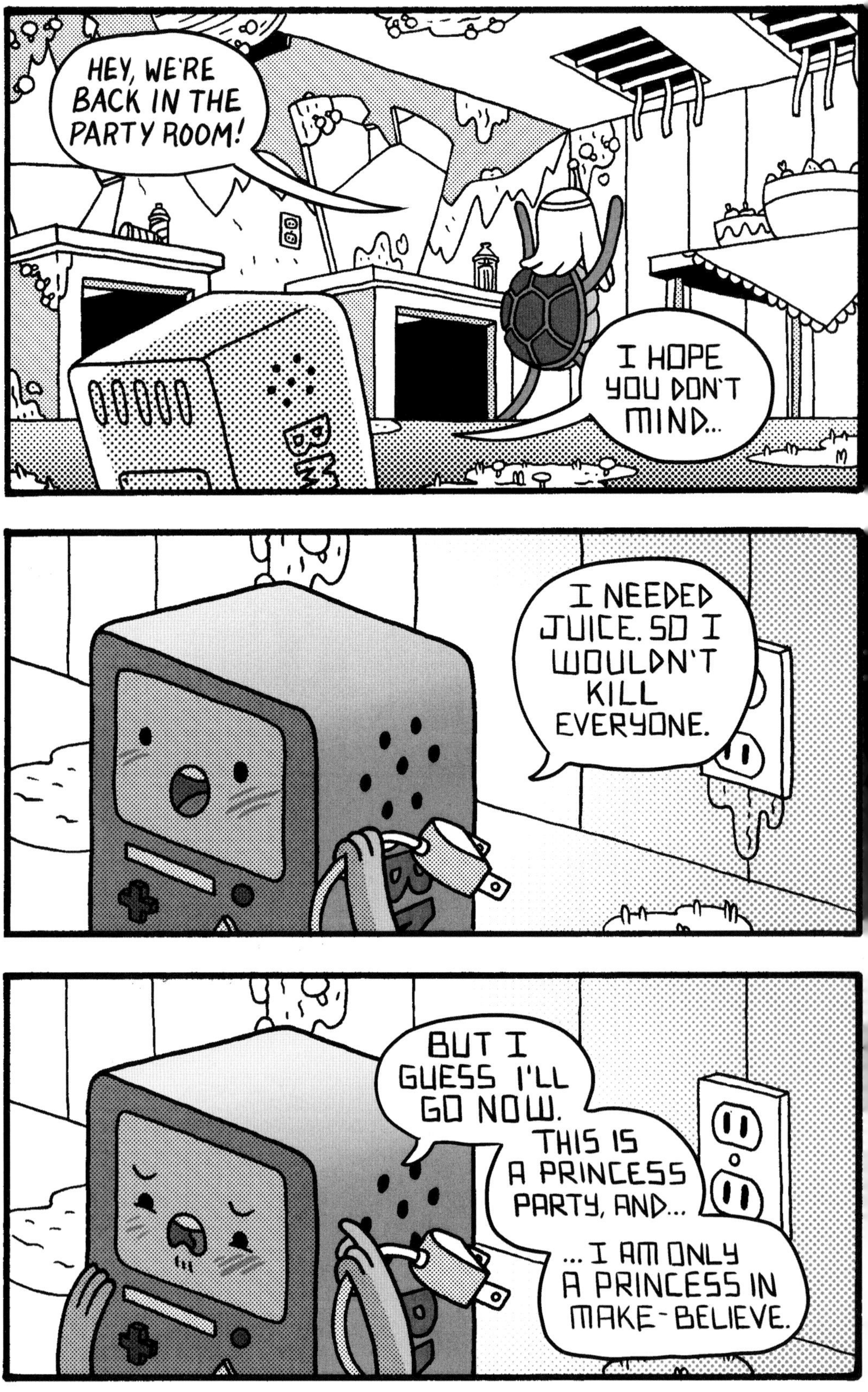
HEY, WE'RE BACK IN THE PARTY ROOM!
I HOPE YOU DON'T MIND...
I NEEDED JUICE. SO I WOULDN'T KILL EVERYONE.
BUT I GUESS I'LL GO NOW.
THIS IS A PRINCESS PARTY, AND...
... I AM ONLY A PRINCESS IN MAKE-BELIEVE.

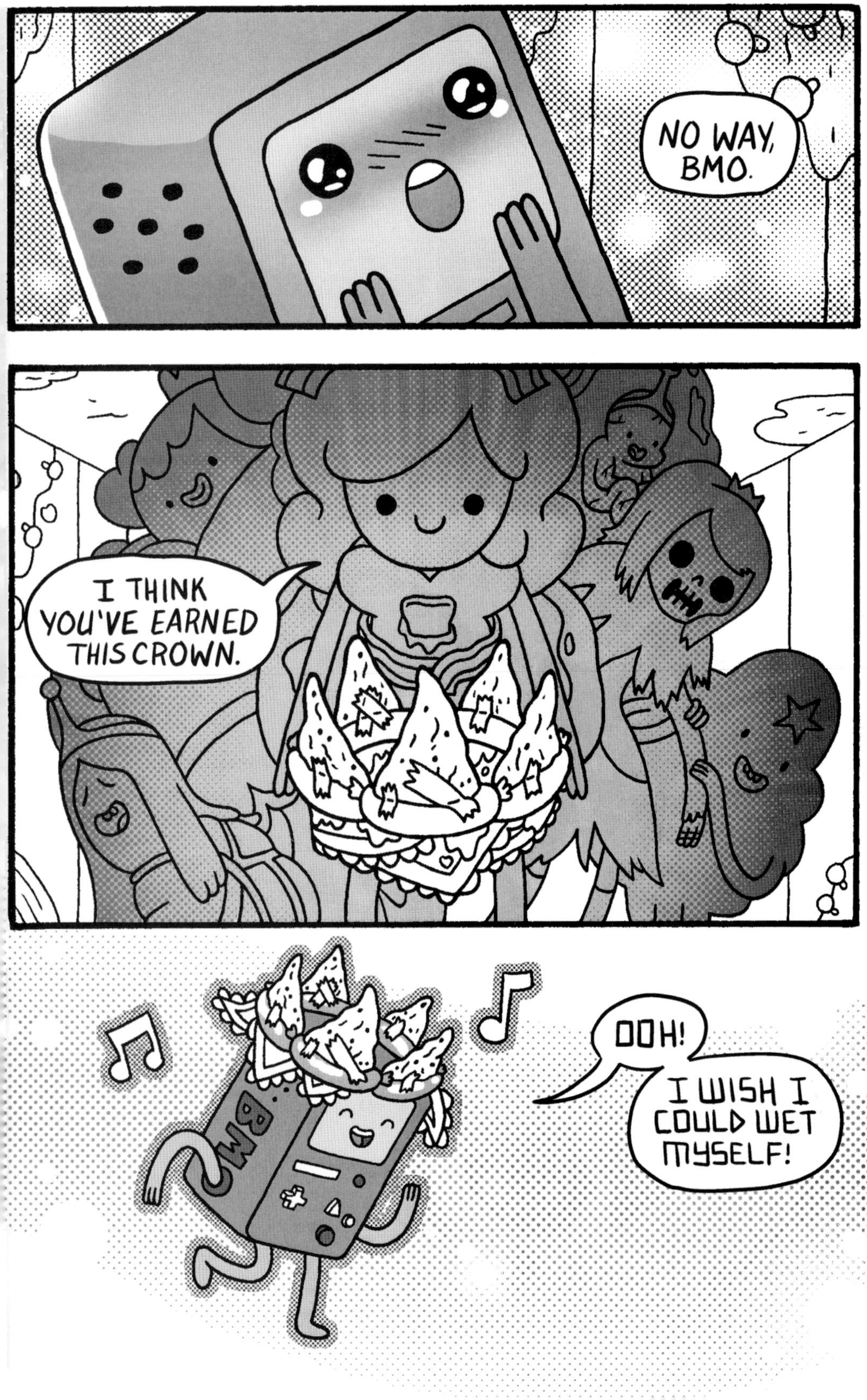
NO WAY, BMO.
I THINK YOU'VE EARNED THIS CROWN.
OOH!
I WISH I COULD WET MYSELF!

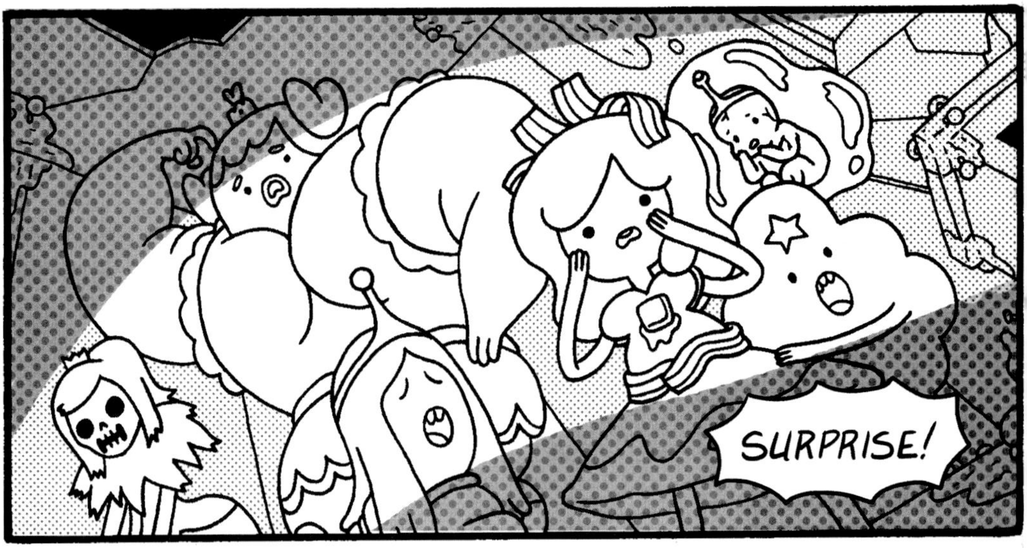
SURPRISE!

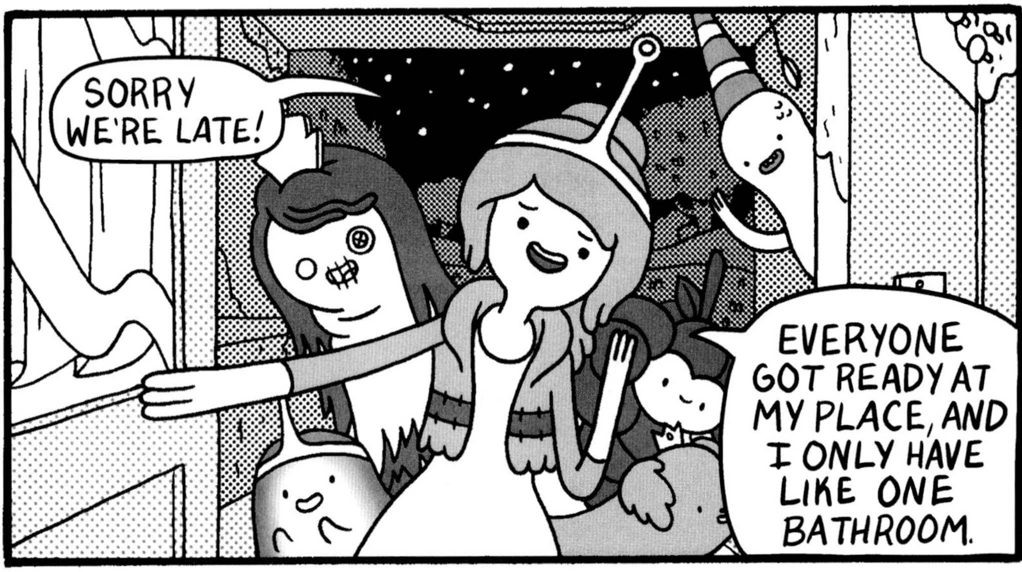
SORRY WE'RE LATE!
EVERYONE GOT READY AT MY PLACE, AND I ONLY HAVE LIKE ONE BATHROOM.

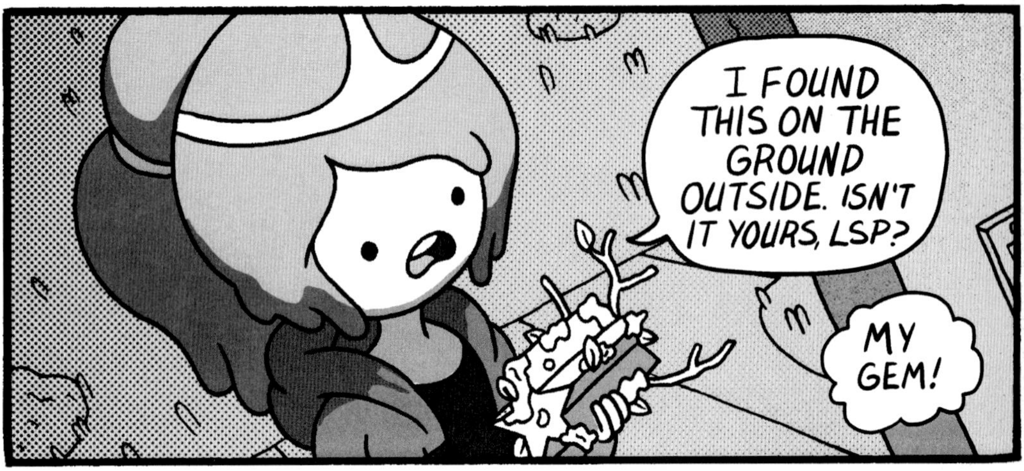
I FOUND THIS ON THE GROUND OUTSIDE. ISN'T IT YOURS, LSP?
MY GEM!

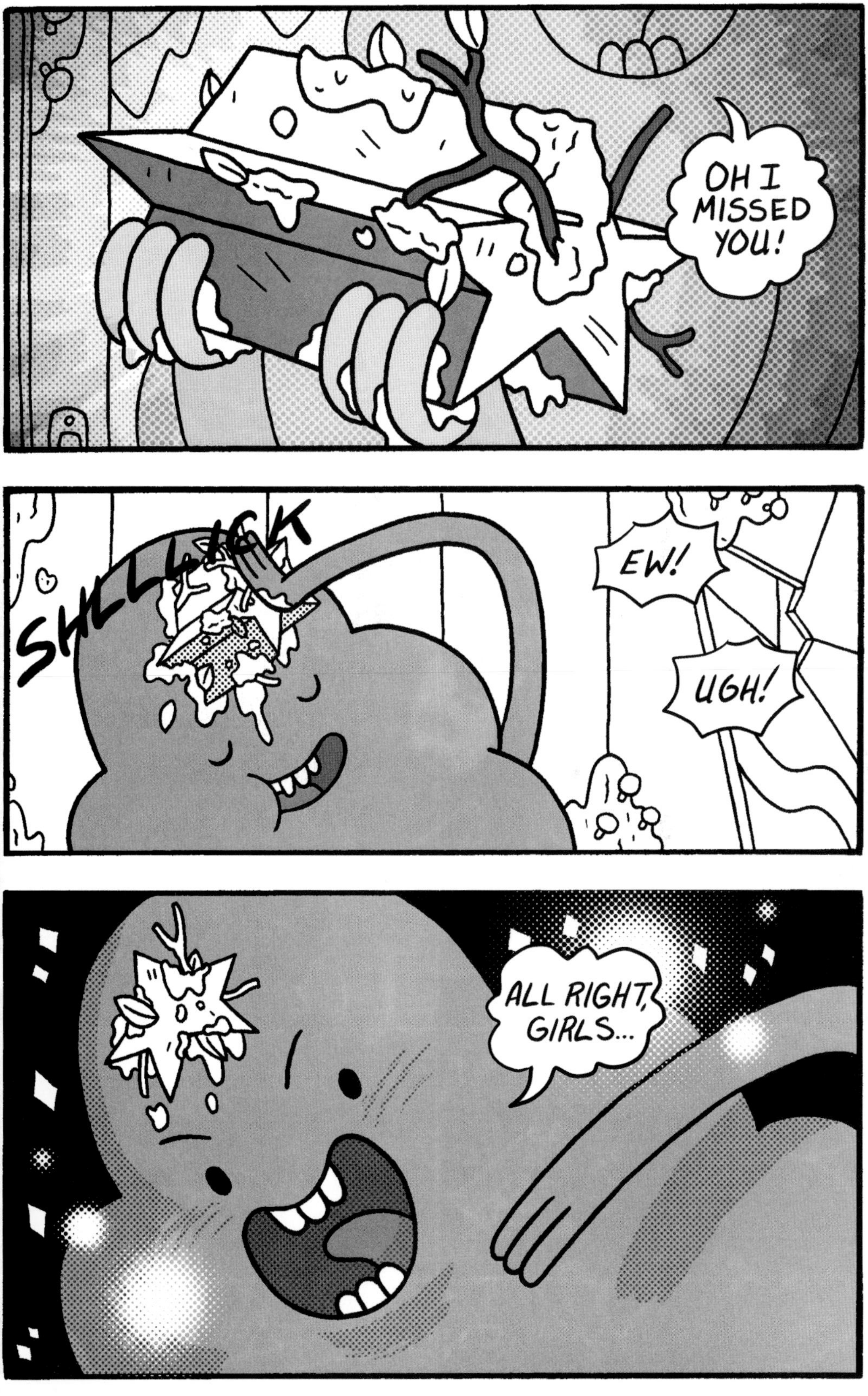
OH I MISSED YOU!
SHLLLICK
EW!
UGH!
ALL RIGHT, GIRLS...

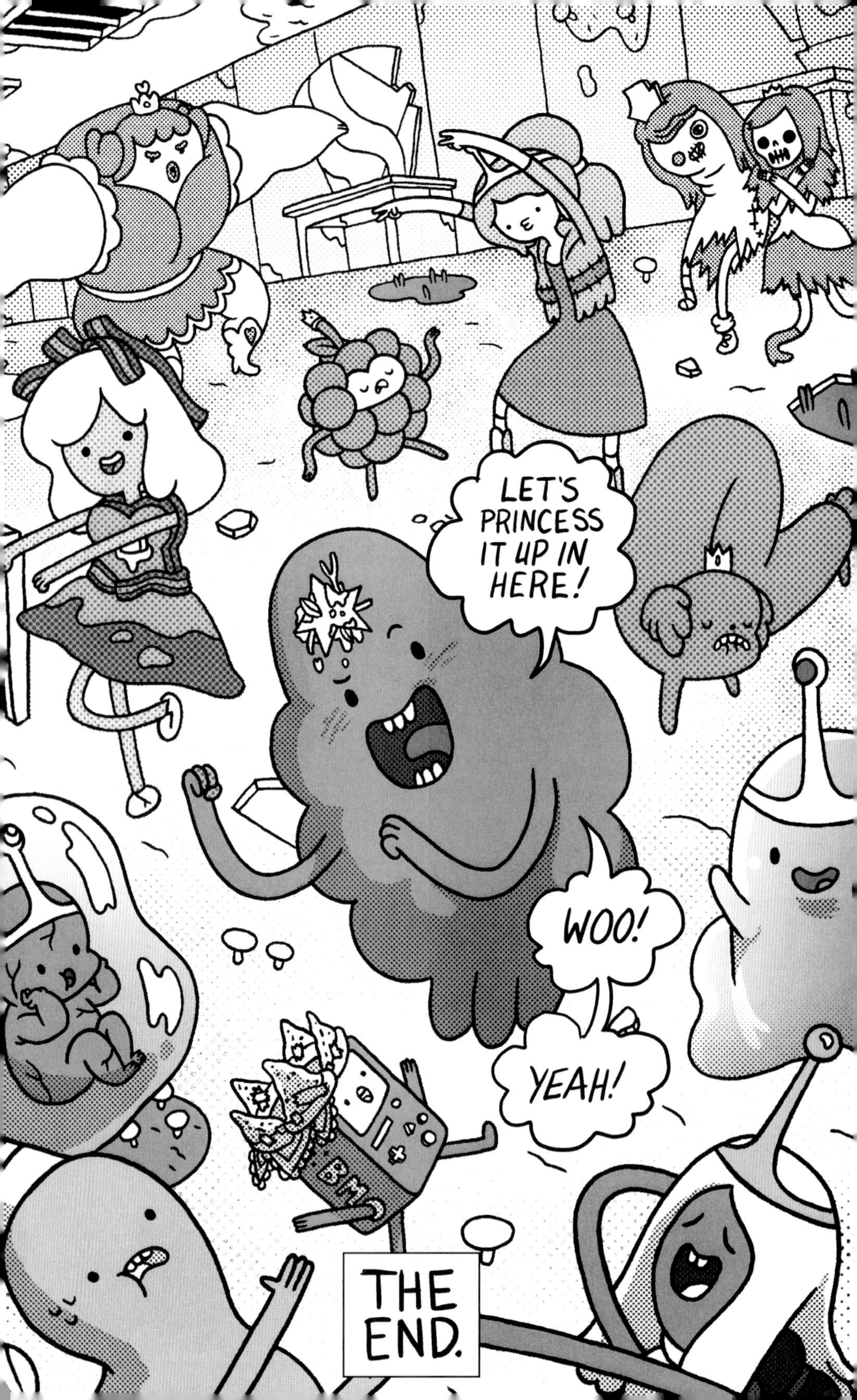
LET'S PRINCESS IT UP IN HERE!
WOO!
YEAH!
BMO
THE END.

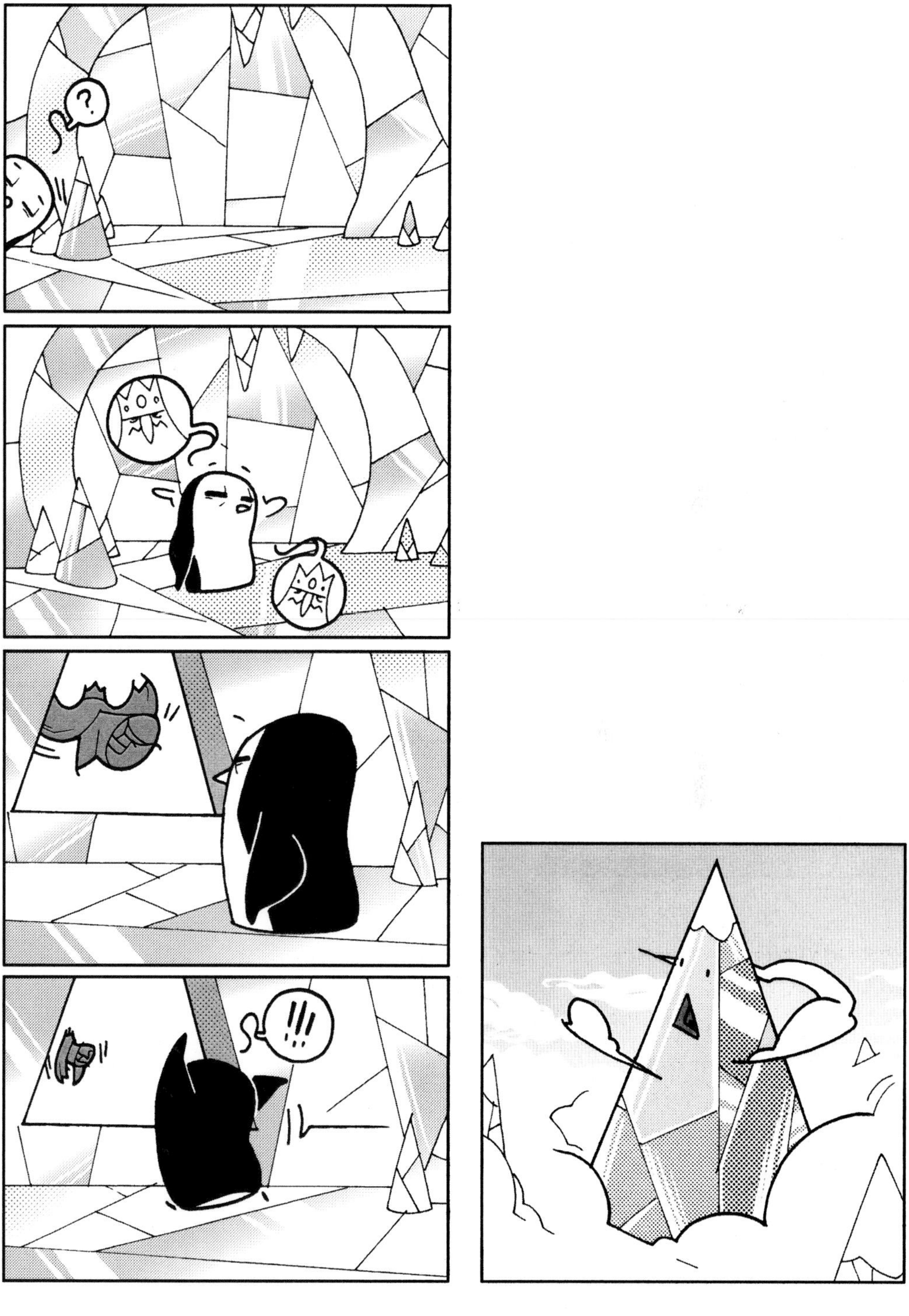
?
!!!

ICE KING
BREAKING STUFF
EVIL
CRAZY BEATS

THE MIND OF GUNTER

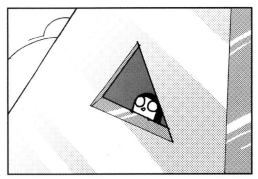

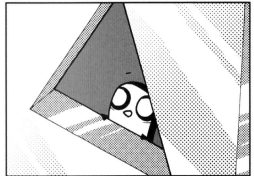

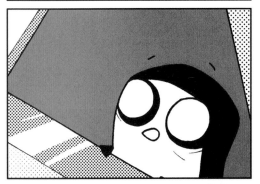

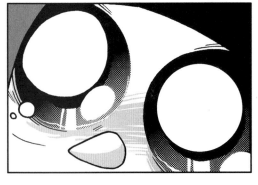

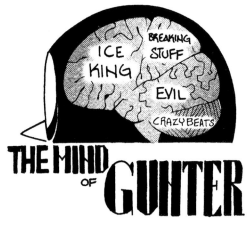

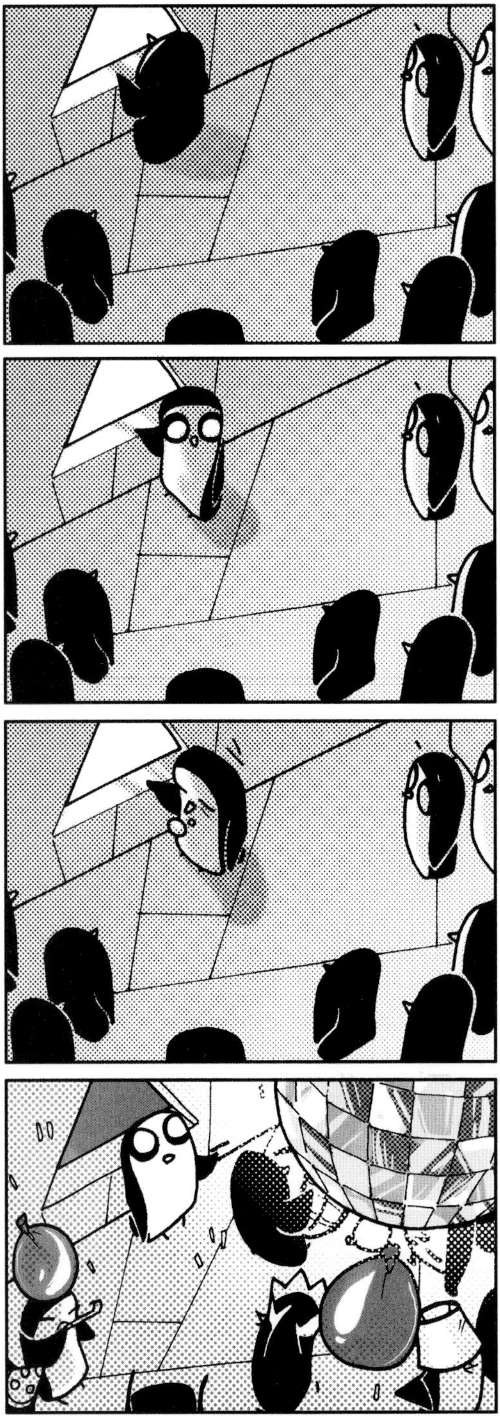

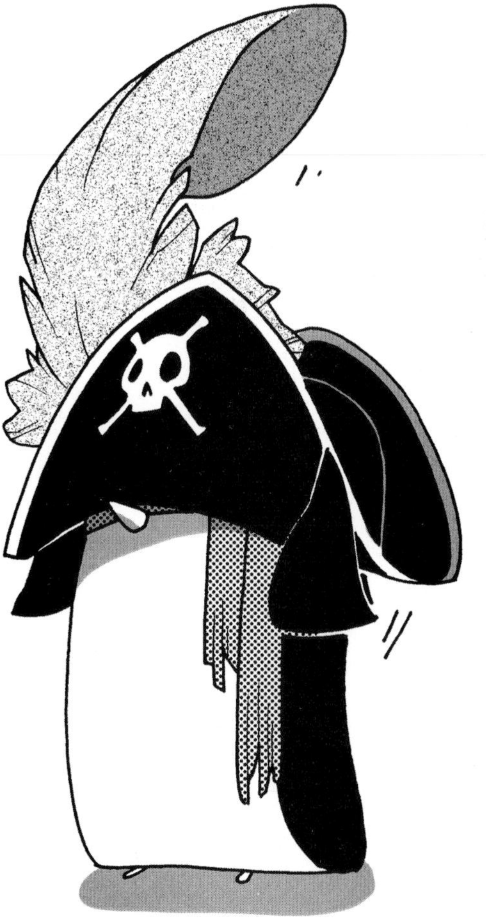

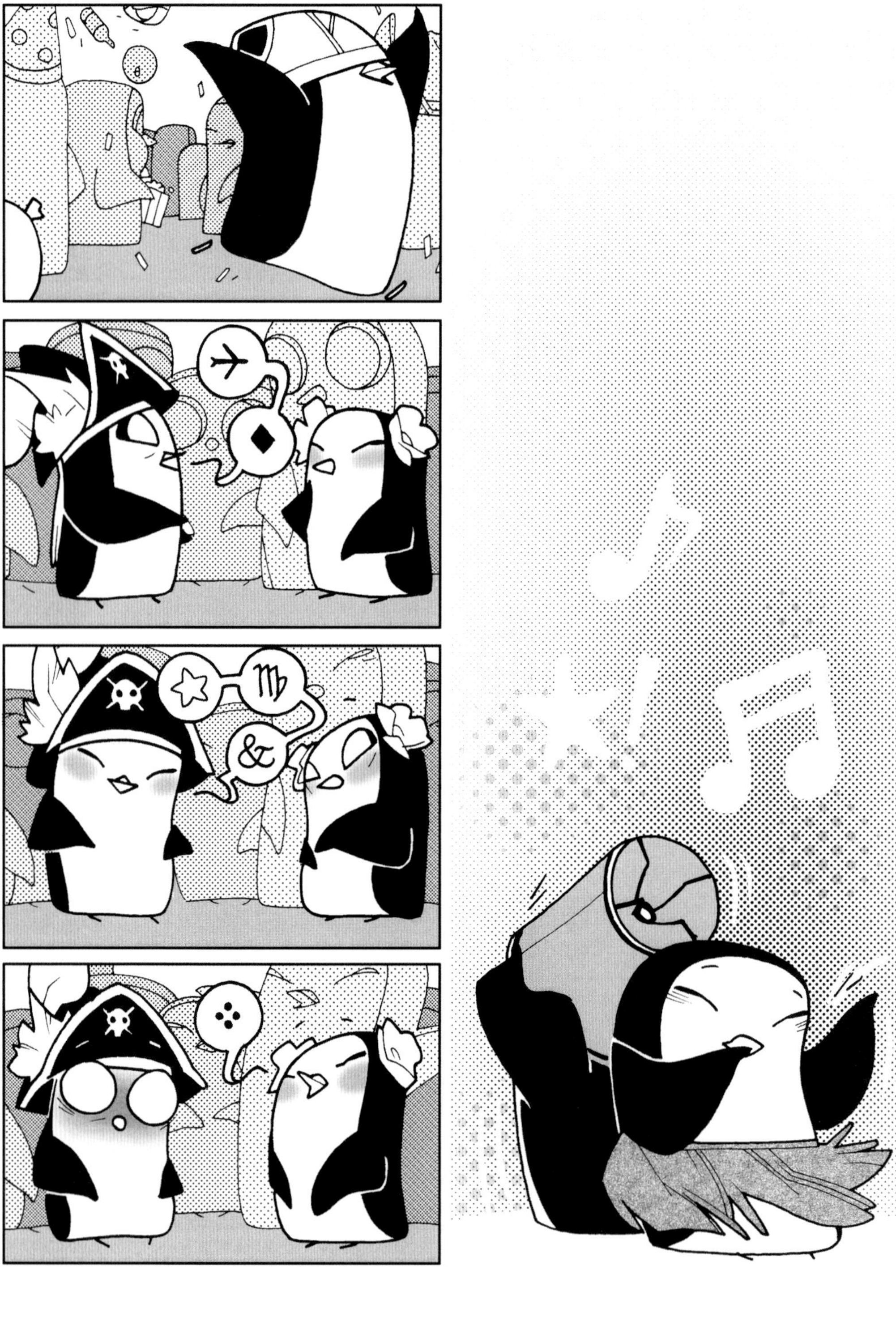

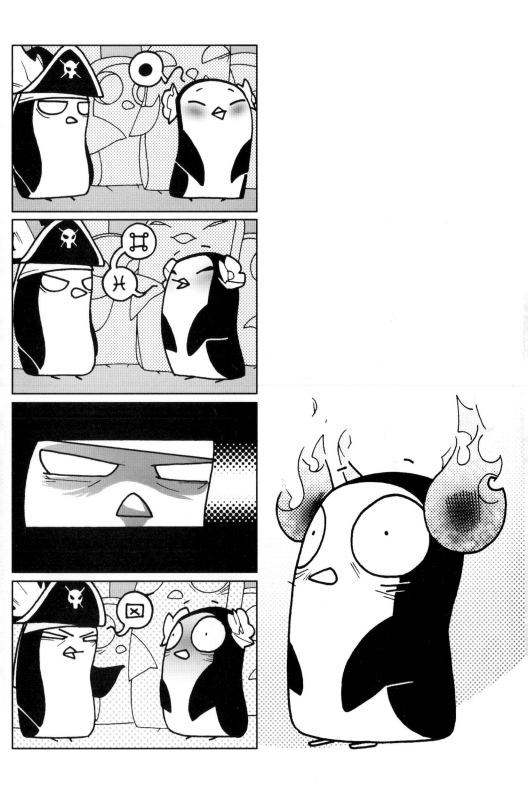

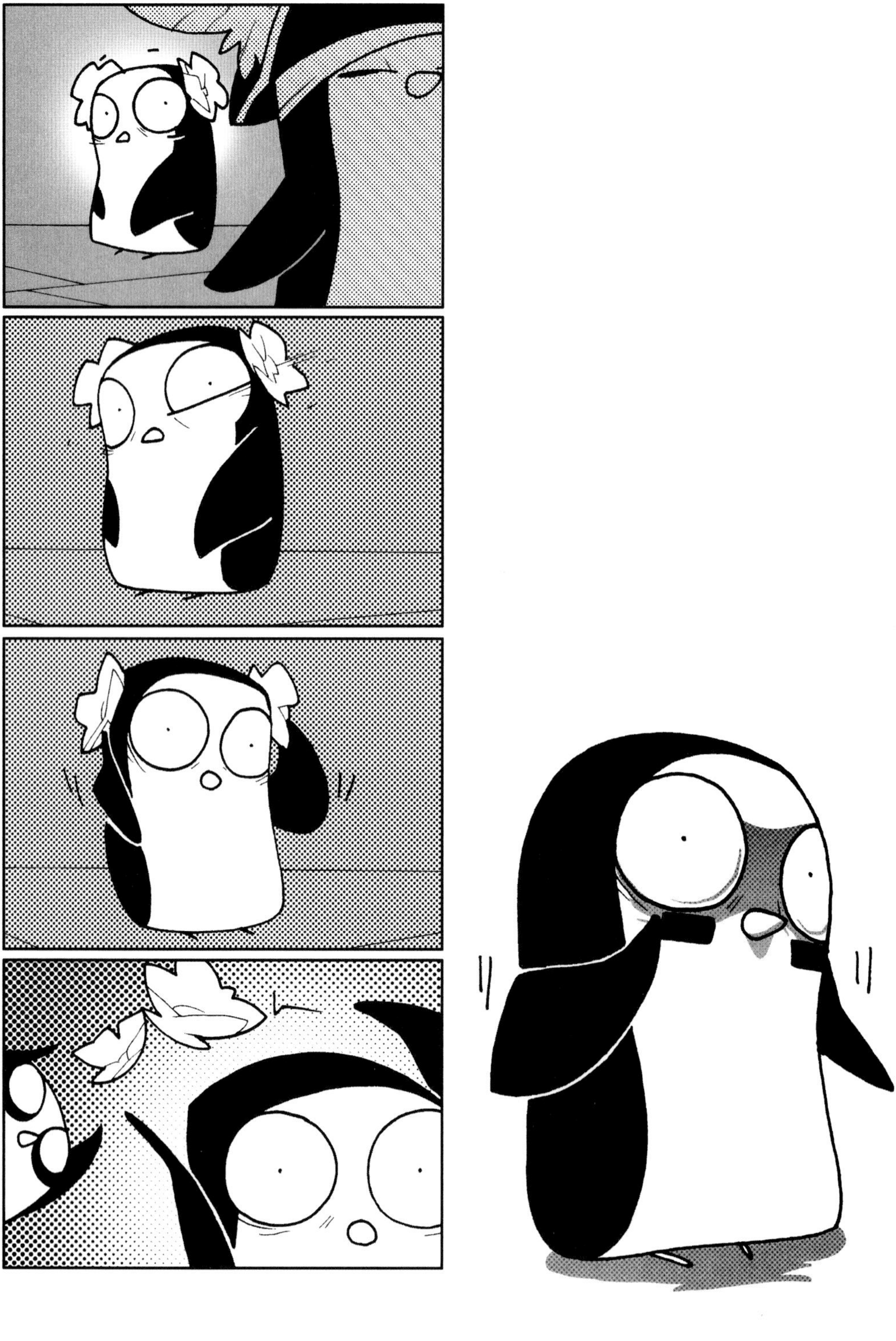

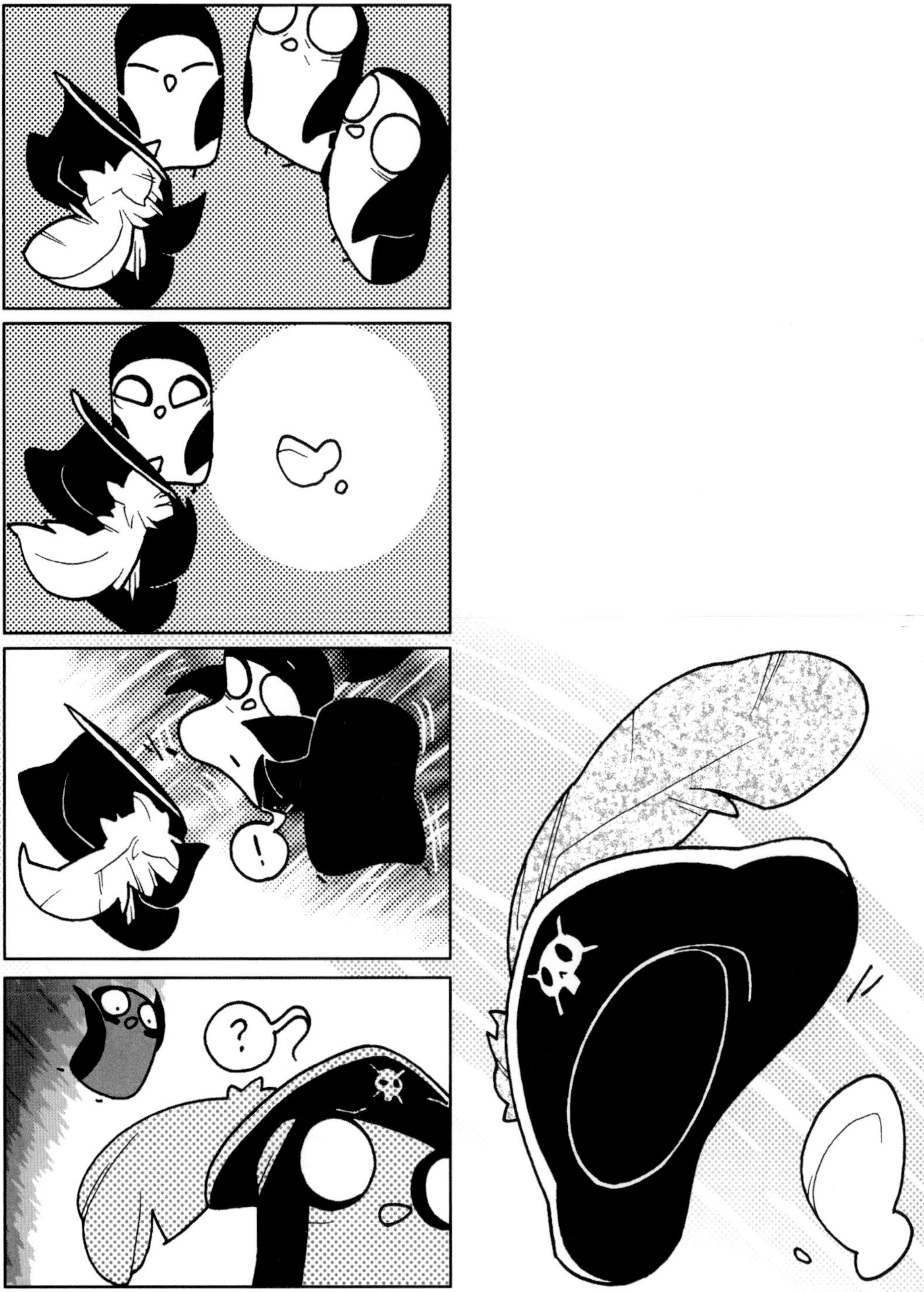
!
?

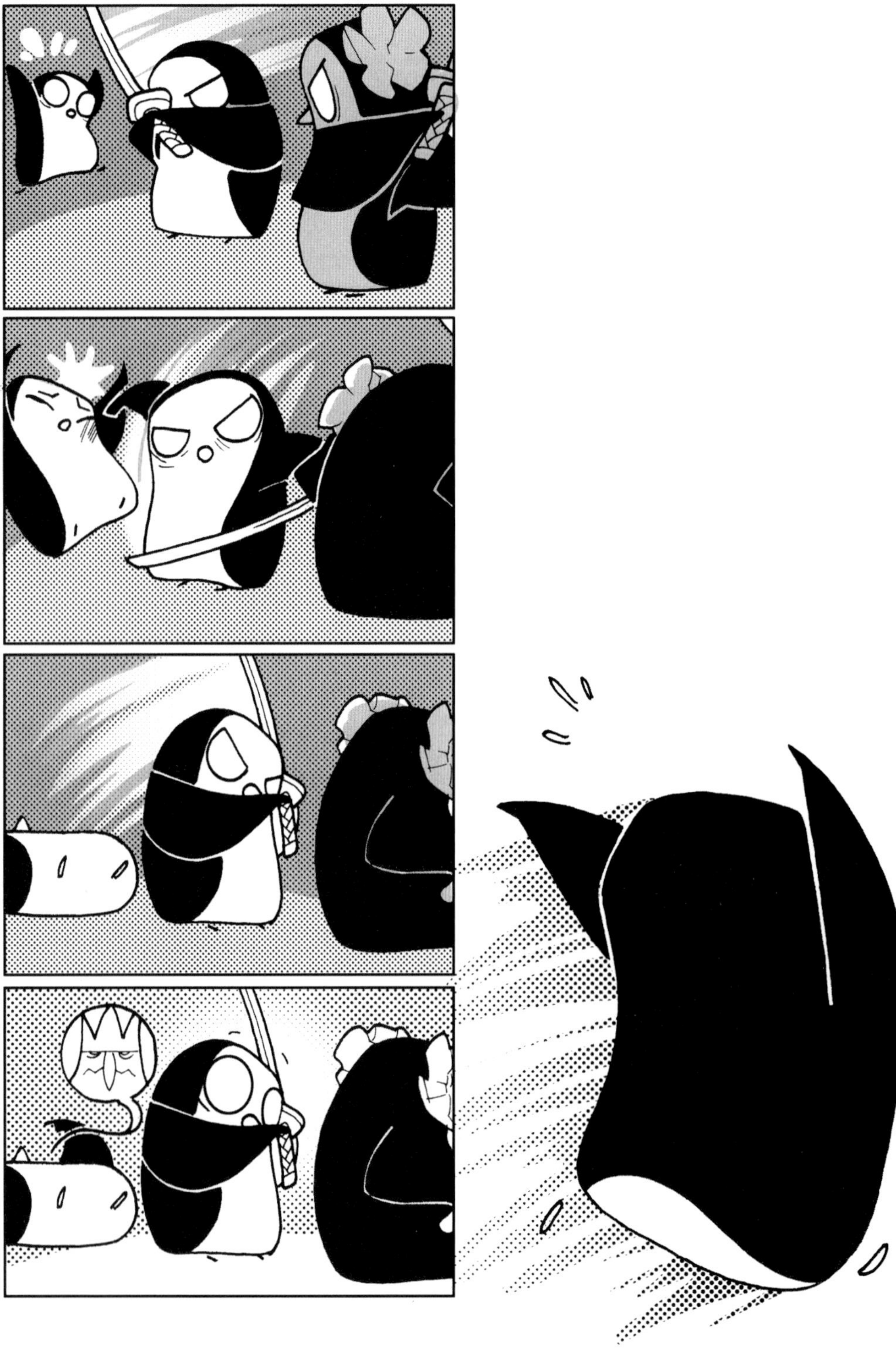

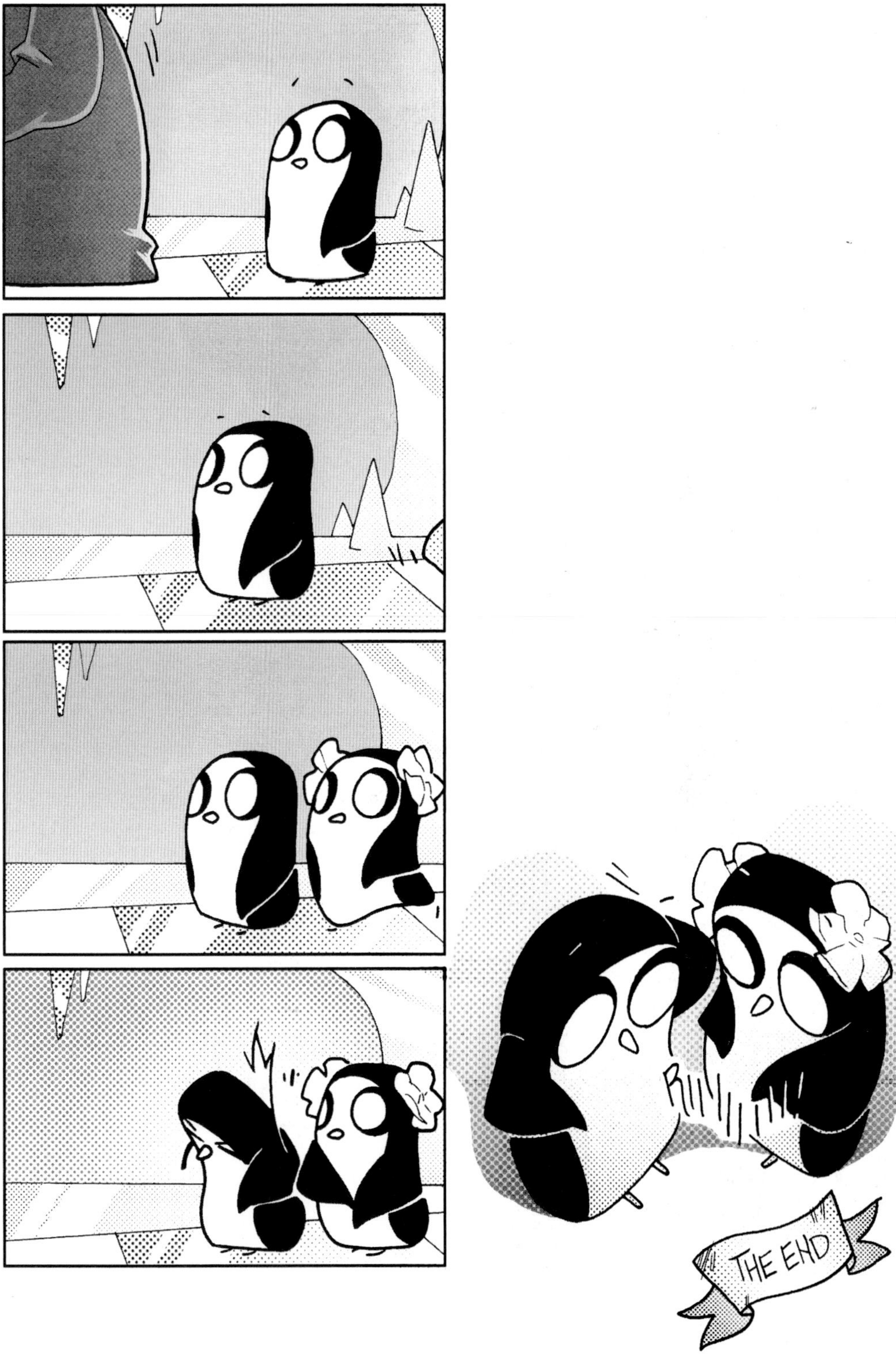
THE END

ADVENTURE TIME™

VOLUME 3

SPRING 2014

Written by KATE LETH

Illustrated by ZACK STERLING